A
VIGIL OF SPIES

THE OWEN ARCHER SERIES
BOOK TEN

CANDACE

DIVERSIONBOOKS

Diversion Books
A Division of Diversion Publishing Corp.
443 Park Avenue South, Suite 1008
New York, New York 10016
www.DiversionBooks.com

Copyright © 2008 by Candace Robb
All rights reserved, including the right to reproduce this book or portions thereof
in any form whatsoever.

This is a work of fiction. Names, characters, places and incidents either are the
product of the author's imagination or are used fictitiously. Any resemblance to
actual persons, living or dead, events or locales is entirely coincidental.

For more information, email info@diversionbooks.com

First Diversion Books edition July 2015.
Print ISBN: 978-1-68230-109-8
eBook ISBN: 978-1-62681-983-2

To all those with the courage to open their hearts.

ACKNOWLEDGEMENTS

I would like to thank Anthony Goodman for his insights into Joan of Kent, shared over a long, happily drawn out lunch on a warm afternoon in the courtyard of St William's College, York; Carolyn Collette for generously sharing her research on Joan; Laura Hodges for her expertise in the clothing of the period; Lorraine Stock for tracking down an obscure but important article about Alexander Neville; Laurel Broughton for finding just the right epigraph from Geoffrey's pen; Barbara Johnson for asking the right question about what Thoresby means to me. My friends on Chaucernet have been sources of ideas and information for the character of Geoffrey Chaucer and details of the age. I wish to thank Georgina Hawtrey-Woore and Patrick Walsh for early input on the manuscript, and Joyce Gibb for a thorough reading of the complete draft. I am, as ever, grateful to my husband Charlie for his support behind the scenes.

GLOSSARY

coney: rabbit

cotehardie: a tight tunic for men, a long tight-fitting gown for women

girth: cinch on a western saddle

jupon: a tight tunic, usually without sleeves

Order of the Garter: a society of lay knights founded by Edward III in 1348-9, dedicated to St George, its device a blue garter; the first group including 26 knights

scrip: a small bag, wallet, or satchel

solar: private room or rooms on an upper level of a house

staithe: wharf

surcoat: an outer coat, or garment, usually of rich material; if wearing armour, this would be worn over the armour, whereas the jupon would be worn under the armour

…certeinly a man hath moost honour
  To dyen in his excellence and flour,
  Whan he is siker of his goode name;
  Thanne hath he doon his freend, ne hym, no shame.

Geoffrey Chaucer,
The Knight's Tale

Oh! what a tangled web we weave
  When first we practice to deceive!

Sir Walter Scott

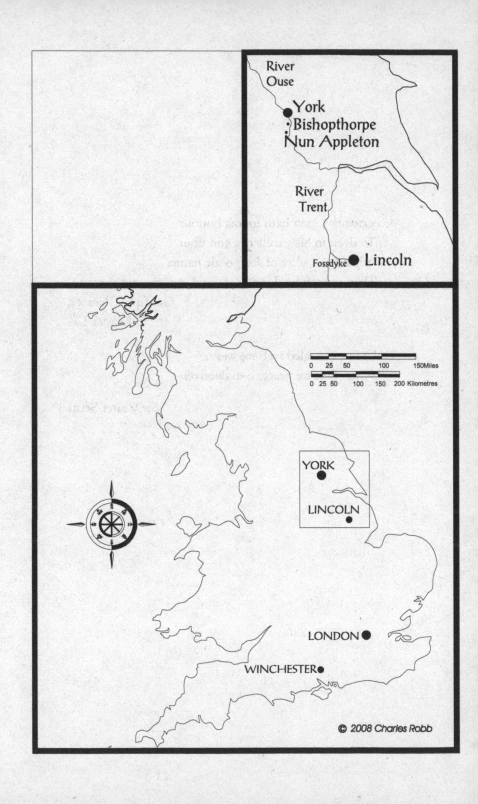

River
Ouse

● York
Bishopthorpe
Nun Appleton

River
Trent

Fossdyke ● Lincoln

0   25   50   100   150 Miles

0   25 50   100   150   200 Kilometres

YORK ●

LINCOLN ●

LONDON ●

WINCHESTER ●

© 2008 Charles Robb

PROLOGUE

BISHOPTHORPE PALACE,
LATE SEPTEMBER 1373

Archbishop Thoresby held up his hand to silence Brother Michaelo's arguments. 'God's will does not align with ours, Michaelo. We tried and failed. The chapter will not choose my nephew Richard to succeed me. It is finished.'

Though His Grace's voice was weak, his personal secretary heard in it the clear resolve. He reminded himself of the fourth step of humility in St Benedict's rule, *To go even further than* [simple obedience] *by readily accepting in patient and silent endurance, without thought of giving up or avoiding the issue, any hard and demanding things that may come our way in the course of that obedience…We are encouraged to such patience by the words of scripture: Whoever perseveres to the very end will be saved.* Bowing, Michaelo began to back away from the great bed.

'I had not realized how much you had set your heart on Richard succeeding me,' said Thoresby. 'Why, Michaelo?'

In his mind's eye Michaelo was back at the wretched day ten years earlier when he lay at the entrance to the abbey oratory, his forehead pressed to the cold, indifferently cleaned tiles, while his brethren shuffled past him. A few stumbled on his robes, one grazed his foot, another kicked his right hand. Then came a long silence in which his attempts to pray that this prostration might signal his repentance and his humility were overridden by his self-loathing. He could not believe that God wished to hear him. Ten years in Thoresby's service had restored his belief, his ability to pray. He'd believed that in the service of Richard Ravenser he would yet be safe from himself.

'I cannot return to St Mary's Abbey, Your Grace.'

'That choice passed with Abbot Campion's death. We spoke of a modest priory in Normandy where you might retreat into silent prayer. My nephew will see to that.'

A small priory in his native Normandy, near his kin, in perpetual retreat. Michaelo knew it to be a wise choice, and yet he doubted his ability to surrender to it. He was but thirty-five, too young to die to the world. He doubted that years of silent prayer and mortification of the flesh could protect him from the inevitable encounter with a young monk who stirred his desire. This was the devil undermining his courage. The devil who knew him.

'God go with you, Your Grace,' Michaelo murmured, then turned and withdrew from the sickroom. Alone in the corridor he slumped against the wall and prayed for the strength to remain by His Grace's side to the end, for the fortitude to resist the terror that bade him flee before despair overcame him. As the archbishop's personal secretary Michaelo had found his way to grace as if residing in the presence of a man of grace had transformed him. But he feared for his strength once Thoresby died, and his death was imminent. The archbishop would not live to see another Christmas, so predicted the healer Magda Digby. Brother Michaelo felt the devil hovering over his left shoulder, whispering darksome thoughts in quiet moments.

His only hope had been in His Grace's winning the dean and chapter's support for his nephew Sir Richard Ravenser to succeed him as archbishop of York. Ravenser had asked Michaelo to serve him as his personal secretary if he won the election. But except for a few of the Thoresby/Ravenser kin in the chapter and their old friend Nicholas Louth, the canons supported Alexander Neville, for King Edward apparently approved of him, or so claimed the Neville family in their aggressive campaign.

Michaelo rubbed his left shoulder. Already it ached with hellish cold.

1

A GOODLY COMPANY

MONDAY

Captain Owen Archer stood in a shaft of sunlight with his lieutenants Alfred and Gilbert, his scarred but handsome face grim as he spoke to them. As Brother Michaelo rushed about, overseeing the preparations for the large and grand company of guests expected to arrive by midafternoon, he caught snippets of the captain's commands. The fair Gilbert was to ride out with a group of guards to surround the company as it approached, and the lanky, balding Alfred was in charge of the guard protecting the perimeter of the manor of Bishopthorpe. Noticing a deep shadow beneath Archer's good eye and how he wearily rubbed the scar beneath his leather eye patch, Michaelo remembered their conversation the previous evening.

Archer had reluctantly admitted that he would miss Archbishop Thoresby, and that he resented the danger Princess Joan's visit presented. With King Edward and his heir and namesake both ailing and the Archbishop of York on his deathbed, the Scots might anticipate sufficient disarray in the northern defences that they could easily seize Prince Edward's wife as she travelled so far north. The French had no love for Prince Edward, who had proven his military prowess on their soil all too frequently, and the new King Robert II of Scotland, having renewed the Scots-French alliance, might enjoy handing Edward's wife to the French king to prove his worth.

'His Grace should have peace in his final days and not be worrying about the possibility of such a disaster,' Archer had said,

11

smacking the table with his hand. 'I would have it so.'

His voice broke with the last words—that was when Michaelo plumbed the depths of the captain's affection for the archbishop. It surprised him. Archer had spent a decade resenting His Grace. Michaelo wondered at this change.

'They say the fair Princess Joan has ever been headstrong. Pray she suddenly changes her mind and rides south,' Archer had added.

But Michaelo welcomed the distraction of a royal guest in the palace. In his opinion it would cheer them all. Though he admitted to himself that the captain and his lieutenants hardly looked cheered.

Breath. I'm fighting my own body for breath. My flesh wants to cease this struggle, but my spirit is not ready. I will soon meet St Peter at Heaven's gate. But not yet, dear Lord, not yet.

John Thoresby, Archbishop of York and sometime Lord Chancellor of England, reminded himself of this when tempted to complain about how weary he was, how frustrated he was with his struggle for full, satisfying breaths. He was still alive, *choosing* to blow on the dying embers to tease out more life, and every moment was precious.

Never in all his long life had he felt so keenly the separation of mind and body. He was a little forgetful, but for the most part his mind was still robust. He felt betrayed by the weakness of his body, which trembled now with fatigue as he adjusted his legs, trying to stretch out a cramp without attracting the attention of the healer Magda Digby, who watched so discreetly from her seat beside the foot of the bed that he sometimes forgot she was there.

'Thou art cramping.' She rose and reached beneath the covers, exploring his calves, then pressing and pulling just the right muscle, showing it how to relax.

Despite his attempt to hide his discomfort from her Thoresby was grateful for her ministrations. 'God bless you,' he murmured.

She made a quiet, chuckling sound.

'He will bless you if my prayers are worth anything,' said Thoresby. Their playful interaction lifted his spirits.

'Thy god may do as he pleases,' said Magda. Clear blue eyes in a wizened face, the wrinkles exaggerated by the smile that engaged all—eyes, mouth, cheeks—she held his gaze for a moment, her expression affectionate, kind, and teasing. Then she nodded, satisfied, and returned to her chair—a stool, actually. But as she was a tiny woman, her spine still straight and strong, she preferred it to the cushioned chair the archbishop's personal secretary, Brother Michaelo, kept offering her, which would leave her feet dangling in the air.

Thoresby had grown fond of Magda. It was such an unlikely friendship that he smiled to himself thinking about it, a pagan healer and an archbishop. Magda Digby was a pagan as far as Thoresby could decipher, always quick to reject his prayers for her, though she gave of herself in a most Christian way. She was a midwife and healer, preferring to work among those who could not afford to pay her. She lived outside the city walls close to the ramshackle huts of the poor on a rock that was an island when the tide rolled upriver— many called her the Riverwoman. Owen Archer and his wife, the apothecary Lucie Wilton, had worked hard to convince Magda to come to Thoresby at Bishopthorpe. She had argued that he had the wealth to hire the best physicians in the realm. But Thoresby had observed firsthand her skill as she worked with a badly burned man a few years earlier, and the experience had opened his eyes to her profound work as a healer among the folk of York and the shire. He had decided he wanted none other caring for him at the end. He also knew she would not fuss, nor would she lie in an attempt to cheer him. There was a time when he'd condemned her, for he knew she helped women prevent unwanted births, tended some people with injuries they wished to hide from authorities, and performed other questionable services for those who could afford it in order to finance her work among the poor. But Thoresby had come to believe that her good works far outweighed those he must disapprove of as a leader of the Church.

All must come to understand Magda Digby for themselves. She was unique.

Unfortunately, his peaceful time in her care was soon to be interrupted. Later this day Joan, Princess of Wales, wife of Edward, the present King Edward's eldest son and thus the future king of England, was coming to Bishopthorpe, bringing with her a highly recommended physician as an offering. Thoresby did not wish to see the physician, but to refuse him might cause too much official interest in Magda Digby's presence. Some might consider her a heretic and oppose her presence or wish her harm, and he would be sorry to cause any discomfort to his newfound friend.

He knew Princess Joan was bringing the physician as compensation for the advice she sought from him. In her letter proposing the visit she had mentioned how the late Queen Phillippa had sought Thoresby's advice in both matters of state and personal issues, and had advised Joan to place her trust in him. Indeed, she had written, he was widely respected for his sage counsel. She need not have bribed him with compliments, for such a journey was not lightly undertaken, and he knew the seriousness of her situation. Her father-in-law the king was aged and vague, her husband Prince Edward had been suffering a wasting sickness for several years, her eldest son had died two years earlier and she feared her son Richard might be called to the throne too soon, being but six years old. Thoresby's goddaughter Gwenllian Archer was that age, and he could not imagine saddling her with adult cares. She was so young, so unformed, so vulnerable. He understood why the princess worried.

Take the boy and your ailing husband and return to Bordeaux, where you were happy, Thoresby was tempted to advise. But Joan was the granddaughter of Edward Longshanks, the present king's grandfather, the daughter of Edmund of Woodstock who had given his life for his brother, and she had been wed to two members of the Order of the Garter. She was not a woman who would run from her duty.

Nor would Thoresby neglect his duty despite Magda's advice to refuse any visitations. In one of his first conversations with Magda he'd realised she had no idea of his status. She was unaware of the extent of his power as Archbishop of York, and hence the fierce competition among the various court and Church parties to have their representative chosen as his successor. Nor did she grasp the weight of his responsibility toward the Church and the government of the realm. No wonder she treated him as an equal, he'd thought, somewhat disappointed that it wasn't a sign of a strong sense of her own personal worth. But when her behaviour did not change after he'd explained his standing to her he was strangely delighted.

'You realise that the Church of Rome is more powerful than any individual kingdom?' Thoresby asked her.

'Magda is aware that churchmen use fear of terrible suffering after death to control most of her countrymen. That has been sufficient understanding of thy power for Magda's purpose.'

Thoresby did not for a moment believe that to be the true extent of her knowledge, but he'd proceeded to explain that his See, or archbishopric, included half of the souls of the realm, and that he controlled an immense wealth as well as the spiritual conscience of half the kingdom. 'And as former Lord Chancellor I have considerable knowledge of the powerful families in the realm, their alliances, their ambitions—these same families expect me to use my influence to guide the dean and chapter of York Minster in their choice of my successor.' Although the selection of the next archbishop of York would affect not only the Church in the realm but also the political climate, it was the duty of a small group of men, the canons and the dean of York Minster, to choose Thoresby's successor. 'I've no doubt that they've spies everywhere trying to discover my intentions, whether or not I'll push harder for votes for my nephew, so that they might know whether to support or undermine me.'

'This does not sound spiritual to Magda.'

'No. If the pope and his archbishops and bishops are carrying out their duties they have little time for the spiritual life.' He dropped his gaze, embarrassed by this admission. In boasting of his temporal power he'd emphasised his spiritual poverty. It was then that he'd realised that he'd sought out Magda not just as a healer but also as a spiritual guide, sensing in her a depth of soul that he no longer found in himself.

'And the princess?' Magda had asked. 'What is her purpose in disturbing thee?'

Something in her voice suggested that she sensed his discomfort and meant to change the subject. Thoresby was grateful.

'Princess Joan might also wish to influence the chapter's vote, but her main purpose is to hear my thoughts on whom she might trust to support her young son if his father dies betimes.'

'These are heavy matters for thy sickbed,' said Magda.

'Ah, but there is a promise of blue sky behind the impending clouds—Princess Joan is one of the most beautiful women I've ever encountered, fair of face and figure, gentle and kind. She will light up this pathetic sickroom. That is a measure of God's grace.'

Magda had found that amusing.

'You leave shortly, Dame Magda?' he asked now, though as he spoke the words he heard them echo in his mind and knew that he'd asked this already, her response lost in his sometimes muddled mind.

'In a little while, Thy Grace,' she said. 'Magda and Alisoun will go to Lucie Wilton's apothecary for physicks and a rest, and then return in a few days, when thy royal visitor is not so likely to take note of common healers.'

She looked him in the eyes as she spoke, not alarmed that he'd forgotten her plans, steady in her resolve, in all things a comfort to him.

A few days. He prayed that he lived so long and was still awake and aware upon her return.

'You will remind Dame Lucie to bring my godchildren?' Gwenllian, Hugh and Emma Archer, the children of Lucie Wilton and Owen Archer, his captain of the guard, were his godchildren, and he was very fond of them.

Magda nodded. 'They will kiss thy brow before thou dost take thy leave if Magda can make that possible. Thou mightst pray to thy god for that as well.'

'You know that I have.' He smiled as he closed his eyes, but opened them with one more request. 'Ask her to bring her adopted son as well, young Jasper. He is an admirable lad.'

'Magda will include Jasper.'

Strange old crow, Magda thought as she glanced around the chamber. Silken hangings and bed coverings, embroidered cushions and finely carved chairs, the finest wines, broths made with the best ingredients—and Magda in her gown of multi-coloured rags in charge. She chuckled to herself. John Thoresby had proven to be an unexpectedly complex man of quiet wisdom, surprisingly inspiring love. She was honoured that he trusted her to care for him—she had not expected to feel so. She would mourn his passing.

Plumes of vapour floated just above the roadbed as the hot afternoon sun shone down on the mud from a week of rain. September had begun with a touch of autumn, but it now seemed like high summer again but for the cool evenings. Though they stood their posts, well aware of their captain's watchfulness, the archbishop's guards squinted against the glare when the steam shifted.

No one was more aware of the glare than Captain Owen Archer, who disliked anything that caused his one good eye to tear, effectively blinding him. Those with two functioning eyes could not appreciate their immense gift—he had not when so blessed. He sent his lieutenant, Alfred, to admonish those whose attention wandered from the road. He wanted no missteps in the plan for his men to encircle the company of the Princess of Wales as they entered Bishopthorpe, ensuring that they and only they entered the yard of Archbishop Thoresby's palace.

Owen heard the travelling party before they rode out of the woods. Horses and wagons, clopping and creaking. The herald sounded his horn as he came within sight of Owen and his men, armed and mounted and commanding the road. Owen bowed and sheathed his sword, signalling his men to begin closing in around the last of the princess's party as it halted. Knights, soldiers, clerics, a nun, and a lady were on horseback, accompanied by several carts. From the cart in the centre hung with gaily-painted fabric, a heavily veiled head emerged and then quickly withdrew. The two knights dismounted—one was much younger than the other. As Owen dismounted he noticed the usual apprehension on their faces as the knights took in his scars, the patch over his left eye.

'Captain Archer.' The older knight bowed. 'Sir Lewis Clifford. And this is Sir John Holand.'

'Sir Lewis. Sir John.' Owen was especially interested in the younger knight, Princess Joan's son by her first husband, Thomas Holand. Joan's marital history had been the talk of the realm on several occasions. As a girl of twelve, being raised in the household of the Earl of Salisbury, she had been secretly betrothed to the young Thomas Holand. But when he was away, making his name and fortune in Prussia, her guardian had married her to his son and heir, William Montague. On returning to England Thomas Holand had petitioned the Pope to overturn her marriage to William Montague in favour of her earlier secret, but still legitimate, marriage to him, and eventually won her back. In widowhood, she had won the heart of Prince Edward and, once again, entered into a clandestine marriage. Upon discovering it King Edward had been furious, having intended to use his heir's marriage for a political alliance outside the realm. But in the end he settled for dissolving the vows made in secret and solemnizing the marriage with a more official, traditional, public ceremony. Joan's sons by Thomas Holand would never be kings, but her son by Prince Edward would in his turn be heir to the throne; Owen was curious how that sat with the half-brother, whether he harboured any resentment, any ambitions beyond his station.

'I am relieved to see a seasoned soldier in charge.' Sir Lewis looked Owen in his good eye; his own were red and tired, and the dust of the road picked out the lines of fatigue on his square, tanned face. 'I had heard you were wounded in the service of Henry of Grosmont.'

'It was my great honour to serve him.' Grosmont had been Duke of Lancaster, a duchy now held by Princess Joan's brother-in-law, John of Gaunt, the second-oldest living son of King Edward III.

'I have heard you had risen to the rank of captain of archers in Lancaster's service. You were much honoured by a noble commander,' said young Sir John.

Though he did not speak it, Owen heard in that last comment Sir John's incredulity that a Welshman had been so trusted. Once again he wondered whether the young man felt shoved aside, one who feels outside the honoured circle being more keenly aware of another outsider.

Someone in the knights' company cut short a chuckle by coughing. Owen glanced up and met the amused eyes of Geoffrey Chaucer. His stomach knotted. Geoffrey's presence was a surprise, and not a pleasant one. The man had a penchant for uninvited interference and a passion for gossip. The latter was of concern to Owen not only for what might transpire at Bishopthorpe but also for what had happened in the past. Geoffrey and Owen had once travelled together to Wales in the service of John of Gaunt, the Duke of Lancaster. Geoffrey knew that Owen, a Welshman, resented the treatment of his countrymen by the English, and he might know that Owen had been approached to stay to help his people. He was also well aware of how Holand's implied comment would rankle.

'God's grace was upon me,' said Owen, returning his attention to the knights. 'Sir Lewis, Sir John, His Grace the Archbishop of York is honoured to welcome Her Grace the Princess of Wales to his palace of Bishopthorpe. Your travelling party is now in his protection.' In truth, the troop of Owen's guards led by Gilbert, his second most trusted man, had shadowed the company since noon, but the escort was now visible and solidly surrounding it. The safety of the beloved wife of Prince Edward, Prince of Wales, Duke of

Cornwall, and Lord of Aquitaine, was worth Owen's life and that of all his men.

'We've had a tragic loss this day,' said Sir Lewis. 'A servant fell from his horse, his neck broken. His body is in one of the carts.'

Here began the trouble Owen had dreaded. He crossed himself. 'Was it an accident?'

'We've no cause to think otherwise,' said Sir Lewis, but his eyes belied his words.

Owen's scarred and blinded eye prickled and ached with foreboding. 'We will arrange for his burial if you wish,' he said. He would examine the body, see what he might glean. A long journey without incident, and then a death at the approach to Bishopthorpe meant further danger, Owen was certain.

The knights bowed again and stepped back beside Princess Joan's cart.

Composing himself, Owen greeted Geoffrey Chaucer, who looked plumper and more prosperous than when last they had met. He had regular features and was a well-built man but for his short legs. It was his eyes one noticed, alert and amused, taking in the world and giving little back. He dismounted with a happy grin.

'Welcome,' said Owen. 'I'd not thought to see you here.' Not that it was inappropriate, as Geoffrey was in the household of the king, Joan's father-in-law, but he had not been included in the description of the travelling party.

'I was fortunate to hear about this journey in time to promote my services—my acquaintance with the archbishop's personal secretary and his captain of guard,' said Geoffrey with glee in his voice. He was here to revel in gossip and high drama, Owen guessed. 'It is good to see you again, Owen. I pray I have the opportunity to call on your family in York.'

Although they had worked together on several occasions, they had never met each other's families, except for Owen's late father-in-law, who had travelled with them into Wales. Owen's wife, Lucie, had long been curious about Geoffrey. 'I would like that,' he said.

'Good. So would I.' Geoffrey gave Owen a little bow and

returned to his horse.

With very mixed feelings—relief, anticipation, anxiety—Owen led the company into the yard of Bishopthorpe. The procession moved along smoothly and they were whisked within into the expert hands of Brother Michaelo while Bishopthorpe's grooms and pages helped those of the princess's party see to the beasts and carts.

Owen watched as a noblewoman, blessed with the vitality and grace of youth, climbed down from the largest cart and offered her arm to one who followed, the one he'd glimpsed veiled and cloaked against the dust of the road. White veil, green cloak—the colours of Prince Edward. Sir Lewis rushed forward and lifted Princess Joan out of the cart and onto solid ground. Owen observed the exquisite fluidity of the veils, the green cloak, and the woman's lyrical gait as she approached, and he remembered thinking of Princess Joan as moving with the grace of a willow when he'd seen her at court and at Kenilworth, when he was in the old duke's household. He'd not thought about Kenilworth in a long while, resisting the memories that quickly rose of lost friends.

'She is a vision, is she not?'

Archdeacon Jehannes must have been standing beside Owen for several seconds. His youthful face and his apparent excitement gave him a boyish air. Owen felt a momentary resentment—he was able to enjoy the moment because as Archdeacon of York he was too valuable to the next archbishop to be anxious about his future. But the feeling passed, for Jehannes deserved all the good that came his way.

'The Princess of Wales is pleasing to look on, but her presence is troublesome in the circumstances,' said Owen.

'I agree.' Jehannes grew serious, shaking his head as he watched the approaching group. 'I do not entirely understand why His Grace agreed to this excitement. He has sought calm and equanimity in our evening conversations and in the Bible passages he chooses for me to read. Perhaps he welcomes a fair distraction, eh? It is not my place to judge—nor did he ask for my opinion.' Jehannes smiled. 'He desires me to escort Princess Joan to his chamber that he might greet her. Pray that all goes smoothly.'

When the princess lifted her veil to receive Jehannes's greeting, Owen noticed the lines around her mouth and eyes and a slackening of the flesh—the little that showed within the confines of the wimple. She was Owen's age or more, in her 40s. Yet her eyes, her complexion, the grace, the smile that lit up her face—even now she was indeed most fair.

Once she, Jehannes, and her ladies passed—one of them carrying a squawking pet monkey secured by a jewelled leash—Owen moved to the body that had been lifted from a cart and placed on the ground. It was wrapped in a heavy cloth. Gesturing toward two squires looking on, Owen ordered them to carry the body to the stables beyond the palace.

'And bring whatever he'd carried on the horse, including the saddle,' he said.

To be powerful is to be isolated from most of one's fellow men—this had been the unhappiest discovery of Thoresby's career. As archbishop and lord chancellor he'd learned that few people approached him in sincere friendship, few gestures were uncalculated. Even his long friendship with the king had changed with his higher status; eventually they could no longer agree to disagree.

In his long life in the Church and at court Thoresby had gathered around him a few people he implicitly trusted. For the rest he maintained a healthy and self-protecting doubt. Few people were who they would have him believe they were. So it followed that he harboured no illusions about the princess's visit, nor did he imagine that those who accompanied her were there without purpose.

'A vigil of spies,' he muttered.

'What, Uncle?' Richard Ravenser said, startled from a doze in the chair beside Thoresby's bed. 'Spies?' Ravenser was Master of St Leonard's Hospital in York and a canon of York Minster as well as a prebend of Beverley Minster, and until Queen Phillippa's death her receiver. Despite his extensive responsibilities he'd been most attentive to his uncle in his illness, clearly out of sincere affection. Though Thoresby often chided his nephew for being a peacock in dress, he trusted him implicitly and believed he would have been a good choice for the next Archbishop of York. Ravenser had said little about his lost opportunity, though his disappointment was plain in his subdued manner—and his chronic headaches had increased in frequency.

'I was reminding myself of what we discussed earlier. We must keep our counsel and pray that the company bides here in peace and then departs in peace.'

'Amen,' said Ravenser.

They both looked toward the door as voices crowded the hall outside.

'It begins,' said Thoresby.

The stables were the temporary quarters for Owen's men and those palace servants who'd been shifted to provide space for the guests. Most slept above in the hay, though Owen and a few others would set up their cots on the main floor in the workroom. It was there he'd had them place the body.

Alfred, Owen's second in command, had appeared, having a good nose for trouble. The balding, gangly man already looked weary. When they were alone, Owen told him what he knew.

'You doubt it is a simple matter of a clumsy rider,' said Alfred.

'Were it anyone else's servant, I might find it easier to believe, but he was the servant of the emissary from the Bishop of Winchester.'

They exchanged an uncomfortable look. William Wykeham, Bishop of Winchester, had drawn trouble to himself a few years earlier on a visit to York. When he'd been Lord Chancellor and a favourite of King Edward he had made many enemies, most importantly the powerful Duke of Lancaster.

'Ah, trouble indeed.' Alfred nodded as he touched the wineskin the dead man had carried on his saddle. 'Perhaps he was drunk?'

'Then someone will have noticed it,' said Owen. 'I hope I am wrong. Come. Let's see what else we might learn.'

In silence, they unwrapped the body. There was little to see. Bruises on his face, and his head and right arm at odd angles.

'Pulled his shoulder out of joint,' said Owen.

They drew off the man's tunic.

Alfred nodded. 'If he was not already dead, that must have hurt like the devil.' He lifted the man's right hand. 'See the palm?'

'Burned by the reins. He held on tightly, eh? I might be wrong, but I would think that a man falling asleep in the saddle would loosen his grip on the reins before falling. Now if he'd died astride...'

'Do you mean his heart stopped?' Alfred considered the corpse. 'In truth, he was not so young, but not *that* old.' Gently, with the back of his hand, he touched the man's cheek. 'I'll be him one day. I don't like to think of that. Do we have a name for him?'

'Will.'

'Poor Will.' Alfred touched the discoloured neck. 'We mean no disrespect.'

Owen wondered what event in Alfred's life had brought on this mood, for he'd often seen dead men before without musing on his own end. It was not like him. 'What of the saddle?' he asked, wanting to draw his second back to the world of the living.

Alfred shrugged his shoulders hard and shook out his hands, as if waking himself, and then hoisted the saddle up onto the table. It was worn but quite serviceable, well maintained, the leather supple, with a pouch for a wineskin and a strap that secured a scabbard— though the latter was empty. 'Look.' He'd turned over the girth where it had come apart.

'Perhaps it snapped from his weight as he fell.'

'Look again,' said Alfred, holding it to Owen's good eye.

Owen brought the lamp closer and saw what Alfred saw. Underneath, the strap had been cleanly cut partway through by a sharp blade.

'Will fell as it snapped,' said Alfred.

Their eyes met. They had no need to voice what they both thought. *Murder.* Someone in the company had wanted this man injured or dead. That was unsettling in itself, but when it was the company in which the Princess of Wales was travelling, that was more than unsettling. The palace was now crowded with high-born guests as impossible to herd as cats, and as opaque.

'Cursed be the day Wykeham was born,' Owen muttered.

'I doubt he cut the strap,' said Alfred with a half-hearted chuckle. 'But now we know we have trouble.'

'We do,' Owen agreed. 'And we don't know whether Will was the intended victim.'

'The emissary?'

'Wykeham's man, Dom Lambert? It's possible. Perhaps once we know the purpose of his inclusion in the party we'll have a better idea whether that might be so. We will also need to find out whether they always used the same saddle.'

'The emissary is more likely to have enemies than his servant.'

'We don't know that.'

Alfred slowly shook his head as he gazed on the corpse. 'Poor man. But truly, who would care about a servant?'

'Say nothing to anyone about this.'

'You know that I won't, Captain.'

'I do, but I feel better for saying it.' Owen coaxed a smile out of his companion. 'Let us see what else we might learn about him.'

In Will's pack were paternoster beads, part of someone's castaway comb, a clean shift and soft-soled shoes. Nothing to distinguish him as a potential murder victim. But he was from Wykeham's household.

'Put his things in the trunk by my pallet,' said Owen, handing Alfred a key. 'Including the saddle. And take care to lock it.' Alfred was again frowning down at the corpse. 'Jehannes will say a mass for him, Alfred.'

'I find myself hoping he was murdered for some crime he committed. I don't like to think he died because he served a servant of Wykeham.'

'You're beginning to think too much. Like me.'

Alfred gravely nodded as he took the key. 'I feared it would come to this.' He broke into a grin, and then bent to collect Will's belongings.

That was more like Alfred.

They moved away from the corpse, telling a servant to ask Archdeacon Jehannes to arrange for the mass and preparation of the body.

'I pray there is no one waiting for Will to return,' said Alfred.

Owen thought it best not to comment, instead attempting to distract Alfred with the business at hand, reviewing the details of the watches. While they talked a servant shook the dust from Owen's jupon. Thoresby had insulted Owen, instructing him that while the guests were present he was to present himself as a minor noble, clean, polite, not sullen, as if he were not in the habit of conducting himself in such wise. He cursed to think of it now as he washed his face and hands before donning his clean jupon.

In his days as captain of archers Owen had enjoyed feasts, enjoyed drinking with his men and then catching the eye of a pretty woman to bed afterwards. Surely those days had not been as carefree as they appeared now in his memory, but he sometimes had to work at recalling the bad times. It was not that he chafed at his present life; he loved his wife Lucie and his children beyond anything he might have imagined. And when with Lucie he still enjoyed such celebrations, proud to show her off—her beauty, her quick wit, her grace—and he was always glad to snuggle in bed with her afterwards sharing his impressions, amazed by how much more she had observed than he had. But now, being responsible for the safety of the feasters, and with a corpse in the stables and murder in the air, he looked forward with little joy to dining with them. Even more than was his habit he must watch how much he drank, he must watch his tongue, he must be ready to move if anyone misbehaved.

The two nuns in the princess's company appeared with two servants—they were to take charge of the body. Owen thanked them and headed to the hall.

When he entered Bishopthorpe's great hall he was amazed that within a few hours of the arrival of so many guests most of them were already seated and feasting. The guests were seated facing inward at trestle tables arranged in a U, the servants bustling about within filling tankards and delivering trenchers and platters of meat. Owen's stomach growled as he turned his head slowly, sweeping the crowd with his half-vision seeking Brother Michaelo, who was adamant about the order of guests. Owen did not intend to cause a fuss by taking a seat on the wrong bench, an argument with a frenetic Michaelo not worth the time saved. His gaze came to rest on Thoresby at the high table on the dais beside Princess Joan and he wondered whether the archbishop had heard of the servant's death.

Archbishop Thoresby looked pale, and his deep-set eyes were over-large in his illness-ravaged face. His elegant robes provided some heft and colour to his otherwise skeletal frame, but he was funereal beside Princess Joan's magnificence. Her cotehardie was of a costly blue silk, the neckline low, exposing plump, milk-white shoulders, and her surcoat, embroidered with fleur de lis, was ermine-lined despite the early autumn warmth. Delicate gold brooches secured her sleeves, and a gold circlet held her gossamer veil. Who would not be beautiful in such attire, Owen wondered. Her features were even and her eyes expressive, her hair a honey gold that was doubtless enhanced in the Italian fashion, with lemon and exposure to the sun. He'd once argued with Geoffrey Chaucer about her reputation as the most beautiful woman in the realm, and Geoffrey had insisted that Owen had only to speak to the princess to understand the claim, for she surpassed all but Blanche of Lancaster in grace. Owen looked forward to testing that theory. For now, he was relieved that she had been safely delivered into the hands of Michaelo.

And suddenly there he was, Brother Michaelo, elegant in the Benedictine robes tailored for him in his native Normandy, standing beside Owen with an air of having alighted on the spot for but a heartbeat. 'All is well, Captain?'

'At present,' Owen lied. 'The hall looks crowded—this great

hall!' He would never have believed it.

'Even so, you have a seat at the second table. His Grace insists I treat you as a knight.' The monk's tone made it clear that he considered it a mistake.

'I would that Lucie might be here,' said Owen. His wife was a knight's daughter, and he often wondered whether she regretted marrying beneath her, forsaking such honours.

'Dame Lucie would grace the gathering,' said Michaelo. 'But I've no time to rue what might have been. Another time. Come.'

Owen cursed as he realized he was being guided to Geoffrey Chaucer's bench.

Michaelo paused to say, 'Master Geoffrey requested that I seat you by him. As it was at the very table to which I'd assigned you I accommodated him. I apologize if you find it uncomfortable. I know that the two of you had your differences in Wales.'

Brother Michaelo had accompanied them on that journey, though Owen had not thought his relationship with Geoffrey had become uncomfortable until after the monk and Owen's father-in-law had been left at St David's.

'I'm honoured that Geoffrey sought my company,' Owen lied, as there was nothing to be done. 'By meal's end I'll have a head full of gossip concerning all in the company.' It might prove helpful.

Michaelo's long, expressive nose quivered. 'I pray you will share what you learn, in gratitude for my making it possible. And for seating you despite the dust on your surcoat and mud on your boots.' He sniffed as he backed away.

There was no pleasing him. Owen might have saved his time and effort—but he reminded himself that he'd done it for Thoresby, not his pompous secretary.

'God go with you,' Owen muttered.

As Geoffrey shifted on the bench to make room for Owen, Michaelo motioned for a server to fill a tankard for him.

'Brother Michaelo has not aged a day in the four years since we met,' said Geoffrey.

'He has not aged a day since I met him ten years ago,' said

Owen. 'I have wondered whether he made a pact with the devil.'

Owen and Geoffrey toasted one another and exchanged insults about their respective changes. Then Geoffrey grew serious.

'I see we come not a moment too soon. John Thoresby is much diminished in flesh.'

Owen nodded. 'I had not expected to see him in the hall again. The effort is a gift of great price for the pleasure and honour of Princess Joan.'

'You can see that the princess is well aware of that,' said Geoffrey. 'Look how she bends to hear him, offers him food.'

Owen watched for a few moments and saw indeed how she bowed her head close to Thoresby to listen, lifting her veil to do so, and then offered a titbit of food at the end of a jewelled knife as she replied. Her expression was that of quiet joy, neither silly nor smotheringly concerned. Thoresby's eyes seemed brighter than Owen had seen them in a long while.

'It appears he finds it worth the sacrifice,' said Owen, his heart lightening a little. His changed feelings toward Thoresby kept surprising him. He'd spent most of his time in Thoresby's service wishing he served elsewhere, but now that the archbishop was dying Owen's heart felt heavy with grief. He did not wish to think about that. 'Since you and I last met, Geoffrey, I have been blessed with a second daughter. My family thrives. How go your son and wife?'

'They are well, God be praised. Though neither of them are as delighted by our new quarters over Aldgate as I am. Pippa is accustomed to the spacious palaces of the royal family. She is not fond of London.' He skewered a piece of meat.

Owen chewed a mouthful of tender coney spiced with just the right amount of ginger, washing it down with wine of a quality he was not often served. He could not deny that as far as the dining there was much to recommend this visitation. He tried not to see Will's corpse in front of him.

Needing a distraction he lowered his voice to ask, 'What can you tell me about the members of your company? What of Lewis Clifford?'

Geoffrey chuckled. 'He composes dreadful poetry, but is otherwise an upstanding member of Prince Edward's circle.' He, too, spoke in a voice loud enough to be heard over the background clamour of a crowd feasting but soft enough to avoid being overheard by the others at the table. 'You met the princess's son John Holand, who struts about as if unaware he's an untried youth. He is most attentive to Lady Sybilla, one of his mother's ladies. The one with the gurgling laugh.'

Owen had noticed her, a plump woman with inviting lips and bold eyes—the one who had ridden in the cart with the princess. 'Isn't she a married woman?'

'Yes, poor man, elderly, surely cuckolded. The other lady is Eleanor, quick-witted and practical. Everyone in the company seems at ease with her.'

She was a petite, attractive woman, with compelling eyes and a graceful carriage. She seemed familiar. Owen had a vague memory of flirting with a woman much like her long ago, and yet not like her, for this woman's eyes bespoke suffering and his memory conjured a merry woman, free of cares.

'She has a tragic air about her,' said Owen.

'Which is perhaps what puts all at ease—suffering invites confidence, eh?' Geoffrey chuckled. 'As you see, Princess Joan surrounds herself with people pleasing to look on. I was not her choice!'

When Owen had first met Geoffrey he'd found his habit of self-deprecation annoying as he was pleasant-looking enough—there was nothing about him that Owen found silly except that he enjoyed belittling himself. He glanced back at Lady Eleanor, trying to decide whether she was old enough for him to have bedded her perhaps fifteen years earlier. It might be she, grown subtle with the years, more beautiful burnished by time…He shook himself out of the memory.

'What can you tell me of the sisters?' Owen asked.

'Dames Katherine and Clarice, Cistercians—but of course you see that in their pale habits—from Nun Appleton. They are to assist

Master Walter, the physician, in the archbishop's sickroom. Be wary of Walter, for he is quite the gossip.'

Owen noticed that the cleric sitting beside Geoffrey had grown quiet, as if straining to hear their whispered conversation. He'd wondered about him when he'd taken his seat, a striking man, large dark eyes, well-defined lips, high cheekbones and a long, elegant nose, pale hair curling about his tonsure, all his features well-proportioned and pleasing. A mature angel was what had come to Owen's mind, and he'd been surprised that Brother Michaelo paid him no attention, handsome men being his weakness. Owen looked at Geoffrey as he nodded toward the man.

Geoffrey understood at once and, leaning back so that the man and Owen might make eye contact, said, 'Dom Lambert, allow me to introduce you to His Grace's Captain of Guard, Owen Archer.'

So this was the murdered man's master. Owen bowed to the cleric, whose expression was coolly polite, allowing a mere hint of a smile.

'Dom Lambert comes with an embassy from William Wykeham, Bishop of Winchester,' said Geoffrey.

'Captain Archer.' Lambert bowed his head. 'Bishop William has spoken of your brave efforts on his behalf.'

'I am honoured,' said Owen, though he imagined that much of what Wykeham had said was the opposite of complimentary. They were not friends. 'My condolences on the death of your servant.'

The handsome face softened a little. 'May Will rest in peace,' he murmured, crossing himself.

Owen was trying to think of a tactful way to ask whether Lambert thought the servant's death an accident when Brother Michaelo swirled to a halt across the table.

'His Grace requests your presence, Captain Archer. For a moment only.'

'Fortunate man,' Geoffrey whispered. 'You are to be introduced to Princess Joan.'

As Owen rose he lifted his cap and raked a hand through his hair, a subconscious reaction to being presented to a great lady.

'Approach him as I have approached you, from the opposite side of the table.' The servants' side, Michaelo meant. Owen cursed—like Thoresby, Michaelo behaved as if Owen had no experience of courtly manners.

Sir Lewis sat to one side of Thoresby and Princess Joan to the other. Beside her was her son Sir John, beside Sir Lewis was Lady Sybilla of the gurgling laugh, fair hair caught up beneath a veil almost as translucent as the princess's. She looked interested in Owen as he approached, one hand fluttering over her low-cut bodice. He forced his attention back to His Grace, who had just noticed him.

'Archer. Come.' Thoresby waved him closer. 'I would introduce you to my esteemed guest, the Princess of Wales.'

The archbishop's voice was faint, his eyes slightly unfocussed. Owen wanted time to reverse. He wanted his overbearing, devious archbishop back. He wanted to resent this man, not pity him, especially not mourn him.

Thoresby was saying something to Princess Joan about her need for a sergeant of the household, and as she smiled sweetly she was closely studying Owen.

'I understand,' she said, 'that you rose to captain of archers in Henry of Grosmont's service, and that when you were blinded he educated you so that you might serve as his spy. So that he might be in two places at once.' She paused with her head tilted to one side, awaiting a response.

Owen could not think what to say, too busy wondering whether it was Thoresby or the old duke who had spoken of this to her and amazed that either would divulge his role, which depended on secrecy.

'You are taken aback,' she said, with no attempt to hide amusement. 'We all have eyes and ears in our service, Captain, and make it our business to know those of our peers.'

He'd prided himself on being inconspicuous. He felt shamed. Slighted. 'Your Grace,' he said, bowing to her. 'I am honoured to be known to you.' He felt mute and awkward; in addition to the unexpected topic with its unpleasant revelation, he found it difficult to hear and be heard across the table and over the cacophony of music, voices, barking dogs. 'Your safety is my only concern at present.'

She bowed her head. 'I am confident that I am in good hands.'

Thoresby nodded him away. As Owen returned to his seat his head cleared enough for him to wonder whether he had been recommended to join the princess's service after Thoresby's death. Though it would of course be a great honour it was nothing he wished for. Yet how could he refuse the woman who might be his future queen if God spared her husband? He only half heard the rest of Geoffrey's gossip as he filled his belly, trying to focus on the excellent fare rather than his worries about the future. When he could eat no more, and long before he could drink no more, he departed to check on his guardsmen.

When Thoresby wished to rise from the table, he found as often happened of late that his feet seemed curled and twisted and quite impossible to set flat enough on the ground to gain purchase. God played with him, allowing him the ease to come to the feast but not to leave it on his own two feet.

'Who would you have assist you, my lord?' asked Joan in a perfectly composed tone of voice, as if she were asking his preference in the dishes set before them. He wondered whether she was practised in this from seeing to her husband, whose illness must colour their marriage in all ways.

'Archdeacon Jehannes, if you would be so kind as to catch his attention,' he said.

As the Archdeacon of York was seated just beyond Sir John on the princess's other side, it was a request Thoresby felt easy making. He heard Jehannes send a servant for Brother Michaelo. He was grateful, for he would need a man at either elbow.

God's blood but he was exhausted. The effort required to sit upright was becoming too great and he might fail at any moment.

And yet he felt it had been worth it, to sit here in his hall sharing a meal with the beautiful and gracious Joan of Kent. She was already queenly, and he regretted that he would not live long enough to see her husband crowned.

It was a clear night, cool but not unpleasant, the moon a barely discernible slice. Gazing up at the stars Owen felt a wave of melancholy. All in all, his life had improved during his time in Thoresby's service. He'd married Lucie, they'd been blessed with children, he had a place in the community of York, a respectable place. Now an uneasy change was in the air, and it saddened him. The feast had conjured memories of his life before York, when he served the old duke, Henry of Grosmont, at his palace of Kenilworth, and that, too, had brought on melancholy—or perhaps the melancholy was actually caused by the presence of death, that of Will the servant, and the imminent death of the archbishop.

Owen sat outside the barracks with a tankard of ale ready to share with Alfred when he appeared, to refresh them as they reviewed the first day of this ordeal.

From the moment he'd learned of the princess's visit Owen had disliked the timing. He understood that Thoresby's failing health was all to the purpose, that the princess wished to consult with the archbishop while she still might about whom she could trust in the North should Prince Edward die and her young son become king—evidently a very real possibility. She was right to hurry, as Geoffrey had noticed—only days before her letter arrived Thoresby had called in his kinsmen to witness his will. But surely a letter might have sufficed, delivered by someone implicitly trusted.

Thoresby had noted Owen's disapproval and grimly asked what better time he might propose. The news had seemed to buoy the archbishop's spirits—some colour had returned to his cheeks and his eyes had sparkled when he spoke of Princess Joan.

In an unusually companionable moment Thoresby had confided

to Owen that he had not originally approved of the marriage of Edward and Joan, that he'd believed Prince Edward had shown a lack of the stuff that kings must be made of in secretly marrying his father's cousin. The heir to the throne was expected to make a strategic alliance with his marriage; he should not marry for love. That had been reason enough to disapprove the marriage, but it was all the worse for the scandal of Joan's first marriage, which had also been secret, and she so young she'd not had the courage to admit to it when her guardians had arranged another marriage—the annulment had been the occasion of much gossip.

But Thoresby had said he'd come to admire Joan of Kent despite her romantically irresponsible marriages, and he was pleased that she would seek him out for advice. Owen prayed it did not prove Thoresby's undoing, that his end might arrive in a more peaceful moment.

Brother Michaelo sauntered over to where Owen sat. 'Might I join you for a moment?' he asked. 'The air is deliciously cool and abundant.'

Owen slid over to make room for Michaelo. 'How goes His Grace?'

'He is abed. Jehannes and I practically carried him he was so exhausted.'

'Stubborn to the end,' said Owen.

Michaelo sank down with an air of exhaustion and sorrow, allowing his shoulders to slump for a moment before catching himself and straightening. In that brief collapse was manifest the monk's sincere grief over his master's illness. 'What do you make of the servant's death?' he asked with false briskness.

'I don't know,' said Owen. 'I want a messenger to take the dead man's pack and wineskin to my wife.'

'I'm to send a messenger by barge to Dame Magda in the morning, after Master Walter the physician has conferred with His Grace. I understand the Riverwoman is at your home. You might use the messenger for your purpose as well, if that will suit you.'

'That would serve me very well.' Owen rose. 'Thank you. I'll bring them to you.'

'Not tonight. I cannot predict who will assail me when I return to the hall. They'll be safer with you until morning.' After a pause Michaelo asked, 'So you doubt that the servant simply fell off the horse?'

Owen considered telling Michaelo of the cut strap, but there was no need. 'Had he been anyone else's servant, I might believe it was an accident, but the servant of Wykeham's emissary?' Owen shook his head. That seemed sufficient information for Michaelo.

'You never did trust Wykeham.'

'Can you recommend that I should?'

It was Michaelo's turn to shake his head. 'I thought he would never leave that autumn when he retreated to York to lick his wounds after being coerced to step down as Lord Chancellor. His Grace would clench his teeth and forget to breathe when the bishop was in the room. And in the end his ingratitude!' Michaelo took a deep breath and sharply exhaled, as if blowing the memory away. Then he sighed again. 'The handsome Dom Lambert is without a personal servant now. I've asked Jehannes's man to assist him.'

So he had noticed the emissary. Owen smiled as he settled back down on the bench. 'You are a most excellent host,' he said.

'All must go smoothly while the Princess of Wales is here. Sweet Jesu, is she not a vision of beauty and grace?'

'She is indeed beautiful,' said Owen. 'Prince Edward is a most fortunate man in his marriage. Would that his health were better.'

'Do you believe the rumours that Lancaster has his eyes on the throne?'

'Whether or not I believe them is of no importance. It worries me that the clerics all around me believe them. If they did not, why would anyone care whether Alexander Neville is the next Archbishop of York? They dislike him because he is Lancaster's man.'

Michaelo coughed. 'There is more beneath their displeasure, Archer. I read the letters when Alexander Neville was fighting for the archdeaconry of Cornwall. I witnessed the King's fury over what Neville was doing in Avignon, whispering in the Pope's ear against our king's choices, presenting petitions listing his complaints without the king's permission—well, of course, since he knew full well that in all things he was going counter to the king's interests.'

'I had no idea.'

'I intend to be far from York if Alexander Neville is chosen.' Michaelo softly moaned. 'God help us, Archer. That he is considered now is a sign of the king's disinterest in his duty, God forgive me for my disrespect in saying so.' He crossed himself.

'I'll not hand you over to the sheriff,' Owen teased, 'though you've added to the worry that's burning my gut.'

'You are worried about having a murderer among us.'

'I am, and you've just pointed out to me afresh what an unsettled time this is. I did my best to enforce peace by convincing His Grace to send away his kin and the clerics from York Minster.' Owen trusted the two who remained—Thoresby's nephew Richard Ravenser because he knew Princess Joan, and Thoresby's former personal secretary Archdeacon Jehannes because the archbishop found him a comforting presence in the wee hours, when he would read scripture to distract him from his wakefulness. 'Most of the guards have served under me in the archbishop's household for at least a year. And the few I added for this occasion I chose with care.' He said nothing for a while, looking up at the stars. It had been a tense day, and now with the spectre of trouble in the crowded palace, the rich food—he needed to move about in the night air before he might sleep with ease. He rose. 'I need to walk. I've waited for Alfred long enough. Would you care to join me?'

Brother Michaelo shook his head as he rose. 'I must see to the guests. Bring the items to His Grace's chamber when you wake. And please, Archer, do not blame yourself for any troubles here. You have done all you could to keep the peace, and I have all confidence that you will continue to do so. His Grace could not ask for a more loyal captain and steward. It is the circumstance that is to blame. The death of the second most powerful churchman in the realm must needs be a time of strife, as everyone tries to influence the chapter at York Minster. Wykeham would have done better to send an emissary to the dean at the minster rather than the archbishop.'

'You believe Wykeham sent Dom Lambert with information to sway the choice of Thoresby's successor?' Owen asked.

'What else could it be?'

'But quite ineffectual?'

Michaelo shrugged. 'His Grace has washed his hands of it.'

'Can he truly be indifferent?'

'Now that his effort on the behalf of Sir Richard has failed? Yes, he can. He has made his peace with God, each breath requires painful, exhausting effort—' Michaelo's voice trembled—'His Grace is now beyond caring who succeeds him, though none keen on influencing the choice of his successor believe that. In the past he would have tried again, indignation spurring him to stronger measures, and they know that.' He turned away from Owen, dabbing his eyes. Then, with forced gaiety, he said, 'Ah. One of the princess's ladies is abroad seeking the fresh night air. Lady Eleanor. Did you know that the other, Lady Sybilla, is a Neville by birth?'

'No, I did not. Do you think she cares who succeeds John Thoresby?'

'A cub out of that ambitious den of foxes? I've little doubt her family campaigned for her presence on this journey. Lady Eleanor, however, is said to be one of the princess's favourites.'

'Geoffrey Chaucer said all in the company find her agreeable.'

'Your friend Geoffrey. He is retained by both the king and the Duke of Lancaster. Have a care what you share with him,' said Michaelo.

'I always do,' said Owen.

'I pray you sleep well,' said Michaelo, and with a little bow, he swept away.

Owen stood for a moment watching Lady Eleanor stroll back and forth beyond the hall door. Something about her was so familiar. He had a fleeting memory of a chase through the gardens at Kenilworth, a bedchamber deserted in the middle of the afternoon, lavender scented sheets, a tinkling laughter that seemed ethereal. He'd yet to hear Lady Eleanor's laugh. How solemn she was, how beautiful. Now she cocked her head, a sweet, graceful gesture, and he knew for certain it was the woman he had pursued for days, obsessed with her, and finally bedded, oh so long ago. The next day she had been spirited away. With a sigh, he headed away from the palace. He had enough troubles with a murderer loose in the palace.

2

WHOM TO TRUST?

TUESDAY

The birdsong woke Owen at dawn. He lay with his eye still closed thinking that for the birds to sound so loud he must have forgotten to close the shutters before coming to bed. He should rise and close them or Lucie and the baby would be chilled. As he fought his way out of the fog of sleep he became aware of a continuo of snores and sighs closer than the birdsong, and gradually he remembered he was not at home in York but in the archbishop's stables at Bishopthorpe in the company of his men and some of the household servants. He need not worry about a shutter being ajar; he was not responsible for the comfort of all these folk. With that thought he turned over to settle back into sleep, but a familiar tension in his neck and jaw reminded him that he'd gone to bed worried. In a few heartbeats he remembered the death of Dom Lambert's servant, the cut strap, and the items that he wanted Lucie and Magda to examine.

'Awake at last,' someone said.

That was sufficient to bring Owen fully awake. He propped himself up on one arm and discovered Geoffrey Chaucer sitting at the foot of his pallet looking quite recovered from his journey and last night's wine. He wore no hat and his wet hair still held the marks of his comb. His clothing was finely made but drably coloured as was his custom—a jester and poet in a magistrate's costume.

'Why are you here?' Owen asked, dreading more bad news.

'I am curious whether you believe Lambert's servant's death

an accident.'

Remembering how irritating he'd found Geoffrey's awkward attempts to help his investigations in Wales Owen had no intention of confiding in him. He groaned. He'd too little sleep, and it was too soon upon waking to have to work at avoiding a conversation. He felt round on the floor for his boots, which were not where he usually put them.

'Do you see—' he glanced up.

Geoffrey was dangling the boots at arm's length. With an impish grin he handed them to Owen. 'I'll wait here while you empty your bladder.'

'That's a comfort to me,' Owen muttered. The man's early morning good humour irritated him.

Outside, Owen found few but the birds and several servants stirring. The sunrise washed the sky in watery blues and pinks but had not yet lit up the ground, which was vague with the mist of the dew rising. In the short time it took to relieve himself Owen felt the damp seeping into his leggings. His joints creaked in complaint as he walked back to the barracks and his mind churned through insults and slights that might inspire Geoffrey to leave him alone.

Geoffrey still sat on Owen's pallet with his chin tucked into his chest, eyes closed, seemingly asleep. But he looked up as soon as Owen was a few strides away.

'So you don't believe it was an accident?' Owen asked as he continued to dress, strapping on his belt, tugging a comb through his hair.

'Had it been anyone else's servant, perhaps. But Dom Lambert is the awkward addition to the company, someone who might have unpleasant business with the archbishop.'

He'd expressed Owen's thoughts precisely. Perhaps Geoffrey could be of help. 'Has he been treated differently from the others?'

'On the journey he kept his counsel and removed himself for quiet prayer when we halted.' Geoffrey screwed up his face. 'Now that I consider it he was often out of sight of the group.'

'Did anyone accompany him?'

'I wish I'd had the sense to notice.'

'Did his servant Will go with him?'

Geoffrey shook his head. 'No. He stayed with the other servants.'

'It was the servant, not Dom Lambert, who fell,' Owen pointed out. 'You say you can imagine why the master might have been killed, but what about the servant?'

'I'm assuming Lambert bears letters from Wykeham, and perhaps someone thought the servant carried them.' Geoffrey shook his head. 'But that would explain a theft, not a servant's death.'

'Men do fall off their mounts, Geoffrey.' Owen picked up his own pack in which he'd stuffed the smaller bag containing the servant's belongings, having removed the damaged strap from the saddle before he'd gone to sleep. 'I must attend His Grace. You are welcome to nap on my pallet.'

But of course Geoffrey fell in step with him. 'I know the guests. You don't.'

'And what are we going to ask them—why did you push poor Will off his horse?'

Geoffrey laughed. 'Why not? The question might startle someone to confess.'

Owen laughed as well. He'd forgotten what an agreeable companion Geoffrey could be, and the irresistible laugh the man had, as if mirth bubbled up in him from a deep, deep well.

More servants were moving about now out in the yard, and the heavyset nun stood outside with the physician, Master Walter. She had her head bowed as she listened to him, nodding now and then. The physician spoke with a frowning earnestness, punctuating his words with grand gestures that took up a great deal more space than his short, slender, almost childish body would in repose. Owen and Geoffrey greeted the pair as they passed. Once in the hall, Owen bid his companion a good morning—whispering, for most still slept on the pallets lining the floor. This time Geoffrey said nothing, merely continuing on down the aisle that led to the fire.

Weak and often slight of breath, Thoresby had arranged to have his bedchamber moved from the solar above to his parlour beyond the great hall. Owen skirted the sleeping guests and found a cluster of servants outside the chamber door listening to instructions from the second nun. Tall, slender, with an authoritative air tempered by a melodious voice, she seemed absolutely in command. Brother Michaelo answered to Owen's knock and drew him into the room, hastily closing the door.

'Dame Clarice will be my undoing. She is contradicting all our arrangements, and inspiring me to extreme measures to silence her,' Michaelo hissed, a tensely held bundle of righteous indignation. 'If you wish to speak to His Grace you must be quick; Master Walter will be here in a few moments.'

'How is His Grace?'

Michaelo lowered his eyes, shaking his head slightly. 'As you see.' Without the animation of his irritation the monk's exhausted state was more obvious, lines extending from inner eye to chin on either side of his mouth, shoulders sagging.

'I need not bother him,' said Owen. 'I have the items we spoke of.' Owen opened his pack and handed Michaelo the smaller one. 'If I could have writing material I'll write a message for Lucie.'

'Is that Archer?' This morning Thoresby's voice was hardly more than a frail wheeze.

Owen crossed himself and then tried to shake off any posture of grief, swallowing his emotion as he strode over to the bed. 'It is, Your Grace.'

Richard Ravenser sat in a chair beside the archbishop, balancing rolls of parchment on his elegantly draped lap.

'Good morning, Captain.' Ravenser did not smile. He was a younger version of his uncle and looked this morning as the archbishop had when Owen had first met him—having them side by side emphasized for Owen how frail the old man was who lay just beyond Ravenser. Thoresby's grizzled head propped on pillows, his watery eyes, the burst blood vessels on his cheeks from his frequent coughing—all this immeasurably saddened Owen.

'Sir Richard,' Owen bowed his head to Ravenser, then forced himself to make eye contact with Thoresby. 'Your Grace.'

'We know about Dom Lambert's loss,' said Ravenser, clearly hoping to cut Owen short.

But Owen had his duty. 'His servant, yes. His saddle was weakened, Your Grace, the girth cut partway through.'

The emotion that passed across Ravenser's face made it clear he'd no idea that Will's death had not been an accident. 'God help us,' he said. 'This is troubling news.'

'It need not lead to more trouble,' said Thoresby speaking softly, 'now that the company is here, surrounded by my guard.'

'It was likely someone in the company who fixed the saddle,' Owen said.

'Then you have a heavy responsibility, Archer,' said Thoresby, his voice a little stronger.

Of course he would say that. 'I am sending his pack and wineskin to Lucie. If there is anything else unusual, my wife will find it.'

'Good,' said Thoresby. 'We shall tell Lambert when we see him later.'

Without hesitation Owen shook his head.

'We should not tell him?' Thoresby seemed to perk up even more. No matter how ill he was he did not like to be contradicted.

'I advise keeping this to ourselves,' said Owen. 'I would rather the company knew nothing of this until I have something to tell them.'

'I'll consider this.' Thoresby looked and sounded annoyed.

Owen wished he might insist that it be kept from the visitors, but of course he could not, having no right to do so. But he could plant seeds of doubt. 'As for Lambert, there is always the possibility—though it might seem unlikely at present—that he is guilty.'

Thoresby began to cough and Ravenser leaned over with a cup of something—Owen guessed honeyed water.

'Uncle?' Ravenser straightened with a surprised expression that softened into a bemused smile. 'He's laughing,' he said to Owen.

'The pretty Dom Lambert arranging for his servant to fall off his horse,' Thoresby gasped.

Ravenser grinned. 'It does paint an improbable picture.' He grew more serious. 'But what if he asks for his servant's possessions?'

'With all the guests and extra staff it is difficult to find anything at present. Make that excuse until we are at ease with telling him what we did with them or a messenger returns them.'

Ravenser nodded, looking relieved.

Owen was for the most part gratified that Thoresby and Ravenser seemed comfortable with his suggestion. He excused himself to write a message to Lucie, and afterwards departed.

A low stone wall warmed by a hot sun, lavender spears moving in a breeze so subtle he would not be aware of it were it not for the bobbing of the bloom-laden stalks. Thoresby fought to remain in the memory of his garden in York, but someone kept calling to him.

'God's blood, what do you want?' he growled, opening his eyes to a stranger with very blond nose hairs. He'd never seen such fair nose hair. 'Who are you?'

'Master Walter of Lincoln,' the man said.

Dear God, the physician. Thoresby groaned. He'd insulted the man whom the princess had brought as a gift. 'Forgive me. I was in such a pleasant dream of summer.'

Walter moved far enough away for Thoresby to see more of his face. He was a man of middle years, though his small stature gave him a boyish air.

'I am sorry to have interrupted your dream, Your Grace.' Walter's smile was intended to look kind, but it was the unpleasant kindness of someone who believes he's dealing with an idiot. 'I have come to examine you.'

'I know your purpose in coming to Bishopthorpe.' Thoresby wanted the man to know he knew where he was. 'The Princess of Wales believes you might heal me, though I've never heard of a cure for old age.' He was sorry for that last snipe the moment he uttered it. There was no need to spoon feed the physician an excuse to neglect his duty. 'I did not mean to sound so ungracious,' he added. 'I am yours to command.'

It was a tedious experience, though not as physically uncomfortable as some of Magda Digby's probing. Master Walter did not pry Thoresby's eyelids quite so wide as she had, nor did he scrape his tongue or press in as many tender areas. The physician seemed to consider his astrological charts as more likely to know what ailed Thoresby than his body might, though Walter did exhibit some fascination with a flask of archiepiscopal urine, studying it, sniffing it, swirling it about. Thoresby thought the physician's pale hair, including eyebrows, eyelashes, and apparently facial hair made him look oddly infantile. That and his unusually small frame. His appearance did not inspire confidence.

'Your Grace, you need only say so and I'll banish him from the chamber,' Brother Michaelo whispered while Walter was far from the bed.

'He means me no harm,' said Thoresby. Michaelo's obvious discomfort amused him for a while. But gradually his efforts to breathe quietly so as not to alarm the physician made his head pound and Thoresby wished he might nap.

'Is it true you've been cared for by a pagan midwife?' Master Walter asked at one point, as he was sniffing Thoresby's mouth once more.

Of course it was impossible for him to speak at that moment, so he ignored the question.

When Walter sat down to consider his charts once more he said, 'You do not wish to comment on the rumour of the midwife, Your Grace?'

Impertinent little man. 'I could not while your nose was in my mouth. Pagan? I suppose she is. Midwife? She is that, but much more.'

'Might I ask why you would choose such a woman to attend you?'

'I doubt there's a soul in York without a story of her remarkable skill as a healer. I myself witnessed her faultless care of a badly burned man.'

'He is alive?'

'No. But his passing was peaceful, for she had made it so.'

Walter sniffed and grew quiet. Thoresby wished he had the breath to tell Master Walter of Magda's soothing compresses and tisanes, how her mere presence calmed his feverish thoughts. But he did not. He allowed his eyes to flutter shut, and searched for the warm summer garden, the drowsy drone of the bees.

'Your Grace?'

The infernal Walter again, he of the blond nasal hair. 'I am here.'

With much hesitation and astrological nonsense Master Walter declared Thoresby beyond the turning point, facing imminent death. 'It is a matter of easing your passing with prayer and pleasant surroundings,' he concluded.

This sentence was no surprise to Thoresby. Though he managed to rally for stretches of time almost every day, he felt closer to death each time the weakness returned. 'It is a pity that you wasted your time.'

'I do not consider it a waste, Your Grace.'

'You are kind. I beseech you, rest now, enjoy your time in my home. You need not hover about my chamber. I shall send for Dame Magda,' said Thoresby. 'Michaelo? Did you hear?'

Michaelo bent to him. 'I did, Your Grace. I have a messenger waiting for the word to depart. The bargeman awaits him.'

'You would bring back the pagan?' asked Master Walter in a voice sharp with disbelief. 'The sisters will be ill at ease with her.'

'Then the sisters may return to their cells,' growled Thoresby. 'I did not ask for them. Michaelo, send for Dame Magda and her apprentice.'

With an impatient sniff—the man must exhaust those pale nose hairs—Master Walter began to gather his things.

'What killed the servant?' Thoresby asked.

Master Walter glanced up with a frown. 'Your Grace?'

'His Grace is concerned about Dom Lambert's servant,' said Michaelo. 'He wishes to know what you think caused the man's death.'

Thoresby nodded his thanks. He would expend no more energy on speaking with the physician.

'He fell off his horse, Your Grace,' said Master Walter.

Thoresby shook his head at Michaelo and gestured for more.

'We know that, Master Walter. But was his neck broken? His back? Did he hit his head?'

'I believe his neck broke,' said Master Walter. 'But it matters little to him.'

'It will matter to Wykeham,' Thoresby breathed.

'He made it so far, and then fell off his horse,' said Michaelo. 'Did someone arrange it? Did someone wish to deprive Dom Lambert of his guard?'

'Guard?' Master Walter shook his head. 'He was but a servant.'

Michaelo opened his mouth, but Thoresby shook his head. The physician was clearly disinterested in the death, and uninformed.

'I shall rest until the Princess of Wales arrives,' Thoresby said, closing his eyes.

Not so long ago Thoresby would have felt as did the physician, that a servant's death was of no consequence, but not this particular servant's, and not in the circumstances. A member of the princess's travelling party meeting such an ambiguous end—no, he never would have found that of no concern. The physician was a fool.

With the grace of one brought up to adorn the royal court, Princess Joan approached Thoresby's great canopied bed in a swirl of pale silk and pearls, flowing into an elegant obeisance, bowing her veiled head to receive his blessing. He drank in a sensual bouquet of roses and spice; as his sense of smell had faded of late, she must be heavily perfumed for him to be able to name the flower. He wondered whether she'd found out about his paltry sense of smell and ensured that she wore enough.

'How do you find the physician?' Her look was searching, no doubt hoping for approval of her offering.

It pained Thoresby to disappoint her, but he had vowed to speak no untruth for the time left to him. He had little strength as it was, and he would not waste it on a lie. 'Master Walter believes me to be beyond his help, my lady.'

Her grey eyes sparked. '*Mon Dieu*! He said this to you?'

Thoresby heard the Aquitaine in her speech; it was said she had wept most bitterly to leave Bordeaux and return to England when her husband's ill-judged campaign in Spain ruined his health and his ability to rule Gascony. Thoresby made so bold as to touch her hand as he smiled his reassurance.

'I saw it in his shoulders, his eyes, my lady.' He saw no reason to distress her if he could truthfully reassure her. He waited until she calmed a little. 'I am grateful for your concern. Touched by it, and honoured. But I assure you I have made my peace with my Lord and Saviour. Death holds no terror for me. I do not fear it.'

But Princess Joan was not a friend of death. 'I cannot believe there is nothing he might do.' In her sorrowful expression Thoresby saw that she was at war with Death—no doubt because of her husband's failing health.

'Be at peace, I pray you, my lady,' said Thoresby. 'I would rather learn in what way I might be of some assistance or comfort to *you*.'

She sighed and delicately perched on the chair a servant had placed beside the bed. The whisper of her silken garments delighted Thoresby, the sound imparting a beauty to the moment. In her lovely grey eyes he saw the weight of her position in the realm, and the sorrow she bore about her husband's illness. God had not been kind to Joan and Edward.

'Sweet lady, I would clear the sorrow from your brow.' Because he was an old, dying man he could say such things to a princess.

She honoured him with one of the saddest smiles he'd ever seen. 'Your Grace, I fear for my family. I fear—' she bowed her head. He thought of swans bending to their young. In a moment she faced him again with those pained, sad, beautiful eyes. 'You know how I lost my father.' It was little more than a whisper. 'You know how my father Edmund, the Earl of Kent, was cut down by Queen

Isabella and Roger Mortimer.'

'What is this? Such an old sorrow eats at your heart?' asked Thoresby.

Joan's father Edmund of Woodstock had been the half-brother of Edward of Caernarfon, the former king and father of the present king. Edward of Caernarfon had been deposed by his wife Isabella and her lover Roger Mortimer, and was rumoured to have died in captivity. But Joan's father Edmund had been convinced that his elder half-brother was alive, and he had won powerful backing for a plan to rescue Edward. Thoresby had been a young man at the time and had been surprised by the support the Earl of Kent had gathered, for he'd had a reputation as a young man quick to excite but also quick to lose interest. Indeed some had considered him a poor risk as he'd initially supported Isabella. From his present vantage point Thoresby understood that brotherly love had overcome all else, and that whatever Edmund's reputation, what he'd professed had been more than plausible to those courageous enough to stand up against Mortimer and Isabella. In any case, Edmund had been brought before Mortimer and condemned without the trial appropriate to a peer of the realm, then executed by a convicted criminal—the only man willing to risk his soul to do the chore in exchange for a pardon.

'This is my fear, Your Grace,' said Joan, her voice stronger, but still breathy, as if afraid to speak her fear too loudly. 'My Edward, my beloved husband, suffers so because of the sins of his grandmother—scheming against the anointed king, betraying her marriage vows with Roger Mortimer, and finally plotting her husband's murder. I fear that our son Edward died before his time for the same sins. I fear we are cursed, Your Grace. I have come seeking your counsel as to what we might do to make reparations. How can I save my family, Your Grace?'

The emotion in her voice, how it tightened on the last question—this broke Thoresby's heart. These were heavy cares, too heavy for anything but a well-considered reply. He would not insult Joan with empty reassurance. 'I had not considered such a curse, my lady.'

'His grandmother, the queen, committed a great sin,' Joan whispered. 'And the precedent she set—an anointed king brought down by his consort and her lover—' she broke off, dabbed at her eyes with a heavily scented cloth. 'Who is to protect our surviving son Richard if my husband dies betimes?'

'This is why you have come? To ask whether I believe God would judge your family in such light?' asked Thoresby. 'To receive a penance that might release you?'

'*Mon Dieu*, I sound so selfish.'

Her blush was not so becoming as it had been in her youth, but Thoresby found it endearing. 'I must pray over this, my lady.'

'Thank you, Your Grace.' Now she looked uncomfortable, fidgeting on the chair. 'But there is more, Your Grace. And now, having already embarrassed myself, I am hesitant to continue.'

'You may speak your heart to me.'

She fussed with the hanging end of her jewelled girdle, smoothing a coil of gold thread. 'I am concerned about your successor,' she began, speaking softly, keeping her eyes on the thread. 'Our brother Lancaster wants Alexander Neville to bear the crosier of York, as does the pope. They are of like minds in this.' Now she looked into his eyes. 'But I am afraid, Your Grace. You know of the rumours concerning the ambitions of my brother-in-law. Perhaps the Nevilles are merely his pawns. Alexander's eldest brother John is not only steward of the king's household but holds a lifetime retainer in Lancaster's household as well. I fear—I cannot tell whether they will allow one of theirs to serve my Edward—or our son Richard—faithfully.'

'Alexander Neville.' Thoresby closed his eyes, feeling suddenly too weary to speak. 'I would not choose him to succeed me. When he fought for the Archdeaconry of Cornwall he seemed to me arrogant and Godless.' The king had ordered Thoresby to arbitrate in the contentious situation. Neville had done nothing to deserve any of his positions, preferring to lurk around the pope in Avignon rather than to hone his skills as a priest and prove himself a man of God. Much of his earlier preferment had been transferred to him on the death of his twin brother, who had been a much more deserving man. 'I had hoped the rumour that the Duke of Lancaster supports the pope's nomination was in error.' He realized that he had not addressed her concern. 'But I cannot believe the duke would prove disloyal to Prince Edward, his own brother.'

'I pray that you are right, Your Grace.'

So did Thoresby. 'I grieve that such concerns weigh on your mind, my lady. The death of a member of your company must also weigh heavily.'

She blinked and drew her brows together, shaking her head. 'You speak of the servant? Winchester's servant?'

Thoresby nodded.

Her eyes crinkled into an affectionate smile. 'Oh, Your Grace, that was just a silly accident. Imagine—riding all this way and then sliding off his horse on the last day of the journey here. They say he rode tilted to one side for a long while, and then just slid off.' She clapped her hands. 'I am not in mourning for a servant.' Her smile faded and her eyes grew serious once more. 'My worries are for the realm, for the safety of our people.'

Her response surprised and disappointed him. Where was her heart? And even if she found it difficult to care about a servant, such a death suggested danger to the company. Indeed, there were many reasons she should care about the servant's death, but Thoresby chose not to exert his energy to speak them, for Joan was clearly uninterested. He merely nodded.

'I have tired you,' she whispered, touching his forehead with her scented cloth. 'I shall await your summons.'

As Thoresby watched her glide from the room he felt sad, disappointed by her chilly indifference. Perhaps he was a foolish old man, but he believed in the unconditional and universal compassion of the Blessed Virgin Mary, and he cherished the belief that there were living, breathing women of her ilk. He'd thought the Princess of Wales a paragon of compassion and love, that she of all women, married twice for love and so beautiful, would care about the death of a servant and about the safety of her company. He wanted her to be perfect in this. But he'd learned that she was merely human after all.

Brother Michaelo and Archdeacon Jehannes prayed with him midday, and then Thoresby napped for a little while.

'Wake me when Dom Lambert comes to see me. I should like to read what Wykeham has sent, and to talk to his emissary.'

Sleep eluded him, and he tossed so much that Jehannes took a seat by him, his eternally youthful face exuding concern.

'Is something troubling you? Do you need something, Your Grace?'

Thoresby considered the question. 'The death of Lambert's servant is troubling me. I wish to confer with Archer. I want to hear his thoughts on it. On what it might portend.' He wanted to be reassured that someone saw the potential danger in the incident.

Jehannes nodded. 'We shall send for Archer as soon as Dom Lambert has spoken with you. He is here, Your Grace.'

Thoresby had not heard the door. Michaelo and Jehannes grew skilled in silencing the world for him. Or perhaps what seemed to him sometimes unbearably enhanced senses were truly impaired, and his hearing was not nearly as acute as he believed it to be.

Jehannes now stepped aside and invited Dom Lambert to approach the bed. Thoresby was again startled by the cleric's beauty, which he found disconcerting in a plainly dressed cleric. He glanced over at Brother Michaelo, at once sorry for having done so, for the man was staring transfixed by Wykeham's emissary. Lambert, for his part, looked anxious. Joan had mentioned that it was the young man's first official mission.

'*Benedicite*, Dom Lambert. I was grieved to hear of your loss,' said Thoresby.

'*Benedicite*, Your Grace. I—Will had served me well and faithfully for many years. I shall miss him. May he be welcomed into the Lord's embrace.' He spoke in a breathy voice.

'Was he a clumsy horseman?' Thoresby asked.

The cleric stared at him for a moment, as if he hadn't understood the question. Then, with a widening of his eyes, he shook his head.

'I would not have described him so. No, Your Grace. Nor was he the drunkard some have suggested.'

Michaelo indicated that the emissary should sit. By the time Lambert had settled, Jehannes had also taken a seat near him.

'We understand that you bring letters from Bishop William of Winchester,' said Jehannes.

'I do, Dom Jehannes.' Lambert turned toward Michaelo, who motioned to the servant standing at the door with a small case to come forward. The servant handed Lambert the case and backed away. Opening the hinged lid, Lambert withdrew a rolled parchment from which dangled the seal of the Bishop of Winchester. 'Your Grace.' He began to hand it to Thoresby.

'Your Grace, would you prefer that I read it aloud?' asked Jehannes.

It was their practice of late, but Thoresby wished to handle this letter, to taste the words himself. William Wykeham, Bishop of Winchester, was a troublesome man, but Thoresby felt a bond with him, and for him to have sent an emissary under the protection of such a lofty travelling party signalled a message of some importance.

'I'll read what my eyes permit,' he said.

Almost at once, Michaelo delivered his spectacles and brought a lamp closer, then untied the roll for him.

'Bless you, Michaelo,' Thoresby murmured as he adjusted the frame on his nose and looked over the letter. 'Ah, he recommends the Bishop of Exeter—Thomas Brantingham—as Archbishop of York,' he said as he began to read. 'A good choice, but that he is only recently bishop. Still, he is a Yorkshireman.' Thoresby silently read further. Wykeham wanted to ensure that he knew of all the nastiness connected with Alexander Neville's insistence on taking his seat at the archdeaconry of Cornwall. Thoresby thought it strange that Wykeham should think he did not know about it, having been commanded by the king to handle the case. Wykeham had sent additional documents that provided detail and proof of Neville's unacceptable behaviour, particularly regarding something that involved Thoresby's family, a pointless but vicious effort. His own family. He could not imagine what that might be. He glanced up at Lambert. 'You have further documents?'

The emissary nodded toward the case, and Thoresby noticed several rolls.

'Do you know the contents?'

'I do not, Your Grace.'

Thoresby nodded and continued the letter. Wykeham pointed out how the king's sudden approval of Neville as archbishop suggested a complete change of heart regarding the man, and such a turnaround was very unlike the king. Wykeham thought it was rather another instance of Lancaster's power, and that of Alice Perrers, the king's mistress. 'Perrers,' Thoresby groaned, apparently aloud, for Michaelo muttered a curse and Jehannes crossed himself. He laid the letter on his lap, took off the spectacles, and rubbed his eyes. 'Bishop William sounds troubled, and presses me to see to this with some urgency. Of course, it might simply be that he fears I'll die before advising the king.' He lay back on the pillows. 'Brantingham. I do like the man. What do you know of him, Dom Lambert?'

The emissary actually blushed to be asked, which made Thoresby wonder at Wykeham's choice of this man for the mission. He was young, too pretty for his own good, and apparently well aware of and embarrassed by his lack of experience.

'Your Grace, the bishop has been a guest at Bishop William's palace in Winchester a few times, but I know little of him. I can say that Bishop William consults with him on issues regarding his part of the country, and clearly respects his opinion.'

'So you are part of Wykeham's household?' When Lambert nodded, Thoresby added, 'Tell me—what is your position?'

'I assist his personal secretary, Your Grace. Purely a minor deity.' His smile was disarming.

Thoresby chuckled, glad that he had found a way to relax the man. His position in Wykeham's household meant that he was deemed trustworthy. He nodded toward Jehannes. 'Let me hear these supporting papers. He writes of something personally disturbing.' He looked at each man in turn as he said, 'Whatever the matter, word of this does not leave this chamber.' All three nodded, and Michaelo ushered the servant out of the room.

Lambert held out the case to Jehannes. The archdeacon asked whether there was an order in which they should be read. 'They were placed in here as you see,' said Lambert. 'The bishop's secretary is an orderly man, so it is most likely that he placed them in order.' He touched the one beside the letter he'd already presented. 'I believe this would be next.'

Jehannes thanked Lambert in his kind way, and then lifted the roll, untied it, and gave an uncharacteristic grunt as he unrolled the document. 'There is nothing here but hints of words—it has been scraped.' He held up the parchment for all to see. 'Do you know if the secretary had reused parchment?'

'Certainly, he would have. But these were not documents he created. They had been given to Bishop William by Bishop Thomas of Exeter.'

'Perhaps he sent along a blank parchment,' Jehannes murmured, not convinced. He lifted out the next roll, untied it, unrolled it, and held up yet another blank parchment. 'Is this some sort of jape?'

Lambert blanched. 'How can that be?' He reached for the unrolled parchments, handling them as if they might spit at him, turning them this way and that. 'I don't understand. Your Grace, Archdeacon, Brother—I cannot—The case was ever on my saddle during the day, in my bed with me at night.' His voice trembled.

'Is it possible you picked up the wrong case?' Jehannes gently queried.

'No. I watched the secretary place them in here. And the letter— Bishop William's letter was in here. No. This can be no accident.'

'Unlike your servant's fall,' murmured Thoresby.

Lambert looked him in the eyes and apparently disliked what he saw, for he dropped his gaze to the blank parchments. 'Do you think—? *Deus juva me*, if someone wanted these...But how someone could make him fall while riding amidst all the others...No one has said they noticed anything.' His pretty face shone with sweat.

Thoresby tired of him. 'Pity we've no idea when the documents were switched or scraped.'

'You've not looked at these documents while travelling?' Jehannes asked, a trace of incredulity in his tone, unusually blunt for the gentle archdeacon. He, too, must find Lambert tiring.

Lambert shook his head, his fair curls bobbing, though those that touched his forehead and temple soon stuck to his sweat-slicked skin.

Thoresby closed his eyes. 'Michaelo, bring Owen Archer to me. Jehannes, Lambert, you will stay here.' As Michaelo departed, Thoresby opened one eye and asked Lambert, 'Have you no natural curiosity? You never once attempted to peek at the documents? You asked no questions?'

Lambert did not blush now. All the blood seemed drained from him, and his paleness was quite unearthly. 'No, Your Grace. To peek would have been dishonest, to ask—it was not my place to ask.'

Thoresby wondered what Wykeham had been thinking to use an idiot as an emissary.

Owen was conversing with Sir John and Sir Lewis in the hall, recounting his days in the service of Henry of Grosmont and enjoying it far more than he would have imagined possible, for Sir Lewis proved congenial and curious, and Sir John seemed interested despite his superior air. He'd intended to speak to all in the party, one by one, about Lambert's servant, in the hopes of easing his mind about the incident, though he could not imagine what would make him comfortable about the cut strap. But he'd not made it past the two knights. In fact, he'd yet to ask them about the incident.

The moment he noticed Brother Michaelo's elegant figure winding through the crowd, his face frozen in a polite smile, Owen knew something untoward had happened. He said a silent prayer that it not have to do with Wykeham's emissary. He turned back to his companions and tried to pick up his train of thought, but Michaelo was already at his side, touching his arm.

'Sir John, Sir Lewis, I fear I must deprive you of your companion. Captain, His Grace would see you at once in his chamber.' Michaelo's eyes were anxious, his speech clipped with agitation.

Fearing Thoresby was in danger, Owen immediately took his leave of the knights, and as they walked he asked Michaelo the details of the trouble. He'd placed a guard outside the archbishop's chamber window and another at his door, but he worried that was not enough.

'Important documents have been stolen. Bishop William chose a fool for an emissary. A beautiful fool, but a fool for all that.'

Owen cursed under his breath. First a dead servant, now missing documents—though he'd feared worse. 'Who is with His Grace?'

'Dom Lambert and Archdeacon Jehannes.'

'I think Sir Richard should be present as well.' Ravenser was his uncle's proxy when Thoresby's strength flagged.

'I'll find him. You know the way.' Michaelo turned back into the crowded hall.

Owen slipped into the archbishop's chamber, then paused a moment, listening to Thoresby's laboured breathing. Jehannes and the emissary quietly sat by the great bed, heads bowed as if in communal prayer. The door behind him opened, and Ravenser and Michaelo joined him. Now Jehannes and Lambert noticed the arrivals.

'Thank you for thinking to include me, Archer,' said Ravenser.

'Come. Let us see what we can learn,' said Owen, approaching the bed. 'Your Grace.' He bowed. 'Archdeacon, Dom Lambert. I've asked Sir Richard to join us.' Thoresby looked suddenly dreadful, exhausted by the day's visitations. 'Perhaps we should first allow you some rest, my lord.'

The old man shook his head. 'Time enough for that soon. Jehannes, show Archer.'

The archdeacon opened a case that sat on the bedside table and drew out a parchment roll which he handed to Owen. 'Open it,' he said.

Unrolling it, Owen thought for a moment that he'd somehow

turned it about, but flipping it over found that both sides were blank. 'What is this?'

'It should have been a document from the Bishop of Exeter, revealing something about Alexander Neville that would convince His Grace that the man should not be the next Archbishop of York,' said Jehannes, his expression unreadable, and by that Owen knew how troubled he was, for he'd always been able to read his friend the archdeacon, even in the chilly days of their first acquaintance when he was Thoresby's personal secretary.

Owen looked at Lambert, who had been watching him but now quickly averted his eyes with a self-betraying blush. 'When did this happen, Dom Lambert?' Owen asked.

The man shook his head. Merely shook his head. Thoresby cleared his throat, and when Owen looked up he motioned him closer.

'He does not know what the documents contained, but I smell the Nevilles behind this incident. You must resolve it.'

'I'll do my best, Your Grace.' Owen straightened and looked around at the others looking at him. 'We should send a messenger to Winchester. It will take time, but we must know what the documents contained.'

'No!' Lambert cried, rising from his chair. 'I beg you!'

'What do you propose we do instead?' Ravenser asked, sounding like his uncle in better days, his tone so biting and cold that Lambert flinched. 'Wykeham will learn what happened in any case, and we must know what he wished to convey to His Grace.'

Lambert clutched some of the fabric of his clerical gown as he looked at each of them in turn, his expression that of desperation. 'Then send me, I beg you.'

'You?' Ravenser turned the one syllable into an insult.

'No, Dom Lambert,' said Owen. 'You have been compromised, and we cannot risk trusting you a second time.' He looked to Thoresby for approval.

'Your Grace,' Lambert moaned, stepping close to the archbishop's bed.

Owen could not help but pity the man even though he had brought such trouble. He imagined the man had expected this mission to make his career, not humiliate him—and possibly be the death of him.

'I shall consider this, Lambert,' Thoresby said in little more than a whisper. 'Now, you must assist Archer in any way you can. He will need to know all that you can tell him.'

'Captain Archer is in charge now,' agreed Ravenser. 'He has our complete trust.'

'You need not fear him, Dom Lambert,' added Jehannes. 'Captain Archer is a fair man, a believer in the supremacy of truth.'

Owen found their praise at once gratifying and embarrassing— and he also knew their confidence in him might be withdrawn at once should he uncover something they did not wish to acknowledge. He had been in the archbishop's service too long to expect otherwise.

The emissary seemed at last to understand that he had no recourse but to acquiesce. He bobbed his head toward Owen. 'I am yours to command, Captain.' He sank back down on the stool and pressed his sleeve to his sweaty brow. Michaelo brought him a cup of wine. 'You are kind. Bless you,' said Lambert, taking a good long drink.

Owen noticed that the emissary and the secretary had avoided looking at one another—even as Michaelo poured the wine his eyes did not wander to Lambert, and Lambert never glanced at Michaelo. Owen also caught Thoresby and Ravenser exchanging a look.

Ravenser said, 'His Grace is weary. Dom Lambert, perhaps you would care to withdraw to the chapel to pray and recover from your unpleasant discovery.'

Lambert rose, looking relieved.

Understanding that they wanted to be free to discuss the situation, Owen grabbed at the moment to ask before the cleric left, 'Dom Lambert, did you and your servant have your own saddles? Did you and he ever trade them? Trade horses?'

Looking at first puzzled, then frightened, Lambert shook his head. 'I rode the same horse all the journey, and I am almost certain the same saddle, though ours were much alike. Very much alike. It is possible that Will confused them. Do you think his fall was arranged? Do you think that I was the one who was to fall?' His beautiful eyes were huge with fear and his face so pale Owen half expected him to faint. But he wondered whether it was fear that he'd almost died or fear of being found out. It was the vigorous head-shaking and rushed denial that bothered Owen.

'I do not know, Dom Lambert. I must consider every possibility.'

Lambert crossed himself. 'I wish I could be certain.'

'As you say, your servant might have accidentally switched them,' said Owen, closely watching Lambert. But the man bowed his head and so hid his eyes. 'You should be quite safe in this household. I would ask you not to walk about the fields.'

'No. I will stay with the company,' Lambert said in a soft, frightened voice.

Once Lambert had departed, Jehannes asked, 'What did you discover about the servant's saddle?' He'd leaned forward, his forearms on his lap, his eyes fixed on Owen's eye. 'Had it been tampered with?'

'It had.' Owen explained. 'Would that the Bishop of Winchester had not sent Lambert, but had kept his own counsel.'

Thoresby chuckled weakly. 'He is your nemesis, eh, Archer?' But he quickly grew serious. 'Richard, you must inform the Princess of Wales of this trouble. And her son and Sir Lewis.'

Ravenser opened his mouth to speak, but seemed to think better of it. He glanced at Owen, frowning in what seemed to be an attempt to communicate something, but said nothing, dropping his gaze to his elegantly sleeved forearms, toying with the buttons.

Owen guessed that he did not wish to be the one to question the princess's trustworthiness—not in the presence of his uncle. But someone needed to voice this; it must at least be considered. Owen felt a responsibility.

'Your Grace, is it wise to move so quickly?' he asked. 'Can you be so certain that Princess Joan had no part in the theft? Would it not be understandable for her to wish to know what Wykeham had sent you?'

Ravenser's face relaxed. 'I am reassured by Captain Archer's clear thinking.'

'I had not considered that,' said Jehannes.

Thoresby growled—softly, but it was an unmistakable growl—from the depths of his great bed. 'Princess Joan told you she has spies, Archer. She's no need to steal or damage the documents.'

'What if all other attempts to discover the matter had failed?' Owen asked.

'We cannot keep this from her,' said Thoresby. 'She will know soon enough. I prefer to inform her.'

'I merely ask because, if another person dies, we might regret having moved with too much haste,' said Owen, aware that he had already lost the argument, but feeling compelled to emphasise the gravity of the situation.

Thoresby grunted and weakly waved them on. 'I must rest.'

Owen bowed to him, as did Ravenser, and with Jehannes they moved away from the bed. Michaelo moved toward the bed, inquiring what the archbishop needed.

'Apparently you trust Sir John and Sir Lewis,' said Owen to the others.

'Certainly what the princess hears, they will soon hear,' said Ravenser, looking uncomfortable. 'I would not say it is necessarily a matter of trust.'

'Who else in the company do you think might be trusted?' Owen asked. He must speak with everyone. He must decide beforehand how to approach them, what to say, what to avoid.

'I was about to ask you about Geoffrey Chaucer, Captain,' said Ravenser. 'You've dealt with him before.'

'I'm not certain of him,' said Owen. 'His curiosity makes me uneasy. And I'm even less certain of the princess's ladies.'

'I agree about the ladies. I have a vague memory that one of them is a Neville,' said Ravenser.

'Lady Sybilla,' said Owen.

Ravenser raised an eyebrow. 'That sounds right. How did

you know?'

'Brother Michaelo told me.'

'Will we send a messenger to Winchester?' Jehannes asked.

'Of course,' said Thoresby from the bed. 'Richard will arrange it. But we'll not tell the fool.' The effort to raise his voice enough to be heard caused a coughing fit.

'God protect him,' Jehannes murmured, crossing himself.

'Even Lambert might have been bought,' said Ravenser. 'I agree that we should not tell him.'

Owen was glad of that. 'So we've only the knights and the princess in our confidence. Good. Have you any idea what Wykeham had wished His Grace to know?'

Ravenser shook his head. 'Only that it involves His Grace—a personal issue.'

'God help us,' Owen said.

'Amen,' Ravenser whispered.

Michaelo looked deeply troubled. Owen had heard him and Lambert whispering at the door, a fast, urgent exchange as the latter was departing. He did not like it.

3

A TRIFLE

LATE TUESDAY

As Owen was passing through the great hall in late afternoon he noticed a fair young man napping on a bench against a wall. Despite wavier hair and a slighter frame, the lad reminded Owen of his adopted son Jasper, and for an irrational moment his heart raced with the possibility that the lad had come to summon him, that there was trouble at home. He'd absentmindedly taken a few steps toward the bench when the sleeper shifted and revealed himself as Master Walter. Owen said a silent prayer of thanks that he had not made a fool of himself and insulted the middle-aged physician in the process. The man must be accustomed to overcompensating for his less-than-inspiring appearance.

Diminutive men like Master Walter were often consumed with anger, and therefore difficult if not dangerous. Owen wondered why Princess Joan had chosen him, what she knew of the physician. As he understood it, Walter was not her personal physician, but someone who had been recommended to her when she had inquired about physicians near York—though Owen did not consider Lincoln to be so very near. He wondered who had recommended Master Walter, and whether he might possibly have a reason to discourage any hope of Thoresby's recovery. Owen could not afford to trust anyone at the moment.

Turning his attention back to the hall, he caught Geoffrey Chaucer's eye and though he looked away at once he knew the damage was done and he would soon have the questionable pleasure of his company. He felt impatient with the crowded conditions that were going to make it difficult to manage private conversations much less prevent interruptions. He was exhausted and frustrated before he'd even begun to question the company, and he cursed the regal size of the princess's entourage. How was he to protect her while distracted by an investigation involving so many? He could place Alfred in charge of guarding the princess, but he was already depending on his second to coordinate the protection of the entire company, both the household and the guests, and he and Gilbert were working well as a team. Of course Sir Lewis and Sir John considered themselves the protectors of Princess Joan, but they were strangers here, unfamiliar with the area.

'What is wrong?' Geoffrey asked, joining Owen just as the latter had resolved to search for the knights to confer with them regarding Joan's safety. 'Your visage inspires thoughts of thunder claps.' He nodded over toward Master Walter. 'Ah, the good physician, or perhaps I should say the disappointing physician. I've heard he has washed his hands of His Grace.'

Owen noticed the physician's eyelids flickering and led Geoffrey by the elbow to a spot farther away. 'Who told you he's washed his hands of His Grace?'

'No one came to me with the news, but I have ears.'

'I believe yours might be the busiest ears in the kingdom.'

Geoffrey chuckled. 'About that you are quite wrong. Mine is idle eavesdropping. You yourself are part of a wide-reaching spy web continually spun by the ambitious and the anxious. I am nothing compared with all of you.' His smile was sly, and not entirely friendly. 'So am I right? Does Master Walter hold out no hope for His Grace's recovery?'

Owen groaned inwardly with the effort to sidestep Geoffrey's insatiable curiosity. He would have liked to think that Geoffrey took information in but did not divulge it, but his own experience disproved that. He chose his words with care. 'Master Walter looks to me like a man who considers his task completed. Have you any idea who suggested him to the princess?'

Shaking his head, Geoffrey said, 'His home in Lincoln is elegant. I don't think he is a fraud, if that is what you are wondering.'

It was not, but Owen did not want to ask such a telling question as whether a Neville had recommended him. Or a Percy—another great northern family who might have a favourite candidate to push forward as the next Archbishop of York. 'How did Master Walter behave when the servant fell?' he asked instead.

'He was one of the first to reach the poor man. He'd cried out when the servant's horse began to bolt, and it was Master Walter who declared him dead.'

'Bolted? The servant's horse suddenly went into a gallop?'

Geoffrey cocked his head and nodded, looking smug. 'So you *do* suspect the fall was no accident. What grudge do you think someone had against Dom Lambert's servant?'

'I cannot imagine why anyone would risk taking vengeance on a mere servant while in the midst of a group of people. But you said the horse bolted. Only *his* horse?'

'Yes. I imagined a bee had stung it.' Geoffrey had opened his slightly owlish eyes so wide as to be comical.

'Now you are playing the fool,' Owen said with irritation.

'I thought to lighten your mood, but I see I've soured it instead. In faith, I did at first think of a bee sting, but somehow, with such a grim result, it seemed too absurd that a bee would cause a man's death. You are very right to question the nature of the incident, I think. I don't know what happened, and no one I've talked to seems to have seen any more than I did. Which is, of course, very suspect, don't you think?' Geoffrey appeared to be holding his breath, waiting for information.

The more Geoffrey talked about the incident the more interested Owen grew in his opinion. 'Why do you say that is suspect? Do you think someone's lying to you?'

Geoffrey made a wry face. 'You are so cautious with me. More has happened, I can feel it. Had someone tampered with the horse? Or perhaps the saddle?'

'Had you?' Owen asked, thinking he might as well.

But Geoffrey's attention had wandered. 'Heavenly mother, forgive my lust,' he murmured as Lady Sybilla approached them, speaking to a servant with much fluttering of her long, silk sleeves, her colour high. 'My lady,' he said, bowing to her. 'Whatever is amiss we shall put it right.'

She looked startled, then blushed prettily. 'Master Geoffrey, I would not burden you with a trifle.' Small eyes and an unfortunately wide nose as well as a slightly overripe plumpness might have condemned Sybilla to invisibility, but what she lacked in beauty she compensated for with attitude and energy, managing to attract men's eyes and invite them to linger.

'It is not a trifle if it troubles you,' Geoffrey crooned.

'It is but a lost brooch. I am certain my maid will find it if she opens her eyes wide enough.' Sybilla waved the woman on.

'Is the brooch of value?' Owen asked.

She blushed again and dropped her gaze to her hands, smiling as if suddenly shy. 'It is of value to me, Captain Archer. But it is a simple trinket, and I cannot think it worth risking someone's life to steal, if that is what you are asking.'

'I pray that your maid finds it and eases your distress,' said Geoffrey, sounding most courteous.

Her companion Lady Eleanor joined them. Owen was again struck by the subtle change in her dark-eyed beauty.

'Is something amiss?' Eleanor asked. She glanced at Owen, then quickly averted her eyes.

'Trouble with my maid,' said Sybilla, who then excused herself and hurried off after the much maligned servant.

'Her maid is dim of wit and has caused chaos throughout this journey. Master Geoffrey, Captain.' Eleanor nodded to them without ever making eye contact and swept away.

Geoffrey turned to watch her depart. 'Did I sense something between you and Lady Eleanor?' he asked.

'It was that plain?' Owen did not like that.

'To me, yes.' Geoffrey smiled at the air and rocked on his heels.

'How delicious.'

With more serious issues to hide from Geoffrey, Owen thought he might be wise to admit to this one. 'We spent an afternoon together long ago after a week of stolen kisses. A very pleasant afternoon that I am not comfortable to remember now—and it would appear that she is also ill at ease about it.'

Geoffrey chuckled. 'And I thought Sybilla the one to watch.'

'She certainly watches all the men.'

Sir John and Sir Lewis now approached. 'Forgive me,' said Owen, 'but I must have a private word with them.'

'Tread carefully with Holand,' said Geoffrey, and then, much to Owen's surprise, he simply bowed and added, 'I am off in search of food.'

Owen greeted the knights and asked if he might talk with them out in the yard.

'You sent Master Geoffrey away,' said Sir Lewis as they moved through the crowd in the hall. 'You do not trust him, Captain?'

'His curiosity worries me,' said Owen.

'It is my experience that he gossips only with his muse,' said Lewis. 'In fact, I was surprised that he knows you. He's never spoken of you.'

Once out in the yard and away from the curious, Owen told them of the lost documents. While he listened John Holand grew increasingly irritated, frowning, shaking his head, and muttering under his breath. One discernible word was 'knave.' Owen noticed that Lewis tried to catch the young man's attention several times.

'Do you think Dom Lambert a knave?' Owen asked John.

'How can you ask that when you've just told us he failed in his mission?' the young knight said with impatience. 'Such a simple mission—deliver some letters to the archbishop. Do I think him a knave?' He sniffed. 'A fool would be more to the point.'

'Sir John,' his older companion said, softly, but in a warning tone.

John shrugged and avoided eye contact with Lewis. He had his mother's features but sharpened, colder.

'Did you note anything about Dom Lambert on the journey

that might help me understand what happened to the documents?' Owen asked.

'I paid him little heed,' John said with a shrug.

'He kept to himself,' said Lewis. 'He was courteous and helpful when needed, but quiet otherwise. Do you distrust him, Captain?'

'I find it best to begin an investigation by distrusting all,' said Owen.

'Even us?' Lewis asked with a wary smile.

'The Princess of Wales and her knights excepted, of course,' said Owen. 'What of the princess's ladies?'

'Is it ever wise to trust women?' John's grin was unpleasant.

His manner surprised Owen. He had seemed reasonably pleasant till now.

'I would advise you to ask the princess about her women,' said Lewis. 'And if you like, I will question my own men. Perhaps someone will have noticed something they'd not thought to report to me.'

'I would be most grateful for your help,' said Owen. 'I had wondered whether your men had been in your service long enough for you to be confident of their loyalty.'

Lewis frowned down at his shoes for a moment. 'Long enough, I pray. My esquire is the most recently added and he's been in my service for almost a year.'

Unfortunately, John had coloured at that question and now exploded with, 'Are you accusing us of jeopardizing my mother's life with my choice of men?'

'Sir John, the captain is merely doing his job,' Lewis said, again in the stern but soft voice. He seemed ever ready to calm the young Holand.

Owen tried smiling at the young man. 'I told you, I begin an investigation by distrusting all. Most find that reassuring.'

To Owen's surprise, the young John Holand responded by turning on his heels and heading back to the hall without a word. Lewis scowled and muttered something unintelligible.

'Is he stormy by nature?' Owen asked.

Lewis shaded his eyes from the sun as he faced Owen. He looked as weary as when he'd arrived. 'That is a more polite description of his behaviour than the pup deserves. He takes care to show only his courteous side to his betters, but the rest of his fellows see smiles one moment, foul temper the next.'

'Is it possible—'

'You wonder whether he knew Dom Lambert before the man joined our company.' Lewis shook his head. 'I am as certain as I can be that he did not.'

Thank God for that. 'Can he be trusted to say nothing about what I've just told you?'

Owen did not like that Lewis hesitated, however briefly, before nodding. But he refrained from questioning it aloud, for he needed the knight's help. He explained to him his concern for the princess's safety.

'My lady was aware that this journey might invite danger, which is why she chose me as her escort. She is my sole concern, Captain. My men and I have vowed to protect her with our lives.'

His voice was thick with pride and devotion, and the speech made Owen easier in his mind about Sir Lewis.

'God go with you, Sir Lewis. I'll be grateful for any information gleaned from your men.' And with no more ado Owen headed for the chapel in search of Lambert, though his mind was caught in the unpleasantness of John Holand. He wondered how well Lewis knew the young man, and how frank he was being about him. He was not easy in his mind about Holand.

He found Lambert lying prostrate before the altar and cursed his luck. He'd hoped that in private the cleric might have more to say. As Owen was about to withdraw into the passageway Brother Michaelo stepped through the doorway and stopped so suddenly it was as if he'd been forcibly halted. He gazed on Lambert with such a haunted expression that Owen felt quite certain that he'd been right earlier to wonder what had passed between the two churchmen. Michaelo's face was not merely the mask of grief that he'd worn of late; he looked secretive and afraid.

Owen drew Michaelo out into the corridor. 'What is troubling you?'

The monk blinked at Owen, looking confused, as if he'd just awakened. 'I don't know what I was thinking, coming here when His Grace needs me. I cannot comfort every waif who comes along. I should return to his chamber.'

'If prayer feeds your spirit, it is good that you are here. You need not engage with Dom Lambert.'

'No, of course not. But I feel that His Grace needs me,' said Michaelo. 'My mind is not at ease. I cannot pray like this. I must go.' He hurried away down the corridor, his dark robes blending him into the shadows.

A day ago Owen would not have doubted that Michaelo was obsessed with being at Thoresby's side. But he felt in his gut that something else tormented the archbishop's secretary this day, and it had to do with Lambert. Owen returned to the chapel and knelt at a *prie dieu*, intending to pray until Lambert rose from his devotions. But like Michaelo, Owen was plagued by a nagging sense that he should be elsewhere. He found himself obsessively reviewing his orders to Alfred and Gilbert, fearing that he'd omitted a crucial item. He closed his eye and tried to calm his mind by whispering Hail Mary's.

'Captain?'

Owen must have drowsed, for he found Dom Lambert kneeling beside him. Prayer would not have prevented him from sensing the man's presence.

'Thank you for waking me,' said Owen. 'I hoped to speak with you away from the others.'

'I guessed that was the reason for your presence. I have questions for you as well. Might we sit rather than kneel?'

They withdrew to a bench near the doorway on which Owen positioned himself so that he could see anyone approaching. He hoped that Lambert would confide more than others should hear.

The emissary smoothed his robes with trembling hands. 'Have they sent a messenger to Bishop William?' he asked, looking toward the altar, not at Owen. 'To inform him of my disgrace?'

'I don't know,' said Owen. 'My concern is the safety of all in the palace. What can you tell me of the company in which you travelled?'

'I know little about any in the company,' said Lambert. 'What do you wish to know?'

'I would have thought it needed no explanation. Did anyone disturb you, ask too many questions, watch you too closely?'

'Geoffrey Chaucer asks too many questions,' said Lambert with a little laugh. 'Everyone seems to find him too curious.'

Owen did not doubt that, but it was of no use—he might find Geoffrey irritating, but he did not suspect him of theft or murder. 'I think you know what I am asking. You are the emissary of William Wykeham, so recently lord chancellor, a controversial man who has been a favourite of our king. You must have been prepared for the likelihood that there would be some in your company of travellers who would be concerned about the nature of your mission, fearing that Wykeham might subvert some of their plans. Did anyone try too hard to befriend you?'

Lambert licked his lips and shook his head. 'I took care to keep to myself. It seemed the safest approach.'

'That must have been difficult, resisting their companionship. I would have thought you might delight in such company. The Princess of Wales is considered by all to be most gracious.'

Lambert drew in his shoulders and tucked in his chin, turtle-like. 'It was not difficult to remain aloof, for I did not feel worthy.'

'Who made you think that?'

'Who made me? No, you misunderstand. All were courteous. But I was thrust upon them, a stranger from outside their circle. I felt I should disturb them as little as possible.'

Lambert's cringing was too awkwardly exaggerated to be believable.

'Dom Lambert, your servant is dead and the documents you were carrying are missing.' Owen made no attempt to hide his irritation. 'How can I help you if you won't confide in me?'

'Would that I had something to tell you,' Lambert almost

whimpered. 'God help me, but I do not know why Bishop William chose me as his emissary. I am out of my depth in this company. I have done all that I could to avoid offending anyone, to ride among them as if of no substance.' He had looked imploringly at Owen, and now looked away as his face flushed crimson.

As an emissary for William Wykeham the man should have known he could not avoid curiosity. Only a simple fool would think otherwise, and Owen knew that Wykeham would not choose a simple fool for this mission. 'Your anguish in His Grace's chamber would indicate that you understood the importance of your mission, Dom Lambert. Surely you realized others would be keen to know what you carried?'

'You think me a fool.'

'No. You would like me to think that, but I don't. I believe you are hiding something, Dom Lambert, and I'm very curious what it is that you do not wish me to know.'

'Why did you ask about the saddles? Had someone done something to Will's to cause his fall?'

Owen found it of interest that this was on Lambert's mind. 'Yes, someone had weakened it. But I don't think it likely that he was the one who was meant to fall off his horse. Do you?'

Lambert crossed himself and shook his head. 'I wish I could help you, Captain.'

Owen would return to that topic. Right now Lambert was too on his guard about the saddles. 'You seem to be acquainted with Brother Michaelo.'

The cleric's sharp breath and an odd tremor in his stiffly held head told Owen that he had touched on something of interest.

'He has been most welcoming to all of us.'

'No more than that?'

Unfortunately, the quiet voices of women drifted down the corridor, and out of the gloom the nuns appeared, their pale habits framing their pale faces.

Lambert rose and excused himself. As he began to walk away he paused. 'I am sorrier than you can know that Bishop William made the mistake of choosing to send me on this mission, Captain.'

'Why do you blame yourself? It might have happened to anyone.'

'But it happened to *me*. *I* failed.'

'Whatever you do, don't wander alone beyond the palace yard,' said Owen.

Lambert nodded and hurried away.

Owen took his time rising, and passed the nuns as he departed the chapel. Dame Clarice was tall and slender, Dame Katherine of average height and plump, a good decade older than her companion. They both nodded and smiled to him. Not far behind them strode Lewis Clifford, looking relieved as he noticed Owen.

'God be praised, I've been scouring the palace and stables for you.'

Owen did not like the tense set of the man's jaw, the urgency in his tone. 'What's amiss?'

'I've two sets of messengers who need your leave to depart— one to Winchester, one to Nun Appleton.'

'You're sending the sisters away?'

Lewis shook his head. 'Her Grace is sending for documents left at the nunnery.'

'What sort of documents?'

'I don't know. My orders did not include an explanation. But she wants them here as soon as the riders can manage.'

'These are trustworthy men who can defend themselves?'

'They are.'

'Give me their names—I'll make sure they are not prevented from departing or returning.' Then Owen changed his mind. 'I'll escort them from the manor myself. Send them to me in the stable.'

'Her Grace has told no one but me, and I chose the men with care,' said Lewis. 'I don't think anyone will waylay them.'

'Have them well armed, Sir Lewis, and I'll escort them. We've had trouble enough already.'

Lewis nodded and departed.

Owen was still stewing over the mysterious documents from Nun Appleton and the failure of Lambert's mission at the evening meal, and had not noticed that Lady Sybilla had sat down beside him until he found her plump hand resting on his.

'Captain? Are you asleep sitting up and with your eye wide open?' Her voice both teased and caressed.

'I beg your pardon, my lady. I was lost in thought.' He was flattered by the intensity of her gaze. Maybe he was not so old as he felt of late. 'Did I miss anything?'

'Besides my presence? No, Captain.' Her smile was dimpled and inviting. Curious how such a plain face could be so appealing. 'I have a message for you from my mistress. She would have you escort her on a hawk hunt in the morning. His Grace has asked her to exercise his neglected hawks.'

'He assuredly did not recommend me. His Grace's falconer is trustworthy.'

'His Grace did not propose you for the hunt, it is true. But my mistress wishes you to accompany her.'

'And you?'

'Of course!'

'Then I shall be delighted.' Owen loathed hawk hunting, but he was most curious about this unexpected request, and a little anxious, recalling her need for a house sergeant. 'Have you found your brooch?'

Lady Sybilla's smile faded. 'No, Captain. It is a pity, for I borrowed it and now I must needs part with a brooch of my own to compensate my friend when we return to Berkhampstead Castle.' She smiled sweetly. 'Until morning.' With a teasingly feminine flick of her skirts she slipped away.

Anxiety about what the future would hold under Archbishop Thoresby's as yet unknown replacement had spread throughout York, not only disturbing the many religious establishments but also the civic groups. Worse was the building grief and the accompanying worry tightening around Lucie Wilton's heart. Her family would lose a friend and powerful ally, as well as her husband's employer. She caught Owen's expression in unguarded moments and guessed that he was wondering what was next for him, who he would be when he was no longer Thoresby's captain of the guard, no longer steward of Bishopthorpe, no longer the archbishop's spy. She also sensed Owen's sorrow. She always feared that another's sorrow might cause them to do something foolish or even harmful to themselves, though she did not fear that in herself. She chided herself for doubting Owen's judgement, but her imagination seemed stuck in the rut of her worries.

In the shop, out in the garden, playing with the children, of late it seemed no matter what she was doing Lucie was preoccupied with weighing possible futures for Owen in her head. She had suggested that he take responsibility for Freythorpe Hadden, the manor she'd inherited from her father. Her steward Daimon presently ran it with little interference from them, with the intention of handing it over to their son Hugh when he came of age—as the boy was not quite four, he would be managing it for a long while. But as Daimon and his wife Tildy now had several children, Lucie thought they would welcome Owen's presence. It would mean he'd often be away from York, but the manor was less than a day's ride away, so all in all it would not be much different from his duties as steward of Bishopthorpe—though the palace was closer to York than the manor Owen's responsibilities often kept him there for several days at a time. But Owen had made no decision, and that worried Lucie. She feared that he would be swept up into the household of the new archbishop—it was possible that whoever succeeded Thoresby would wish to retain his predecessor's proven captain—and that a younger prelate might spend a great deal of time in travel—to his far-flung archdeaconries, to Westminster, to wherever the king was residing—and that he would want Owen with him.

The only time Lucie found it easy to relax was when nursing little Emma, as she was doing at the moment, caught up in sweet, milky daydreams. She had been in this same position in the window seat when Magda and Alisoun had arrived the previous evening. As she had shifted the baby to her shoulder she'd noticed Magda Digby sitting near her on a bench. Now she tensed as she heard a knock on the door, and Emma began to fuss. Lucie bent to her tiny daughter and softly began to sing in order to shut out the sound of her servant Kate answering the door. She saw Kate motion Magda to the door. When the nursemaid Maud retrieved Emma to put her to bed, Lucie sought out Magda. She found her standing in the kitchen doorway to the garden examining a piece of leather. Her eyesight was remarkable for an aged woman, so Lucie guessed the intensity of her expression was a sign of trouble. Earlier Magda had been helping Kate in the kitchen, for the sleeves of her multicoloured gown were pushed up and there was a dusting of flour on one of her cheeks. As she looked up and saw Lucie, Magda slowly shook her head, a silent acknowledgement that something was indeed wrong.

'What is it?' Lucie asked. She noticed a pack on the bench beside Magda and a parchment. Written in Owen's hand, if she was not mistaken.

'Thy husband writes that the royal party has brought trouble to Bishopthorpe,' said Magda. 'See how this girth was cut just deep enough to weaken it, but not so deep as to be seen from the other side.' She held the piece of leather up to the light for Lucie. 'The cut caused it to break, and the saddle to slip.'

The cut was very clear below, and too precise to be accidental. The leather was fine, somewhat worn but supple and strong. 'You called it a girth? For a saddle?'

Magda nodded. 'The saddle of a dead man. He fell, breaking his neck.'

Lucie made the sign of the cross. 'Someone who accompanied the Princess of Wales?'

Magda nodded as she set the leather down on a bench and handed Lucie the parchment. 'The servant of an emissary from the Bishop of Winchester. Bird-eye has explained it in a letter to Magda and thee.'

Wykeham. Owen always expected trouble from him. 'What is he meddling with this time?' Lucie wondered aloud.

'Who is to sit on the throne in York Minster when Old Crow dies,' said Magda.

Old Crow. Bird-eye. Magda referred to both Thoresby and Owen as birds. Lucie had never thought 'Old Crow' fit the archbishop, but now, ill as he was, she found it chillingly appropriate. When she'd last seen him his hands had been fleshless and knobbly, like a bird's claws, and as he moved his dark gown had hung like wilting feathers.

Magda had said when she arrived, 'Old Crow is as he was when thou last saw him. Fighting for his breath, weak, weary, but at peace with himself. He is ready. He has made Magda promise to remind thee to bring the children to him as soon as Princess Joan departs. Jasper as well.'

That had surprised Lucie, for Jasper was their adopted son and not one of Thoresby's godchildren. 'He asked for Jasper?'

'Old Crow has great affection for all thy family,' Magda said.

'I've never understood it, though I am most grateful.'

'Thou hast caught the heart of an old man who regrets that he waited until writing his will to acknowledge his daughter.'

'A daughter?' Lucie had not known Thoresby had a child.

'Idonea,' said Magda. 'There are more, Magda suspects. But this one he knew of from the time of her birth. She bides at a nunnery in Hampole.'

Lucie remembered that Owen had once mentioned a liaison that had caused Thoresby belated trouble when the king's mistress Alice Perrers learned of it and used it to her advantage. 'Did Idonea know of him?'

Magda had nodded. 'Old Crow said that she has oft written letters filled with love for a father she much admires. She wrote that it was enough for her to know her father was an archbishop, and once Lord Chancellor of the realm.'

'He never replied?'

'Nay.'

'He told you of this?'

'He speaks of many things in the night, after Archdeacon Jehannes leaves him. It is not uncommon for the dying to live in the past in their last days.'

Lucie remembered the time Thoresby had escorted her children home from her father's estate, how he'd laughed with them, how they trusted him. She would have expected him to be an attentive father. 'Why did he never write to her?'

'He seems unable to explain his neglect.' Magda had held Lucie's gaze for a moment with eyes soft with sympathy. 'He is an old fool.' She'd described a man resigned to death, his interest in earthly issues already fading, and a household of people trying to hide their grief from him.

'Then perhaps Princess Joan's visit is a gift for all, something to cheer the household,' Lucie had said. 'Perhaps I was wrong to think it selfishly ill-timed on her part.'

Lucie noticed Magda watching her now with a puzzled expression. She'd been standing in the doorway holding the letter and lost in her own thoughts. 'I must be more tired than I realised,' Lucie said, and lifted the parchment to the light.

Owen explained that the leather was from the dead servant's saddle. He asked that Lucie examine the contents of the wineskin he'd sent, looking for poison or something that would have made the servant drowsy and clumsy in the saddle. He asked her to tell Magda anything else she noted about the contents of the pack.

'You are to return tomorrow?' Lucie asked. 'The physician has failed so quickly?'

'Yes. He cannot cure His Grace of old age, so the messenger is to escort Magda and Alisoun back to Bishopthorpe in the early morning. Hast thou time now to look at these items?'

Although she had not expected a cure, Lucie's heart broke a little more with the news. Thoresby was such a part of her life in York that her heavy sadness was complicated by fear that his passing would bring frighteningly profound change. She was glad to have an absorbing task to distract her from her worries. 'Of course. Come— let's take these to the workshop.' She picked up the pack and led the way through the garden to the apothecary. The workshop had been her family's main living area as well as the apothecary workshop before Lucie's late father had purchased the large house across the garden in which she and her family now lived. Her adopted son Jasper and his fellow apprentice Edric now slept up above the shop in the solar. Edric was alone in the shop at the moment, Jasper still at school. Lucie checked to make sure that he did not need her and then sat down to examine the pack. There was little in it, and nothing of much interest. But the contents of the wineskin proved interesting.

'Poppy juice?' Lucie asked as she handed Magda the dish in which she'd poured some of the wine. 'And an earth scent. Mandrake.' She nodded, and then lifted it to her nose once more and sniffed. 'And leek? What would the leek be for?'

Magda sniffed. 'Poppy and mandrake. And water germander.'

'Ah yes, that does smell like leek. Strange. The first two are such common sleeping physicks. But water germander. It helps pass water, eases gout, is soothing on wounds. Why would it be in a sleeping potion?'

'A traveller wishing to carry as little as possible. A night physick to ease gout and bring on sleep.' Magda shrugged.

'I wonder who in the princess's company suffers from gout?' Lucie asked.

Magda nodded.

When they returned to the hall, they found Lucie's elderly aunt, Phillippa, waking from a nap confused, her eyes unfocused. Ever since suffering a palsy several years earlier Phillippa alternated between competence and a vague wandering in time.

'This is one of Aunt Phillippa's difficult days,' Lucie said. She watched as Alisoun slipped out to the kitchen with Gwenllian and Hugh; she knew how Phillippa could frighten them with her confusion. Lucie appreciated the young woman's tact. The children missed her—they blamed the new nursemaid Maud for Alisoun's departure and had not warmed to her despite the woman's best efforts. Magda had not chosen Alisoun as an apprentice—indeed, she'd never felt the need for one. But the young woman had desperately wanted to work with Magda, and when Owen insisted that a woman who could be wet nurse if Lucie required one was more appropriate for the infant Emma, Alisoun had begged once more and was at last accepted. Although the girl was difficult, testy, Magda felt in her gut that she might be a gifted healer. 'The children miss Alisoun. Has she been of help to you at Bishopthorpe?' Lucie asked.

'Maud will win the children in time,' said Magda, as usual hearing all that was behind Lucie's words. 'At first Alisoun irritated Brother Michaelo with her dark looks, but she has won his approval, and in all else has been helpful and quieter than Magda thought she could be.'

'Have you seen proof that she has a gift for healing?'

Phillippa was tugging at her wimple and Lucie hurried over to calm her as Magda replied, 'Alisoun is yet a mystery.'

Later, as Jasper and Edric joined them for the evening meal, Alisoun entertained them with descriptions of the chaos at the archbishop's palace as the staff prepared to welcome Princess Joan and her large party. She was particularly cutting in her descriptions of Brother Michaelo.

'He is not a fool,' Lucie commented. 'From all accounts he was very good to my father on his last pilgrimage.'

'No, he's not a fool, but very funny all the same,' the girl remarked with a smirk.

Lucie resolved to work harder to turn the children's affections toward Maud—the household was on the whole more peaceful without Alisoun's prickly presence.

4

INTO THE WOODS

WEDNESDAY, EARLY MORNING

The air had stilled overnight and heavy mist cloaked the woodland into which Malcolm the falconer led the small party shortly after dawn—Owen, Princess Joan, Lady Sybilla, Sir John, Sir Lewis and a few servants. Malcolm dismissed Owen's suggestion that they wait until the mist lifted, assuring him that Thoresby's hawks were accustomed to the moods of the River Ouse and would hunt well even in a gentle rain. The falconer did not understand that it was the eyes of the guards that were of concern to Owen, not those of the hawks, though he did know that the guards were following them and would provide a circle of protection. As long as they could see…

Owen did not know the falconer well, having had little cause to talk to him in the past, for he had no interest in hawk hunting, preferring to fell the prey with his arrows. He saw no sport in being the beast of burden for a bird's entertainment. Ravenser had assured him that the falconer could be trusted to stay within any bounds that Owen ordered, but it was Princess Joan who had overruled him.

Joan had asked to hunt with the largest female hawk, and to carry her from the start. Owen watched with fascination as the dark-eyed, sharp-beaked hawk perched on the princess's leather-clad forearm threateningly flapped her wings as if testing the princess. Rather than extend the forearm on which the bird sat to keep it at a distance, Joan folded her arm in closer and gently stroked the hawk's chest while softly talking to her. Staring into the princess's unblinking eyes, the hawk quieted. It appeared that Joan had won her trust and respect, and as the party began to ride, the reddish-gold hawk and the straight-backed princess in her deep green gown and hat moved as if they had hunted together for years.

Elegantly garbed in leather leggings and leather tunic over a deep green shirt and sporting a peacock feather in his leather cap, John Holand had also chosen to ride with a hawk, and he too handled it with the ease of an accustomed hunter. Apparently hawk hunting was a passion mother and son shared. Lewis Clifford had his servant carry his bird until he was ready to hunt. He looked even less rested than he had the previous day. Owen wondered what had kept Lewis awake.

With a flirtatious smile and posture but serious eyes, Joan had requested that Owen ride beside her. Sir Lewis had teased that Owen was a married man, and she'd teased Lewis that she detected a touch of jealousy in his protest. Reaching back into his former life, Owen had dredged up laughter and an appreciation for court banter, a lightness that did not come easily for him in the midst of his very serious responsibility for the princess's safety.

Now, as they paused for the falconer and his boys to flush out some game, the princess tapped Owen's thigh to catch his attention. It proved most effective. Owen was immediately drawn to her.

'You are highly regarded by all. Are you aware of that, Captain Archer?' Her lips teased, but Joan watched him with a humourless intensity. He was learning to rely on her eyes for the accurate reading of her message. The rest was her public performance.

'You are kind to tell me so, my lady.'

She made an impatient sound. 'My purpose in telling you is not to be kind, Captain. Two families with great ambition reside in the North, the Percies and the Nevilles.' With her forefinger she stroked the hawk's breast as she spoke. 'I have need of someone up here whom I can trust to listen to and watch these families, and to inform me of their activities—particularly their pursuit of alliances. Their wooing, if you like.' Her smile was almost impish as she glanced sidewise at him. 'Several men have recommended you to me.' She paused for his reaction.

He tried to hide the uncomfortable confusion of interest and alarm pulsing through him. 'I am honoured to hear that, my lady.' As Owen was about to ask who had recommended him, the hawk twitched and ruffled her feathers, something on the ground catching her eye. Several coneys stumbled out of the underbrush.

'Before I depart Bishopthorpe we must discuss this more fully.' Joan bestowed on Owen a last, enigmatic smile. 'For now, the hunt begins.' She let go of her bird, who immediately spread her majestic wings and swooped toward a hesitating coney.

Not interested in watching the attack, Owen quietly dismounted and handed his reins to one of the servants. He stretched and twisted a little until his back felt usable; he did not ride often enough these days to be as at ease astride as he'd been when in the old duke's service. Thoresby had little need to send Owen on long missions away from York. He wondered whether he would travel if he were to spy for the Princess of Wales. He was surprised to feel a little thrill at the thought of joining her household.

Joan's beautiful laugh was followed by an intimate, cooing monologue; Owen guessed that her hawk had killed and returned to her. To so delight in death seemed obscene to him. He'd seen too much of it. He walked away from the hunting party, scanning the woods for his men. He had ordered that half of them be on foot, half mounted—those on foot were quieter and might observe more, those on horseback were faster. Walking very slowly, his eye trained about ten strides beyond the company, he gradually picked out with his half-vision three men, the centre one mounted. All were still but alert, their eyes on the hunting party. He became aware of a fourth, another mounted guard, but this one with his back to the hunting party, watching for intruders. If the circle continued so, and Owen had no cause to think it did not, he was well satisfied. He heard a flutter of wings, the strangled cry of an animal. At least he knew the game would not be wasted. Thoresby's cook would use any game brought to her kitchen.

Through the canopy of leaves a dappled sunshine awoke and

the mist began to writhe up from the ground, causing the woodland to shimmer and pulse. Owen closed his eye, the tricks of the rising mist disturbing him. Since he'd lost the sight in his left eye he'd disliked anything that blurred or negatively affected his vision, uncomfortable about how vulnerable it made him feel. Archdeacon Jehannes had once suggested that this disquiet arose from the very lack of faith that might have caused God to blind him—that God may have blinded him in order to strengthen his faith in his ability to see beyond physical sight. Owen found that interesting but unlikely. God was too busy to play such games with each soul.

'Captain!'

Owen moved in the direction of the shout. As the mist shifted he seemed to see his mirror image approaching him, but realised it was Tom, one of his guards, much younger than Owen, with the same curly dark hair, unusual height, and broad shoulders. Some teased that Tom was Owen's bastard, though no one believed it—at least he was reasonably sure that neither his fellows nor Tom did. As he picked his way along the uneven, mist-shrouded ground the hairs on the back of his neck and a twitch in his blind eye warned him that Tom had found trouble.

'Up there, Captain, in the tree.' His eyes raised up to the canopy, Tom spoke softly, almost reverently.

The woods were unusually quiet, Owen realised. Leading his horse, Gilbert was moving forward on Owen's right. Still unable to see what they were looking at, Owen stepped closer until he saw what spooked the birds to silence. A body hung from a tree, a few feet above the ground, the man's legs gently swinging. He could just make out the groan of the rope against the green wood, a sound that he felt more than he heard.

'God help us.' Owen crossed himself and then motioned to the converging guards to halt. 'Touch nothing.' As Owen made his way through the underbrush another man came into sight, lying on the ground beneath the hanging man, curled in a foetal position, absolutely still. He wore the robes of a Benedictine monk, the elegantly tailored robes of Brother Michaelo. Owen cursed, and his scarred eye tingled with dread.

The ground beneath the tree, a damp mixture of leaf mould and earth, had been churned up by a horse's hooves. Owen saw no horse but Gilbert's. An old ladder lay on its side nearby, as if the hanging man had kicked it away.

Twisted and swollen and shadowed by incongruously beautiful autumn leaves the face did not at once reveal the victim's identity, but the clothes and the fair curls suggested to Owen that Dom Lambert had joined his servant. He drew nearer until he could see the distorted face, indeed the wreckage of Lambert's once-beautiful visage. Owen crossed himself and prayed for the emissary's soul. Whoever had failed to kill him by damaging the wrong saddle would be most pleased.

As for the body curled up near the dead man, Owen could not tell whether or not Michaelo was breathing. For the obsessively tidy monk to lie in the rotting vegetation so startled Owen that he feared he, too, was dead, and he crossed himself as he picked his way across the churned ground to crouch beside Michaelo, gently resting his hand on the monk's neck to feel for a pulse. He was relieved to find a strong pulse, and the flesh warm. *God be thanked.* But it was even more puzzling that Michaelo did not respond either to Owen's touch or to his own name.

Tom moved closer.

'Had you expected this?' Owen asked him. 'Had someone directed you here?'

Tom, looking frightened, shook his head. 'No, God help them, I just now noticed something odd in the tree. I did not see Brother Michaelo on the ground at first. Is he dead as well?'

'No.'

'Thank God.'

As Owen searched his mind for a flaw in his organisation of the guard around the manor, a horse and rider came up behind him, and he held up his hand for them to halt as he turned.

'*Deus juva me,*' Lady Sybilla cried.

Owen silently cursed to see that it was she who had witnessed this darksome sight. She tightly clenched the reins with her gloved hands, her small eyes round with shock. Her mare, sensing her unease, danced a little, and Sybilla let go of the reins with one hand to stroke the horse's mane. At least there was no hawk on her arm to react to her emotion; she'd accompanied the hunting party solely to assist Princess Joan in any way she might.

'Who is it?' she asked, her voice surprisingly steady.

'My lady, return to the others. This is no sight for you,' said Owen, running his hand along the horse's neck to reassure her and then catching the front loop of the rein to turn her around. But Sybilla halted the motion by leaning to one side, the soft, rich fabric of her short green cape pooling over Owen's arm as she peered up to see the hanging man. She smelled of rosewater and her breath was warm and sweet as she turned to speak to Owen.

'Dom Lambert? Sweet Jesu, it is him, isn't it? That beautiful man.'

Absurdly, Owen felt a stab of jealousy as he steadied her horse. He doubted any woman had ever called him beautiful, scarred as he was. Perhaps before he was wounded, but not likely. Christ, he was a fool to care. His grisly find here in the wood had unhinged him. 'I pray you, say nothing to the others, Lady Sybilla.'

'Why say nothing? Who is it?' Sir John came striding up beside Sybilla's horse. He was on foot, still carrying his hawk who was beating his wings as if distressed by being taken away from the hunt.

Sybilla leaned forward over her horse's head, as close as she dared, and when she'd made sure of Owen's attention, pretending to address the horse, she whispered, 'The brooch is a moonstone in silver.' After making a slightly louder calming comment to the horse, she straightened.

Her brief look had been intent, serious, and disturbing, and with her mentioning it now the lost brooch took on a new, ominous dimension. He must later ask what it signified. At present he must see to Lambert's body, and have someone help Michaelo back to the palace. Lady Sybilla and Sir John must leave so that he could concentrate on observing all that he might before the guards released the corpse from the tree.

'My lord, I would be grateful if you would have the servants go ahead to fetch Master Walter and Archdeacon Jehannes while you escort your mother and her lady safely back to the palace.'

Both the young man and his hawk were eyeing the swinging man. 'Dom Lambert, is it? Too humiliated to face Bishop William, I suppose.' His tone was mocking.

Owen felt like slapping him, the pampered pup, but he did not want to deal with the uproar such an attack would cause. 'Please send for Master Walter and Archdeacon Jehannes.'

'What is Brother Michaelo doing there?' Sybilla asked. 'Is he hurt?'

'I cannot tell. I pray you, bring help.'

'Dear Lord, watch over them,' she murmured as she began to move back toward the hunting party.

'What *is* the archbishop's secretary's part in this?' John had stepped closer to him.

Owen stepped between Michaelo's inert body and the princess's son. 'I will find out, I assure you.' He stared at the young man until, with a snarl, John withdrew.

As the lady and the knight moved away, two more guards approached, one on horseback. Owen sent the horseman to ride back to the palace with the hunting party and return with Jehannes and Walter, as a reinforcement in case Sir John found the assignment beneath his dignity. Owen ordered Gilbert to keep his horse outside the area beneath the hanging tree while he studied the churned ground.

Now that Owen knew Michaelo was alive his mind was awash with questions, implications, suspicions and concerns, as if a great dam had burst. If Lambert had taken his own life, Owen faced an uncomfortable question: Had he pushed the emissary too hard, a man who had been desperately fumbling for his balance after having been felled by his weaknesses? He had not sensed such a profound despair in Lambert, but perhaps he had not wanted to acknowledge it. Owen had been angry that his prayer for calm in Thoresby's last days had been rejected, an anger aimed most passionately at Wykeham for sending trouble with the princess. It had been Lambert's misfortune to represent Wykeham—Owen might have been gentler with a member of Princess Joan's household.

My sweet Lord, forgive me if I had any part in this man's despair.

And Michaelo—what was Owen to make of his presence beneath Lambert's body? Had he anything to do with the man's death? Remembering the looks exchanged between Lambert and Michaelo, their whispered conversation, Owen was sick at heart. He'd often feared that Michaelo's discipline to forgo sins of the flesh was but a varnish, and as it aged might become dangerously brittle. Perversely, he was also irritated about the inconvenience if Michaelo could not supervise the household—it was just the sort of ridiculously mundane concern that often came up in moments of crisis—it was more comfortable to complain about day to day frustrations than to face the larger implications.

Owen forced his attention to the evidence before him. He considered the toppled ladder, an old thing dark with damp and moss. It would have sunk into the damp woodland floor beneath Lambert's weight, but there was no mud clinging to it. But for the moss it was quite clean. There had been a thick covering of leaf mould that might have protected the legs from sinking, acting as a carpet over the mud, but the horse had disturbed it—unless the horse had come afterwards. It was also possible that Dom Lambert had not taken his own life, but that his executioner had placed the short ladder there to make it look as if the emissary had done so. A chilling possibility, for it suggested danger for all at the palace. Brother Michaelo? Had he gone mad and murdered Lambert, then swooned to see what he'd done? Owen did not think a madman would have the forethought to bring the ladder, nor did it seem possible that such a brief acquaintance could inspire Michaelo to cold-blooded murder. He had spent too many years in deep penance for that.

Or had he dammed up his passions for so long that it had taken little for the dam to break? Who could ever answer such a question but God? Owen was certainly not up to the task.

Gazing up, he realised that Michaelo could not have managed it alone. Yet Michaelo was a solitary soul, and the thought of him recruiting someone to assist him in hanging Lambert was ludicrous.

If it had been suicide, the horse that had churned up the ground would be found wandering. Now there was something Owen could search for—the horse. A horse that had returned without a rider.

But a rider had taken it from the stable sometime in the night, and no one had yet come forward to report it. Owen had surrounded the manor with guards and posted them at intervals within the grounds. More than one of his men should have witnessed Lambert's movements from palace to stable to tree. And Michaelo's movements should have been noticed, though he was so ubiquitous it was almost understandable if a guard had discounted it—but all the guards he'd passed? How careful had Lambert and Michaelo been to move without stirring the air? Why?

Murder or suicide, it was a violence that should not have been possible during this vigil. Someone should have interrupted it.

But stare as he might, he could not tell whether there had been one horse or several—if Lambert had used the horse to help him into the tree he might have fussed with it, causing quite a lot of movement.

Crossing over to where Gilbert stood beside his horse, Owen told him to take a good long look at the scene. 'I want you to question the men on duty last night. Describe to them what happened here on their watch. Describe it in all its horror. God help us, that should make them talk.'

Gilbert, grim-faced, nodded. 'I will, Captain.'

Owen turned back to Brother Michaelo. In all this while, he had neither moved nor made a sound.

'Come help me, Tom.'

They picked him up—he was awkwardly limp—and carried him to an undisturbed area well away from the tree. Although he remained limp as if in a deep sleep or faint he'd begun to murmur something. Owen caught fragments of Latin prayers. Perhaps Michaelo had an injury he could not see, or had been sedated with something similar to the concoction that had caused Will's fatal fall. Michaelo's breath revealed nothing unusual, but hours might have passed. Stains were difficult to detect on his dark habit, but it smelled strongly of leaf mould, so he might have been lying there for a good part of the night. Gently Owen felt his skull, and lo and behold, discovered a substantial lump which could explain Michaelo's faint—indeed, moderate pressure elicited a moan. Owen would see that he was watched for signs of serious injury. Now he considered yet another possibility—that Michaelo had witnessed a murder, in which case, he might be the next victim—unless it seemed he was presumed the murderer or the cause of Lambert's suicide. For now at least he was safe with them, but Owen would need to arrange for him to be under constant guard. He must think how to protect him. Christ, he must think how to protect His Grace and the princess as well.

Leaving Michaelo still murmuring disjointed prayers, Owen motioned for Gilbert to bring the horse close so they could ease Lambert down onto its back. He was still slightly warm and not yet rigid. Owen guessed he'd died several hours before dawn. He checked whether the knot was unusual, but found nothing to distinguish it.

Tom climbed into the tree with a knife to cut the rope, while Owen and a third guard grasped Lambert's legs to ease his pull on the rope and prevent him from swinging. When Tom had finally severed the noose he held the rope as Gilbert, Owen and the other guard lowered Lambert's body onto the waiting horse. Owen was trying to decide whether to wait or to lead the horse back to the stables when Jehannes and Walter arrived, accompanied by Alfred.

'What a cursed mission,' said the physician as he dismounted and joined Owen. He was so short that as he stood next to Dom Lambert's body sprawled over the horse his head was level with the corpse's.

'Brother Michaelo?' Jehannes crouched beside the archbishop's secretary. 'What are you doing out here? His Grace has been asking for you.' When his presence and his words did not rouse Michaelo from his trance-like prayer, Jehannes looked to Owen. 'How does he come to be here? What has happened to him? His robes are damp and smell of the woods.'

'We found him curled up beneath Dom Lambert, as if in a deep sleep from which we cannot wake him,' said Owen, half-expecting Jehannes to laugh at such an absurd story.

But the archdeacon nodded with a gravity that reassured Owen. 'Hence your grim visage.' Jehannes blessed Michaelo and then rose and went to Lambert. He proceeded to administer to him the last rites.

'I'll see to Brother Michaelo in a moment,' said Walter, studying the corpse as Jehannes prayed over it. 'Dom Lambert's neck is broken, of course. He looks as one might expect from strangulation and then—' the physician turned away, shaking his head. 'It is a horrible sight.'

'When we bring him to the barracks I would have you examine his body for other injuries,' Owen quietly commented, for Walter's ears only.

The tiny physician made a show of distaste as he regarded the body. 'Do you think someone had already wounded him? That this was simply the final act? Scourge, crown of thorns, lance through the side, then hanging?'

Owen found his sacrilegious use of the imagery of Christ's execution offensive. 'I'm implying nothing so crass, Master Walter. I simply meant that I need to know as much as possible about Dom Lambert's last hours. His corpse might have much to tell.'

'Or nothing more than that he hanged himself and the weight of his body pulling at the rope did the rest. I don't like to examine him further,' said Walter, both his throat and his face seeming to tighten against the prospect. 'This is not what I came to Bishopthorpe to do.'

'I did not expect you to find it pleasing, Master Walter. It is a duty, not a pastime.'

Jehannes motioned Owen aside, his expression not merely grieved but troubled.

'Dom Lambert was to share my bed last night,' he said, speaking as quietly as possible, 'but as far as I can tell I slept alone. My servant, who was seeing to Dom Lambert as well, is quite certain I slept alone.' The palace was crowded and all must share beds or chambers. Jehannes searched Owen's face for his reaction, then nodded at his distress. 'I pray Dom Lambert did not lie with Brother Michaelo. I noticed how they spoke, how they looked at one another.'

'I did as well.'

'Not that I believe that Michaelo would do this.' Jehannes's eyes begged Owen to reassure him. 'He would have tried to dissuade him from taking his life, not encourage him.'

'I pray you are right. I'd hoped that years of penance and service to the archbishop had changed Michaelo, purged him of his sinful passion.' Later Owen would confide in Jehannes for he trusted him above most men, but for now he thought it best to express suspicion. Indeed, it was possible he misinterpreted Michaelo's injury. 'Still, they say once one has murdered—or attempted murder—the barrier is far more easily crossed. He *did* try to poison Brother Wulfstan many years ago.'

Jehannes was shaking his head. 'He had been under the influence of an evil man.'

Owen rubbed beneath his patch, his scar prickling as it did when he was deeply troubled. 'I agree. It was a different time, he was young, and Archdeacon Anselm had poisoned his mind. But if he has sinned, I worry how that might again poison his mind. He would be so ashamed. Listen to his prayers.' Owen cursed under his breath. 'His Grace needs Michaelo here and whole. The household needs him as well. There will be confusion and disorder enough when the company learns of what we've found here.'

Jehannes crossed himself. 'I know. I've ordered my servant to keep his tongue about Dom Lambert's absence, which he will.'

'It will be more difficult for him once he hears of this.'

'I trust him, Owen. He will not fail me.'

'Impress upon him the grave danger we all face here.'

Jehannes nodded.

Working to compose his mind for the work at hand, Owen

thanked Jehannes for telling him of Lambert's not having slept in his bed that night. 'And thank you for riding out. Has the hunting party returned to the palace?'

'Yes. The princess wishes to talk to you as soon as that is possible. She understands that you cannot predict when you might go to her, but she will wait for you. Her son began to protest, but she silenced him with a look.'

Master Walter knelt down beside Michaelo, who had curled himself up once more and grown quiet. He sniffed his breath, lifted a hand and felt his pulse, probed along his back and his stomach, lifted an eyelid. Sitting back on his heels he considered the man for a few moments, and then startled Owen by suddenly clapping several times.

'Holy Mary, Mother of God!' Michaelo cried out, struggling to sit up. He blinked rapidly as if having difficulty keeping his eyelids up, and his movements were erratic, uncontrolled, unbalanced.

Owen stepped forward, but Jehannes was quicker, crouching down and taking Michaelo's hands, stroking his head.

'Peace, Michaelo. You are among friends.'

Michaelo looked at Jehannes, then all around, shaking his head. 'I don't understand,' he said, speaking barely loud enough for them to hear, his voice hoarse. 'What is this place? Why am I here?'

Owen crouched down beside him. 'What do you remember?'

Michaelo closed his eyes and dropped his chin to his chest, hiding his face. He began to mutter a prayer.

'You will have time for prayer after you talk to me, Michaelo.'

Though he did not intend to thoroughly question him here, Owen wanted to make a good show of it. He thrust a fist beneath the monk's chin to lift his head, and when Michaelo tried to turn away he slapped him. Holding his burning cheek Michaelo glared at Owen.

'At last. What happened here, Brother Michaelo?'

'Why—' Michaelo paused to clear his throat, wrinkling his nose at the state of his sleeve.

'I found you lying in a faint beneath Dom Lambert's body,'

said Owen.

'*Deus juva me,*' Michaelo whispered, fear widening his eyes, constricting his throat. 'Hanged? It was not a dream?'

'What do you remember?'

Michaelo shook his head and then pressed his hands to his face.

Owen leaned close and whispered, 'Say nothing to anyone but me.' Then he pretended to attempt to pry Michaelo's hand from his face.

Michaelo sank to the ground moving his hands to the back of his head and pressing them there with such strength they could not be pulled away without injuring him.

'Damn Wykeham,' Owen hissed. He looked up at Jehannes, who had looked on with sorrow. 'Will you take Brother Michaelo in hand if Master Walter says he can be moved?'

'Take him away,' said Walter. 'I believe his wounds are better tended by a priest.'

Jehannes nodded.

'If he is guilty, he must face his judgement. If he witnessed something he may be in danger,' said Owen, 'and so might you.'

'I am not afraid, my friend. This I gladly do for you.'

Owen pressed his shoulder. 'God go with you.' He thanked God for a man so trustworthy as Jehannes.

He called Tom over to bring a horse for Michaelo and Jehannes and to assist the former in mounting, and then left them to join Alfred where he stood beside the hanging tree.

'I cannot explain how this could happen. You should hang me where he was swinging.' Alfred's hands, fisted, were pressed to his gut as if he would eviscerate himself.

'I can't spare you at the moment,' said Owen. 'You will have to bide your time for penance.' He slapped Alfred on the back. 'I pray we suffer no other such losses.'

'The ladder—he hanged himself?' Alfred finally brought himself to face Owen.

'I don't know. He would have had to fetch a horse and ride out here—surely someone saw him—someone besides Michaelo. I've ordered Gilbert to question all those on guard last night. The ladder looks like something he might have found out here. God help us if none of the guards noticed anything for that would paint yet another problem. No one is to leave the manor, Alfred, and none are to be admitted but Magda, Alisoun, and Sir Lewis Clifford's men who will be returning from Nun Appleton. See to it.' He need not mention the messenger to Winchester—he prayed that by his return, which would take a while, they'd know what had transpired. But he must send yet another messenger to report Lambert's death to Wykeham. He mentioned that to Alfred.

With a nod, Alfred went off to begin passing orders to the guards.

Master Walter chose to walk back to the palace with Owen.

'The walk will help me forget Dom Lambert's face,' he said.

'And prepare you to see it again.'

The physician shrugged. 'A moment of peace is better than none, Captain. The air in the wood is fresh, cleansing.'

'I'll have no peace until I know what happened there.'

'God grant Brother Michaelo the strength to tell you, and soon.'

Something about the physician's tone caught Owen's attention. 'What are you thinking?'

'I have never before seen a hanged man, Captain, so it may be my ignorance, but the bruises on Dom Lambert's neck seemed too wide to be the result of the rope's pressure.' He lifted his own long-fingered hands to his neck and pressed his thumbs to his throat, raising his eyebrows as he met Owen's gaze.

'You think he was strangled?'

Dropping his hands, Walter shrugged. 'As I said, I have never before examined a hanged man.'

'I will look more closely.'

'Brother Michaelo seems to run the household. Has he been long in His Grace's service?'

'Almost ten years.'

'I understand he fell under the influence of Dom Jehannes's predecessor as Archdeacon of York.'

'Anselm. Yes. But Brother Michaelo—' Owen caught himself before he denied the possibility that the monk might be guilty. 'It is difficult to accept that he might have strangled Dom Lambert.'

'Perhaps he had fallen under the influence of another manipulative man.' Walter tapped his teeth as he thought. 'But if there is truth to the rumour that Dom Lambert failed in his mission for the Bishop of Winchester, then I should think it more likely someone is trying to silence him.'

Owen had been turning that over in his mind. It seemed possible that whoever stole the documents might not want Lambert to remember something that in hindsight seemed suspicious.

'I pray Michaelo regains his wits,' said Owen. 'How did you choose the sisters you brought to assist you?'

Master Walter made a surprised sound. 'You don't think either of them strangled Dom Lambert and then hanged him?'

'We don't know that only one person committed the crime.'

'Would a crowd not be noticed?'

'Would not two men and at least one horse be noticed?'

Walter nodded. 'I see your point. I'm afraid I can tell you little about the sisters. They had already been chosen, and I was simply told they would assist me if I had need of them. I had never met either of them.'

The physician paused to stare up into a great oak, his hood falling back, his neck straining as he looked up, up. 'Soon these colourful leaves will turn brown, drained of moisture, and what this morning is a soothing whisper will be a sorrowful rattle causing one to shiver and think of the grave.' He lowered his head and took a breath that seemed to expand him for a moment. Then he shook his head, his eyes sad. 'I see so much death, Captain. I have looked into the eyes of Princess Joan's husband, the once magnificent warrior Prince Edward, and I have seen that his death is very near. I was one of many physicians summoned to examine him. That is how Her Grace knew me.'

'Thank you for telling me without my needing to ask.'

Walter nodded. 'I count myself fortunate that I have no

acquaintance with the Bishop of Winchester. *He* seems a dangerous man to serve.'

Owen had not expected the physician to be so talkative. 'It was a great honour to be summoned by the Prince of Wales.'

'I have served his brother, the Duke of Lancaster, when he is in the shire,' said Walter, his voice less comfortable. 'I also serve the Bishop of Lincoln from time to time, as well as his esteemed guests. I've travelled with him to York on occasion. In fact, I knew your wife's late husband—Nicholas Wilton? You *are* married to Dame Lucie, are you not?'

'I am.'

'You are nothing like her first husband. I say that with no intention of judging your worth against his, I pray you do not take offence. I merely wished to express my delight that Dame Lucie, about whom Nicholas spoke with such love and admiration, was accepted by the guild. They can be harsh with widows, and it is so unfair when we know that husband and wife worked together as one.'

It had been Archbishop Thoresby's influence that had kept the apothecary in Lucie's hands. 'God has smiled on my family,' Owen said.

'As I recall the evil Archdeacon Anselm who led to Brother Michaelo's downfall had a part in Nicholas Wilton's death.'

Owen remembered Geoffrey's warning about Walter being a gossip.

'Anselm? Not that I can recall.'

Though he did not look as if he believed Owen, Walter merely shrugged. 'I am curious about this healer the Riverwoman. I cannot think how His Grace came to know her. Does Dame Lucie know anything about her?'

On another day, when his mind was less weighted with serious problems, Owen would have laughed at the physician's transparent appetite. But today he merely found it burdensome, yet another hurdle to clear. 'There was a time His Grace forbade Dame Magda to enter York,' he said. 'But he has since witnessed her skill. All who do come to respect her.' He was uncomfortable with the direction in which the physician was going with his questions, and glad that they were approaching the stables, a scene of milling people calling to one another, horses being shifted, and supplies being moved. Alfred looked up from a conversation with Gilbert and caught sight of them, waving to make sure Owen saw him. Sir Lewis and one of his men stood nearby, watching the activity and talking.

'But this Riverwoman is not a Christian,' Master Walter was saying, apparently intent on pursuing the topic.

'No, Dame Magda is not a Christian, but she would give her life for another's if that is what she deemed necessary. Perhaps she does not need all the prayer that most of us require to teach us to love one another.' He bowed to the physician, who frowned as if trying to decide whether he'd been insulted. The safety of the palace was Owen's first priority, not the professional pride of the little physician. He joined Alfred.

'Is there anything else Gilbert should ask about besides whether anyone had seen Dom Lambert or Brother Michaelo since the feast?' asked Alfred.

'Other riders last night—one or several. Someone carrying a ladder in the woods.' Gilbert had a good mind and was liked by everyone. The men would talk to him if they would talk to anyone. 'Come to me with anything you learn,' he said to Gilbert and then moved on to Sir Lewis and his man. As he reached them he heard them discussing Princess Joan's wish to be kept informed of his progress in discovering how Lambert had died.

Lewis glanced up. 'Here he is.'

'I pray you, assure Her Grace that I shall keep her informed,' said Owen.

Sir Lewis nodded. 'Captain, what do you think? Was Dom Lambert murdered?'

'Perhaps,' said Owen.

'By Brother Michaelo?'

'I pray he is innocent.'

'I understand there was a ladder?'

'Yes. The murderer might have used it, or Dom Lambert might have hanged himself. Either way he is dead and a messenger must be sent at once to Winchester.' Yet another. He wondered whether Wykeham would regret his interference.

'I had not thought of that. Forgive me for delaying you.' Lewis seemed embarrassed.

'Do you know where Archdeacon Jehannes has taken Brother Michaelo?'

'To the monk's bedchamber, I believe.'

Owen thanked him but did not depart at once, mentally scanning the list of those in Princess Joan's party to see whether he had any more questions for Lewis. There *was* someone about whom he was curious. 'Lady Eleanor did not join the hunt this morning. Is that unusual?'

'She is ill at ease around the hawks, Captain.' And Sir Lewis was quite obviously ill at ease about the question, though perhaps he was merely still uncomfortable with Owen's abruptness. 'You cannot be thinking that she hanged Dom Lambert?'

'I merely asked. Eventually I hope to be able to account for everyone's movements last night and this morning. Have you known her to avoid hawks before?'

'I don't recall her presence on any hunt. No.' Lewis shook his head. 'I cannot remember ever seeing her with a hawk.'

Owen nodded. 'You have been most helpful, Sir Lewis.' He noticed Richard Ravenser crossing the yard toward them. 'Commend me to Her Grace. Meanwhile I have commanded my men to allow no one to leave the manor.' He bowed to Sir Lewis and his companion and then went to reassure the archbishop's nephew that he was doing all that he could to ensure the safety of Princess Joan and Thoresby.

Ravenser nodded to Lewis and moved aside with Owen. He looked haggard and uncomfortable with the moderate glare of the weak sun, as if he had not slept, or was unwell. 'Dom Lambert's death. Brother Michaelo's presence. This is very bad, Archer.'

'I consider it worse than "very bad", my lord. In this crowd, with the future queen and a dying archbishop here it is a dangerous situation. I have ordered the guards to allow no one to leave the manor. But of course I do not know whether the murderer is still here, or whether there *is* a murderer—or more than one. And if Michaelo is innocent, I've no idea who the murderer might be, or indeed who might be the next victim. If Michaelo witnessed something, then he might be in danger.' Owen stopped, realizing he was only heightening Ravenser's anxiety when what was most needed were calm heads. 'Who is with His Grace now? With Brother Michaelo indisposed…?'

Ravenser pressed the heel of his hand to one eye and softly groaned.

'One of your headaches?'

'God's blood, I've no time for this affliction.'

'Do you have the physick you need?'

'Yes.' Ravenser took a deep breath and forced himself to open both eyes, blinking rapidly. 'You asked—One of the sisters is with my uncle. I'd not seen Brother Michaelo yet this morning—of course now I know why, and Dom Jehannes was called away, so it fell to me to read to him. Pray God Dame Magda returns soon. His Grace is tired but unable to rest quietly. Only she is able to comfort him when he is so agitated.'

'God willing she will be here before nightfall,' said Owen. 'Does His Grace know of this latest death?'

'No. I heard of it only when I came out for some air.' Ravenser shaded his eyes with his hands. 'Brother Michaelo. Do you think he—?'

Owen glanced around to check that he could not be overheard, and when he was satisfied he said, 'I doubt that he is guilty, and I pray that I am right. But I will pretend to suspect him. Do not be surprised to hear it.'

'Why the pretence?'

'For Michaelo's safety.'

He seemed to understand. 'My uncle took him as his secretary for reasons other than fondness,' said Ravenser, 'but over time I believe he's come to have a deep affection for him. It appears he symbolises for my uncle the power of penance, renunciation of sins, redemption. I fear my uncle's reaction to this news.'

Owen had much the same concern. 'I'll go to His Grace after I've seen Michaelo. Rest, my lord. His Grace needs you whole and healthy. I will tell him what happened, and I'll make sure someone he trusts is with him at all times until Dame Magda arrives.'

'God be thanked that my uncle has such a loyal and worthy captain.' Ravenser pressed Owen's arm. 'God go with you. I'll be in my chamber if you have need of me.'

Owen bowed. Ravenser departed with a little groan.

5

FALSE INDULGENCES
WEDNESDAY

It was only mid-morning, but Lucie found herself oddly clumsy in the workshop as if she were pushing on past a reasonable time to cease her labours for the day. She found her thoughts straying too often to the farewells in the gloomy dawn. While her neighbours in Davygate had yet slept, or perhaps groggily stoked their fires, she and Jasper had stood in the quiet street helping Alisoun and Magda secure their packs on the horses the messenger had brought for their short journey to the staithe from which the archbishop's barge would take them to Bishopthorpe.

Her face still creased from sleep and her voice a little hoarse, Magda had said, 'Be ready for thy summons. Old Crow will not linger once the princess departs.'

'May God grant His Grace the time to bid farewell to those he loves,' said Lucie.

'John Thoresby will not die until he has seen the children,' said Magda. She had taken Lucie's hands and held her gaze for a long while, as if passing strength and comfort to her. 'Nor will thy family fall apart upon the death of Old Crow. Thou knowest that for a false fear.'

Did she? Late last night, when the rest of the household had been long abed, Lucie had confided in Magda, telling her of her dread of the changes to come with Thoresby's death. After she'd laid bare her heart she'd waited for Magda to comment, but instead her friend had silently watched the fire.

'My fear is selfish,' Lucie had finally said, thinking she had made a fool of herself.

Magda had put an arm around her and smiled into her eyes. 'Old Crow has given thee much. But thy happy family has a life of its own.'

When looking into Magda's eyes, Lucie could see the folly in her fear. But now, hours later and without her friend's inspirational presence, she found the fear creeping back up to hang over her shoulders and weight every gesture with dread.

Owen entered the palace by the door leading from the kitchen into the hall, hoping to reach Michaelo's small chamber without further encounters with the guests. Sir Lewis and Geoffrey stood just beyond Thoresby's chamber door with their backs to Owen, but they did not turn around when he quietly lifted the tapestry being used for the door to Michaelo's makeshift chamber and let it drop behind him. Michaelo sat on his cot, his hands pressed together in prayer, and Jehannes broke from his prayers to nod at Owen.

'*Benedicite*, Owen.'

'*Benedicite* Jehannes, Michaelo.' At his name, the monk lifted his eyes to Owen. A sudden thought, almost discarded, begged to be acknowledged. Michaelo might not have the strength to have lifted Lambert himself, but he might have helped Lambert commit suicide. Owen would be remiss to rule out that unwelcome possibility. 'You must tell me what you remember, Michaelo.'

The monk took a deep breath, trembling as he exhaled. 'I don't deserve your trust.'

'I do not need your humility, Michaelo. What I need is for you to tell me whatever you can remember.'

Nodding, Michaelo closed his eyes and bowed his head for a moment, covering his mouth as if to force it to pause for thought. After a while he straightened and faced Owen. 'Lambert was distraught, desperate for a place to hide. I meant merely to hold him, nothing more. It was compassion that moved me.'

Owen could see from Michaelo's blush that it had become more. Too much more? He thought it best not to interrupt him to press for a confession. Patience would best serve his purpose. He would hear all in time. For now he had less delicate questions.

'Think, Michaelo, did anyone see the two of you together? Might someone have waited for him? Followed him from your room?' Since Thoresby had moved to the ground floor Michaelo had been sleeping in this screened area beside His Grace's room on the farthest side, near the corridor to the buttery and pantry. Normally it would be a quiet place at night, but with so many guests and their servants to accommodate, pallets were set up in the pantry and the corridor after the evening meal. Someone would be noticed if they stood about, but a clever lurker could make it seem as though he had been assigned to sleep there.

Michaelo looked distraught. 'May God forgive me. I was concerned only for Lambert. I thought we were discreet, but how can I know?' He glanced at Jehannes and back at Owen as if seeking reassurance. 'I can't bear the thought of his having left my bed, and then in agony searching for the rope.' Tears fell down the monk's cheeks unheeded. 'He'd been humiliated by losing the documents, he carried a heavy guilt about trading horse and saddle with Will because the horse was testy, and then he lay with me—a man, a *monk*...' Michaelo shook his head slowly and moaned again, his face a mask of remorse.

'The compassion became passion?' Owen softly asked.

'*Mea culpa, mea culpa, mea maxima culpa,*' Michaelo moaned, beating his breast.

Owen caught Michaelo's hand and waited until he had his attention. 'You take too much of the burden on your own shoulders. Lambert was a grown man. You have not suggested that you forced him.'

Michaelo opened his eyes wide. 'Forced? Of course not.'

'Then he shared the blame with you. He *chose*, just as you did.

You must calm yourself.'

'Calm myself?' Michaelo's voice cracked.

'Lambert's servant was murdered, Michaelo, I have no doubt of that. And now, what I've just learned from you is that Lambert and Will switched horse and saddle. It was meant for Lambert to die. I think it much more likely that far from taking his own life last night Lambert was murdered—the intended victim was finally dispatched. His murderers want us to believe as you do, that he took his own life. They made it look that way.'

'Pretty words, Captain, and if I had any faith in them I would thank you. But I'll never forget that Lambert wept after we lay together. He *wept*.'

'He might as well do so about the tenth time as the first. Did you think of that? Perhaps like you he had promised himself never to sin again—and then did. What then? Is it then all on your conscience?'

Michaelo finally looked up, his expression one of disdain. 'Why are you doing this? Why are you exonerating me?'

Why indeed was he comforting a sinner? For a selfish reason— Thoresby needed Michaelo. But Owen was saying nothing that he did not believe—Lambert could have refused Michaelo.

'His Grace needs you, Michaelo. You must not desert him now.'

'He has Dame Magda and that solemn young woman.'

'You are his ballast and his comfort.' Owen let that sink in for a moment.

'You believe Lambert was the intended victim all along, Captain?'

'Now that I know of the switch I've no doubt he was. Help me, Michaelo. What woke you?'

'His being gone.'

'How long? Was the bed warm or cold?'

'I'd heard him weeping, and I pulled the covers over my head.' Michaelo spoke slowly, hesitantly, as if horribly weary. 'I must have slept again, for the bed was cold where he had lain.'

'I ask you again. What woke you?'

Owen watched as Michaelo tried to think back to his waking, then realised what the question implied.

'Someone wanted me to wake then,' he whispered.

Owen nodded. 'And then what happened?'

Michaelo passed a hand over his eyes as if to conjure the scene. 'I hurried from the palace and heard something at the stables. It was quiet, all the company asleep. I don't recall seeing any guards. And then I saw Lambert and a woman slipping from the stables with a horse.'

'Just as you stepped into the yard?'

Michaelo slowly nodded. 'Yes. I see. You think they appeared on my arrival. The woman was dressed in the finery of the princess's ladies.'

'You were meant to see Lambert—or someone dressed like him. Are you certain it was Lambert you saw? And what of the lady?'

Michaelo looked down, rubbing his forehead, slowly shaking his head. 'I don't think I could swear as to whom I saw. It was too dark.' He shook his head. 'Too dark.' Curling his long-fingered hands into fists he angrily punched the pallet to either side of him. 'May they rot in hell, whoever they are,' he groaned.

'Yes,' agreed Owen, 'but who are they?'

'I wish I knew. I followed them, but lost my way in a copse, then followed sounds. By then—dear God, Lambert was hanging.' Michaelo covered his face with his hands.

'And you were struck from behind?'

Michaelo did not respond, and Owen waited for him to regain his composure.

'He has been through a difficult night,' said Jehannes, who had sat with head bowed, his lips moving in prayer.

Michaelo raised his head. 'It is no more than I deserve. As for your question, Captain, yes, I was struck from behind and knew nothing until you found me. Do you think I'm in danger?'

He had certainly been so last night, Owen thought. 'I think it likely, and the worst of it is that you do not know who your enemy is. Nor do I. I don't trust Holand. Or the women—I trust Princess Joan, for the most part. She would not need to come all this way to kill Lambert. As for my men, I'm not sure I can trust any of them.'

'Surely you can trust Alfred,' said Jehannes. 'And you've come to entrust more to Gilbert.'

Owen almost argued for distrusting even Alfred and Gilbert, but his heart refused. 'Yes, Alfred and Gilbert I can trust.' He thanked God for that. 'Here is how you must behave, Michaelo. Play silent and torn with guilt. Stay away from the company as much as you can. Indeed, you would do best to remain in His Grace's chamber.'

Michaelo shook his head. 'I cannot hide, Captain. The household needs me. But I will behave as one shamed—it will be no performance.'

Jehannes spoke up. 'That will be painful, Brother Michaelo, for surely you will feel their anger. From what I've seen of him John Holand might well express his contempt without discretion.'

Michaelo gave Jehannes a weak smile. 'It does not matter. Truly. I will offer it up as my penance. And when His Grace has passed on, I'll hie to Normandy and spend the rest of my days in penance.'

Owen did not choose to argue, knowing how stubborn Michaelo could be. Instead he instructed both to be ready to move Michaelo's pallet into Thoresby's chamber when he sent word, which would be soon.

The corridor was fairly quiet when Owen crossed the short distance to Thoresby's chamber and silently opened the door and slipped in. God must have guided him in his stealthy entrance, for he found something he might not otherwise have witnessed.

Thoresby's breathing was at first all he noticed, loud despite the bed curtains being pulled shut. He must be asleep, because when awake the archbishop preferred the curtains open—he said he'd have sufficient privacy very soon. Owen was angry that the archbishop was unattended and was about to go fetch Michaelo when a sound farther in the room caught his attention, a rustling of cloth. Holding his breath, Owen moved toward the sound. Just beyond the bed the lid of a large trunk stood open and one of the nuns, black veil and pale habit identifying her, was sitting on the floor, legs crossed beneath her, leaning against the trunk, a lamp beside her, and was frowning down into a book on her lap. If she was a thief she was inexperienced, allowing herself to become so absorbed in reading that she did not notice his approach. He could not imagine that she might need any items stored in the trunk, but he would not have thought she would require a book. Moving closer yet he saw the book was a breviary or prayer book, with annotations scrawled along the margins.

'Have you His Grace's permission to read that?' he asked in a quiet voice, so as not to startle her.

But she did startle, and in scrambling to her feet she dropped the book and brought the lid of the chest down on her hand.

'Who goes there?' Thoresby cried out from within the bed.

'Dame Clarice needs my help with one of the trunks, Your Grace,' Owen said. 'I pray you, rest easy.' He picked up the book and noticed that the marginal notes were in Thoresby's hand. 'What right have you to read this?' he demanded of the nun, keeping his voice low.

Standing beside the chest, Dame Clarice was ministering to her hand, rubbing it, flexing it and moving it about. 'Nothing seems to be broken.' She glared up at Owen. 'What right have you to sneak up on me?' Her words challenged but when she saw Owen's anger she backed up a few steps and dropped her gaze.

'I've every right, as the archbishop's captain of guard.' He shut the chest, but placed the book on top intending to look at it more closely after he'd seen her out of the chamber.

She smoothed her gown and felt about to make sure her veil was secure. Her habit was tidy and tailored for her tall, thin frame. Owen realised she was a handsome woman but for thin lips and sunken eyes, and to fuss with her appearance in such circumstances suggested vanity—the Brother Michaelo of her convent.

'It's a mere prayer book,' she said with a sullen, wounded expression.

Thoresby peered through the bed curtains. 'What has she done?'

'It is pointless to play the fool with me,' Owen said to the nun, 'I cannot believe you would be of such feeble wit as not to realise that the belongings of the Archbishop of York are not yours to explore at your whim.'

'A spy,' Thoresby said with disgust.

'No!' Clarice cried. 'I thought to find something inspiring to read…'

'Get out of my chamber, you pathetic liar.' Thoresby frowned and then withdrew.

'I'm no thief. I was merely reading,' Dame Clarice whined.

Someone knocked once and entered the room. Owen groaned to see Geoffrey Chaucer.

'I'd hoped to find you here,' said Geoffrey.

Owen shook his head at him, hoping he would withdraw, but the man merely looked with interest toward the nun.

'His Grace ordered you to leave,' Owen said to her.

'Who is to attend His Grace if I leave?' she demanded. 'I was sent here to sit with him.' She'd assumed a defiant posture and her facial expression and voice were alive with righteous indignation.

'I ordered you out of here,' Thoresby said from behind the curtains. The effort caused him to cough.

'His Grace is my concern,' said Owen. He took Clarice's elbow and escorted her to the door, shutting it tight behind her.

He considered doing the same with Geoffrey, but distracted himself from his irritation by busying himself with checking that Thoresby had honey water within reach. Opening the bed curtain he found the archbishop lying back against his pillows.

Thoresby waved Owen away. 'I need to catch my breath.' He held a cup to his lips as he closed the bed curtains.

Owen withdrew, calmer now.

'That did not seem a friendly exchange with Dame Clarice,' said Geoffrey when Owen turned to him.

Patience, he coached himself. 'I can't say that I'm feeling any friendlier toward you than I did toward her. What are you doing here?'

'Forgive me, but with Archdeacon Jehannes seeing to Brother Michaelo and Sir Richard Ravenser abed with a headache, I thought perhaps you might need someone to sit with His Grace. And from what I just witnessed, you do.'

Geoffrey's knowledge of everyone's whereabouts astounded Owen. 'Do you know everything that happens in this palace?' He wondered why Geoffrey paid such particular attention to Thoresby's close companions.

'I don't know what happened to Dom Lambert, or what Brother Michaelo had to do with it.'

Owen was not ready to enlighten him. 'Dame Clarice had searched through at least one of His Grace's trunks—wanting something to read, she said. She must not be left alone in here again. Perhaps neither sister should be.'

Geoffrey glanced over at the trunk. 'One of the nuns in our company so bold as that? What do you think she was searching for?'

'I doubt it was just the book.'

Following Owen's gaze Geoffrey crossed to the trunk and picked up the book. 'It seems innocent enough—devotional reading. She showed poor judgement in opening a trunk—' he gave a short laugh. 'Listen to my foolishness. A stranger trespasses in the room of the Archbishop of York and I make excuses for her because she is a nun.'

Owen had his own suspicions. 'How did you come to enter just when you did? How do I know you hadn't arrived to help her?'

'Help her? Are you mad?' Suddenly quite serious, Geoffrey glanced round, found a bench well away from Thoresby and motioned Owen to join him.

Reluctantly, Owen settled beside him. 'Why *are* you here?'

'I've recently become a squire of King Edward's chamber,' Geoffrey frowned down at his shoes, his short legs never quite touching the ground when he sat, and seemed to weigh his words.

'A squire of the king's chamber? I'd not realised you'd risen so high.'

Geoffrey sniffed. 'My wife was so close to the late queen and her sister is unpleasantly close to Lancaster, so I do not flatter myself that I've risen on my own merit. Now, as to why I am here, I'm privy to conversations expressing much concern about Prince Edward's failing health as well as the king's. We may be moving into quite difficult times if both fail. I believe Princess Joan has already mentioned her need for a spy here in the North, someone to watch the Percy and the Neville families, eh?' He arched his eyebrows and nodded at Owen as if nudging him to the point.

It took but a heartbeat for Owen to guess. 'You? It was you who suggested I might be that spy?'

'Lancaster supported my recommendation, for you served him well in Wales. Do I hear irritation in your voice?' Geoffrey shook his head at Owen. 'I am disappointed that you are not pleased. Owen! Your lord is dying. I have found you an honourable post that will allow you to stay in Yorkshire with your family.'

'I need no position.'

'Oh? You'll just wander about Freythorpe Hadden and annoy your steward? Or will you play apprentice to your lovely wife in the apothecary?'

'That is my concern.'

Geoffrey threw up his hands. 'I thought I had found a way to thank you for saving my career at Cydweli. Without you I would have failed in my mission for Lancaster.'

'Thank me?' All this time Owen had thought their parting had been uneasy, with Geoffrey distrusting him for his Welsh sympathies.

'Of course.'

'In faith, that is generous of you.' Owen searched for a neutral question. 'You came here to encourage me to work for Princess Joan?'

'Yes! You are a difficult man, did you know that?' Geoffrey scratched his head. 'So where were we? Oh yes. You asked whether I'd entered this chamber to assist Dame Clarice in her search of the archbishop's belongings. No, I did not. In fact, I shall report her trespass to Princess Joan—you are right to be disturbed by her activity. And you are wrong to distrust me.'

Perhaps it was time Owen trusted Geoffrey. He could use the assistance of someone in the princess's party, and he could think of no good reason to doubt the man's intentions. 'I am particularly concerned after two members of her travelling party have died, possibly both murdered.'

'Murdered?' Geoffrey shook his head. 'I feared as much. I was almost certain that you thought Will was murdered, but Lambert? They said it looked as if he'd hanged himself, that there was a ladder.'

'There are bruises on Dom Lambert's throat that fit a man's hands, not a rope.'

'By Saint Foi, someone strangled him and then hanged him?'

'I think so.'

'Not Michaelo?'

'I pray not.' Owen hesitated, then with a prayer that Geoffrey proved trustworthy he continued. 'Even though I am almost certain of his innocence I've told him that I shall behave as if I'm watching him. He may be in danger. After I've spoken with His Grace, Michaelo will move in here, and he'll stay at least until Magda and Alisoun return.'

By now Thoresby had pulled back part of a bed curtain. Despite the warmth of the room he clutched a mantel around his shoulders. 'Michaelo is in danger? Has this to do with the nun you caught in here?'

Owen opened the curtain wide. 'I don't think Dame Clarice is involved in Michaelo's trouble, Your Grace. She had taken one of your books from a trunk she had no cause to open.'

'What book?' When Owen handed it to him Thoresby did not look at it at once, but said, 'She tried to be pleasant enough, but I disliked how closely she watched me. Had I not succumbed to pride in dining in the hall on the princess's arrival I would not be so weary today and would have been sitting with the curtains opened wide, not prey to a little sneak.' He looked at Owen's companion. 'Master Chaucer, is it not?'

'Your Grace.' Geoffrey bowed. 'I came to offer the captain my help.'

'Help, yes. I've little doubt he'll need some.'

Only now did Thoresby glance down at the book in his hands, squinting at first, though of course he did not have so many books that he would need his spectacles to distinguish which this was, and then widening his eyes, his face taking on a most haunted expression.

Alarmed, Owen asked, 'What is it, Your Grace?'

Thoresby held the book to his heart and bowed his head for a moment. 'God in heaven, of all the books—' He checked himself with a shake of his head and took a deep breath. 'We'll talk of this later.' He set aside the book on the small table next to the bed and gave his attention to Owen. 'Tell me what has happened.'

'Might we have some time alone?' Owen asked Geoffrey. 'I'll not keep any information from you.'

Though he did it with clear reluctance, Geoffrey withdrew from the chamber without argument.

Owen's caution was rewarded. As soon as the door closed behind Geoffrey, Thoresby picked up the book he'd set aside, and with trembling fingers he plucked at the top edge of the front cover where there was a slit in the leather. Owen felt a cascade of needle pricks across his scarred eye as he guessed the purpose of Thoresby's effort to spread the slit and slip his fingers inside.

'Had you hidden something in the binding?' he asked, hoping for a negative response. The theft of Wykeham's documents was as yet unsolved.

With a curse, Thoresby handed the book to him. He did not look Owen in the eye, but kept his gaze lowered. 'I've too little feeling in my fingertips. Is there a folded parchment slipped inside on either side of the board?'

Owen felt about. 'Nothing.'

Thoresby sighed and lay back against the pillows. 'If it was there, she's taken it, that cursed nun. But I cannot be certain it *was* there. I've moved it so many times.'

'What, Your Grace?'

'A letter. A love letter I foolishly kept. *From* Marguerite.'

Owen knew of whom he spoke. She had been Thoresby's most-beloved mistress—and King Edward's mistress as well. Years ago a memento of that liaison had fallen into the hands of the king's present mistress, Thoresby's nemesis at court. 'Is it the letter that Alice Perrers used—'

Thoresby shook his head. 'That one was from me *to* Marguerite.'

He chuckled. 'That letter would have shocked the little sneak. This one might leave her sighing. There is a great deal of sighing in nunneries.'

Although evidence of past misbehaviour could hardly hurt Thoresby now, Owen was unable to share in his amusement. Anything out of joint was a threat to the safety of His Grace and the princess. 'Where else might you have hidden it? If we check all the possible hiding places we'll know whether she has taken it. We can then search her.'

Thoresby frowned. 'That is the problem, Archer. I've moved it so many times, always back to this book, but I've shifted it to scrips, boxes, cushions, clothing, other books, and not all the items are at Bishopthorpe. In truth, I cannot recall when I last looked at it.'

'That is not helpful,' Owen accidentally muttered aloud.

'I'm aware of that, Archer. The nun is a sneak in any case and I'll not have her in my chamber again.'

'I agree.' But Clarice might now be in danger—or dangerous.

'Tell me what has happened. It must be something sinister indeed for you to have sent Chaucer out of the room. I should have thought you would trust him. Or does he know too much about your activities in Wales?'

Owen ignored the last comment. For several years Thoresby had been playing an annoying game of cat and mouse with him, hinting at something that he knew about Owen's trip to Wales but never admitting to how much he knew. The most he could know was that Owen had been aggressively urged to join a Welsh rebellion against English rule. He could not possibly know how close Owen had come to taking part in the rebellion unless he could read Owen's mind. It made Owen all the more curious about the significance of the book Clarice had chosen.

'I'm concerned about Dame Clarice's transgression, Your Grace,' said Owen. 'Not knowing what it might involve I thought it best to discuss it without Geoffrey, and I am glad that I asked him to leave.'

'I should think he has more important concerns than my losing a letter from a mistress long dead, Archer. But I'd put the book aside while he was yet here and would not have discussed this in his presence. Still, I believe him to be worthy of your trust. Do you have good cause to doubt that?'

'I'd found his presence at this vigil suspicious, Your Grace, but he's just told me he's a squire of the king's chamber.'

'He is indeed, and has recommended you to Her Grace, Princess Joan.'

'So he said.'

'You doubt him? Don't be a stubborn fool, Archer. Now come, pour me more honeyed water.'

Owen did so, and helped Thoresby sit up more comfortably. It was painful to see how the archbishop's hands shook. He stank of sweat and had sour breath, this man who would bathe daily had he not considered such luxury sinful. His illness seemed to Owen a terrible indignity.

Once Thoresby was settled in relative comfort, Owen took a chair near the bed.

'In any case,' said Thoresby, 'I doubt that either Princess Joan or Sir Lewis would have agreed to Chaucer's presence in the party if they did not feel certain of his loyalties. In fact, he and Lewis Clifford are fast friends.'

That was an interesting titbit. 'And yet someone has murdered a servant and now—'

'Tell me.'

'There has been another death,' said Owen. 'Dom Lambert.'

'In God's name,' Thoresby whispered. 'The timid emissary? No wonder you are so ill at ease. How?'

Owen briefly described how they had found Lambert in the woods. He regretted how Thoresby's eyes seemed to sink deeper into his almost cadaverous skull as he listened.

'What monster came on the heels of Wykeham's emissary?' Thoresby sighed and closed his eyes for a moment, raising a hand to keep Owen at his bedside. 'The princess is safely back in the palace?' he asked.

'She is, Your Grace,' said Ravenser from the doorway, 'and her women and the knights.'

'I am grateful for that,' said Thoresby.

'Your head is better?' Owen asked as Ravenser entered, bringing up a chair to join them.

'I could not sleep—but your wife's powder has eased it enough that I can bear it in here where it is not so bright.'

'I heard you say that Michaelo might be in danger, Archer. Where is he?' asked Thoresby. 'Is he involved in Lambert's death?'

Owen and Ravenser exchanged a look.

'Your Grace, I found him lying beneath Lambert, in a faint,' said Owen.

'There is talk about Lambert and Michaelo,' said Ravenser.

'That old curse come back to destroy our peace? Damn the man. How dare he succumb?' Thoresby coloured and began to cough.

Ravenser helped him to some more of his drink. As Thoresby settled back on the pillows, his nephew shook his head.

'How could Lambert and Michaelo move past all the guards? And a murderer?'

'It would have taken more than one person to hang him, I think,' said Owen. He told them what Michaelo had seen.

'One of Her Grace's women.' Ravenser rubbed his temple. 'If it involves her company, that makes it all the worse, all the more dangerous.'

'I agree,' said Owen. 'I have a man questioning all the guards. Perhaps someone did not realise what they were witnessing.'

'Where do their loyalties lie, my guards, now that I am dying?' Thoresby paused, taking a shuddering breath. 'I told Richard when the princess's party arrived that the vigil of spies had begun. But I would imagine some in the guard compromised their honour months ago.'

Owen felt a chill. He'd reassured himself that he had chosen all of his men with care, and those he had not chosen had been hand picked by Alfred. But he had not sat down with each one and sounded them out as to how they felt about their service with the archbishop coming to a close. Though Thoresby was the most powerful representative of the Church they would ever encounter, Owen imagined the guardsmen's devotion to him had far more to do with livelihood and protection than with religious awe. He'd not thought to speak to each individual about that.

'I pray you are wrong in your suspicion, Your Grace, but I will not depend on that.' Would talking to each one have made a difference, Owen wondered.

'What of Michaelo?' Ravenser asked. 'If he is not guilty, did he witness a murder? Is he in danger?'

'I'm worried about that as well,' said Owen. 'If it please Your Grace, when we are finished here I thought to bring him here, to move his cot in here with you.'

Thoresby nodded. 'I took him as a penance, and I will honour that as long as I may.'

'I have told Geoffrey and Jehannes that I do not believe Michaelo murdered Lambert, but I think it is to our advantage to behave as if we're uneasy about him. Michaelo has agreed—though he refuses to quit his duties.'

'Stubborn man. But how have you already decided his innocence?' asked Thoresby.

'By a painful lump on the back of his head. He was meant to be found.' Owen explained to them the timing, and then rose. 'I've much to do.' He wanted to find Dame Clarice.

'I do not envy you your responsibility,' said Ravenser, searching Owen's eyes, plainly aware of his discomfort. 'I imagine you will have John Holand's temper to deal with—he seems the sort to express his fear with temper tantrums.'

'I've dealt with his sort before,' said Owen.

'God go with you, Archer,' said Thoresby, blessing him. 'You could not protect me from this vigil. When the ambitious sense the imminent death of someone in power, they cannot stay away. Even had the Princess of Wales not come, we would have had spies all about us. I would trust no one to keep the peace at Bishopthorpe as I trust you.'

'Your Grace.' Owen bowed, and felt the weight of the archbishop's trust on his shoulders. He prayed that he was worthy; he feared that he was not.

Of Ravenser Owen asked, 'Would you be willing to stay here until Brother Michaelo comes?'

Ravenser nodded. 'I will gladly sit with His Grace.'

Owen was grateful for the easy escape. Thoresby's comments about his guard had brought on a cold sweat. It had been years since he'd felt so unsure of himself, so overwhelmed. Of course his guards might be making arrangements for their lives after Thoresby's death. The next archbishop would have his own loyal servants. He might not even choose to live so near York as Thoresby had.

Once outside the archbishop's chamber Owen paused to tell Jehannes and Michaelo that Thoresby agreed that his secretary should share his chamber, and then he headed for the chapel in the hope that Dame Clarice would be there doing penance and he might ask her whether she'd removed anything from the book. She would no doubt refuse to answer, but in her manner he might glean the truth. As he walked he managed to calm himself with the thought that Alfred was ever alert to grumblings among the men. But he'd no sooner calmed a little than a very unwelcome question occurred to him—what of Alfred's loyalty? After Owen, Alfred was the one who would lose the most prestige, the most comfortable wage. He had spoken often of late of a young widow in York. How would he provide for her? Owen had been a fool to not have considered this. Yet surely he was better off with the men who had served with him all these years rather than a new, untried group with even less cause to be loyal. He'd often trusted Alfred or Gilbert to escort Lucie or guard his home and they'd never betrayed his trust. Lucie. How Owen wished she were here. He needed her calm head to help him think this through.

As he stepped into the chapel he felt a chill, a sense of time having collapsed, or waking to discover the past day had been a dream and he was standing in this door as he had the previous day. Prostrate before the altar lay—no, this was a woman, not the ghost of Lambert. Unfortunately it was not Dame Clarice, for this penitent wore expensive silks. Her veil covered her head so completely that he could not be certain, but it must be one of Princess Joan's ladies.

'Lady Eleanor has lain so for hours.'

Owen had not noticed Geoffrey sitting near the door, cross-legged on the floor, as if taking his ease.

'I've checked on her several times,' said Geoffrey. 'Earlier she was on her knees before the altar, folded over as if crumpled in pain, weeping so piteously I did not like to disturb her. I withdrew before she was aware of me, and I spun out some time walking in the garden before returning, and yet when I did return, she had still not moved. Her sobs were as deep and wrenching as they had been earlier. At least now she is quiet. Perhaps she has exhausted herself.'

'Why do you suppose she is here?'

'Perhaps she is frightened by the two deaths in her travelling party?' Geoffrey rose. 'But you must come with me to the garden. Dame Clarice is there. With Princess Joan.'

Would she show Joan the stolen letter? Owen rejected that suspicion as soon as he thought it. That she was with the princess alleviated some of his sense of urgency, for she was as safe as he could possibly make her in Joan's company. But he still needed to question the nun, and then to talk to Alfred, to ask Lady Sybilla about the brooch—the list seemed endless and uppermost in his mind was the need to stop the deaths now. He sensed a great wound in the community here in the palace with blood flowing unhindered. He must stanch that flow.

Yet here was a woman who might be she whom Michaelo had seen last night. He wanted to at least see her face. 'First let us see whether Lady Eleanor needs assistance,' he said. He crouched beside her, and although the crackling of his knees and ankles sounded to him like explosions in this quiet room she remained motionless as if unaware of his presence.

Owen softly called her name. When she still did not respond he placed the flat of his hand on her back to feel for heartbeat and breath. Now she stirred with a strangled sob.

'Are you unwell?' Owen asked.

With a shimmering swirl of silks Eleanor rose to her knees and sat back on her heels, smoothing her veil, then her gown, all with her eyes downcast—but Owen had already glimpsed red-rimmed eyelids, blood-shot eyes. 'I have been praying for Dom Lambert. And his servant,' she said in a tight, slightly quavering voice.

'You have heard about our discovery in the woods?' Or had a part in it?

'God help us, yes, I have heard.' Lady Eleanor crossed herself. 'It is not my way to be so weak, so easily frightened. But that two have died, one in such a terrible fashion, in the midst of this sorrowful vigil—I can think of little else.' She shook her head as she pressed her fingertips to her swollen eyelids. 'God bless you for your concern.' She did not glance back at Geoffrey, but said, 'I don't like how he watches me.'

'I will take him away, my lady,' said Owen. 'Can I do anything more for you?'

She shook her head.

Something stopped him from questioning her further, a sense that if she were the guilty party it was best she not know how much he already knew. Or thought he knew. He felt as if he were juggling feathers in a windstorm.

'I'll leave you to your prayers,' he said, rising.

Geoffrey glanced back as they stepped out of the chapel. 'Of the two ladies, I find her the most disturbing.' And then he suddenly grinned impishly. 'I hope I am the first to tell you that a villager has come with a horse he found grazing in his field. Dom Lambert's horse.' He looked pleased at Owen's surprise. 'You see? I *am* of use to you. But first come to the garden. The villager is already gone, so you've no need to rush to the stable.'

But they came upon Alfred, who had been watching the doorway. 'Captain, I've news.'

'If it's about the horse, I've already told him,' said Geoffrey.

When Owen and Alfred both glared at him he backed away. 'I'll be just outside in the yard. Don't be long.'

'He's told you? About Dom Lambert's horse?'

'He has.' Owen did not bother to hide his irritation.

'You're not relieved? You're not thinking that there is no murderer, that we need not worry?'

'I'm thinking we might have a very clever murderer who is playing this like a chess game, moving his pieces with great care.'

Alfred was nodding. 'My thoughts as well. The man—Sam is his name—said he knew it was too fine a horse to belong in the village fields, and he'd heard of the great company that had arrived the other day, so he brought it here.'

'What did you think of this Sam?'

'Something in the way he spoke was too assured, as if he'd practised his lines.'

'And you let him go?'

'What could I do? He'd returned the property that was not his and everyone seemed to believe his story. If I'd questioned him too closely—'

Owen patted his shoulder. 'Good. I'll go to the village to talk to him.'

'There's more. Gilbert brought me a fool who had not thought it of any importance that he'd seen Lambert and Michaelo leave the stable with a horse last night.'

A witness at last. 'Lambert and Michaelo?'

'So Matt claims.' Alfred shrugged and shook his head, a slow, weary gesture.

'Matt?' Owen had almost sent Matt off many times for falling asleep on a watch or exaggerating reports. 'You don't believe him.'

'I rarely do, and I don't believe that with so many men watching only Matt saw Lambert and Michaelo.'

And Michaelo had seen Lambert with a woman, a woman dressed in the finery of the princess's ladies. Owen nodded. 'So we've no witnesses yet.'

Alfred grunted. 'I'm grateful to see we agree, Captain. I wondered whether I was just looking for trouble, wanting it for some queer reason.' He ran a hand through phantom hair. 'But what is happening here, Captain? Who is this clever murderer? Where the bloody hell were our men?' He spit and returned to the tired shaking of his head.

'It's possible that someone has offered them money or positions elsewhere. They know that the archbishop is dying, and that the new one will choose his own men.'

'I hate to think that they are so easily bought.'

'I feel the same.'

Alfred cursed. 'It *does* makes sense. How could we be so blind?' Again Alfred raked his scalp. 'I thought I knew them, all of them. Now I feel I've been a fool to think so. I should have taken care to pair one who has served under us for a long while with one of the newer men. Why did I think a few months was long enough to test loyalty?'

'It's not your fault, it's the change—the death of an archbishop is no small event. Maybe it's worse than that—our king is old, Prince Edward is very ill and his own son is but a lad. The prospect of a child king brings out the predators. Everyone is choosing sides, hoping to be in the new regime.' Owen stopped, realising that he was saying aloud what he had tried not to think about.

Alfred looked defeated, his eyes frightened. 'What are we to do?'

Owen wished he believed he had an answer to that, but Alfred need not know the depth of his unease. He thought it best to calm his second in command.

'None of this might have mattered had His Grace refused to extend his hospitality to the princess. We could not have foreseen such a visitation, such temptation for the men. We must have faith that no one wants guards who cannot be trusted. My hope is that the men have agreed to be silent, nothing more.'

Alfred did not look comforted. 'But they might be concealing murderers.'

'They may choose not to think about that. A man will accept much in order to provide for his family.'

'Traitors.' Alfred spit into the hay.

'Loyalties are never so simple as we would like them to be, Alfred. What if you were already wed to your pretty widow? What if you had a child to feed?'

Owen could read in the slump of his friend's shoulders that he understood the point.

'So what do we do?' Alfred asked.

'Round up the men who were on the night watch. Gilbert must have been too gentle. I'll talk to them.'

'They're sleeping.'

'They don't deserve to.'

Alfred bobbed his head and departed.

Geoffrey waited without, and hurried Owen along to the garden. Beneath a linden tree sat the princess and the nun in tense, albeit whispered, discussion. Dame Clarice was weeping. She looked pale and pinched—frightened. The princess gave her a little shake, imperiously angry.

Owen and Geoffrey withdrew to a quiet corner beneath the eaves.

'What do you make of that?' Geoffrey asked as if he'd just shown Owen something delicious.

'I had not realised that Dame Clarice and the Princess of Wales were acquainted,' said Owen, 'but that did not look like a conversation between strangers.' It might explain why Master Walter was simply told she was to assist him.

'Nor had I. I'd not seen them together.'

Owen sank down onto a bench. 'I feel as if my mind is under siege.'

Geoffrey sat down beside him. 'Dame Clarice had helped herself from a chest in the archbishop's chamber. Is it possible that she was sent there by Princess Joan to look about, and having been discovered by you is now being lectured on the fine art of being clever enough not to be caught?'

'A tidy summation,' Owen said. 'It might even be true.' Though surely a love letter was of no interest to the princess. He thought about Lady Sybilla and the brooch, Lady Eleanor weeping in the chapel, Dame Clarice reading Thoresby's book and possibly stealing the letter. The other sister had yet to misbehave. 'But would Princess Joan have kept this from you, Geoffrey?'

In his companion's eyes Owen saw the absurdity of his question. 'I cannot expect her to consult with me on everything, Owen. I doubt even her ladies know all. Certainly my wife did not know all that was on Queen Phillippa's mind.'

Her ladies. 'I forget that your wife was one of the ladies of Queen Phillippa's chamber,' said Owen. That might prove helpful, though at the moment he could not think how. It might help to know how a woman like Joan chose her ladies. 'For all her delight in hawking, it is strange that Princess Joan chose two ladies who do not share her passion.'

'Two?' Geoffrey looked at him askance. 'You are misinformed. Lady Eleanor keeps several hawks. She is often teased about her passion for those beautiful creatures and the delicate hoods she has made and decorated for them. But Lady Sybilla, now she cares nothing for the birds. You would enjoy hunting with her—I've never seen a woman as skilled with the bow as she.'

Sybilla's worth rose several notches in Owen's mind. 'I would not have guessed that of her. But now you mention it, she does have an admirable posture.'

Geoffrey cocked an eyebrow and chuckled. 'I thought you would find that enticing.'

But what he'd said of Eleanor disturbed Owen, begging the question of Lewis's motive in telling him something so easily revealed to be untrue. 'This is puzzling—Sir Lewis said that Eleanor does not hunt.'

'He did?' Geoffrey snorted. 'A peculiar deception. He most certainly knows of her hawks. Perhaps he thought one question might lead to another and you would discover he's bedded her. Though why he would want to deceive you in that or in anything I cannot imagine.' He looked troubled.

'Lewis and Eleanor?'

That brightened Geoffrey. He chuckled. 'Oh yes. The heat

had built for quite some time. I am almost relieved that they finally coupled and cooled the air about them.' He glanced in the direction of the chapel. 'I did wonder whether her tears were over her sin. Or perhaps that the passion is spent.'

'I suppose that explains some of it.' Owen rubbed the scar beneath his eye patch. 'What matters to me is that Lewis lied. I'd hoped I might trust him. I don't know in whom I can place any trust.'

Geoffrey had grown solemn. 'That is the crux of the problem, I agree. I thought Dom Lambert seemed trustworthy. But of this I can assure you—Lewis Clifford is an honourable man. I can vouch for him. And where the princess's safety is concerned, I am certain you may still trust her son John as well.'

Owen noticed the qualification regarding John—where his mother was concerned. 'What of her ladies?'

Geoffrey sagged a little. 'I am certain she chose them with care, but to what purpose I would not pretend to know. Binding their families to the young heir to the throne? Queen Phillippa chose some of her ladies for reasons other than her fondness for them.'

'I wish I knew more about Dom Lambert. Did he comport himself as a priest?'

'If you are asking whether he lived chastely, I daresay he did not. Women were drawn to him, and he did not demur.'

'Women in your travelling party?'

'That is the only experience I'd had of him. I must tell you in all honesty that I saw nothing to suggest that he lay with anyone on the journey, but there was much flirtation, and again, there are Lady Eleanor's tears to make me wonder. Perhaps she thought if only she had bedded Lambert last night...No. I am creating tales without substance.'

Had Michaelo seen Lambert with Eleanor, Owen wondered. 'What of men? Lambert and other men?'

Geoffrey turned on the bench. 'Brother Michaelo.' He nodded. 'It is unfortunate. I must point out to you that all eyes had been on Dom Lambert, so almost everyone knows that he spent some time in Brother Michaelo's bed—for there's little else in that enclosure—

last night. If either you or Brother Michaelo think it is a secret, you are mistaken.'

'Christ have mercy.' Owen leaned back against the wall and closed his eyes, trying to collect his thoughts. 'But wait—that is all to the best. With Michaelo now the subject of gossip they'll jump to conclusions.'

'It might be best to keep him out of sight, eh?'

Owen shook his head. 'He refuses. With the palace filled with important guests the household staff needed his guidance.'

'Lewis and John will not like that.'

Owen cursed.

Geoffrey leaned close, asking in an earnest tone, 'How might I help you, Owen?'

He considered Geoffrey, wondering whether he should tell him of Marguerite's letter to Thoresby. But it did not seem necessary, for Geoffrey would surely tell Owen if he heard of something so unusual. 'Listen to the gossip. Watch especially Dame Clarice and the ladies Sybilla and Eleanor. If you hear *anything* you think I should know of, come to me. Time is our enemy.' Straightening, Owen felt the tension in his back. 'I must leave you now. I face the unpleasant task of letting my men know that I suspect some of them of protecting those behind Lambert's death.' In the silence after his words a sorrow welled up in Owen's heart and he bowed his head. He had faced and accepted that Thoresby's death would cause a great upheaval for him, but he had not been prepared for this possible betrayal—of him and Thoresby. It was as awful as if the pall bearers had dropped the casket and abandoned the archbishop. As awful and as infuriating.

Geoffrey watched him with concern. 'I see that it is a bitter thing, to suspect your men of treason. May God be your strength and your guide in this.'

Though grateful for the sentiment, Owen was rendered speechless by the anger that had closed his throat, and he merely nodded to Geoffrey and departed.

• • •

A crowd had gathered around the great doors of the stable. Gilbert broke away from the crowd and moved toward Owen scowling, though he smoothed his expression as he caught his captain's eye. Gilbert was a squarely built, sturdy man.

'Captain, I've already talked to the men. As you commanded.' There was an angry edge to his voice.

Owen almost growled at him. 'And the only one to speak to you was Matt. It's a game with him, and he's played it too often for me to believe him.'

Gilbert frowned. 'I didn't know.'

'I'm surprised you didn't. But now you do. Has Alfred gathered the others who guarded last night?'

'In the stables.'

'Good. Take care of this crowd. Send them off to their duties.'

Inside the stable a bleary-eyed, cranky group awaited him, some sitting on the hay, others lounging against the walls. Owen decided to launch right in to his purpose in meeting with them and then depart for the villager's house. They could come to him on their own, with as much stealth as they desired, once he'd returned.

'I won't keep you from your rest for long, men. Look round you. There are twenty of you, and more than half of you have much experience in this household. I trusted you to do your duty. Yet right in front of your eyes at least two men left the palace and went into the woods last night—one of them came here and saddled a horse—' He interrupted himself to ask Alfred, 'It was saddled?' With Alfred's nod, Owen resumed. 'And apparently not one of you witnessed anything of any significance. You don't look refreshed, but you don't look as if you're recovering from stupors caused by strong sleeping potions in your ale. I want to hear of anyone you noticed moving about. *Anyone.* I'll be the judge of whether it's important.' He held up his hands as Matt and another man would speak. 'I don't want you to say anything to me now. Come to me on your own. But let me say this—I thought all of you had wit enough to realise the importance of your mission. Your lord, the second highest Churchman in the realm, has entrusted you to guard the wife of Edward, Lord of the Aquitaine and Prince of Wales and *your next king*. I expect you to guard his lady with your lives. If someone has promised you a post in their guard as a reward for betraying your duty here you have been most cruelly used, for they've taken you for the fools you must be. They would hardly hire someone they knew could so easily be coaxed to betray them in turn. I'll leave you with that cold truth.'

Turning to Alfred, Owen ordered his horse saddled and then strode out of the stables before the fire in the pit of his stomach inspired him to beat someone senseless. In the yard he found Archdeacon Jehannes talking to Gilbert. The crowd had dispersed.

'How is Brother Michaelo?' Owen asked.

'Sleeping. Master Walter gave him something to help him rest, concerned that he'd been weakened by his night in the woods. Sir Richard has remained with His Grace until Michaelo wakes.'

'Would you care to ride with me to the village?'

Jehannes smiled. 'I would welcome a ride.'

Owen ordered Gilbert to have a horse saddled for Jehannes. He thought the villager might feel more comfortable with the gentle, sweet-faced archdeacon. From years of experience Owen knew that some people never relaxed in the presence of his scarred soldierly appearance—neither were all comfortable with his height or his Welsh accent.

As Jehannes stood with Owen outside the stables, waiting for the grooms to bring out their horses, he expressed his relief to be escaping the tensions of the crowded palace for a little while.

Owen laughed. 'I expect quite some tension at the villager's house.'

'But of a different kind. I am curious—why are we riding? We might walk and be there and back again before vespers.'

'To impress the family,' said Owen, 'and to allow us to hurry back if we've learned anything. Nor do I wish to be long away.'

Jehannes said nothing for a little while. 'Forgive me if you do not wish to speak of it, but I sense great anger in you—you looked as though you could make thunder when you strode from the stables, and you were so curt with Gilbert.'

Owen could hardly have expected that his fury would not be noticed, yet he was sorry Jehannes had seen him so. 'I'll not attack you.'

Jehannes laughed. 'I did not think you would. But perhaps you'll confide in me as we ride?'

'Gladly. I could use a good dose of your calm wisdom.'

Indeed, as Owen slowly rode from the palace he was already calming. The feel of warm sun on his back eased his spirits, and the pleasant, almost crisp breeze was a subtle sign that autumn was adding its breath to the summer breezes and starting to cool them. He could imagine Gwenllian and Hugh introducing the baby Emma to her first snowball. It was good to think of how happy his household was, with the new baby and Lucie so strong and back to her clear-witted self again.

'It is good to see you smile,' said Jehannes, tearing Owen from his reverie. 'I find it a pity that the household is so glum, for His Grace is quite happy. He's made his peace with God and he is ready to be relieved of his fleshly body.'

'I'm paid to be suspicious, not happy,' Owen reminded him.

He wondered whether Thoresby would be aware of autumn this year, or if he would be trapped now in his great bed until God called him. He remembered the times he'd come upon the archbishop in one of his gardens, sitting on sun baked stones enjoying the quiet hum of insects. He wondered whether when struggling for his next breath Thoresby ever wished that it might be redolent with the perfume of flowers.

'There is a woman in the princess's party who keenly watches you, have you noticed? The Lady Eleanor?'

'She watches me?'

Jehannes read something more than indifference in Owen's voice or on his face, for he said, 'You are not strangers?'

'I'd not seen her since I left the old duke's service. I trust she's praying that I say nothing of having bedded her many years ago.'

'Oh!'

'Once. I think only once.'

Jehannes sighed. 'I would remember every breath in the embrace of such a lady.'

'I am not proud of my former ways. Her presence has not been easy on my conscience.'

'I'll say no more about this.'

Owen nodded. But he was glad Jehannes had spoken. He'd not noticed that Eleanor watched him. He changed the subject.

'The nun Clarice may have stolen a letter from His Grace, one from Marguerite,' said Owen. 'I wish I knew why.'

'Why in heaven's name did he keep such a thing?' Jehannes asked the sky. 'Why did Michaelo befriend the handsome Dom Lambert? Their weaknesses are their undoing. Perhaps this is the meaning of original sin. We each have a flaw that will destroy us if we relax our vigilance.'

'I do not like to think God was so cynical in our creation,' said Owen.

'Is the nun's theft the cause of your anger?' Jehannes asked.

'No.' Owen moved his horse a little closer to Jehannes. 'I think that some of the guards may have betrayed His Grace's trust. And mine.' He confessed his fears.

'May God lead them to confess,' said Jehannes when Owen grew quiet.

'Aye.' Owen spent the rest of the ride telling Jehannes of his purpose in visiting Sam.

At Sam's house they learned from his wife that he was out in the fields. While one of the girls was sent out to fetch him, the goodwife invited them to sit on a bench in the kitchen garden and she would bring them some ale. The house was simple wattle and daub, a longhouse shared with the livestock, with one small, shuttered window opened to the lovely day. No doubt the goodwife thought it too crude and dark for the likes of them. And yet Owen had been in her shoes in his youth and knew that keeping the lord's men outside was also a safeguard against their noticing poached meat hanging from the rafters or other items out of place. If Sam had been paid for his part in the concealment of Lambert's murder Owen might find some evidence of new wealth in the house. He listened closely, and soon heard a clatter that allowed him to rush in, asking whether there was anything he could do to help.

The poor woman was on a stool trying to tuck a hefty sack of grain into the corner above a beam and a small tear was leaking corn as she pushed. A girl a little older than his own Gwenllian, perhaps nine years old, held a very full pitcher of ale and watched her mother with uncertainty—should she serve the guests or help her mother?

Owen was beneath the goodwife in one stride, tall enough to finish the task for her, tucking the hole upright.

The light in the house was too dim and smoky to allow him to see subtlety in her expression, but by her quavering *God bless* it seemed clear to him that she knew that he knew what he'd seen.

'Mary, take the ale out to Dom Jehannes,' said the woman, wiping her hands on her apron and then reaching for two bowls.

A baby slept in a cradle by the fire. And over the fire hung a fine new pot—no charring or dents. A fine piece of ironwork.

'Forgive me, I do not know your name,' said Owen.

'Janet,' said the woman, tugging on her wimple to straighten it.

'Dame Janet, I am here because of the death of the man whose horse your husband returned to Bishopthorpe yesterday.'

'Death?' Janet breathed, lifting a calloused hand to her throat.

'Hanged in the archbishop's woods,' he added.

She quickly lowered her hand. 'So that is why his horse was wandering. Poor man.'

'He was a man of the Church.'

'A priest? Like the one without?'

'Not so high in the Church as my companion, the Archdeacon of York, but a cleric,' said Owen. 'The dead man had been entrusted by the Bishop of Winchester to carry important documents to the archbishop. I very much fear that he was murdered, Dame Janet. That is why we wish to speak with your husband.'

'God have mercy on his soul,' she whispered. 'You think my Sam killed him?'

'I did not say that. He may have seen or heard something that will help us catch the murderer.' She'd be of no help if she felt she needed to protect her husband. Owen made a show of looking around the longhouse with a half smile. 'I grew up in a house much like this.'

'You?' Though she looked him up and down and shook her head, she seemed more at ease.

He nodded and smiled down at her. 'In Wales. I am a long way from home. Now I live in the city—in York, with my wife the apothecary. Our home is much different from this.'

'Dame Lucie mixed a salve that saved my Sam's arm when he was badly scalded,' Janet said.

Mary stuck her head in the door. 'Ma, are you bringing the bowls?'

With a nervous laugh Janet hurried past him, then paused in the doorway to urge him to join Jehannes in the garden for some ale.

Owen joined her, but stayed in the doorway. 'You've come into some wealth of late, Goodwife. I pray it had nothing to do with the dead man's horse.' Though how they might have spent it so soon... 'I hope that someone did not come to your Sam a while back, promising more if he would assist in whatever way was necessary?'

The woman reddened, but said nothing.

'I am racing against time. I promise you that if you help me I will punish neither your husband nor your family. You have my word.'

She bowed her head and crossed herself. 'He did it for our souls, Captain Archer. They told him that the new Archbishop of York would grant us indulgences for his help, that it was God's work. But if they killed the bishop's man—How could we hope for God to honour such ill-begotten indulgences?' Her eyes welled with tears. Indeed, she looked quite frightened. 'We'll be cursed instead!'

'Did your husband mention any names?'

As Janet shook her head the infant in the house began to cry. 'Mary, see to little John. Go along.'

As Owen stepped aside to let the girl pass, he noticed a lad of about seven eyeing the horses from a careful distance. That was four children and two adults to feed so far, and he decided that he would not tell anyone about the grain he'd seen, or the pot. The indulgences were enough to report, and they would deprive no one of nourishment.

Beyond the horses, he now saw a man he presumed was Sam loping across the road. Owen said a silent prayer of thanks for the opportunity to coax the information out of Janet, for he could see by the changing drama of anger, fear and calculation on his face as he approached that Sam was cut from a very different cloth than was his wife. He looked an opportunist. The Nevilles must have been delighted to find him.

'Captain Archer, I did not think to see you here.' He wiped grimy sweat from his brow with a sleeve and muttered to the girl who had fetched him to bring him a bowl of ale. He glanced at his wife's face and his jaw tensed as she bowed her head and shrugged.

Now he returned his gaze to Owen, who took the opportunity to introduce Jehannes.

'Archdeacon of York?' Sam said.

'I have come on a difficult mission,' said Jehannes. 'I fear that you may have mistakenly helped a murderer to escape punishment.'

'What?'

Jehannes told Sam almost precisely what Owen had told Janet. The woman stood with tears of gratitude in her eyes as Jehannes added, 'I fear that he or his helpers might have told you that they represented the future Archbishop of York, and that you might be rewarded with indulgences. It is their custom to make such false claims. Am I right?'

'I—' Sam turned to his wife in a fury. 'What did you tell them?'

Janet backed from him and, hugging her arms to herself, began to weep.

'Cursed woman,' Sam spat.

Owen grabbed him by the shoulder and unceremoniously led him a little away from his family. 'Don't make me change my mind about revealing the source of your extra grain and new pot, you thankless cur. I thought to ease your family, seeing no harm in that. But if you persist…'

'A murderer, you said?'

'And the victim an envoy of the Bishop of Winchester. Your greed has led you into a cursed trap and now you've sold your soul. There will be no indulgences won by you for this foul deed.'

'But he said—'

'He said what he knew would win you over. Who was he?'

Sam shrugged and spit to the side. 'Curse you, all of you high blooded bastards.'

6

MISSION TO NUN APPLETON

WEDNESDAY EVENING

Unfortunately, Sam knew little of the man who had offered money and indulgences except that it was a different man who'd come with the horse in the early hours past midnight, banging on the door, simply instructing Sam to deliver the horse midday to Bishopthorpe with the tale of finding it in the fields. The one who had paid him several days earlier had spoken like a noble, using some foreign words; the man who came in the night spoke like a man of the shire.

Owen and Jehannes had returned to the palace knowing little more. On the ride back Owen fell to brooding about Sybilla and Eleanor, two enigmatic women who seemed to invite mystery.

God was looking after him, for as he entered the palace yard he spied Sybilla, her blue silk gown and gold surcoat bright against the dark wood of the stables. She appeared to be talking to one of the grooms about two young dogs rolling about in play nearby. Lifting laughing eyes to Owen, she momentarily rendered him reluctant to broach a serious subject and dim that smile. There were all too few smiles in the palace at present.

'Captain Archer. I've been admiring the puppies. They've captured my heart.' Sybilla's round face and short stature animated by her excitement made her seem childlike.

'I trust His Grace would be willing to part with one—if you would like to carry one back with you,' Owen said.

She beamed with joy, clapping her hands as she exclaimed, 'I shall ask him!' She pointed to the larger and rowdier of the pair and playfully commanded the groom to guard him with his life.

'I will, my lady,' said the young man with a wink at Owen.

'My lady, might we walk away from here and talk a moment?' Owen took a few steps toward the gardens.

With a quizzical look Sybilla bowed her head and followed. Overhead, clouds were gathering, and the late summer garden was dreary with dry, rotting leaves, flowerless stalks, drooping blossoms gone to seed. Sybilla's bright clothing only emphasised the faded mood of the garden.

When they were well away from anyone who might overhear, she said, 'You want to know about the brooch.' She glanced up at him with a tiny, apologetic smile. 'I have teased you with it.'

'Why, my lady? It seemed a very odd time to speak of it in the wood this morning, unless the brooch is connected to Dom Lambert's hanging.'

She crossed herself. 'I did not mean disrespect. I pray they are not connected.'

'The corpse made you think of it?'

'I do not know what to think. My intent was that *if* you were to encounter it, you would know that it meant something. Do you see?'

'Not at all. Why would I come upon it?'

She wrapped an arm round his and led him to a far bench beneath a linden.

'I fear a friend is in danger, and I am—prying.' She shrugged. 'Hoping to find out how I might help without breaking a promise to say nothing. I'm not very good at it.'

'The friend for whom you fear is the owner of the brooch?'

She nodded. 'It will probably turn up among a servant's belongings, but I cannot help but worry, with all that has come to pass on this journey, whether the loss of the brooch is more significant. I thought that if you came across the piece, then I would know where her danger lies—or whether I am worried over nothing more than a greedy servant.'

'Who is this friend?'

'I cannot say.'

Owen was losing patience. 'Two men have died, my lady. If you believe her to be involved in their deaths you must tell me.'

'No. I pray you, forgive me for mentioning the brooch.' She fussed with her surcoat, kicked a leaf out of the way with her pretty shoes, then looked him in the eye, all hint of teasing gone. 'My concern might be much ado about nothing. And then I could not forgive myself for breaking my promise and perhaps compromising her reputation.'

'I'm assuming you speak of your companion, of Lady Eleanor.' He watched Sybilla fight to conceal her reaction, but it was clear to him that he'd guessed right. 'What sort of danger do you think she's in?'

She was quite visibly upset, teary-eyed and flushing crimson. 'Why did I mention it?' she cried.

'What danger, my lady?'

She took a deep breath. 'Betrayals of the heart, Captain.' She rose. 'Forgive me for distracting you with my petty concerns. God go with you.'

'I don't believe you think them petty, my lady. There is a sadness in Lady Eleanor. Is she content in her marriage?' Owen asked, hoping to learn more of Sybilla's thoughts, seeking the key to the change in Eleanor.

Sybilla brightened a little, apparently amused by the question. 'Is anyone content in their marriage, Captain? Are you?'

'I am most content in mine, my lady. Aren't you?'

'Would that I were, Captain. You are a most fortunate man, and your wife a most blessed woman.' She nodded to him and turned to leave.

He frantically searched for a way to ask more without revealing his past acquaintance with Eleanor. 'So she is not content?'

'In her position here, yes. But her home is a cold place.'

'The brooch is from a lover?'

'No! But—' Sybilla hesitated, then said quietly, 'It might have been given to one.'

'And therein lies the danger?'

Sybilla looked mortified. 'I pray you, ask no more.'

'Do you know where I might find Lady Eleanor?'

Frightened eyes searched his face. 'God in Heaven! You would tell her of this conversation?'

'Do you take me for a cur, my lady? Of course I would not so betray you. I would enquire as to her recovery from this morning's fright. She was most affected by Dom Lambert's death.'

'I believe she is in the great hall, talking to Sir Lewis,' said Sybilla, and with another nod, hurried down the path.

The sun was beginning to set, and a fine mist fell from the sky seeming to tease tendrils of fog from the river. The brightly dressed Sybilla seemed an exotic bird in the dying light, flying down the path toward the stables and the puppies she coveted. Owen guessed that the woman was not the silly pet she pretended to be, but was rather a shrewd woman who knew how to use her effect on men. He wondered why she'd sought to distract him with this matter of the brooch.

He sank back down on the bench to consider how to approach Eleanor, and was deep in an argument with himself when he noticed an oddly flickering form approaching. He crossed himself and whispered a prayer. Blinking to clear his vision in the dying light, Owen realised it was Magda Digby, her multicoloured gown catching the occasional glimmer of twilight in the swirling mist. He felt his mood lift as she stepped lightly along the stone pathway seemingly waking nature up as she came, the water pooled in the lady's mantle leaves shimmering as her skirts brushed them, the rosemary releasing its heady scent into the air as her hands swept past. Her presence healed even before what she would consider her work began.

'Magda, I am more relieved to see you than I can say.'

'It would not be fitting to say Magda is delighted by thy greeting,' she said with a concerned tilt of her head. 'Thou'rt in need.' She moved aside to allow Alisoun to step forward and deliver into Owen's hands the pack he had sent with them.

'I am glad to see you as well, Alisoun.' To his surprise, Owen meant it. As often happened, Magda's naming of his state made him more aware of it. He was glad to have these two allies present.

Never reticent, Alisoun asked outright, 'What has happened here, Captain? As we passed through the hall we heard whisperings of another death. A hanging.'

He settled the pack on his lap as he considered how much she might need to know, but realised that she must know enough to be safe and to recognise information that might be useful to him. 'You heard rightly. We found the Bishop of Winchester's emissary hanging from a tree in the archbishop's woods this morning. He might have taken his own life, or someone might have gone to some trouble to make me think so.'

'May he rest in God's grace,' whispered Alisoun as she bowed her head and crossed herself.

She had grown up in Magda's company, Owen thought. Although she looked as gangly and sharp-edged as ever, her slender neck seeming too fragile for her adult-sized head, there was a quiet about her now that invited one closer than before.

'I count on you to pass on to me anything you hear that might help me discover what happened,' said Owen. 'His name was Dom Lambert. It was his servant who died when his saddle failed the day the company arrived.'

Alisoun looked him in the eye and nodded once. 'Thank you for trusting me, Captain.'

Magda smiled to herself, but Owen saw it. Then she grew solemn, studying Owen's face, shaking her head. 'Thou art weary of heart, Bird-eye. To blame thyself will help no one.' She settled down beside him and took his hand in both of hers.

The simple gesture brought him great warmth. He realised he'd been feeling deathly cold.

Glancing up at Alisoun, who was blinking against the drizzle, Magda said, 'Hie thee to His Grace's chamber, and have a servant fetch thee some food and wine. Sit close to the brazier and dry thyself. Magda will have need of thee in the days to come. Thou must not catch a chill.'

As Alisoun moved to obey, Owen made one more request.

'There are two sisters here, in pale habits and black veils. I do not want them alone in His Grace's chamber at any time, for any reason, particularly the younger one, Dame Clarice. If either should question your refusal to leave them alone with His Grace, send them to me.'

Alisoun frowned, but did not ask why. She simply nodded, then bobbed to them and hurried off.

'She is maturing in your service,' said Owen.

'She is,' said Magda, a smile in her voice. 'She is a lesson in trusting thy gut about someone. Magda doubted up here,' she tapped her head, 'but believed down here,' she pressed her stomach. 'She was patient when Magda stopped to help an injured man on the way to the barge. She uttered not a word of complaint.'

Owen found it almost beyond belief, but said nothing.

A gust of wind shook the tree overhead, sending down a shower of moisture, but Owen did not find it unpleasant enough to warrant moving, and apparently neither did Magda.

'The nuns are not to be trusted?' Magda asked after a comfortable silence.

'No.' Owen told her about Dame Clarice's disturbing behaviour and that she might have stolen something—so he distrusted her and yet at the same time could not rule out the possibility that she might be the next victim if someone wanted what she'd taken and chose to silence her after relieving her of it. 'It comes down to trusting few in the visiting company. Even fewer of my men—I fear they may have fallen prey to greed, money offered to them to betray His Grace and help those who hope their man will replace him as archbishop. Money and indulgences as well, I've just learned.'

Magda's barking laughter rang out, but she did not smile. 'Blessings for betrayals. Thy religion can be sadly amusing, Bird-eye. But in truth, thou dost deserve better from thy men. Thou'rt loyal and good to them. Magda is sorry to hear of their falseness. What of the physician?'

'I have no cause to distrust him, but neither do I have proof that I can trust him, so I prefer to be cautious.'

'Perhaps the physician and the nuns will leave now that Magda and Alisoun have returned?'

'No. I'm allowing no one to leave. Until I have found the murderer, I cannot risk that.'

Magda stretched out her legs and yawned. 'Magda will nap for a short while, then sit with His Grace through the night.' She squeezed Owen's hand. 'Thou wast right to think this visit from the Princess of Wales ill-advised. Two dead, and at least one of those deaths was hastened by someone.'

'You found poison in the wine?'

She tapped the pack on Owen's lap. 'Magda and Lucie found that the wineskin holds a sleeping potion—poppy, mandrake, and water germander. A strong potion, though not a poison.'

'I doubt he had chosen such a drink for travel,' said Owen. As ever, the proof that someone had arranged a mortal accident angered him. Poison was the coward's way to rid himself—or herself—of an inconvenient person.

'Nay,' said Magda, 'thou hast a murderer here at the palace. The germander could be thy most helpful clue, for it is most often used for gout.'

'Gout?' Owen was surprised. 'I've seen no one I would guess was so afflicted. Perhaps you might observe the guests, Magda.'

She patted his hand once more and shifted on the seat with a little groan. 'Magda prefers making a journey on her own two feet.'

Owen realised she'd said nothing about her time at his home. 'My family is well?'

Her blue eyes brightened. 'All but for missing thee, and Lucie grieves Old Crow's imminent passing. For all his sins, he is well-loved by thy family, eh Bird-eye?'

'Much to my surprise,' Owen agreed. 'I wish Lucie were here. I worry that I'm too angry to observe with the care I should. She calmly listens and advises me when I am so.'

'Anger can cloud thy vision,' said Magda, nodding. 'Remember that violence rises out of fear and pain. Remember as well that Magda is here if thou shouldst need her.'

'I depend on you.'

'Thy family will come bye and bye, sooner than thou wouldst like, but not so soon as to help thee with the murderous guest.'

As always, Owen felt that in her words she hid a knowing that went beyond observant common sense. Yet he knew she would deny any gift of prescience.

He told her in greater detail about Lambert's death, the evidence of strangling, and Michaelo's involvement. He also told her about Sybilla and the brooch, curious what she might make of the woman's behaviour. 'Did she seek to distract me from my investigation, or am I seeing guilty behaviour where there is none?'

'Magda hast not yet met this young woman, but from what thou sayest, she might be honest in her concern about a friend, fearing the woman might trade this small treasure for trouble.'

'Why did she tell me of it but not tell me all?' Owen wondered.

'She told thee of her promise. And yet she broke it, little by little. Have a care—thou might be wise to doubt her explanation.'

'And the nun Clarice—though I warned Alisoun against her I cannot discount the possibility that she might have taken something that the murderer or murderers might want.'

'Old Crow wants peace and he is instead surrounded by the fearful and the desperate. Thou hast a heavy burden, Bird-eye.' Magda rose and stretched her arms up toward the darkening sky. 'That cloud is about to open. Magda is off to nap. Thou art surrounded by friends as well as foes.'

Owen thought it a frustratingly vague encouragement. But he had no time to sulk. Going to the great hall in search of Lady Eleanor, he discovered her seated at a little distance from Sybilla and Joan, a piece of needlework forgotten on her lap. She seemed lost in her own thoughts.

'My lady,' he said, bowing to her.

Eleanor's lovely face with its high cheekbones, large, dark eyes, and wide, expressive mouth glowed for a moment as she gazed up at him. Then, as if catching herself, she glanced down to fuss with her embroidery.

'The light is too dim now for stitching, my lady.' He sat down near her. 'Have you recovered from this morning's darksome fears?'

When she looked up, her eyes shimmered with tears. 'You don't remember me, do you, Captain Archer? Owen?' She whispered the last.

'Remember you? Sweet lady of course I remember you. I thought surely you would not remember me—or would not wish to.' He smiled gently and her embarrassment dissolved.

Still a little tearful, she said, 'I hear you are happily wed to an apothecary.'

Owen nodded. 'I came north in despair after the death of my lord and to my surprise I found a blessed new life. We have three children of our own and a foster son.'

'I am happy for you, Owen. I have a son as well, a bonny boy.' Though she smiled, tears fell down her cheeks. 'But now that I've done my duty…' She looked away, delicately dabbing at her eyes with the edge of a long sleeve. 'Forgive me. I'll say no more.' She took a deep breath and turned back to smile on him. 'In your presence I fear no harm, Captain. Would that we might have walked away from Kenilworth hand in hand.'

'Your life is so unsatisfying?'

'Worse than that. Far worse than that. But you asked whether I'd recovered from this morning's despair. I am sorry that you witnessed me in such a state. My husband loses patience with me when I fall into my dark moods. He lectures me on trusting in God's grace.'

'What causes them, my lady?'

'I pray you, call me by my Christian name.'

'Eleanor,' Owen whispered.

She looked long into his eye. 'I recall the story of your blinding. When we were together you were so angry, your wounds so fresh. I've often wondered whence came the woman's anger, what more there had been to her story.'

Owen had been wounded by the mistress of a Breton prisoner

he'd protected and released. Catching the man when he'd returned, sneaking through the camp to slit the throats of the valuable prisoners, Owen had attacked him in a rage at his ingratitude and his own poor judgement, and the woman had come to her lover's aid, slicing Owen's eye.

'Whence came her anger?' he said. 'I was part of the invading army, my lady. We were at war. I'd attacked her love. That all seems plain enough.'

Eleanor shrugged. 'As for *my* story, I trust no one in my household but my son. There is no one on whom I might depend. That is the bleak truth of my life, Owen.'

'You've no one?'

She must have caught a gesture from Princess Joan, for she bowed to her mistress and said to Owen, 'I forget myself. My lady wishes you to attend her after the evening meal.'

Owen turned to the princess and bowed. 'I will be there,' he said to Eleanor. 'Have you confided in the princess?'

'She is aware of my unhappy state. To my shame most of my travelling companions have witnessed my despair. I am heavy company.' She forced a smile. 'And now you must go, or we shall provide the gossip for the evening.'

He took his leave of Eleanor then, having no heart to ask about the brooch. He'd thought of another aspect of Sybilla's concern about the piece of jewellery—that she might think it had been given as a bribe or payment, and could have been sold in York. He considered whom he might trust to take the barge to York in the morning and talk to the goldsmiths, who might hear of such a transaction. It might be useful in general to listen for any rumours of the events at Bishopthorpe. The person who came to mind was Archdeacon Jehannes, to whom all felt safe in confiding. He found him meditating in his chamber and apologised for interrupting him, but he soon discovered that his friend was eager to learn of Owen's progress in the investigation. After telling him all he'd learned, Owen proposed to Jehannes the trip to York.

Even a man as ready to do anything for His Grace and all his friends as Jehannes baulked at the thought of a river journey in the autumn damp. 'Not tonight, surely?'

'This is not meant as a severe penance, of course I meant in the morning. You might begin at the York Tavern with a comforting tankard of Tom Merchet's ale and Bess Merchet's memory of people's conversations the past few days.'

Jehannes's eyes brightened and he smiled. 'Indeed, this begins to sound like a blessed respite from this besieged place.'

Anticipating that the presence of the Princess of Wales would insinuate itself in some marvellous way throughout the palace of Bishopthorpe, Alisoun was disappointed to find the archbishop's chamber unchanged. It was still overheated, dark, and tinged with the smell of the sickroom, though the latter only faintly, for Brother Michaelo was skilled in tempering the odour with fragrant fires and aromatic oils.

Brother Michaelo, however, seemed alarmingly changed. Wilted. Hollow-eyed.

'*Benedicite*, Alisoun,' he said, rising from his seat beside the archbishop's great bed, his smile oddly sad, as if she reminded him of happier times now gone.

'*Benedicite*, Brother Michaelo,' she said. 'Dame Magda is with Captain Archer. She sent me to arrange her things.'

'Are you hungry? Thirsty?'

She nodded. 'Dame Magda told me to have a servant bring food.' She glanced at the servant who stood ready at the door.

'Yes,' Michaelo nodded to him, 'some food for this young woman. And for Dame Magda?'

'She said she would nap a while, and then attend His Grace,' said Alisoun.

Michaelo motioned for the servant to see to it, then led Alisoun away from the sleeping archbishop to review with her His Grace's condition during her absence. Alisoun wondered whether the archbishop had surrendered to his fate with the physician's diagnosis, but Michaelo did not allude to that and she was not comfortable asking him. When she had eaten a little and arranged Magda's trunk of physicks, she offered to sit by His Grace.

Michaelo seemed most grateful. 'I will leave you then and go make certain the servants are seeing to the evening meal. With so many guests, they are easily confused.'

He stopped in a far corner to drop something on a cot that had not been there before. She wondered whether that was a sign that the archbishop needed more constant attention.

A quiet time ensued, interrupted only by one of the sisters the captain had warned her about inquiring whether Alisoun would like some company. It was the older one, Dame Katherine, and Alisoun saw no harm in her presence as long as she was not left alone in the chamber. They sat quietly for a long while, the nun praying, Alisoun spinning. When Thoresby woke and asked for some wine, the sister departed, having exhibited no suspicious behaviour. The archbishop seemed genuinely glad to see Alisoun. She did not find him at all diminished by the gloomy prognosis of the princess's physician. In fact, he seemed as calm and matter-of-fact as before, though he sought to reassure her that she need not feel threatened by the deaths of Dom Lambert and his servant. She appreciated that he treated her as a responsible adult.

When Magda arrived in Thoresby's chamber she told Alisoun that she was free to do as she wished until dawn.

'Magda has rested. She looks forward to a quiet night in His Grace's company.'

Alisoun had grown accustomed to the friendship between Magda and Thoresby, and understood when she was in the way. But it was difficult, despite her admiration for Magda, to believe that the elderly woman could remain awake all through the dark, quiet, uneventful hours.

'I do not mind returning earlier.'

'There is no need. Thou couldst dine in the great hall with the company,' Magda suggested.

Alisoun knew she was welcome in the hall. But once out of the chamber she was drawn out into the evening. Hastening out the door to the kitchen yard, she turned toward the river gardens. She was making her way beneath the eaves when someone grabbed her arm. She turned toward a man who stood so close she could smell the wine on his breath.

'What a pretty poppet. Where have you been hiding?'

By his elegant dress she guessed that he was one of the knights in the company. He thought her easy prey.

'I am no poppet,' she hissed, yanking her arm from his grasp. 'I am apprentice to Dame Magda Digby and of the household of Captain Archer.'

He took a step backward and swept her a mocking bow. 'Sir John Holand, stepson of Prince Edward.' Then lunging for her, he grabbed her round the waist and pulled her close.

Her heart pounding, she said, 'You have had too much to drink, sir, and will regret this behaviour. Go now.' She was about to bring her knee up into his groin when she heard voices just ahead.

He must have heard them as well, for he suddenly released her and with a chuckle moved back toward the kitchens.

Alisoun hurried on.

'It is I who should leave, being the one who has given offence, however unwittingly. I pray you, stay and rest awhile.'

Two women stood in the shadows of a lovely porch facing the gardens, one of them a nun. Alisoun did not think it was Dame Katherine, but it was difficult to be certain and she did not wish to stare. The speaker wore elegant attire. She sounded as if she were trying to lighten her companion's mood—there was a hint of teasing affability in her tone.

Welcoming the refreshing coolness of the gentle rain on her face and in no hurry to return to the palace, where she might encounter Sir John, Alisoun moved on through the gate and into the autumn gardens. She found just enough shelter on a stone bench beneath a tree and was calming down when footsteps on the gravel path set her heart pounding once more. She shrank into the shadow and apparently succeeded in becoming invisible because a woman in the habit of a Cistercian nun rushed passed her without so much as a glance or a hesitation. The drizzly twilight did little to illuminate the nun's face, but her sobs were enough to make Alisoun curious, particularly after having heard the sweet consolation in the lady's voice in the porch. If this was Dame Katherine Alisoun wondered what had happened to her in the short while since they'd parted in the archbishop's chamber. If it was Dame Clarice she was even more anxious to discover what was wrong, considering Captain Archer's warning about her.

Stepping with care over the damp spots on the path and ducking beneath the branches growing heavy in the mist, Alisoun followed the nun out beyond the cultivated gardens and into the fields. She was soon shivering as her damp skirts clung to her ankles and the moisture ran down into her shoes. But she did not hesitate until the nun approached the edge of the woods—remembering Dom Lambert's death among those trees, Alisoun did then pause. Her curiosity was not strong enough to lure her there at twilight.

But the nun had also halted. Now Alisoun could see that she was taller and thinner than Dame Katherine—this must be Clarice. She stood quite still for a while, and then slipped her fingers up a sleeve. Apparently not finding what she'd thought was there, she checked the other sleeve, and then her bodice, her movements increasingly frantic.

'Bitch!' she muttered. 'Trust no one, Clarice, no one. You know that, you fool.' After more frantic searches of her clothing the nun groaned as she tilted her face upward to the soft mist and shouted, 'Damn her! And damn him for calling me a spy and a thief.' Her voice broke into a sob and she bowed her head and covered her face with her hands, her continued muttering impossible to understand.

Alisoun was undecided whether to reveal herself and attempt to comfort the woman, or to withdraw and allow the woman time to regain her composure.

But in the end it was not hers to decide. The woman made a loud, choking sound, startling Alisoun, who was already quite nervous about being so close to the edge of the woods. Clarice was clutching at her throat with one hand, stretching the other out in front of her as if to reach for help. She stumbled forward a few steps, coughing more forcefully now, as if she was trying to clear her throat, and then she spun around in the opposite direction, took a few hesitant steps and tripped on her skirts.

Before Alisoun could reach the poor woman a man in the princess's livery rushed forward, knelt to lift Dame Clarice and rose with her in his arms. He noticed Alisoun and nodded to her.

'I'll take her to her chamber. Fetch Master Walter.'

Alisoun gathered her skirts and ran back to the palace.

As Owen stepped into the kitchen yard a maidservant and one of his men unwound from an embrace and joined him, arm in arm.

'We'll walk with you to the stables, Captain,' said Ned.

Owen read fear in his eyes. The young maid's as well. He knew she was a laundress and occasional kitchen maid, but knew nothing more about her, not even her name. He led them into the stables to a quiet spot on the ground floor, away from those sleeping off the night watch—which should have included Ned, he realised.

'You've something to tell me?'

Ned nodded. 'Ann and I both, Captain.'

'I spurred him to speak, Captain,' said Ann, 'and he planned how we might come to you without anyone guessing our purpose.'

'Dom Lambert's murderer might not want us to talk,' said Ned.

Owen hoped their information was as helpful as they seemed to hope and fear it was. 'Go on.'

The young woman took a deep breath as she met Owen's gaze. She had a plain face but for large, deep blue eyes that drew one in.

'My pallet is so near where Brother Michaelo is sleeping that I feared he'd stumble over me in the dark,' she said. 'But all who were sleeping there worried about folk moving about, so we agreed to keep a lamp burning while we slept. The night Dom Lambert died,

I saw him creep from Brother Michaelo's bed.'

Owen crossed himself. 'God bless you for telling me this, Ann. How did he look?'

'I thought he might be weeping,' she said. 'He made a noise like a sob and hurried out the door where we just met you. I was falling back into sleep when I heard a woman's voice out in the kitchen yard, and Dom Lambert answering, or at least I guessed it was him.'

'Could you hear what they said?'

She shook her head. 'Later, Brother Michaelo's habit brushed my arm as he passed. I could not tell you how much later.' She shrugged. 'That is all.'

'How did he look?'

'Hurried.'

'And you, Ned?'

'I saw Brother Michaelo walking in the fields before dawn. I thought nothing of it—he is everywhere on the manor.'

'He was alone?'

Ned nodded. 'And empty-handed. I wish I could tell you more.'

'I am grateful to both of you,' said Owen. In a louder voice, he said, 'I'm warning you, Ned. Sleep with the others on your watch. You can court Ann after Her Grace's company departs.'

With grateful smiles the couple parted, he to climb up to his pallet, she to scoot out the stable door.

Owen lay down on his cot to consider this new information—it would seem to support Michaelo's story. He wished Ann had been curious enough to peek out the door and identify the woman who'd spoken to Lambert, but perhaps someone else would come forward. Before long he'd returned to his fear about the loyalty of his men, reviewing how he had come to hire each one, searching for the telling detail. Unfortunately there were some he could not recall. Some had been added by Alfred while Owen was away in Wales. Some had been in Thoresby's guard before Owen joined it.

John Holand found him still lying there, wrapped in his worries.

'You lie there doing nothing? The Princess of Wales is making excuses for you and how do I find you?' His fine clothing was misted with rain and when he shook his head he sprayed Owen.

Owen closed his eye and reminded himself that strangling the son of a princess would bring ruin on Lucie and their children. 'I may appear to be idle but I am considering possible changes to the arrangement of my guards.'

'We looked for you in the hall. We expected you—you had supped there the previous evening.' He stank of wine and was already unable to give his full attention to another's response.

'I thought Her Grace would prefer to enjoy her evening meal in peace,' said Owen. 'I have much on my mind. I would be too grim a guest at the table. Nor can I spare the time for a long feast. Should I understand by your presence that the company has dispersed so early?'

'You cannot spare the time,' John growled. 'But you've plenty time to lie abed.'

Perhaps it was Sir John's unlined, unscarred face that made Owen react to him as an impertinent boy, but that he was not—he was twenty-one and no doubt knew his way around the court circle. Owen must have a care. A drunk courtier was often an unreasonable courtier. They stared at each other with caution.

John was the one to look away first. 'I'll escort you to my lady,' he said. 'Remember your station.'

Owen decided that it was best to take that as an order and acquiesce.

Princess Joan had been given Thoresby's former bedchamber up in the solar, a lovely, spacious room. Brother Michaelo had managed to arrange the one large bed and several smaller ones to give the princess and her ladies some privacy from one another. Tapestries from Thoresby's other nearby residences had been brought to Bishopthorpe and the chamber walls were festive with scenes of hunting and winemaking.

The princess's ladies and a pet monkey had been sitting with her on the bed, and Geoffrey Chaucer had been sitting nearby spinning a tale for their delight, eliciting laughter and applause. Owen was sorry when his presence dampened the much-needed cheer and dispersed the gathering. Eleanor and Sybilla took John and withdrew to another part of the room, and Geoffrey bowed and took his leave. Fortunately the monkey went with the ladies—Owen did not trust the exotic little beasts.

Princess Joan thanked Owen for coming. She still wore the beautiful green silk gown that shimmered in the candlelight. She sat quite upright on the bed against a mound of cushions, her outstretched legs draped with an embroidered coverlet. A small cushion peeked out from beneath the coverlet, revealing that one foot was propped up.

After the polite greetings, Owen inquired whether the princess had been injured.

Her laughter was sweet. 'No, God be thanked. It is enough that I am an aging woman who does not heed her physician's advice, Captain Archer. Riding and hunting this morning were excellent activities for me, and had I strolled in the garden for a while this afternoon and eaten a little less at supper I might be quite comfortable tonight. But I sat this afternoon over my embroidery, ate and drank too much at supper, and now my ankle and foot ache.' She laughed again. Though her face was rounded and softened with age, her forehead was smooth, her eyes bright, and her entire face alive with her mood. She was lovely to behold. 'God forgive my petty complaints. I am not so sinfully self-absorbed as I might sound. I have indeed thought of little else than that poor Dom Lambert since you found him. He was a lovely, courteous, gentle man. Have you learned anything about what happened?'

Rich food, idleness—Owen was distracted, thinking that Princess Joan was very possibly the one using water germander for gout. But when she asked again whether he had learned anything he hastened to satisfy her concern—such as he could.

'As you know, Dom Lambert suffered much embarrassment yesterday when he presented the archbishop with blank parchments. His mission for the Bishop of Winchester failed, it is possible that he took his own life.'

Princess Joan made a sympathetic sound. 'Or perhaps he

despaired over that *and* his shame over lying with His Grace's elegant secretary, a man known to have unnatural passions.' She adjusted her foot a little, then met Owen's eyes. 'There is little I do not know, Captain. What was Brother Michaelo doing at the feet of the hanged man?'

'I do not yet know, Your Grace. He says he was concerned about Lambert and followed him there. Someone overcame him and he woke confused.'

'And do you believe him?'

'I think it unwise to believe anyone without witnesses or some evidence.'

'And no one saw anything last night?'

'So far someone has reported seeing Dom Lambert leave Brother Michaelo's chamber, and another saw him take a horse from the stable. It is possible he was alone. Another saw Brother Michaelo walking through the fields, also apparently alone. It is little to go on.'

With a sigh, Joan gazed thoughtfully at the bed's canopy as she idly twisted and released a silk scarf. 'You say he felt shamed by the failure of his mission.' She nodded. 'That I find within reason. But then for someone who had already brought notice on himself to risk sneaking out in the middle of the night with so many eyes supposedly watching all our movements, to have the presence of mind to move silently and manage to climb the tree, bring his horse beneath it—still in silence—oh I forgot, there was the ladder, yes, he need not have used the horse beneath him.' She sighed, then looked at Owen. 'But the horse must still be kept quiet until the deed was done. If the horse whinnied he might have been discovered by one of your men in the midst of hanging himself—well, you see why I find it an unsatisfactory explanation.' She punctuated her conclusion with a flutter of the scarf. 'Brother Michaelo may be speaking the truth.'

Owen was at once filled with admiration for her careful reasoning and with despair for the renewed certainty that there was a murderer in their midst.

'I do see, Your Grace, and I am worried about your safety and that of all your company.'

'Except for the murderer.' She laughed, then made a face. 'Faith, you must think I make light of this, but it is my remedy for fear when my dear husband is not at my side to protect me.'

Owen found it a strange comment, for he could not imagine that Prince Edward had been at her side so very often, at least before his illness, and now from all accounts he would find it difficult to protect her. Perhaps it was a story she told herself to feel safe.

'I do wonder whether the same person killed both Dom Lambert and his servant Will. If it would please you, I would inquire, Your Grace—did you bring with you a sleeping potion?'

'I assure you I carry all manner of potions, Captain.' Her expression was suddenly wary. 'Why do you ask?'

He explained what Magda and Lucie had found in the wine skin.

'The healer has returned from York?'

He did not believe for a moment that she had not been informed about Magda's return, but he must play along with her. 'Yes. I spoke with her earlier.'

'I look forward to meeting her. And your wife is an apothecary.' She smiled and nodded as if giving her approval. 'A woman made master apothecary. I am glad to hear of such an accomplishment.' She seemed lost in thought for a moment. 'But I am certain that what the servant carried in his wineskin was not from my stores, Captain. How could it be?'

'Such confidence might be just what the murderer depended on—that we would not dare to search the physicks of the Princess of Wales.'

He was relieved to see her struck by his reasoning.

'I'd not considered that. You may be right. I am reassured by your clear thinking, Captain. What would you have me do?'

'I hoped you might agree to show Dame Magda the medicines you have with you.'

'I see no reason to refuse your request, Captain. Lady Sybilla will assist her.'

'Might Dame Magda come directly to you, Your Grace?'

She raised an eyebrow. 'You do not trust Sybilla?'

'If someone stole from you, Your Grace, it was someone who knew what was there. A physick might easily be misplaced.'

She straightened a little. 'Send Dame Magda to me in the morning. I shall keep the trunk containing my physicks by me, and she shall look through it in my presence. No one will know that she is to come, so no one will know to remove anything.'

Owen thanked her. She stared at him for a moment, then suddenly reached forward and gently brushed his eye patch. He flinched, a reaction he found it impossible to prevent even so many years since his wounding.

'My dear Tom, John's father, lost an eye in combat. So did our dear friend Sir John Chandos. Did you know you shared such august company in your affliction?'

Her choice of words pained Owen—he preferred people to consider it an injury and not an affliction, despite his own fear that his blinding was God's punishment for his sins, but he understood that she meant to put him at ease. 'I am honoured that you place me in their company, Your Grace. I remember Sir Thomas Holand a little. He was greatly admired by all who served under him. I saw Sir John Chandos only from afar. Their wounds did nothing to diminish them. But it is different for an archer—my skill was all I had.'

'Archbishop Thoresby is fortunate that your lord the old duke knew you had far more to offer than just skill with your bow. But forgive me. I should not have called it an affliction. Neither my first husband nor Sir John liked anyone to call attention to the scars on their faces.' She tilted her head and smiled as she studied his face. 'You are a handsome man, Captain. The scar merely adds the spice of danger to your appearance, which women find exciting. But then you know that, I am sure.' She glanced over in the direction of her women, though the screens hid them, and then back to Owen. 'I've seen Eleanor watching you. And I saw you two confer so prettily in the hall before dinner.'

'You tease me, Your Grace.'

Joan smiled and waved her scarf. 'In matters of the heart, teasing is innocent, Captain. You are a married man, she a married woman, so a little excitement can be refreshing. But I see I embarrass you and I shall desist. Had you any more news for me?'

'I would beg a question, if it please you, my lady. I wondered how you came to choose the sisters from Nun Appleton?'

All teasing left her visage and again she grew wary, resuming the nervous twisting of the scarf. 'I said we must have some sisters to assist Master Walter, and they were provided, with assurances from the abbess of their character.'

'You know neither of them?'

Her expression was carefully blank. 'I trusted their abbess.' But she clutched the scarf and held herself terribly still. 'Why do you ask?'

'Forgive me, Your Grace, but I was in the garden earlier and saw you from afar in conversation with one of the sisters, Dame Clarice. I heard nothing that passed between you, but I saw from her face and your stance that it was an uneasy exchange.'

Joan had closed her eyes and sat without as much as a muscle moving for a long while. Owen began to think he'd been dismissed, but he could not bring himself to rise. Princess or no, he felt she owed him at least a feeble lie.

'I had not met Dame Clarice before she joined our travelling company,' Joan suddenly said in a quiet, unemotional tone. 'Nor had I heard of her even so recently as a month ago. Her part in this situation—' she hesitated, then continued, 'her part will be revealed in a few days, I promise you. Events here have led me to send to Nun Appleton for information that might assist you. For now you need only to know that she is not a murderer. Indeed, I fear that the murderer might wish her harm. I have men watching her at all times.'

'Not earlier today,' said Owen. 'I found her quite alone with the archbishop, searching through a chest of his belongings.'

She looked surprised. 'Searching his chamber?' She took a deep breath. 'Foolish woman. But my men know that when she is in the archbishop's chamber she is quite safe—though I'd assumed there would always be someone present in addition to His Grace.'

'I have arranged for that to be so from now on,' said Owen. 'Is she in danger because of her search of His Grace's chamber?' The princess had expressed surprise, but he did not believe her.

'I knew nothing of that. Why should that endanger her?'

'I hoped you might know, Your Grace.'

'What do you think she took?'

'A personal letter.'

Joan bowed her head and touched the scarf to her forehead, effectively hiding her expression from Owen. 'If you like, I'll send for her and see what I can discover.'

'I would be grateful for that, Your Grace.'

'Meanwhile, Dame Clarice should not cause you any more trouble.'

'At the moment I'm more concerned about what you just said—that she might be in danger, Your Grace. I pray you, tell me what I need to know about her.'

He could see at once that he'd pushed too hard, and he silently cursed himself.

'You forget yourself, Captain Archer.' She was suddenly stern and imperious. 'The welfare of the people of this realm tempers all that I do for I am the wife and mother of your future kings. I know what is best here. I have told you all that you need to know. I will order her to return anything that is not hers, and I shall see that you are present when I reveal the reason for her presence here in the palace.' She softened her tone. 'For now, I am reassured by your sense of duty, and you may rest assured that she is watched by one of my men. May God watch over you and bless you for coming to see me.' She bowed her head and called for a servant, who was slow in responding because he was distracted by a messenger who'd just arrived.

'He has returned from Nun Appleton, Your Grace,' said the servant.

'Excellent.' Joan saw Owen watching with interest. 'You shall know all tomorrow, Captain. You are dismissed.'

Owen quietly withdrew, though beneath his calm he was in

danger of exploding with the frustration of dealing with the princess. Imperious, petty, enjoying her little mystery—damnable woman.

The nuns. God had been guiding him in his stealth when he'd come upon Dame Clarice in Thoresby's chamber. Owen crossed himself.

'Captain?'

He turned as Alisoun stepped into the dim light from the sconce by the chamber door.

'What is it?' he asked. 'You look worried. And wet.'

Her veil was limp with damp and the scent of wet grass and soil rose from her hem.

'The sister Dame Clarice fainted out in the fields. One of Princess Joan's servants carried her back to the palace. She was struggling for breath. Master Walter has given her something to calm her.'

'Out in the fields? How did you both come to be out in the fields at this time of day?'

'I was in the garden as she rushed through, seeming very upset. I did not think she should run off like that alone. And I remembered what you had said about the sisters.'

'Was there anyone else? A servant?'

'The man in the princess's livery came rushing forward to assist Clarice as soon as she fell. He must have followed her.'

Owen nodded. 'I'll put a guard by her door.' One of his own men. 'Thank you, Alisoun. You have been very helpful.'

With the ghost of a smile, she turned away, but suddenly turned back. 'Stay a moment, Captain. I'd forgotten the porch. I saw her first on the porch that faces the gardens. She was with a woman in elegant dress, and—' she stopped, shaking her head. 'I think it was Clarice on the porch—it was one of the sisters.'

'Tell me what you can.'

'The lady was comforting the nun—she suggested that she stay and rest a while.'

'This lady—was she dark or fair?'

Alisoun shrugged, and he could read the frustration in her

brown eyes, her furrowed brow. 'I could not see her clearly.'

'Slender or stout?'

'Not slender, I think—but her clothes—just as with the nun, I can't be certain.'

'I am most grateful to you, Alisoun.'

'Really?' Despite the tears of frustration in her eyes she almost smiled. 'I did not wish to interrupt you with Her Grace, but I wanted to tell you as soon as I might.'

'God go with you,' said Owen. 'Go dry your clothes by the kitchen fire and ask Maeve for something warm to heat you within.'

Alisoun bobbed her head and walked slowly away down the corridor leaving a trail of wet boot prints.

Owen fought down anger—he should have had one of his men follow Clarice. But who could he trust? For a long moment he considered returning to the princess with this latest news of the mysterious Dame Clarice, but in the end he desisted, admitting to himself that his sole motivation for doing so right now would be to shock the princess into revealing all she knew about the nun, and he was fairly certain that it would fail. Princess Joan had a strong will and she'd already made it quite plain that she believed she knew what was best. He feared it would also cost him too dearly—that she would not cooperate with him again.

Outside Thoresby's chamber Gilbert caught up with Owen. 'Captain, I've something to tell you.'

'You've found a guard who saw something,' Owen guessed.

'I have. Fiddler John says that he saw Dom Lambert leave the stable with a horse, and with him was Lady Eleanor.'

Owen's heart sank. The voice in the kitchen yard—had it been Eleanor out for one of her walks in the night air? 'Is he certain that it was the princess's lady?'

Gilbert nodded. 'The dark-eyed one.'

It was a most unwelcome report. 'Send him to me in the stables later.' Owen took a step toward the archbishop's door, then turned back. 'No one else had anything to tell you? Only Fiddler John?'

Gilbert shook his head. 'He's the only one who said aught to me. Perhaps they are waiting for you to settle for the night, and they'll come to you.'

'When they're least welcome,' Owen said with a curse. They'd had ample opportunity when he'd gone back to the stable while the guests dined in the hall and only Ned and Ann had come. 'But I thank you. Well done, Gilbert.'

The guard withdrew.

Owen entered the archbishop's chamber. Michaelo lay on the cot, apparently asleep. Magda and Thoresby were quietly talking but broke off and looked toward him with interest, making space for him near the great bed. He told Magda of his meeting with Princess Joan, and that she'd agreed to have Magda attend her in the morning.

'I am glad she has agreed,' said Thoresby.

Owen told them of Dame Clarice's faint, and that Master Walter had given the nun something to help her sleep.

'I am uneasy,' he added. 'For her to be overcome so soon after searching this chamber, my mind misgives. Did someone poison her so they might search her?'

Magda frowned thoughtfully. 'Not all poisons are meant to kill. Magda will look in on her in the morning.'

'I would be grateful,' said Thoresby. 'Despite her transgression I would not have her suffer in such wise. We've had enough death in this palace.' He turned to Owen. 'But how would anyone know she might have stolen something—I'm assuming that's why they would wish to search her?'

Owen described his glimpse of the altercation between Clarice and the princess in the garden. 'It is possible that someone overheard them.'

Thoresby groaned. 'Too many people. Why did she bring such a large company?'

'There is more.' Owen told them of Lady Eleanor's prostration in the chapel, and the sightings of Lambert in the corridor, the woman's voice in the kitchen yard, Michaelo's walk in the fields before dawn and Dom Lambert departing the stable with a woman, with one guard naming her as Lady Eleanor. He regretted upsetting

Thoresby, but it was his duty to inform him. 'What I do not yet understand is how, if they left together and Michaelo followed, even losing his way how did they manage it so quickly before he reached them?' Owen suddenly felt a great weariness.

As if she read his mind, Magda said, 'Thou hast a body that demands food and rest, Bird-eye. See to thyself. Magda will see to the young nun in the morning. Thou hast done enough for one day.'

Owen was only too happy to leave the two of them to their nocturnal musings.

Out in the kitchen he discovered a consolation gift in the presence of Master Walter. The physician was enjoying one of Maeve's meat pies as she smiled on him. She was always grateful to satisfy a good appetite. As soon as she saw Owen, she rose to assemble a meal for him.

'I just heard about Dame Clarice,' Owen said as he sat down beside Walter.

Walter nodded to him in greeting, washed his food down with some ale, and then said, 'She will sleep through the night.'

'God grant that she wakes in the morning,' said Owen.

Halting the pie halfway to his mouth, the physician eyed Owen with alarm. 'That she wakes? I saw no sign of poisoning. Is that what you fear? Have you cause to believe she'd been poisoned?'

'I am relieved that you believe her to be in no danger,' said Owen.

'Who would poison one of the sisters?'

'We must all pray that I can soon answer that, Master Walter. To whom do you entrust the physicks that you carry?'

'*My* physicks? Why, my manservant Jonah carries them.'

Owen had noticed the servant, at least as old as Walter and at least twice his size, with the look of a soldier rather than a manservant. 'He has been in your service a long while, has he?'

Walter nodded. 'I know him better than I do my own children. He's not only a loyal and hardworking servant, but his mere presence frightens would-be attackers and convinces clients to honour their bills.' He laughed, but it was nervous laughter. 'Why do you ask? Do you think someone would steal from me? Or has?'

Owen was glad that Maeve and her kitchen maid were having a loud conversation by the crackling fire as they worked, for he did not want anyone but Walter to hear what he was about to ask. 'Do you carry poppy, mandrake, and water germander?'

'Of course I do. All physicians do.' Walter grunted as he turned a little on the bench—though his diminutive build made him look boyish he was not, and he moved with the stiffness of his age. 'Now you've confused me. I might guess that you believe Lambert's servant had been slipped a strong dose of poppy and mandrake that made him too languorous to sit his horse. But the germander? Bloating? Gout? He did not seem one to suffer from that. It is a rich man's disease, not that of the servant of a bishop's clerk—' He hesitated, frowning. 'Though I *have* treated a disappointingly large number of monks for it. And the occasional manservant of a wealthy master.'

Maeve set a tankard of ale and a meat pie before Owen, returning at once to her maid and commencing her loud discourse. Owen said a silent prayer of thanks for her discretion. Walter seemed lost in thought at the moment, and Owen took the opportunity to bite into the pie. The aroma had awakened his stomach juices, and he was not disappointed. It was manna from heaven, hot, spicy, rich, the meat cooked to a tenderness that melted on his tongue. He wished he were alone to savour this.

'Maeve, you work miracles every day,' he called to her.

She glanced over her shoulder, beaming.

'We were talking of gout,' Walter said.

'We were talking of poppy, mandrake and water germander,' Owen said. 'My wife and Magda detected all three ingredients in the remaining wine in Will's wineskin.'

'In his—God in heaven. How unlike me not to notice he suffered from gout. How did I fail to notice that?'

'I do not mean to suggest that Will suffered from gout, Master Walter. Even if he did, and he also had trouble sleeping, he would not carry such a mixture to drink while riding, eh?'

Owen chewed as he watched understanding dawn on Walter's face.

'Oh, yes, I see.' The physician wiped his forehead. 'I am weary and not thinking as clearly as I might.'

'I'm sorry to have disturbed you at your meal,' said Owen.

They ate companionably for a moment.

'Would you permit Dame Magda to look at your physicks?' Owen asked.

Walter wiped his mouth with a cloth. 'I'd heard she'd returned.' When Owen said nothing, Walter went on. 'To what end would you have her look at my supplies? I do not mix anything until it is needed. She could see that I have poppy, mandrake, and water germander, but I have already told you that I do.'

'I see. And you trust that your servant Jonah would be aware of anyone attempting to take anything?'

'Oh yes. He is proud of my trust. He believes that it raises him to a position quite superior to other servants.' Walter smiled with affection. 'I thank God for Jonah.' He was quiet again for a while, eating a little more. But suddenly he turned to Owen. 'If Will's wine was made to cause his accident, does that mean that Dom Lambert's supposed suicide *was* murder, that I was right about the bruising on his neck?'

'What do you think?'

'That it would so follow.'

Owen nodded. 'So do I, despite the horse in the villager's field.'

'Which would mean that not all of your guards are honest,' said Walter, lowering his voice.

Meeting the physician's searching gaze, Owen said simply, 'Not at present.'

'God help us.' Walter crossed himself. Fear was writ plainly on his face.

'Amen,' said Owen. He fought the urge to soften what he'd just admitted, a strange compulsion, for the situation was as serious as Walter seemed to have just realised.

The physician had been staring into his cup. 'I've lost the thread of our conversation. You are concerned about Dame Clarice? That she might have been poisoned like Will?'

'I have the word of someone I trust that Dame Clarice may be in danger, and Alisoun's description of the nun's fall suggested to me that she'd suddenly become ill.'

'I will request samples of her urine as soon as she wakes,' said Walter, pushing the remaining piece of pie aside. 'And I'll bleed her on the morrow for good measure. God help me if I did not pay enough heed to her condition, if I gave her something that will help the poison along.'

'How could you know if Alisoun did not describe it clearly?'

He guessed that Walter thought some of the blame might be his. Certainly Owen's words did not seem to calm the physician, who rose with a nervous energy and bade him good evening, then thanked Maeve for her excellent pie. 'I'll sit with the young sister tonight,' Walter mumbled as he crossed the room. 'I want to be there if there is a change.'

When the door closed behind the physician, Maeve left her maid and settled her large body across from Owen. Reaching for Walter's abandoned tankard, she tilted back her head and drained it of ale.

Owen did likewise with his tankard.

'Did the sisters from Nun Appleton take their meals in the hall today, Maeve, or in here?'

'I've no idea where they dined midday,' she said, 'but they favour a cold, light repast in the evening, which I give them in here.' Her broad, pleasant face creased with concern. 'Has one taken ill? Is that what you and the physician were discussing?'

'Yes. Dame Clarice.'

'Poor soul! But I cannot think of anything she had of me that would sicken her.' Maeve had straightened and tucked in her chin, refusing responsibility.

'You were here all the time? No one else might have slipped something into the food?'

Maeve bristled. 'I cannot think how.'

Owen held up his tankard. 'Join me in another?'

Maeve hesitated, but soon relaxed. 'It is late enough. Everything else can wait until dawn.' She called to the kitchen maid to come fill their tankards.

Quiet had settled on the palace. If he strained his ears Thoresby could hear the water lapping at the river landing, the shriek of a coney as an owl swooped down on it in the orchard, the cats settling by the mouse holes, watchful, ready to pounce. Most of his life he had treasured this time of night if he found himself awake, rarely annoyed by any break in his sleep. But tonight his mind kept turning to the scene he'd imagined over and over, the handsome Dom Lambert, a rope already draped round his shoulders, climbing a tree and methodically testing for a branch that would hold his weight long enough to crush his windpipe. Because he had not sufficiently guarded Wykeham's letters and someone had stolen them? He had not thought Lambert so distraught over the loss that he would commit the ultimate act of despair. Considering the servant's death, Thoresby thought it more likely that Lambert had been murdered—that someone had murdered him in a way that would look like suicide.

But perhaps with a little too much wine clouding his thoughts Lambert had been unable to imagine standing up before William Wykeham and admitting his failure. Perhaps Lambert had put all his hope in the esteem he might garner by completing this mission. Perhaps Wykeham had promised him a promotion on his return. Thoresby wondered how it would be to serve Wykeham, a man so ambitious who had so recently been bitterly disappointed and was now so determined to win back the heart and confidence of the king. He would be impatient with failure, perhaps worse than impatient.

Thoresby returned to the image of the man with the rope draped around his shoulders, perhaps weeping as he drunkenly scrambled into the tree, the wine igniting his imagination, convincing him that death would be far easier than facing his master. What must it feel like to lose all hope? Thoresby's stomach clenched. He knew what it felt like, for he felt it now. Master Walter held out no hope for him, suggested no remedy for his failing body. His heart raced and the blood pounded in his head. He gasped for breath.

The lamp had been moved near the doorway and his bed curtains were closed. He lay in darkness like the grave and he did not find it at all comfortable.

'Dame Magda?'

'Magda is here.'

He found it interesting how she responded as if another were reporting her presence.

Thoresby tugged at the curtains. 'I would have some light.'

Without fuss or argument the small, elderly woman drew aside the curtain, standing on tiptoes to tug it wide, then brought the lamp closer, setting it on a table near the stool on which she sat her night watch. She helped him sit up, then adjusted his pillows to support him in a more upright position. She smelled of smoke, spices and earth, a not-unpleasant combination.

'Art thou thirsty?' she asked. 'Fear dries the throat, eh?'

'How did you know?'

She smoothed his forehead, her bony hands reassuringly warm, her touch comforting. 'Thine eyes.'

He reached for her hand and she in turn firmly grasped his, her warmth and strength flooding up his arm to his heart. 'God resides in you,' he said.

'Thou hast strange ideas.' She accompanied the comment with a gentle smile. 'Rest thine eyes whilst Magda mixes a soothing powder for thy wine.'

'I was imagining myself climbing the tree to die,' he admitted to her before he let go of her hand.

'Hast thou ever thought to take thine own life?'

Thoresby paused, trying to remember. He never answered her questions thoughtlessly. There was something about her that inspired him to search deep within for his answers. He believed that in doing so he learned much of value. 'No. I cannot recall a time when I despaired of finding a way out or grasped at death as an acceptable solution.'

'Magda thought not.' She slipped her hand from his and gently felt for his pulse. After a pause, she nodded and let go of him.

Her touch reminded Thoresby of his long ago beloved. He had lain with other women after her, but Marguerite had been able to soothe him with the gentlest touch, or a thoughtful word spoken at the precise moment he needed to hear it. Marguerite. She'd been much in his dreams of late, a sweet presence. He wished he could remember where he'd last hidden her letter. He cursed his failing memory. He had not liked how foolish he felt with Archer, not being certain whether the nun might have stolen the letter.

'And you, Dame Magda?' he asked, not wanting her to move on just yet. 'Have you ever tried to take your life?'

'A violent death is not a good death. Worst of all, by thy own hand. How might thy spirit ever find rest?'

Thoresby crossed himself. 'God help all who despair.'

'But thou knowest Lambert did not take his own life. He was strangled, or so says Bird-eye.'

'Oh! Yes. I'd forgotten.' Was that a better death? Then he remembered—it was Michaelo about whom he worried. Caught by his old demon, would his secretary take his own life?

'Does Michaelo sleep?' he asked.

'Aye. Like a babe,' said Magda.

She withdrew to the table at which she mixed her physicks, set up near the brazier on which a pot of water always steamed. Thoresby closed his eyes and extended his prayer for all those who took their lives, or were in danger of doing so. He had never felt such compassion for those lost souls as he did now. He wondered if there was something he might have done in his lifetime to comfort them, to teach them that God loved and forgave them. When Magda placed a steaming cup in his hands he was grateful for the warmth.

She settled on her stool, gathering her multicoloured gown about her, and as she moved the cloth the flickering light from the brazier made the pattern shift and ripple, as if it had come alive.

Sometimes Thoresby imagined the odd movement of her coloured clothing to be a spirit presence that hovered about her, bequeathing her power.

'Thou must drink it to benefit,' Magda said with a gentle smile.

He sipped and found the warm, slightly sweet liquid comforting.

'I have opened my heart to you about my daughter,' he said, not wanting her to withdraw into herself. He was not yet comfortable with sleep. 'Now I would learn something of you. Why do you speak of yourself as "Magda", not "I"? It is as if you are outside yourself. I don't understand. I remember your granddaughter Tola—she did not speak so.' Magda's granddaughter had been wet nurse to Lucie and Owen's son when they had sent the children to the country to escape the pestilence.

'No, Tola does not speak as Magda does. She has no cause.'

No cause. Thoresby felt a thrill of anticipation as he swallowed a bit more of the warm, sweet concoction. It soothed his throat. 'I knew there was a tale behind it.' He fidgeted, seeking a more comfortable position. His back did not like so much lying abed. 'Would you tell me?'

He sensed her hesitation, though it was brief.

'Magda Digby once forgot that her gift as a healer was for all folk, not only those she thought worthy folk. She forgot that her opinion must count as naught, that she must step aside from herself. *I* is not for a healer.'

'You neglected someone? Refused them healing?'

'Much to Magda's shame.' The pain in her voice moved him.

'I have conjured bad memories. Forgive me, my friend.'

She patted his arm.

'I would say you have long since made reparation for your very human error,' he said. 'You are remarkable for holding to such an ideal.' He coughed and silently cursed his weak body, for he was enjoying the conversation.

'Magda is not remarkable,' she said as she tapped the cup to remind him to drink. 'She is merely a vessel for healing, and she had not surrendered her pride as completely as she should have.'

Thoresby drank again and felt his limbs relaxing. 'Our duty is difficult to know, Dame Magda. I doubt that many of us ever fully understand our purpose, and if we do, few of us have the courage to embrace it without occasional rebellions. Even Christ questioned God's purpose in the suffering he was about to endure.' His last sentence came out in such a tortured whisper he feared she would not be able to hear it.

She touched his forehead. 'Magda is glad to hear that this man thou callest a redeemer was not cursed with perfection.'

In the firelight Thoresby could see her teasing smile. In anyone else, such irreverence would make him uneasy. Perhaps it was that he sensed no malevolence in her.

Magda had just stoked the fire in the brazier and returned to her chair beside Thoresby's great bed when she felt a draft on her neck. Turning, she could just make out a tall, slender figure enter the room. By the grace of his movements Magda recognised Brother Michaelo, the black swan. She was accustomed to his nocturnal vigils at his master's bedside and seldom let him know that she was awake—she rarely slept during the night when sitting with the dying. The patient's condition could turn suddenly, and she should be awake for that. But tonight, she had thought him sleeping peacefully in the corner. As the monk drifted down onto a chair near her, she almost gasped aloud at the wave of sorrow and pain that arrived with him, and the cold damp emanating from him. She guessed he'd been lying on the damp stone floor of the chapel, as those devoted to the Christian god often did.

'Magda is also wakeful,' she said in a quiet voice, not wanting to startle him and wake Thoresby.

'I just wanted to rest in his presence,' said Michaelo, a great weariness in his voice.

'It is peaceful here,' said Magda. 'Thou hast taken much care in making thy master comfortable in his last days. He is blessed to have thy devotion.'

'He lifted me out of a terrible darkness. He has been my redemption.' His voice broke and he covered his face with his hands.

Magda said no more, leaving him to his sorrow, sensing his need for solitude.

7

MISSED OPPORTUNITIES

AFTER MIDNIGHT AND INTO THURSDAY MORNING

Sharing ale with Maeve had done nothing to quiet his mind. After leaving the kitchen Owen had been drawn back into the palace, but the crowd of pallets occupied by snoring servants that lined the corridor outside Thoresby's chamber reminded him that he would find few awake at this hour. Most had eaten and drunk their fill and would be worthless even if he could wake them. Still, he had an angry urge to race through the palace waking all and dragging them to the hall to be questioned en masse. How dare they sleep when he could not for fear that more would die. How could they sleep? Did they think they were immortal?

Sybilla and Clarice—is that who Alisoun had seen in the porch? He stepped out into the kitchen yard and discovered Geoffrey sitting on a stool, his ink-stained fingers curled around a bowl from which steam curled into the chilly night. He nodded at Owen.

'Maeve told me you'd just left her.' He held out the bowl. 'We can share this if you like. A tisane of fennel and I'm not sure what else. Maeve assured me it would cool my belly without killing me.'

Owen settled beside him and took the bowl in his hands, letting the steam clear his head, then sipped it before handing it back. 'You were at the evening meal in the hall?'

'I was.'

'Were the ladies Eleanor and Sybilla there?'

Geoffrey nodded slowly, then grunted. 'Sybilla left early. Very early.'

'She was in Princess Joan's chamber afterwards, when I arrived.'

Geoffrey nodded. 'Not long before you appeared she returned, rosy-cheeked from a walk outdoors, I presumed.'

'And Eleanor?'

'We left the hall together. I was in her company all evening until you arrived in the princess's chamber. Later I saw Sybilla in the hall with one of the men who'd ridden to Nun Appleton, and Eleanor was out here in the yard for a while—she enjoys some evening air before she sleeps.'

'God's blood,' Owen groaned in frustration, raking his hands through his hair and then tugging on it as if he could wake his brain. 'Which one?'

'I'd heard that the nun you'd caught trespassing in His Grace's chamber had taken ill while we were in the hall for the evening meal. You don't think Sybilla responsible?' He looked incredulous.

Owen told him what Alisoun had seen. 'Though I've also had a disturbing report about Lady Eleanor. One of my guards claims to have seen her leaving the stable with Lambert the night he died.'

Geoffrey crossed himself. 'Eleanor? Have you spoken to her of this?'

'No.'

'I saw you with her in the hall earlier in the evening. Sir Lewis growled to see her look on you with such affection—and you her.' Geoffrey tilted his head, trying to get a good look at Owen's expression.

'I remind her of the time she was free and all happiness seemed possible. Can she be so desperate as to commit murder? Why? How would these deaths benefit her?'

'The bitter wife, a common theme in courtly discourse. They are usually too despairing to act.'

'Perhaps Sir Lewis might know more of her situation. Something that might align her with the Nevilles?'

'I'll speak with him.' Geoffrey put a hand on Owen's forearm and paused, waiting for Owen to look at him. His eyes were serious, his expression concerned. 'What if she is part of this crime, Owen? Will you forget the past and confront her?'

Owen shuddered to think of it. 'Reluctantly, Geoffrey. But I will do it if I must.' He reached for the bowl and took another drink, though he knew his gut was beyond such gentle ministrations. 'Speak to Sir Lewis and watch them both, would you?'

'I will. How is the nun?'

'Master Walter has her sleeping, and I've agitated him enough that he'll watch her closely.' He handed the bowl back to Geoffrey and rose. 'I'll try to sleep now.'

Geoffrey stood as well. 'I doubt either of us will sleep well.'

'With two murders and now the nun how are all those within sleeping so soundly?'

'They put all their trust in you.' Geoffrey chuckled at Owen's expression. 'I am teasing you. They are all drugged with drink. It is not a natural sleep.'

'But they do expect my men to keep them safe,' said Owen. 'Yet I wonder which of my men are to be trusted. And that poor nun—'

'She was trespassing, Owen. Remember that.'

'I'll have Alisoun sit with her. Michaelo can attend His Grace when Magda is resting. With you watching the ladies I'll have a little peace of mind.'

Geoffrey reached up and grasped Owen's shoulder, looking long and seriously at him, glancing away only as the night's peace was shattered by a company of drunken singers staggering into the yard from the gardens. 'To have your trust means much to me, my friend. I'll do my best to deserve it. And for the moment I'll save you from an encounter with that nasty drunk, John Holand. I saw him and his companions earlier. Hie thee to the stables!'

With a nod of thanks, Owen hurried away from the approaching voices. It was a little heartening to know that carousers were threatening the privacy of any who hoped to slip about unnoticed in the night.

In the stables he lay down, but he could not rest. His heart beat in a crazily uneven staccato, his head buzzed with too many worries battling for prominence, and his skin crawled with anticipation of trouble that could come from anywhere. After what seemed hours of tossing about desperately praying for a comfortable drowsiness to pull him under, he gave up and rose. So be it. He stepped out into the chilly night. Clouds segmented the sky, alternately revealing small fields of stars, hiding others, slowly changing the patterns until Owen felt unsure of the steadiness of the ground beneath him.

Energy built up in him and he began to walk, needing the movement. He found himself just outside the chapel, and stepped within to pray for guidance.

Kneeling before the Lord, he felt humble, lost, insignificant.

Magda had once suggested that his blinding had been the wound that allowed the healer in him to come forth. Now he found himself smirking at the absurdity. He'd been blinded as a sign that he was blind to some kernel of wisdom that would allow him to be whole.

And then he'd been swept up in the service of John Thoresby, against whom he'd proceeded to struggle and fight for ten years, righteously judging the archbishop as a man whose ambition blinded him to compassion, love, the healing of the people in his care.

Jehannes knelt down beside Owen. 'You are also wakeful?'

Owen nodded. 'And God seems distracted.'

He could see Jehannes's smile in the soft light from the sanctuary lamp.

'He cannot be distracted,' said Jehannes. 'You have not the ears to hear at the moment.'

They knelt side by side, silently pursuing their own thoughts, for a long while. When Jehannes finally rose, Owen followed.

'Sir John Holand woke me,' said the archdeacon.

'I heard him as well.'

'He wanted to know what you intend to do to protect his mother and her ladies, as well as the nuns. He grows more hostile toward us with every mishap. He was furious when he saw poor Clarice being carried in last evening, convinced that she'd been raped and murdered. He has an unsubtle wit.'

'I count myself fortunate that for the most part he's kept his distance from me.'

'Perhaps it's his fortune—or he's smarter than he behaves. I imagine you would take some satisfaction in thrashing him.'

Owen could not help but chuckle. 'Oh, that I would.' He stretched. 'God watch over you on your journey to York.'

'I pray that He inspires me, that I do not fail you. Are you certain you want me to return in the afternoon even if I've learned nothing?'

'Yes. I need you here—there are so few I can trust.'

Jehannes nodded and wished him a good night.

But Owen had no intention of returning to his pallet. He could wait no longer to inquire about Clarice's condition. Stepping out into the pre-dawn dark he hesitated. Dame Katherine might yet sleep. But it was no time for courtesy. He resumed his walk across the yard and entered the pallet-lined palace, heading up to the small chamber in the solar where the nuns were lodged. He was relieved to see one of his men standing without, wide awake and ready to challenge him until he recognised Owen.

'You're up betimes, Captain.'

'I haven't slept.'

'The physician and the midwife have been wakeful as well. They've both come to see the sisters.'

The plump Dame Katherine opened the door looking hollow-eyed and rumpled, her face carrying the pattern of a wrinkled surface on which she'd rested, the lamp in her hand dangerously tipping.

'What is it, Captain?' She clutched at the neck of her gown as if protecting her throat.

Owen steadied the lamp. She seemed startled by his touch, but she held the lamp steady now.

'I am concerned about Dame Clarice,' he said. 'How is she?'

Katherine shrugged. 'Asleep. As she was when Master Walter came a little while ago, and Dame Magda before him. Why is everyone so worried?' The nun shifted to rub the top of a bare foot against the back of her standing leg.

Owen took the opportunity to push past her and into the small chamber.

'Captain, you should not be in here!'

He ignored her. 'It did not concern you that she was carried in from the fields in a faint?' Owen took the lamp from her and set it down on a small table, kneeling to listen to Dame Clarice's breathing, relieved to find it steady, easy.

'At Nun Appleton we are accustomed to her fits of temper, Captain,' Katherine said in a loud whisper. 'I tried to tell the physician so last night. And that pagan healer.' She let go of the neck of her gown to cross herself. 'I would not allow her to touch Dame Clarice.'

Then Katherine was a fool, but so was her abbess to send on such a mission a woman who suffered frequent fits.

'Despite what you say, you do seem worried,' he noted. And she was plainly very tired—but then, he was her third visitor. 'Were you the one who put her to bed?'

'To be sure, I was! And you should not—'

'I have reason to believe she might have taken a letter from the archbishop's chamber. Did you find anything like that?'

Katherine seemed to debate with herself, opening her mouth as if to answer, then looking away. At last she drew out a small parchment from her sleeve, but she hesitated when Owen held out his hand.

'His Grace is anxious to have it back in his possession,' said Owen. 'Have you read it?'

'Just enough to know it was not hers,' said Katherine, shrugging her shoulders forward as if to protect her heart. 'But—' She bit her lip and frowned at the letter. Her hands were rough and her nails caked with dirt. She was not a pampered nun.

'I pray you, trust me, Dame Katherine. My purpose is the safety of all this company.'

Shyly, she seemed to force herself to look him in the eye. 'I did not find it on her when I first removed her wet gown. It was not

until later—after all the fuss had quieted down and we were alone—
that I found it tucked into the sleeve of the gown I'd hung over a
stool by the brazier to dry.'

He was grateful that she had decided to trust him. 'Who was
in here?'

'Master Walter, one of the princess's retainers—the one who
had carried her from the garden—and one of the princess's ladies—
she seemed to know the man, a maidservant who accompanied the
lady, and a kitchen servant...I believe that is all.'

'Which of the princess's ladies?'

'The fair-haired one—not the pretty one. Sybilla? I think that is
what they called her—Master Walter and the retainer.'

'And the man's name?'

She shook her head. 'I don't know. He was fair as well.'

It would be easy enough to find out who had brought her into
the palace. 'Could you describe the maidservant?'

'She was very ordinary, Captain.'

'And the kitchen servant?'

'A young man, with a tooth missing right here.' She tapped the
spot in which one of Maeve's long-time helpers was missing a tooth.

'So you think one of them brought in the letter?'

'They must have. I removed the gown and draped it over the
stool, arranging the sleeves so they would dry. I would have seen
it then.'

'I am most grateful for your help.' He took the letter from her
and as if it had been all that was holding her up she slumped down
onto a stool.

'I've never known her to faint after one of her fits.' She spoke
softly, glancing behind her as if gauging how loudly she might speak
without waking Clarice. 'I was frightened when she was carried in,
so pale and lifeless. And when Master Walter returned after he had
given her the sleeping potion, wanting to listen to her heartbeat, I
feared he knew of some mischief that had befallen her, something
that the pagan healer's girl had not thought to tell me. This morning
he means to bleed her and wants a sample of her urine. But he says

I've nothing to worry about.'

'Did he seem concerned after listening to her heart?'

She nodded and crossed herself. 'Everyone is worried because of the letter, isn't that it?'

'She was foolish to steal something from the Archbishop of York,' said Owen. As Katherine began to sputter something, he changed the subject. 'You say that she often has fits of temper. Do you know the cause of her anger?'

Her rosebud lips pursed, Katherine considered her response. 'It is hardly worth speaking of. She resents the fact that she was not given a choice in her vocation, that she was sent to the convent so young she remembers no other life. This journey has certainly not appeased her in any way. Quite the contrary, in fact. I fear that being here and seeing the princess and her ladies has filled Clarice with impossible yearnings.'

Owen could imagine how that might be, the luxurious clothing of the princess's entourage, their pretty language, the sumptuous feast, the gorgeous tapestries and fittings of the palace. She would see nothing so elegant in the nunnery. 'I am sorry for her.'

Katherine did not look moved. She sniffed. 'There is nothing out of the ordinary about it, Captain. Except that three of you have been troubled enough to inquire about her in the middle of the night. Is there more to it? Did something *happen* to her last night? Was it not her usual fit of temper? Did someone try to kill her for the letter?'

'I know no more than you, Dame Katherine. I think it likely that the deaths of Dom Lambert and his servant have touched us all in different ways. Perhaps healers see omens in unusual faints such as hers. I am charged with the safety of all here, so I respond to unusual behaviour. The letter disappearing and then reappearing is admittedly cause for grave concern.'

She crossed herself. '*Deus juva me.*'

'I do not know your abbess, but I question her judgement in sending a woman prone to fits of anger on such a mission, to attend a dying archbishop in the company of the Princess of Wales.'

'My abbess is a good and noble woman, Captain. It is not my place to question her decisions.'

The tight-lipped reply was no more than he'd expected. She was naturally and perhaps admirably guarded in her criticisms of her superiors.

She tried but was unable to suppress a yawn. 'I would sleep a while. Master Walter said he will be back this morning to bleed Clarice.' She took a step backward and reached for the door handle.

'Then I shall leave you to rest a little before he returns,' said Owen. 'I will send Alisoun Ffulford to you, the young woman—'

'I know who she is, Captain. I assure you, I can care for my fellow sister.'

'I've no doubt you could in the peace and safety of your nunnery, Dame Katherine, but this palace is neither peaceful nor safe at present.'

The woman looked almost amused. 'And that girl can protect me?'

'She is an expert archer, Dame Katherine, and skilled with a dagger as well. I'll see that she has a dagger—her bow would be of no use in this small space.'

'Ask her to be quiet,' the nun snapped as she closed the door behind him.

As Owen moved away he tried to remember whether he'd seen Sybilla in Joan's chamber when he was leaving the room the previous evening, but his irritation with the princess must have blinded him to anything else, for he could not recall any but the returned guard and the servant who had announced him. She'd been there earlier, but it was quite possible that while he spoke to Her Grace Sybilla had slipped away to return the letter after reading it.

In the kitchen a sleepy Maeve handed him a bit of cheese and a small, crusty loaf of bread.

'Would you like cider or ale?' she asked.

He felt blessed by this abundance, having expected to find the kitchen help still asleep and nothing more at hand than perhaps a cup of water and if lucky a crust of bread. 'I think cider this morning. I'd not thought to find you at work so early. We shared that ale late last night.'

She looked at him askance. 'I would sleep late when I've such a company of folk to feed? I'm lucky to rest at all.' With a nod to him, she added. 'Should I worry that both you and Dame Magda are up betimes? I pray there is no more trouble.'

'Not so far, but I've trouble enough.'

With a knowing nod she went about her work.

Now Owen saw Magda sitting near the fire, a bowl of cider on her lap. She seemed to be drowsing. He settled beside her and while he ate, watched Maeve and several kitchen helpers move about in what seemed a well-rehearsed dance between ovens, caldrons, and tables, organising the ingredients for the day's meals. It was a comforting performance and the chills of the night receded a little despite all the nagging questions that remained. The warm bread and cider helped as well.

Remembering the letter, he opened it and skimmed it, smiling at the sweet, affectionate tone. The writing was a clumsy scrawl— of course Marguerite would not have dictated to her chaplain or secretary such an intimate letter to Thoresby, already a bishop. He wondered whether Thoresby was yet awake. He wanted to place the letter in his hands.

A quiet voice said, 'Dame Clarice will recover.' Magda was now sitting upright, regarding him with her clear blue eyes.

'God be thanked,' said Owen. 'Is His Grace sleeping?'

Magda nodded.

Owen tucked the letter beneath his tunic. 'Would you walk with me in the garden a while?'

Without a word she rose and accompanied him out into the yard.

The damp of the previous evening was held close to the ground by low clouds, though it was not raining. Owen had thought it would feel good to pace off some energy in the garden while waiting for the household to awaken, perversely regretting that another hawk hunt had not been arranged for the morning. He would have welcomed the distracting activity.

Once they were well away from the buildings he asked Magda what she had noted about Clarice.

'Magda saw her whilst she slept the sleep of Master Walter's physick. It was as if seeing her through a thick veil—of little worth. But there was no poison in her breath, and no hint of it in her eyes—Magda lifted the lids, and looked at her fingernails, her tongue, her feet.'

'So what happened?'

'Thou hast witnessed men fall ill from a drink that would simply help most sleep, eh, Bird-eye? Magda thinks Clarice was meant to drowse but the drink made her ill. She might have taken it willingly.'

Owen told her about the letter Clarice had taken and its mysterious reappearance.

'She was to sleep in the garden while someone read it?' Magda shook her head. 'Clumsy, but possible.'

'I've told Dame Katherine that I would send Alisoun to attend Dame Clarice, to nurse and guard. I thought Brother Michaelo could sit with His Grace when you are resting.'

'Magda is glad thou art giving him such responsibility for his master. His devotion will keep him safely in the chamber. He slipped out last night, Magda does not know for how long, making his bed look as if he was tucked up beneath the blankets.'

'Damn him. What was he doing?'

'Magda knows not.' She looked grave.

'I'll talk to him when I return the letter to His Grace. I'll go now.'

He cursed Michaelo as he headed back down the path to the palace. What aggravated and enervated him was a sense of missed opportunities and time rushing on—toward another 'accident'? He wished he'd watched Michaelo more closely. He wished he'd questioned Dame Clarice more when he'd found her alone in Thoresby's chamber. He wondered what she'd done to anger Princess Joan, and whether it was the princess's anger that had brought on her own temper in turn. Clarice was angry that her family had sent her to the convent while still a child. If Dame Katherine knew that, then most likely so did her abbess, and she'd made a grave error in choosing such an embittered young woman for a mission on which she would be exposed to a palace and a princess, the trappings of a life any dissatisfied young woman might yearn for. He wondered whether Dame Clarice had approached Princess Joan about leaving the convent, or had perhaps set her heart on one of the young men here at the palace. As for Michaelo, he prayed that the monk had merely been praying in the chapel.

A few pallets remained in the corridor, not yet stacked in the corner for the day. Owen could hear the servants and squires moving about in the hall. In Thoresby's chamber Michaelo knelt at a *prie dieu* near his pallet, and Alisoun sat with some sewing near a window, glancing up to nod a silent greeting. The curtains of the great bed were still closed. Owen drew a stool up beside her and explained what he and Magda had agreed, that Alisoun would go to the sisters. He watched the light dim in her eyes, her jaw tighten.

'Why me?' she asked, softly, so as not to wake Thoresby, but her irritation was plain.

Owen knew that he had but one chance to convince Alisoun of his sincerity. Once she'd taken offence she would not be stirred. 'I need you there because you are both a healer and a warrior, and I trust you,' he said.

Her usually wary eyes widened in surprise, and she blushed, dropping her gaze to her embroidery as if to hide her confusion.

Praying for the right words, Owen leaned closer and said so softly he saw her strain a little to hear, 'I've precious few I can trust at present. And being a woman you can remain in the chamber. Will you help me, Alisoun?'

For a moment he thought he'd failed. But at last, without looking up, she nodded. She stayed very still for a few more heartbeats, and when she raised her head on her so-slender neck her eyes glistened with tears. 'I will be honoured to be of service, Captain.' A tremulous smile lit her face, and for the first time Owen saw the beauty in her that his son Jasper saw.

'If you need help, if you encounter something that you think I must know at once, use the guard—he is just without in the corridor. Don't hesitate to ask for anything. I could not forgive myself if anything happened to you.'

She nodded once. 'Shall I go now?'

'Yes. Go softly. Dame Katherine's sleep was disturbed throughout the night and she is resting until Master Walter returns. Do you need assistance? Have you much to carry?'

'No, I can manage.' She ducked her head in confusion as he helped her gather her sewing and spinning. He walked with her to the door, and just outside asked, 'Has Brother Michaelo been in there all the while?'

Her eyes now met his. 'Yes. Do you not trust him? Even Brother Michaelo?'

'I trust his devotion to His Grace,' said Owen.

'He was asleep when I relieved Dame Magda, and since waking he has been as you saw him.'

'Good. Ask the servants for anything you need, Alisoun. My mind is much eased knowing you'll be up there with the sisters.'

She was smiling as she made her way down the corridor. Owen prayed she would be safe.

Back in the chamber, Michaelo rose from his devotions and greeted Owen.

'I am glad to find other souls awake and about at this hour, for I weary of my own company,' said Owen.

'You'll soon tire of my company,' Michaelo said. His tone was uneven, as if his throat threatened to close around his words. 'I should not burden you.' He took the seat Alisoun had vacated, shrugging and fussing with the drape of his habit, the peace of his prayer gone, already ill at ease. 'I heard a little of what you said and was pleased for young Alisoun.'

'It was not an easy decision to send her. I meant all I said about her being most suited for the task, but it means that you must be here whenever Magda is away.' Owen observed Michaelo's increasing agitation. 'You see my dilemma.'

'You can trust me to ensure that His Grace is attended at all times,' said Michaelo. 'I worry about the household, but so be it. Soon none of that will matter.'

'There is more on your mind. Tell me.'

Michaelo closed his eyes and shook his head, his face constricting as if he were in great pain. 'I am accursed and so ashamed. I am the devil's plaything. How I can possibly believe Our Lord will hear my prayers? And how can I look His Grace in the eye? He made possible my redemption and now, after all this time, I have betrayed his trust.' Michaelo shivered and hugged himself, and would not meet Owen's gaze.

It was his refusal to look him in the eye that reminded Owen to be on his guard. It was not an attitude from which to offer comfort, but then Michaelo did not inspire such an impulse, he who sneered at the slightest shortcomings in others. Even now, though Michaelo was apparently wretched with humiliation and despair, Owen was too aware of that other side of him. Indeed, Michaelo fussed with his habit as if disgusted with himself. Like the guards, Michaelo might succumb to a bribe—he'd been disappointed in the chapter's indifference toward Ravenser. It was possible he'd back a Neville.

'What was the nature of your betrayal?' Owen asked.

'I have already told you,' Michaelo moaned. He stilled his hands by crossing his arms and tucking his hands into his sleeves. 'I knew by Lambert's looks that he shared my passion, but he did not speak it. Nor did I. I must have thought to fool myself and him by suggesting a cup of wine and a chance to unburden his heart, to speak of his failed mission. But our flesh overcame our chaste intentions. Dear God.' He dropped his chin and took a sobbing breath though his crossed arms held him rigid.

Owen waited.

Michaelo groaned. 'I have undone all I'd achieved with my penances for my former sins. I have thrown away my salvation for a night of passion. I cannot believe it now. I prayed when I woke that it had been a dream—a beautiful, passionate dream, *but only a dream*. But I would not then have been lying in the wood. I would do anything to undo it.'

The pain in his voice moved Owen. 'I've yet another reason to curse William of Wykeham's part in this.'

'No. I am the one to blame. But bless you for listening and not judging me.'

'You may yet regret confiding in me. More questions.'

Michaelo nodded. 'I will answer all I can.' Still he held himself rigidly with his crossed arms like a corset about his torso.

'Was Lambert worried that night? Frightened?'

'Yes, yes, and tormented by his clumsiness as Wykeham's emissary—he believed his career was ended, that Bishop William would never trust him again with anything of consequence. But that night he also felt haunted by his servant Will.'

'You said he had traded horse and saddle with Will because his horse was agitated?'

Michaelo bowed his head for a moment as if thinking how best to present Lambert's deed. 'He was embarrassed. He suffered sores—haemorrhoids—and the horse's fidgeting caused him much agony. I believe that his humiliation over his affliction blinded him to the need to examine the horse. And then the beast threw Will. Fear, self-loathing—they warred in Lambert. He seemed beset by devils, buffeted by storms, cursed by his own stupidity. I would not have been surprised had he taken his own life.'

Michaelo painted a pathetic man, and Owen realised how little he'd taken into account all that Lambert had suffered in so short a time. 'Were you worried when you woke to find him gone?'

'Worried? No. God help me, I was relieved. I prayed he was as ashamed as I was.' Michaelo paused, meeting Owen's gaze, his face haggard, so unlike the self-possessed man he'd seemed in Thoresby's service. 'Did I drive him to his murderer? He said that you had told him to stay at the palace, not to risk venturing into the fields. Why did he go out there that night? Who was the woman? Dear God. Oh dear God, I'll never know, I'll never know.' His breath caught and the moan that followed deeply affected Owen.

He wanted to believe Michaelo's pain, his remorse, his innocence of anything but lust.

'I want you to remain here, in this chamber, as much as possible. I have enough to contend with without Sir John or someone else attacking you. I need you here, do you understand?'

Michaelo's eyes searched Owen's face with a growing expression of panic. 'You think it possible that I am guilty of Lambert's death.'

'In truth, I cannot think how. But until I have solved his murder and that of his servant, and know whether Dame Clarice fell ill by someone's agency, I will not allow myself to believe anything that I cannot prove. I am sorry, Brother Michaelo, but that is how it must be.'

The great bed creaked, and Thoresby peered out from the curtains scowling, his face puffy and wrinkled from sleep. 'In God's name, confess to murdering Lambert and let us all feel safe in our beds, Michaelo.'

The monk blanched and bowed his head. 'I would confess if I were guilty, Your Grace, I swear to you that I would. But though I am guilty of much, I had no hand in the murder of Dom Lambert.'

Thoresby stared at his secretary for a long while, a weariness in his face, as if he were revisiting concerns he'd thought he'd moved past, and finally nodded as if satisfied, his expression clearing. 'This is no time for reverie, Archer,' he suddenly barked. 'Ask young Alisoun to help me with my cushions. Has something happened to the nun?'

'I've sent Alisoun to sit with Dame Clarice,' said Owen. 'But I can assist you.'

Leaving Michaelo, Owen opened the curtain wider. As Thoresby's energy fluctuated it was difficult to know how much help to offer when, but Owen thought he would attempt to assist him in easing his position. Michaelo joined him and together they adjusted Thoresby's cushions until he pushed them away, impatient with their fussing. Only then did Owen hand him the letter. After a quick glance at the contents, Thoresby pressed the parchment to his heart.

'God bless you for finding this and returning it to me, Archer.' The tender relief on his face softened his entire visage. But it was only a momentary mood. 'The nun had taken it?' he asked sharply.

'She did, much to her misfortune.' Owen described Dame Clarice's condition, Dame Katherine's story and Magda's assessment. 'I asked Alisoun to act both as healer and guard.'

Pressing his long, bony fingertips to his temples, Thoresby sighed. 'What foolish sentiment tempted me to keep this letter from a woman so long dead? The nun had no right to take it, but had it not been there she would not have been tempted.'

'No one placed the book into her hands, Your Grace. I am more concerned about whether someone ordered her to search your chamber, and what she was looking for.'

'I am too close to death to care about much, Archer.'

'But she found the one thing you held dear,' Owen said. 'I don't like that.'

'You don't think Alice Perrers is behind this?'

Owen almost laughed at that, Thoresby's fixation on the king's mistress, as if all that went wrong in his life could be traced to her. 'I have heard nothing to connect her with the choice of your successor, Your Grace,' he said. 'I merely meant that I fear Clarice might have been instructed in her search by someone who knows you well.'

'Nevilles, you mean.' Thoresby closed his eyes. 'Perhaps I should simply write to the chapter a letter supporting Alexander Neville as my successor, and ask Brother Michaelo to read it out at supper. It might save lives.'

'And ruin others once you've passed on,' said Michaelo.

Thoresby grinned, his eyes still closed. 'That is not my concern.'

Never in all her years had Magda Digby imagined conversing with someone as close to the king as Princess Joan. But here she sat, holding the delicately fleshed hands of a woman who had lived her life with others' hands doing her work, her only scars the genteel results of threads and needles and the beaks of falcons, as this so-alien woman allowed fear, anger, pride, hurt, an abundance of emotions to flash to life, rage about her being and subside. Magda had merely shown the princess that in the small trunk in which she carried her physicks about on her progresses there were two powders that might quite easily have been combined to create the sleeping potion mixed with water germander that she and Lucie had detected in Lambert's servant's wineskin. It was Joan herself who quickly connected that with a fear she confessed to having fought hard to ignore—that one of her women, either one of her ladies or a maid, had withdrawn her loyalty.

'I've felt a dangerous chill draft in the cocoon spun round me,' she said, 'but I've turned my back to it as if I could protect myself in such wise. I've refused to acknowledge it, to speak its name and make it true.' She had spoken with deep yet quiet emotion, without self-pity or any apparent hope of engaging Magda's sympathy.

Magda sensed the tremendous burden this woman carried, wife of the king's eldest son and mother of a future king. 'Thou art a great lady who rises to thy duties without resentment and with fierce courage. To catch a traitor will be painful for thee, but thou hast the heart for it.'

Joan looked into Magda's eyes for a long while, then took a deep breath. 'I have not felt such comfort in a long while, Dame Magda. To be in your presence is to feel the solace of sanctuary. I'd heard you were a pagan, but I feel Divine Grace in you.'

Grace could be interpreted many ways. God was another matter. Magda accepted the compliment.

'What would you have me do about my doubts?' Joan asked.

'Watch thy people and tell Owen Archer of anything thou canst not explain.'

Again, Joan quietly studied Magda for a dozen heartbeats before responding. 'So many here place their trust in the handsome Captain Archer. You do as well?'

It was Magda's turn to consider an impression she received as the princess asked that question, that Joan meant to invite Owen into her household. Magda doubted that such a position would sit easily with him and considered saying something to ward off the princess, but of course it was not her decision to make.

She merely nodded. 'Magda trusts him.'

'My son John does not like Captain Archer, and I teased him that he sees his father in him, still resenting his efforts to discipline his temper. My first husband Tom lost an eye in battle. Faith, I wondered whether I trusted Captain Archer so quickly because of his resemblance to Tom. But you and the archbishop—truly everyone here speaks so highly of him. I fear my son John is a poor judge of men. In truth, I fear for him in all ways. I should have taken better care in choosing his companions as he was growing up.'

'A child will find his own way.'

'Have you any children?'

'Two. Magda's son is dead, and her daughter found her own path.'

'I lost a son as well. But I still have three, and the youngest will someday be king. I must be strong for all three of them, and for my husband Edward.'

'A woman's strength is a fearsome thing, eh? Thy gout. Dost thou knowest that walking, dancing, riding, all these pleasures will go far to take away thy pain?'

The princess's cream complexion bloomed with roses and she was suddenly shy, dropping her gaze. 'I do. I've allowed the weight of my husband's illness and my fears for the future to send me to my bed, where I drink sweet wine and mead and eat far too much. My physician says that I have unbalanced my humours.'

'Magda is glad to hear thou hast a wise physician.' She pressed the princess's hands before releasing them.

'Would you come to see my husband?' Joan impulsively asked. 'You could return with me.'

Though the thought of such a journey amused Magda, she did not laugh. 'Magda appreciates the honour such an invitation carries, but she is needed here, amongst those who cannot send for the finest physicians. Thou hast no need of a country midwife.'

Joan looked stricken. 'You are no country midwife, Dame Magda.'

'Fear not. Thou hast strength and grace in thee.' Magda bowed and took her leave.

Richard Ravenser invited Owen to join him by the fire in the hall while breaking his fast. Though Owen had already eaten, he took the opportunity to eat a little more while reviewing with the archbishop's nephew all that he knew. Ravenser was so busy seeing to his uncle's archiepiscopal duties that they'd had little chance to talk.

He flicked breadcrumbs from his chest and fussed with an elegant silk sleeve as he listened. 'You've learned precious little of use,' he muttered. 'You must have Her Grace's men snapping at your heels.'

'No, except for an outburst from John Holand when he escorted me to his mother's chamber I've been left alone. I should count myself fortunate that I've not seen more of Holand.' As soon as he'd said that, Owen realised that it was strange. 'Though he was attentive on the day he arrived. Why would he avoid me?'

'Curious,' said Ravenser. 'That *is* curious. I would have expected him to follow you about demanding satisfaction.'

Owen noticed Master Walter enter the hall and excused himself to go talk to him. The physician nodded when he saw Owen approaching.

'I hoped to find you here,' said Walter. 'I wanted to tell you that there is a scent and a discolouration in Dame Clarice's urine which I cannot identify. I don't know whether it is poison or she merely consumed something that sickened her. I do not believe her life is in danger, but I took the precaution of bleeding her.'

'So she seems better this morning?'

'I did not say that. She is silent, unmoving, and her breathing is too quiet. I had another thought—that these are the signs of one in a trance or—if you believe such things—under the influence of a spell.'

'Do you believe such things?'

'When nothing else makes sense, I find myself wondering.' Walter removed his hat and patted his forehead, then ran a hand through his fair hair before covering it again. 'Though I would deny it to my patrons.'

'Dame Magda also observed Clarice, and she proposed that something had been put in the sister's food or drink to make her drowsy, but for her it was too much, or it was something that would not sicken others but did her. In short, that it was not another attempt at murder.'

'God be praised if she is right,' said Walter. 'She is a clever woman, the midwife. That does indeed sound quite possible and is a comfort—of sorts.' He rubbed his cheeks, as if to revive himself.

'You look as if you need to find a place for a nap,' said Owen. 'The barracks are quiet as the men take turns sleeping. I trust you could find an empty pallet.'

Walter's face smoothed out with relief. 'Bless you, Captain. That is just what I need.'

'I am headed there myself,' said Owen. 'I'll walk with you.' He meant to talk to Fiddler John himself concerning his report to Gilbert about the two he'd seen leaving the stables.

Breath had never seemed so precious as it did now, and Thoresby thanked God for each one. He also thanked God for each awakening. He had made his peace, but he wished to live long enough to see Princess Joan on her way and to welcome his godchildren in turn. It was much to ask. He doubted now the wisdom of having agreed to Joan's visitation. Had he known that she sought advice regarding her fear that her family's ills were the result of Divine retribution for the slaying of her father and uncle he might have been more honest with himself, admitted that he was too weak and exhausted to summon the wisdom that she sought. But he'd proudly agreed to advise her and now found himself with little to say, which weighed heavily on his conscience considering how through his self-deceit he'd put his household and her company in grave danger.

He particularly blamed himself for putting Brother Michaelo in harm's way, albeit inadvertently. He'd known his secretary was weak in spirit, but here again Thoresby's own pride had betrayed him, had convinced him that Michaelo would not dare sin while he who had given him a chance to redeem himself yet lived.

His intentions had been generous, charitable. He sympathised with Joan's situation, the wife of an ailing prince and an under-aged princeling. But it was all going so wrong. He'd disliked his painful and humiliating sense of vulnerability when he'd awakened and found Archer with Dame Clarice, the cold sister from Nun Appleton, the one who had watched him with disturbing intensity. When Archer had said he'd caught her reading his breviary Thoresby had felt helpless. Now he'd proof that she'd done more than that—she'd stolen the love letter he'd hidden in it. He shivered and pulled the mound of covers up under his chin. Perhaps he should place more of the blame on Princess Joan for having included in her company those who were almost strangers to her.

Owen and Walter were walking past Thoresby's chamber when Magda stepped into the corridor. Already tiring of flitting from one person to another this morning, Owen once again excused himself. Fiddler John could wait, and Walter was only too happy to withdraw to the barracks alone. Magda nodded to Owen and gestured to him to walk with her.

Out in the garden she raised her arms overhead and took a deep breath.

'It is unpleasantly hot in His Grace's chamber,' Owen said, settling down on a bench.

'The fire in his body cools,' she said. 'Magda would rather walk than sit, Bird-eye. Come along.' She did not wait for his opinion.

But her stride was short enough that it cost him no breath to fall into step beside her. 'Did you talk to Princess Joan?'

Magda nodded as she considered a fork in the paths. She chose the river walk, which seemed the choice of most walkers. Perhaps in winter one would choose to move inland, away from the icy river.

'The Princess of Wales is a most gracious lady. Magda found powders that might have been added to the dead man's wine with little fuss, and without further prompting the princess admitted that she has sensed a traitor among her ladies and servants, but knows not who it might be. She has promised to watch and tell thee aught that seems amiss to her.'

Owen had not expected so much. 'I am glad that she said so, and grateful that you saw her.' He found it dissatisfying to talk to Magda in motion, unable to watch her expression, note the subtle sounds and see the gestures as she considered his words. Reaching a bench, he said, 'I hope you've cooled off enough to agree to sit for a moment.'

She had walked on, but paused now, and seemed to sniff at the air before she turned back to him. 'Thou hast something darksome on thy mind.'

'Yes.'

Looking back at the palace she shook her head, a sad shake, as if regretting her thought. 'Darksome is a subtle current beneath the surface of this company, Bird-eye.'

Owen reflexively crossed himself.

'Aye, beware,' she nodded. 'Come. Magda has the strength to listen to one more tale before she finds a place to rest.' She led him to a stone wall at the edge of the rose garden. 'Tell Magda thy trouble.'

He told her of Lady Eleanor, being more honest with her about their past than he had been earlier and that she might have been with Lambert when he took the horse from the stables. 'I don't want to believe she murdered Dom Lambert.'

She turned to him on the bench, her wrinkled face set in a thoughtful frown. 'Thou hast a difficult role, Bird-eye. Magda has ever sensed the weight of it on thy broad shoulders. Magda has not met her, but as Lady Sybilla expressed, loyalties can be terrible burdens. Magda senses thou'rt sad about Michaelo as well.' Before he could speak she held a finger to his mouth. 'No, Magda understands. Thou dost fear that he is not the redeemed soul thou hast believed him to be.' She took his hand, looking down at it, smoothing the skin on the back. 'Hast thou ever thought that what Black Swan feels for men is simply his nature? Nothing to punish him for?'

'God condemned sodomy.'

'Men wrote thy bible. Men lead thy church. Men create unnatural laws that cripple their fellow men so that they might control those they do not understand. Thy church has made many such laws, and good men who serve thy church suffer for no good cause.'

'Are we still talking only of Michaelo?' Owen heard more emotion in her voice than he would have guessed she would have for the monk.

Magda said nothing, but letting go of his hand she turned away from him, toward the river. 'How different might Black Swan's life have been if he had been permitted his love for men, Magda does not know. She does not know him well. The sin that brought him to Old Crow's attention was about far more than carnal love. He had given his power to a man who was consumed by hate.' She looked back at Owen. 'Hast thou looked into thy heart and judged him so harshly? Or her, this woman thou didst once embrace? Or dost thou merely fear thou wilt not be happy when thou dost discover the murderer?'

'My heart?'

She placed a palm on his eye patch. Her body heat relaxed the muscles beneath his patch.

'Thy wounding forced thee to look within. Magda has seen thy hand fly up to thy wounded eye as if it has suddenly spoken to thee with a pain that has no source that thou canst detect.'

He often felt a shower of tiny pains like hundreds of pin pricks over his eyelid and the scarred socket. He'd interpreted it as dread, which he supposed might be a kind of knowing.

'I do feel something. But what does that have to do with Brother Michaelo's confession? Or Lady Eleanor's possible guilt?'

'Didst thou sense a lie in their words?'

He'd felt there was much that Eleanor was not saying. And Michaelo—he felt the man was telling him more than was necessary, which made him suspect that he meant to distract Owen. But Magda seemed to be suggesting that he try to open his heart to Michaelo's suffering. It was difficult, for he kept seeing him lying beneath the tree on which Lambert had been hanged.

'I am sad for Michaelo, but I cannot afford to believe that he is entirely innocent and will cause no more trouble. I pray that he is true in all things but his sin with Lambert. But I cannot let down my guard with him. As for Lady Eleanor, I don't know what to think about her. I must have a doubt, else why would I be sitting here worried that she might be a murderer? There is a desperate yearning in her behaviour toward me, making too much of an afternoon long ago.'

'Gifts, skills, talents—they torment folk with riddles. Thou must learn through practice, as thou didst learn to be an archer.' Magda cupped his chin in her hands. 'Thou'rt a good man, Bird-eye. Courageous, true, and gifted with inward sight.' She dropped her hand and gave him a coy smile that forced a smile from him. 'And if Magda had met thee when she was young, she would have done anything to share thy bed.' She barked again as she rose. 'And now Magda must sleep.'

As she hurried away Owen realised that she had flirted with him to distract him at the last moment, preventing more questions that would delay her rest. The flirtation reminded him of Sybilla.

In the hall, he found Sybilla discussing the day's plans with one of Her Grace's servants. Although he stood near her being rudely obvious about waiting to talk to her she ignored him until she was finished, and then turned to him with the sweetest of smiles.

'Captain Archer. What do you think? His Grace has said he is pleased to grant me the puppy.'

How skilfully she lightened the mood around her, Owen

thought, like a musician plucking out a cheery tune that tickled one into a jig. But he could use her topic to woo her out into the yard. 'Shall we bid your new friend good morning?' he asked, crooking his arm.

She took his arm and stepped lightly through the milling guests and out into the yard.

'Sir John made a fool of himself last night, did you hear him?' she asked rather loudly as they passed him berating his squire for a stain on his boots.

'I am partially blind, not deaf—though I would have been glad of the latter last night. I wondered why he'd found his drink so irresistible as to let it take command of his senses, if yesterday's events so disturbed him.'

'He needs no excuse, Captain.' Sybilla nodded at Sir Lewis, who was talking to one of the grooms.

'I understand that you sat with Dame Clarice out on the porch last evening shortly before she fell ill,' said Owen. 'Had she also been drinking too much?'

Sybilla fought hard to mask her surprise with laughter. 'Now *that* would be an intriguing pairing—Clarice and John.' She made a comical face and rolled her eyes. 'They're both champion complainers. But to answer your question, Captain, no, the poor woman was drinking her own bile. She is a tragically bitter young woman. I thought she needed a friendly ear, but I found to my discomfort that it was not my friendship she wanted. My finery, my very station in Her Grace's company offends her, but not morally. She resents having been sent to the convent by her mother and her unknown father rather than having been set up in a noble household. So much for a life of prayer bequeathing grace and beatific joy.'

She sniffed and flipped her skirts, stepping directly in front of Owen and facing him, forcing him to stop. 'I did not think that you sought me out to ask about the dogs,' she said, no longer smiling. She'd manoeuvred them to an empty part of the yard. 'Princess Joan asked me to watch Dame Clarice, and so I did as I was told, bearing her insults so long I wanted to scream. But I did not poison her in retaliation for the poison of her words, Captain.'

'I am glad to hear that. What of her complaints? Were they only of you?'

'She complained of her fate in general, Captain. She did not name her poisoner if that is your question.'

'Why do you speak of poison, my lady? I said nothing of that.'

He saw by the tightening of her silk-clad shoulders that she realised she'd stepped into a trap.

'Master Walter and Dame Magda both believe she fell ill by eating or drinking something that sickened her quite by chance,' he said. 'Did she seem ill when you talked?'

Sybilla shook her head. 'No. But she did suddenly quit the porch. I confess I was relieved to see her go.'

'And she did not eat or drink while you were there?'

'To be honest, I cannot remember.'

'Why has Princess Joan asked you to watch Dame Clarice?'

'I am reliable. Now come, Captain, we've been serious quite long enough and it's time to see my charming puppy.' She took his arm and tried to pull him in the direction of the kennels.

But Owen did not move. 'You misunderstood my question. I've no doubt you were an excellent choice, but why is the princess concerned about Dame Clarice?'

'I've no idea. I did not think to ask.'

'Do you know why she sent messengers to Nun Appleton yesterday?'

'You must ask her, Captain. Neither Eleanor nor I were privy to what she told them.' Prettily pouting, she tugged on his arm.

'I've also learned that you went to Clarice's chamber when she was carried in from the fields. Why?'

Sybilla, still pouting, tilted her head as if trying to see him from a better angle. 'What is this, Captain? Do you think me heartless? I was concerned for her.'

'You've just told me that you lost patience with her insults.'

Shrugging, she toed a pebble. 'She is a bore, Captain, but I sympathise with her complaint, her fate being one I narrowly escaped.'

'Do you know who carried Dame Clarice into the palace last night?'

'It was Douglas, one of John Holand's men. He's been favoured by Princess Joan on this journey. I do not think he'll be long in her son's household.' With a sigh, she tugged again on his hand. 'Come now.'

'Go on, my lady. I am not good company today.'

She dropped his hand. 'You disappoint me, Captain.'

'I pray you will forgive me for that, my lady.'

He bowed to her and headed back to the palace. He must talk to the guard who had been following Clarice and discover why Princess Joan had both Sybilla and a guard following the nun. It was a simple matter to have him pointed out.

'Of course I noticed Lady Sybilla, Captain. I've not the strength to *not* notice her,' said Douglas. They laughed companionably. 'But Her Grace had not mentioned that she, too, was watching Dame Clarice. I am not, in truth, of that household.'

'I understand that. But Princess Joan finds you useful.'

'My master has little need of me while we are here, and does not like his men idle.'

Owen sensed a hint of resentment in the man's tone. 'Could you describe exactly what you witnessed last night?'

Douglas's description of the event was very like Alisoun's.

'Did you notice a parchment? Perhaps in her hands? Did she drop anything as you carried her?'

Douglas shook his head.

'Did anyone approach you? Did you stop? Talk to anyone who might have touched her?'

'As I passed my master he taunted me for ravishing a nun. I cannot recall whether he touched her.'

John Holand. That was an uncomfortable possibility. 'Anyone else?'

'As I walked she grew heavier and heavier, and I did not notice much beside putting one foot before the other.'

• • •

The night watch had already bedded down for sleep, but as Owen stood at the top of the loft ladder allowing his good eye to adjust to the dimness he noticed two men talking quietly on the nearest pallet. They sneaked glances at him several times, and then one rose and approached him.

Duncan was one of the older guards, a pious widower who had told Owen that he considered guarding the archbishop a form of worship. He asked whether Owen had a moment to talk to him.

'That is why I am here,' said Owen, 'in the hope that someone will come forward with some detail—a sound, a movement, anything—that might help me understand what happened the night Dom Lambert died.'

'Stephen and I were just talking.' Duncan gestured for his companion to join them and put his arm round the younger man, as if determined to hold him there. 'We were beyond the place where the poor man died that night, out toward the village, and so we thought anything we might have witnessed would be of no use to you. But Stephen told me about the villager finding the horse.'

'You hadn't known?'

'When I sleep, I sleep soundly, Captain. Nothing wakes me, not even a horse.' He grinned.

Owen sank down on a bench and folded his arm, signalling that he was ready to listen. 'Tell me.'

Duncan nodded to Stephen to go first.

'I heard a man and a woman arguing about something she'd given him. She wanted to know what he'd done with it and was none too pleased when he said he'd sold it in York. "For to pay for all this. What did you think I would do with it?" he spit at her and she hissed back something I couldn't make out. But they did not part friends, I can tell you.'

Owen of course thought of the brooch. 'Did you hear what the item was?'

Stephen shook his head. 'Nor could I see them. And they talked in whispers—loud whispers, but all the same, I don't think I'd know them if they spoke plainly.'

'Thank you, Stephen. Was this toward morning?'

'Aye. Still dark, but I could hear the birds shifting.'

He wanted to ask why in God's name the man had not come forward with this yesterday, but held his tongue. He'd spoken up now, and he should not be punished for that.

'And you, Duncan?'

The older man glanced round, then stepped closer, and leaned toward Owen's ear. 'I swear I heard your second lieutenant Gilbert say something, and a woman answer him. It was a fleeting thing. I think she moved on past me toward the village, and he moved toward the palace. But it's troubled me. I'd swear it was him.'

'What were they saying?'

'He said something like "they'll find him there and think the worst." And she said, "Poor man."'

'But you saw nothing?'

'Nay.'

This time Owen could not keep himself from asking in frustration, 'Why did you wait till now to tell me?'

'I did not like to think it of him, Captain. Gilbert is a good man, and I reckoned since you hold him second only to Alfred, you trust him.' Duncan shrugged.

He had, that was true, and this accusation was difficult to accept. But Owen pushed that aside. 'Good man, Duncan. Never keep anything from me you think I should know. I will not betray you.'

Duncan nodded. 'I told Stephen as much, that you would protect us if we did our duty. God go with you, Captain.'

'And you and Stephen,' said Owen.

He rose, but for a moment he stood woodenly, unsure what to do next. Gilbert. He did not want to think right now about the significance of Gilbert being a traitor.

'Do you know which pallet is Fiddler John's?'

Stephen pointed to one on the far end.

'One more thing. When Gilbert spoke to you after we found

Lambert—did he not urge you to come forward with anything you might have noticed?'

Stephen looked puzzled. 'He said nothing to me, Captain.'

Owen turned to Duncan, who shook his head.

Cursing beneath his breath, Owen headed over to Fiddler John's pallet and a little too impatiently shook the man, made even angrier by the stench of ale that the man gave off. As Fiddler John woke and opened his mouth, Owen clamped a hand over it.

'Come downstairs with me.'

The man struggled.

Owen's anger had made him clumsy. He whispered, 'Don't be afraid. It's your captain. I don't mean to harm you. I need to hear what you told Gilbert—in your own words.' He was grateful to feel the man relax a little. 'Follow me away from your fellows. I would not wake them.'

John nodded, then scrambled up with the brittle energy the ale still in his belly provided, and stumbled after Owen, awkwardly climbing down the ladder and joining him in an empty area near a side door.

'You gave me a start,' he mumbled, rubbing his face.

Turning a little to spare himself John's noxious breath, Owen was not inclined to soothe the man. 'What did you see the night of Lambert's death?'

'A man and woman leave the stables with a horse, Captain.'

'Can you describe them?'

John hung his head. 'The man, he looked to be dressed like Lambert. The woman was very fine.'

'Could you see her face?' John shook his head. 'Her hair colour?' Another shake. 'What of him?' Another shake. 'So all you saw was a man dressed like Lambert, and a finely dressed woman?'

'That's all I could swear to, Captain.'

'Is that all that you told Gilbert?'

John nodded.

'You're drinking too much, John. Be careful of that. But I thank you for your report. Go on, back up to your pallet. Sleep the sleep of the virtuous.'

With a curse, Owen strode out of the barracks part of the stable and sat down on his own pallet to piece together what he'd learned. Gilbert. Eleanor. Sybilla. Clarice. Michaelo. He felt a growing panic that he was too tired, pulled in too many directions, and was not seeing what was right before him. If only he had Lucie here to talk this over with him. He wished he'd gone upriver this morning in Jehannes's place, but of course his absence was out of the question. Today Princess Joan would explain why she'd sent to Nun Appleton and he intended to be in Thoresby's chamber when she did so.

Though weary to the bone he could not lie still. He needed to pace, and to talk. When he'd left Sybilla he'd noticed Geoffrey talking to Sir Lewis out in the yard. Perhaps he'd learned something about Lady Eleanor. He splashed his face with cool water before he headed back to the palace.

8

A WOMAN'S WOE

THURSDAY MORNING

Idly observing the gardens of Bishopthorpe lining the riverbank as his journey upriver began, Jehannes noticed a pair of servants cutting back the branches of a broad shrub in order to access a breach in the retaining wall. Their clothes already hung heavy with moisture wicked up from the morning mist and the dripping foliage and their shoes sank into the soft, shifting soil that had allowed the wall to crumble. It seemed an inspired theme for a sermon, and Jehannes toyed with appropriate lessons as the landscape changed, the gardens giving way to fields and woodland.

Composing sermons calmed him, drawing him into contemplation of God's laws and Christ's teachings, the ordering of society and the path to inner peace. He was particularly fond of Christ's Sermon on the Mount, a reminder of the rewards awaiting the good, the gentle blessings of a virtuous life. A crumbling foundation—a lack of the cohesive qualities of loving one another, compassion. The corrosive quality of pride, which precluded this compassion, prevented the binding of cooperation and sharing. Alexander Neville's overweening pride that had perhaps tempted Owen's good men away from the bond that had worked well these many years. He'd sensed Owen's pain and prayed that balance might somehow be restored. But with John Thoresby dying, the men were understandably looking out for themselves, feeling their future prosperity threatened, and someone like Neville knew how to feed that sense of vulnerability and offer false security.

This exercise was not cheering Jehannes this morning. He turned to his servant and asked him to join him in prayer. Praying for the suffering and the spiritually floundering was never a waste of time.

Alfred shook his head in disbelief. 'Gilbert? They cannot be right, Captain. Someone sounding like him, surely. God help us, they cannot be right. And he was the one you'd sent to talk to the men—do you think he did as you ordered?'

'No. It was only after I talked to them that a few came to me. We must act on the possibility that they are right about Gilbert. Tell him nothing, Alfred, and set someone to watch him.'

Bowing his head, Alfred groaned. 'I would it were not so.'

'I feel the same. We cannot trust him and heaven knows who else. I am working hard not to curse Princess Joan for coming here.'

Alfred cursed for him. 'And may Gilbert rot in hell if he's betrayed us.'

'I pray he's done all the damage he means to do,' said Owen.

Alfred crossed himself. 'Soon I won't be able to sleep for worry about who's guarding my back.'

Owen could not reassure him.

Lucie woke to a misty morning, chilly and lonely in the big bed. She hugged a cushion as she prayed that Owen would soon be sleeping beside her again. She ignored the prick of conscience that her prayer was selfish, that his return would happen only on Thoresby's death. This morning she wanted her husband, yearned for his strong, warm body beside her, his sweet kisses, the fire he kindled in her.

On rising, she had no peace in the hall—the weather bored Gwenllian and Hugh. They loudly challenged their nurse Maud for insisting that they play in the house rather than kick through the fallen leaves in the garden, and their crankiness—not to mention their shrill young voices—agitated their Great Aunt Phillippa. Lucie had hastened to her workshop behind the apothecary intending to accomplish a long list of chopping, pounding, mixing, and potting. Her apprentice Edric had helped her set up the materials on a large table, and she'd settled down with a sense of quiet contentment to the repetitive work, which freed her mind to meander where it would. She missed Alisoun, who would have managed the restlessness of Gwenllian and Hugh with songs and games. Maud was good with the infant Emma, but she was easily overwhelmed by the older children. As usual these days Lucie's thoughts turned toward the future, considering alternative careers for Owen once Thoresby died—in truth, worrying about them. He might serve the new archbishop, or become more engaged in the management of Freythorpe Hadden, or perhaps become an alderman in the city, or perhaps first a bailiff.

She lifted her head as she heard Edric greet one of Bess Merchet's servants. Concerned that his appearance meant an illness at the York Tavern, Lucie set about tidying her work space in case she needed to rush to her neighbour, closing the jars she had been filling so that Jasper's cat Crowder would not track powders about on his paws or an errant draft would not send them all over the workroom. Her first thought was of Tom Merchet—he had complained of pains in his chest lately but refused to take something to strengthen his heart and quicken his blood. Bess had threatened to slip something into his next batch of ale, but Tom had called her bluff, knowing that she would not risk losing business by sickening her customers.

When Edric announced that Bess had sent for her, Lucie hurried through the beaded curtains with a jar of the powder she'd prepared for Tom.

'Dame Lucie, my mistress thought you would wish to speak to Archdeacon Jehannes. He's come to see her from Bishopthorpe.' Bess's serving lad nodded as if Lucie had expressed doubt. 'In truth, mistress, he came by barge this morning.'

Her momentary relief that she was not being summoned to Tom's sickbed was quickly overridden by anxiety about Jehannes's mission. Lucie set aside the jar so that she might remove her apron and the cloths covering her sleeves, saying a silent prayer that Owen was safe and well as she shook out her veil and brushed her skirt.

'Presentable?' she asked Edric. It was a wicked thing to do to the young apprentice who adored her, to ask him to approve her appearance, but she did not want to waste time searching for a mirror.

Edric blushed and tapped a side of his nose. 'You have some powder right there. All else is perfect.'

Lucie brushed her nose, thanked him and told him to be sure to fetch her at the tavern if he needed her. She doubted she would be long. As she stepped out into the now more substantial drizzle she breathed deeply, welcoming the damp air after working with powders and dried plants. She forced her mind toward the positive, hoping that Jehannes would not feel it was gossiping to talk of the princess and her ladies, for she had a head full of questions, having heard tales of Joan's beauty and the extravagance of her wardrobe and household. The cobbles in the square were slippery, the gentle rain merely dampening the summery residue of dust and debris. A good downpour was needed to cleanse the stones before they were once more made even more slippery by falling leaves from the trees that shaded St Helen's churchyard. As Lucie reached the tavern yard she abandoned her effort at calm, growing more and more anxious about why Jehannes had come to the city, and she was almost running as she reached the tavern door.

There were few customers in the main room. Tom glanced up as he poured ale into a tankard and nodded toward the kitchen.

'Bess swept the archdeacon out there. He's on a mission for Owen—he's assured us that Owen is fine. But Bess thought you'd like to talk to Jehannes yourself.'

'Bless you, Tom, I was stirring up the litany of fears I've collected over the years, all the risks Owen might take and the dangers he might face when on the archbishop's business.' She hugged her old friend, his scent of sawdust, hops and yeast comfortingly familiar, then stepped out of the tavern and across to the large tavern kitchen in the yard behind. She heard the voices of Bess and Jehannes coming from behind a screen that separated her friend's private space from the almost always busy work area. Today was no exception, with the cook and two kitchen servants moving about preparing the midday meal that would be served in a few hours. Slipping behind the screen Lucie recognised trouble in the grave expressions on her friends' faces.

Jehannes rose to greet her, giving her a blessing and reassuring her that Owen was well and Thoresby still alive. He explained that he'd come to ask round the city for news of a moonstone brooch that might have been sold, and he'd hoped that Bess and Lucie might have heard something or could advise him where to search. But he also wanted to make sure they knew the truth of events at Bishopthorpe, so they would know to disregard any false rumours.

'Is my husband sleeping? Taking care of himself?' Lucie asked.

'He is well.'

She could tell that he was not telling the entire truth. 'Has there been another death?'

'Yes, and Owen feels an urgency. He is working against time. I'm to return to the palace today.'

Lucie thought of how early the light faded these days. 'That leaves you so little time.' No time at all to entertain them with descriptions of the fine company and lavish feasting.

'Do begin at the beginning now that Lucie is here,' said Bess. 'Tell us all that Owen has told you. Perhaps something will tease our memories.'

Brother Michaelo's implication in Dom Lambert's death saddened Lucie. She had grown fond of him. He had taken loving care of her father on his last pilgrimage, and he had been kind in his efforts to tell her everything he knew of Sir Robert's experiences on that journey to St David's. It had helped to ease the emptiness she'd felt in losing her father so far away, buried so far away, a place she'd probably never see.

'The sisters from Nun Appleton sound like trouble,' Bess said, 'and the princess's two ladies—can she be such a poor judge of her own sex?'

'I would think her choice of waiting ladies is complicated by family alliances and favours owed,' said Lucie. She was reminded of a conversation she'd overheard in the minster. 'One of the ladies travelling with Joan of Kent is related to the late Margaret Neville, who was the wife of Henry Percy, Earl of Northumberland,' she told Jehannes. 'I did not hear her name, but I wondered whether she might be working to further Alexander Neville's cause. Or for the Percies. Are they for Neville? They will care who is to be Archbishop of York—they rule the north.'

'Though the Nevilles are doing their best to elbow them aside,' said Jehannes. 'I think you must mean Lady Sybilla, who is a Neville.'

'So you already knew.' Lucie was disappointed. 'I've heard nothing about such a brooch.'

'Nor I,' admitted Bess. 'But I've heard much about Alexander Neville.'

'I've yet to hear of another candidate with strong support,' said Jehannes. 'It is strange that he is fighting so hard for something that seems about to be offered to him without a struggle.'

'Much to hide?' Bess suggested. 'They say he was the lesser of twins, and that he has risen so far only because his twin died and his preferments went to Alexander, all undeserved.'

'Does no one care about the spiritual wellbeing of the See of York, of the care of souls?' Lucie wondered. 'Do they all see His Grace's death merely as an opportunity to seize power? Has everyone forgotten that York is more than a temporal seat?'

They all grew quiet at the thought.

Owen had drawn Geoffrey back out into the softly falling rain, which had everyone crowding into the hall so that it had been impossible to find a quiet place where they might talk without being overheard.

The reports from Duncan and Stephen disturbed Geoffrey—Owen could see it in the tension around his wide eyes and the grim set to his mouth.

'God help her if they are speaking of Lady Eleanor,' Geoffrey said. 'Sir Lewis was candid with me about his concern for her. In truth he seemed grateful for the opportunity to talk about his fear that she has become involved in something that has gone too far. She has a gentle, acquiescent nature. He has debated with himself whether to ask her outright and in doing so risk her anger for she also has a temper when frightened. But she has precluded any choice in the matter by avoiding him. He is dismayed by his sense that she is frightened and trusts no one. He describes her eyes as wary, like those of her beloved falcons, and her movements as agitated.'

It troubled Owen to think of Eleanor so benighted. 'So she had not confided in him at all?'

Geoffrey shook his head, shifting on the damp bench. They'd walked out into the gardens, but the rain made it an unpleasant venue.

'If she was party to murder, and to arranging it to look as if Brother Michaelo committed that murder, I do not think she would confide such heartless and unforgivable deeds to Sir Lewis. Theirs has been a playful wooing, nothing deep and enduring.' He shifted again. 'There is a summer-house farther on with benches, though it is likely a fanciful name for something that is doubtless rarely warm and dry so far north and close to that dreary brown river with the ugly name. Still, it might be drier than this. Shall we move on to that?'

'It is the peat that gives the Ouse the brown colour and the name. It is a Norse word.'

Geoffrey gave a little laugh. 'I am delighted to know that, but as I sense that you have much to discuss yet, I require a more comfortable seat.'

They moved on through a box hedge silvery with rain drops and past a bed of lady's mantle, its huge late-season leaves heavy with water. Several leaves drifted down from a hazel as Owen brushed it with a shoulder, and mud oozed beneath his boot where gravel had been worn away over time by many unquiet feet in front of a stone bench.

'I'll confess to you my urge to protect the Lady Eleanor,' said Owen as Geoffrey caught up with him. He'd walked at his long-legged pace forgetting that though Geoffrey had the torso of a man of average height he had short legs.

'What is your secret with women, besides your scarred face and great height?' Geoffrey asked, chuckling. But before Owen could come up with a response Geoffrey sighed. 'I confess I'm more concerned about Her Grace's other lady, Sybilla. She seems less experienced than Eleanor, more impulsive.'

It struck Owen as strange how differently the two of them perceived Sybilla. Owen found her the more manipulative of the two ladies, her behaviour carefully gauged to achieve the effect she desired.

'You do not give Lady Sybilla enough credit,' he said. 'She has a cunning wit.'

'I delight in women of wit and determination. And you are partial to the gentle Lady Eleanor,' said Geoffrey.

Owen grunted his admission.

They stepped into the summer-house, their boots echoing hollowly on the raised planking as rain whispered on the thin roof. Brushing blown leaves from one of the benches Owen lowered himself with a moan.

'The worst of it is not Lady Eleanor,' he said, 'though I'm cross with myself for being too slow to suspect her darksome aspects. But even worse is the betrayal by one of my guards, a young man I trusted with my wife when she needed an escort and I could not accompany her. Gilbert. How had I disappointed him that he turned against me? He'd assisted me in questioning my men here—God's blood, I was so confident in him and his ease with the other men. Now his possible guilt throws doubt over everything I thought I knew.' Owen could not sit still. Boiling up from within, a surge of anger pushed him to his feet and he punched a post.

'Just when we found a dry spot,' Geoffrey muttered, sliding

away from that corner. 'Put your anger to better use than destroying a decorative shed, for pity's sake.' He leaned his forearms on his thighs and bowed his head, pressing his hands into the back of his neck.

'Do you never lose your temper?' Owen asked.

'Of course I do. I think of clever insults.' Geoffrey laughed. 'What else have you learned?'

'I sent Archdeacon Jehannes to York for the day, to try to get a description of the man who sold Lady Eleanor's brooch, if that's what has happened. I pray that Lady Sybilla has not completely led me astray about its existence and to whom it belonged. For all I know the conversation the men overheard was about selling a horse.'

'Nor do you know whether they'd heard the same couple,' Geoffrey noted. 'It seems it was a busy night, despite all your men on guard. No! I pray you, calm yourself.' He lunged for Owen's arm, laughing as he caught it.

'You should have been a jester,' Owen said. 'You have a way of turning the grimmest mood to laughter.'

'It is my best defensive strategy,' Geoffrey said with a chuckle, but his smile faded. 'I do not mean to make light of all this, Owen. I am well aware that we're all in danger until we discover who murdered Lambert and who took the letter from Dame Clarice and then returned it. It would help to recover the documents stolen from Lambert. Do you believe that Gilbert is in Alexander Neville's employ?'

'I fear that is the case.' Owen settled again beside Geoffrey. 'It was John Holand's man Douglas who carried Dame Clarice into the palace last night. Her Grace trusted him to protect Clarice. But why would she also ask Sybilla to watch her?'

Geoffrey frowned. 'I agree it seems a doubling of effort, or as if one is spying on the other is spying on the other. Have you asked Her Grace if she *did* set two to follow Clarice?'

Owen shook his head. 'Not yet. I must tread carefully with Her Grace. She already chides me for questioning her judgement.'

Geoffrey nodded. 'She never forgets her blood and

her marriages.'

'Sybilla seems too eager to assist me. Like Brother Michaelo telling me too much.'

'You don't like Lady Sybilla, do you?'

'You do. That worries me. Do I favour Eleanor so much that I want to distrust her companion instead? To me it seems most likely Sybilla stole the letter from Dame Clarice, then returned it.'

Geoffrey sighed. 'I confess that does seem likely.'

In her dreams Magda realised how she might help Owen. Princess Joan kept him at the distance she maintained from her household servants, which prevented her from confiding in him about Dame Clarice until she formally presented the information to the archbishop. But she might agree to convening the meeting early this morning rather than at her leisure if Magda could convince her of the importance of sharing all that she knew with Owen. She woke after a brief sleep and freshened herself before going to Joan.

The sounds of activity outside the sisters' little sleeping area, both around and below them, stirred Dame Clarice. There was only Alisoun to notice, for Dame Katherine was snoring on the pallet beside her companion. Though pale and shaky, Clarice managed to prop herself up and focus well enough on Alisoun to realise she did not know her.

'Who are you?'

'I've been asked to sit with you. My name is Alisoun Ffulford. I've been assisting the healer Magda Digby with His Grace the Archbishop.'

'Asked to sit with me?' Clarice tried to rise too quickly and apparently met with a pounding head, for she pressed her fingertips to her temples and lay back down with a moan. 'What happened to me?' she asked, her voice much softer than at first, almost a whimper.

'You fainted out in the fields last night, we know not why. The physician Master Walter gave you something to ease your distress so you might heal with a good night's sleep.'

The nun glanced at her companion. 'Dame Katherine was also given something to sleep?'

'No. She watched over you last night.' Alisoun left her seat to pour a drink from a pot on the brazier, then crouched down to hand the cup to Clarice. The nun seemed to shrink from it. 'It is but honey in boiled water, nothing more,' said Alisoun. 'It will refresh you.'

Clarice warily sniffed it. 'I fainted?' The scent must have met her approval for she accepted the cup and took a few sips. Then she wrinkled her nose. 'So sweet.'

'Honey soothes the throat and cleanses the blood. Most people enjoy its sweetness.'

'I've a tooth that sharply complains whenever something sweet touches it.'

'I'll tell Dame Magda. She might know of something that would ease the pain.'

Clarice sipped again. 'It does feel good on my throat.' She sighed deeply. 'I remember rushing from the porch. I remember the fields. My feet were so cold. But then—I can't remember what happened.'

'Had you been feeling ill earlier in the day?'

With a wince, the woman put the cup aside and explored the side of her mouth with her tongue. 'Yesterday.' She groaned. 'It's difficult to think with my tooth throbbing.'

'Rest a while. We can talk later.' Alisoun removed the honey water and sat quietly until Clarice began to fidget.

'I was not ill before I shared a flagon of wine with that plump little harlot who calls herself a lady,' she muttered.

Alisoun tried not to sit too far forward, not to sound too eager. 'You shared wine with one of Her Grace's ladies?'

'Sybilla. A spoiled bitch bragging like a child about the archbishop agreeing to her request for one of the puppies in the kennel. Can you imagine? Dressed in silk, jewels winking in her hair and on her fat fingers, delicate slippers that she did not wish to risk on the garden paths and she must have one of his puppies as well?'

She had certainly regained her voice, Alisoun thought. 'Were you in the hall?'

Clarice pressed her temples. 'My head is pounding.'

Alisoun added water to the small pot on the brazier to dilute the honey and poured a cup of the tepid liquid. 'Thirst can cause your head to hurt after strong wine. Try this.'

'Is that all it was?' Clarice asked. 'Strong wine?' She tasted the water, then drank it down. 'Bless you. That did not make my tooth throb.'

'Are there foods that sicken you? Anything that others can drink that you cannot?'

'The infirmarian complains that my humours treat many remedies as poisons,' said Clarice. 'My mother has also suffered ill effects from the potions of some of the finest midwives and apothecaries.'

So if Sybilla had put something in the wine she might not have meant it to have any ill effect at all. 'Could you taste anything other than wine in the drink?'

Clarice shrugged. 'I did not pay it much heed. She made me angry and I drank up her wine, then felt as if a fire was simmering beneath my eyes. She saw that something was wrong and tried to help me loosen my wimple but I did not like her touching me and I hurried away—I thought I was about to get sick.'

'I don't recall your wimple looking disturbed.'

'I pushed her away.' Clarice frowned. 'You saw me?'

'I was sitting in the garden when you rushed past. One of the guards in Her Grace's company was near. He caught you as you fell in a faint and carried you into the palace. Much fuss was made over you.' Alisoun tried a smile, but it was not returned and she abandoned it. 'It would help me know what you need if you could describe to me how you feel this morning.'

'Prickly in my arms, bitter in my belly, scratchy in my throat. My eyes burn and everything aches. My head pounded when I tried to sit up just now.'

'But you can feel all your limbs?'

Alisoun was sorry she'd asked that, for the fear in Dame Clarice's eyes intensified a hundredfold as she shoved the cup back at Alisoun and proceeded to poke and shake and pinch her arms, legs, fingers, shoulders. But it had been necessary to ask or Alisoun would need to prick her and observe her responses.

'It's all painful,' Clarice concluded. 'I trust that is good?'

'Yes. I am sorry I frightened you.'

'I wasn't frightened.'

Alisoun did not argue, seeing the stubborn set to the nun's shoulders despite her illness. 'Master Walter left a draught that he said would ease the discomfort. Would you like me to mix some in your honey water?'

'I have two healers—the physician and the midwife?'

'I told you they'd made a fuss.' Alisoun smiled again.

'I would like some of the draught.'

For a while, Clarice lay quietly, her face almost peaceful. But suddenly she asked, 'Did I say anything while I slept?'

That was a question to report to Captain Archer, Alisoun thought.

'Not while I've been with you. You've been far quieter than Dame Katherine.' Her snoring had grown louder, as if attempting to drown out their voices.

At last Clarice looked about to smile. 'She's a pig. Can you imagine travelling with her all this way?'

'Nun Appleton is not so far, I think.'

'Far enough in such company.'

Lady Sybilla, a plump, fair-haired woman not much taller than Magda herself but far younger, barred Magda's entrance to the princess's chamber, suggesting that later would be better for a conversation with Princess Joan. But her mistress disagreed, inviting Magda to enter, and Magda saw at once that the princess was still in pain from her over-indulgence of the previous day.

Fortunately she had brought with her an unguent that would be useful. 'Wouldst thou allow Magda to rub some warmth into thy afflicted foot, Thy Grace?'

She showed her the unguent, urged her to smell it, for the scent was pleasant, unlike the unguents that most mixed for gout. Joan hesitantly bowed her elegantly coiffed and delicately veiled head toward the small pot, plainly ready to pull away as quickly as possible. Her brow smoothed as she sniffed a second time.

'It is fragrant enough to wear as perfume,' she marvelled. 'Eleanor, come, smell this. It will remind you of your garden.'

The quieter lady had sat on the bed holding the princess's monkey while trying to be discreet about studying Magda. Now she leaned over and smelled the pot.

'I think perhaps there is some germander, and rosemary and—a drop of rosewater?'

Magda nodded. 'Thou hast some knowledge of scents.'

'A garden can be a source of deep comfort,' said Eleanor. She smiled with her mouth, but her eyes were dark with trouble.

'I thought the stench was part of the healing property of a salve,' said the princess.

Magda laughed. 'A mountebank would tell thee so.'

Joan sighed and sank back against her cushions, a forearm to her forehead. 'I would fain stay in bed all the day, but I think you would advise that I move about, perhaps walk around the hall?'

'Surely not!' the fair-haired doorkeeper exclaimed, fluttering toward the bed.

'You may go amuse yourself, Sybilla,' said Joan. 'I am safe with Dame Magda watching over me.' She waved away the protesting attendant. 'She is a sweet, lovely woman,' Joan said as Sybilla stepped out of the chamber, 'but too clever to trust at present. I yearn to complete this journey and return to Berkhampstead.' She turned to Eleanor. 'You may leave as well. Just put Gaspar in his basket.'

The animal squealed with indignation as he was shut away. With a whisper of silk, Eleanor bowed and departed the chamber.

'Thou hast promised a meeting with His Grace concerning Dame Clarice,' said Magda. 'Walking from thy chamber down to his would begin to move thy blood through thy limbs and prepare thee for thy journey home.'

'I am not well enough for such a visitation this morning, Dame Magda,' the princess said in a petulant tone.

She pretended to be a pampered pet like the angry Gaspar, but Magda knew that the behaviour masked a pride that did not easily bend to the desires of others. Yet Magda must try.

'Thou hast a grave responsibility and with some preparation thou canst indeed fulfil thy promise this morning, Thy Grace.' She sought the woman's eyes. 'Unless thou wouldst prefer to have the archbishop and Owen Archer attend thee here.'

The servant standing near the bed sucked in her breath at Magda's boldness. But Princess Joan merely frowned and seemed to consider the idea.

'I would be relieved to shift this burden to their shoulders,' she said as if weighing the benefit. 'But I would not be so unkind as to ask His Grace to attend me here—his infirmity is far worse than mine. Can your salve ease me enough to sit in grace and dignity in his chamber long enough to tell the tale?' She fixed Magda with her clear blue-grey eyes.

'It will. Wilt thou permit Magda to apply it?'

'Dame Clarice is in danger?'

'Owen Archer believes she may be, and he is seldom wrong, Thy Grace.'

Princess Joan lay back on her cushions. 'My servant will assist you with my slipper.'

Apparently Princess Joan was not satisfied to wait until Thoresby summoned her. He was sorry for that, for he was not satisfied that he had any advice that might be of use to her. 'My dear Princess.'

'Your Grace. I have something important—and difficult—to

tell you.'

Hearing the strain in her voice he looked more closely and saw that she was not smiling and hesitated to look him in the eye, as if she were uncertain she wished to engage with him despite her words. Today she wore a gown of deep blue, a colour that Thoresby associated with the Blessed Virgin. He wondered whether she intended the association, perhaps to reassure him.

'You are not here for my advice?'

She shook her head. 'No, Your Grace, I am here to tell you something that you must know, that it is your *right* to know.'

That struck him as an ominous promise. He glanced down, seeing Ravenser and Archer seated below and to either side of the great bed. Archer looked grim but leaned toward Thoresby and Joan as if determined not to miss a word. Ravenser looked officious, as if prepared to advise, and weary—he carried a double burden these days, his duties and Thoresby's. Behind Joan stood Magda Digby in her gown of many colours, a calm figure in a room busy with tension. Looking beyond them he noticed the day was grey and damp. He wondered what he would be doing were he well.

'Your Grace?' Joan was apparently awaiting a signal to proceed.

'Has Dame Magda counselled you in this visitation?' he asked.

'She has.' Joan glanced back at the wizened healer and her voice softened. 'She has shown me my duty, Your Grace. Might I sit beside you?'

Though he was not at all sure that he welcomed this dutiful telling of something that it was his right to hear, Thoresby thought it best that he accept it.

'I would be honoured, my lady.'

He noticed with what care Joan folded herself onto the chair beside him. He'd not considered that she might be unwell, but he was comforted by the knowledge that Magda would do her best to ease whatever might be afflicting her. He noticed also that she clutched a leather pack such as a courier might use—indeed very like the one in which Lambert had carried his blank rolls.

'Have you found the documents stolen from Dom Lambert?

Wykeham's documents?'

'Alas, no. I had my men fetch the copies held at Nun Appleton, Your Grace.'

This was indeed something he had a right to read. He held out his hand. 'I would see them.'

She did not move to hand them over. He could imagine her using on her son John the maternal look she now bestowed on him—a gentle but firm warning that he must abide by her terms. 'I would rather prepare you with some information.'

'You say these are copies held at Nun Appleton. That is whence came the sisters in your company, one of whom stole something from me. Who is she?'

'Do you remember Euphemia of Lincoln, Your Grace?'

'Of course I do not,' he snapped, growing irritated with her stubborn delay. 'Who is she and what does she have to do with all this?'

'Dame Clarice is her daughter by you, Your Grace.' Joan said it gently and a little breathlessly as if expecting an ungentle response.

Of all the revelations Thoresby might have imagined, this was so far from what he'd expected that he asked, 'Do I understand you to say that Dame Clarice is my daughter?'

'Yes, Your Grace.'

'Clarice. My daughter.' He tasted the idea. It was not so dark a thing, though neither was it immediately pleasing.

He looked down the bed at his nephew, looking startled, having just learned of a cousin he'd not guessed existed. And so soon after learning of his cousin Idonea in the convent at Hampole. Then Thoresby looked at Archer. He could see his mind working, comparing two faces, Thoresby's and Clarice's. He guessed that because one look at his nephew, who was so much a mirror of him years ago, and he'd realised the resemblance. He'd noticed her deep-set eyes, but other families had similar features.

'Yes, I can see the family resemblance around the eyes,' he said. He sensed Joan's relief. 'Did you expect me to deny this? Euphemia of Lincoln.' He shook his head. 'I still do not recall her, but though it be sad to say, I have no doubt that I sired a number of children about whom I was never informed. This Euphemia must have been of noble birth, or at least did not need financial support from me?'

'Yes, Your Grace. The family tucked her away to give birth so that she might yet make a good marriage, which she did.'

'Does Dame Clarice know who I am?'

Princess Joan nodded.

'Why did she not say anything to me?'

'She believes that you were informed of her birth and denied her, Your Grace, but I thought it unlikely that you'd been told. Considering the family, they would not have wanted to risk informing any more people than necessary, particularly you, the father, as you were in no position to wed Euphemia.'

'So my daughter hates me.'

Joan sighed and wagged her head. 'That is a stronger word than I would have chosen, but she is bitter, yes. She resents being given no choice as to her station, no alternative to religious vows. In truth, I do not believe she is suited for the convent, but few are.'

Women's talk. He had no patience for such chatter. 'But what does this have to do with the Bishop of Winchester? Was Euphemia his kinswoman?'

'No. He learned of this from Thomas Brantingham, who showed him papers left to him by his predecessor as Bishop of Exeter. They documented Alexander Neville's campaign to gather information against you in case you seemed to lean toward rejecting his claim to the archdeaconry of Cornwall.'

'He thought to force my support by threatening to expose my sin if I ruled against him?'

Joan sighed. 'He thinks more like a merchant than a noble. Brantingham expressed dismay that such a man might become archbishop.'

'This is just the sort of petty nastiness I would expect from Alexander Neville,' Ravenser said, breaking his silence.

Princess Joan handed Thoresby the pack. 'Euphemia was harassed by Neville's men and her family sent a report and copies of Neville's letters to the Bishop of Exeter to warn him of the man's low character. These are the originals, which they kept at Nun Appleton in case of future need to defend themselves against Neville. As for Clarice, she believes that you knew of Neville's treatment of her mother but refused to help. That, I think, is the source of her deepest anger. As to her search of your chamber, she merely wished to know more about her father. I do not think you can deny that a powerful temptation.'

'And so she stole a letter from one of my other mistresses,' Thoresby said.

'Sweet heaven!' Joan exclaimed.

'She learned little from that. So who scraped or stole Lambert's documents?'

'I do not know. I wish I could tell you.'

Thoresby closed his eyes, his head swimming.

'Might I ask a question, Your Grace?' Owen inquired.

Thoresby had almost forgotten Archer's presence. 'Of me or Princess Joan?'

'Of Her Grace,' said Owen.

'You are most welcome,' said Thoresby. 'I need a moment to collect my thoughts.'

'Your Grace, why did you wait so long to tell us this?' Owen asked.

'I'm curious as well,' said Ravenser. 'Had we known the content of Wykeham's documents we might have known to protect the young woman.'

'I've had my men watching her,' said Joan. 'The captain knows this.'

'And you've had Lady Sybilla watching her as well?' Owen asked.

Thoresby opened his eyes, curious as to how Joan would respond to this questioning. At the moment her lovely eyes were fastened on Archer.

'Sybilla watching her? No. Who told you that?'

'Lady Sybilla.'

Thoresby saw that this gravely disturbed the princess. He also noticed a look pass between Archer and Magda.

'Who knows what you've come to tell His Grace?' Owen asked. 'Do either of your ladies know that you are here with him now?'

'I doubt there is anyone in the palace who does not know that I am here,' said Joan. 'But as to the contents of the documents I've given His Grace, only Sir Lewis knows.'

'Not your son? Or either of your ladies?' Thoresby asked.

'No. As to why I did not tell you of this when Lambert was murdered—I wanted the documents safely here before anyone knew of their contents. I saw no connection between the emissary's death and the theft of the documents—I was certain he'd taken his own life. I still believe I made the right choice.'

Thoresby could see that neither Archer nor his nephew concurred, but he was not certain he disagreed with her. He opened the pack on his lap, saw several rolls, and set it aside, suddenly reluctant to read them. It was not from lack of curiosity—after all this he wanted very much to see what the fuss had been all about. But he sensed that all in the room expected him to *do* something about the documents, and that was the problem. He did not care to go after Alexander Neville, he had not the energy, and his attempts to suggest a man more worthy than Neville to succeed him at York had failed. His family's influence waned in the North. It was the time of the Nevilles and the Percies.

'I shall read them later. What is your concern about Lady Sybilla, Archer?'

Before his captain could respond, Princess Joan struggled to her feet. Magda was there at once to inquire whether she was in pain. The princess gave a weary nod, and sighing, made her excuses to Thoresby.

'I have delivered what I'd intended, the documents and the news that Dame Clarice is your daughter. I trust you to decide what use you will make of the former, and whether you will attempt to make your peace with the latter. If you will excuse me, Your Grace, I am in some pain and would lie down to rest.'

'Of course, my lady. God go with you, and bless you for

bringing these to me.' He patted the pack. 'As for Dame Clarice, we shall see.'

Magda guided the princess from the room, bowing as she caught Thoresby's eye.

They would have much to discuss later, he thought.

When Alisoun saw the elegant woman on the threshold she had to fight for the confidence to assert her authority.

'This is a sickroom, my lady. If you bear a message you may entrust it to me.'

Her words seemed to confuse the woman for a moment. Her dark eyes searched what was visible of the room behind Alisoun, which was very little, then returned to look directly at Alisoun. Her expression brightened and softened.

'I am Lady Eleanor. Who are you?'

'Alisoun Ffulford, apprentice to the healer Dame Magda, who is here at His Grace's request. I've been charged with the care of Dame Clarice.'

The lady seemed more comfortable now, smiling as if hoping to put Alisoun at ease.

'As my lady the Princess Joan has no need of me this morning I thought to sit with Dame Clarice, entertain her with tales of the court. Perhaps you would enjoy a walk in the garden or some pleasant respite from your duty here, Alisoun?'

'I have been ordered to stay, my lady.'

Indecision played across the lady's face as she swayed away and then back.

Clarice spoke up softly from her bed. 'Do sit with us a while.'

'You may rest assured your tales are safe with me,' said Alisoun. 'You need not send me away. I am not a gossip, my lady.'

The lady had the courtesy to blush.

Stepping aside, Alisoun welcomed her into the room. Dame Katherine gave up her place on the bench beside Clarice's pallet and offered the guest some wine, which she declined.

'What about you?' Lady Eleanor asked Katherine. 'Might I entice you to find some pleasant exercise in the hall or out on the porch? This is such a tiny chamber for four of us.'

Alisoun busied herself with adjusting Clarice's cushions while Dame Katherine fussed about her responsibility and then at last bent to Lady Eleanor's will and withdrew in a cloud of disappointment.

Lady Eleanor settled on the seat beside Clarice's pallet, and Alisoun set her own little bench in the shadows. She was most curious about the lady's visitation, a courtesy she could not imagine was totally selfless. Eleanor's dark eyes and hair and the deep greens and golds of her beautiful clothing—the vision of elegance momentarily choked Alisoun with envy until she met the woman's eyes and recognised a deep abiding unhappiness.

'I pray you are feeling better this morning,' Eleanor said to Clarice.

'I am, my lady.'

'My companion Lady Sybilla told me of your bitterness regarding your lot in life,' said Eleanor to Clarice, 'and I thought I might be able to ease your unhappiness by telling you something of the life you were spared.'

Clarice did not mirror Eleanor's gentle smile.

'What would you know of how I feel? How can you know what it is like to be shut away with so many unhappy, unwanted women?' Clarice grimaced and looked away. 'You said you would tell me tales of court.'

'And so I shall, at least one tale. It is of a young woman sent to court to find a husband. By tragic happenstance the handsome young man to whom she lost her heart was her first cousin, and the family laughed at their request to pay the pope for a dispensation.'

'Is this your own story?' asked Clarice.

Again the sad smile. 'You have guessed so quickly. Yes, this is my story, more bitter for me for the example of what might have been my joy had I been born to a nobler family.'

'Prettier gowns?' Clarice snipped.

Eleanor looked at the woman lying on the pallet as a mother might look on a stubbornly erring child, with a smile reflecting empathy. But still there was the sorrow in her eyes.

Alisoun realised she was holding her breath, that something about Lady Eleanor made her expect some unpleasantness.

'I am in the household of a woman, Princess Joan, who married her nephew, the son of her father's brother's grandson, a marriage that required several dispensations, the barriers melted away with money and alliances. But *our* marriage promised no great alliance, nor were we clever enough to bed before asking permission.'

'At least you have had such a love. I've never had the chance.'

'The chance to have your heart torn from your breast, Dame Clarice? To see your love wed to a pretty woman he likes well enough who has given him healthy sons and daughters? To be forced to sleep with a husband old and infirm, scarred and ever stinking of wine? And then to be pushed aside when you had borne the required son, in favour of his former mistress? To give your youth to someone who cared nothing for it? You have no idea how fortunate you are.'

'Did you never find another man you might love?'

'Oh yes, I did. Several. But—they do not love as we do.'

'I find it difficult to pity you. You have had the experience of love, something that has been denied me.'

'I doubt that you would ever have been given a choice in your fate,' said Eleanor. 'I know that you are the daughter of a man of the Church.'

Clarice reddened. 'You stole the documents from Dom Lambert,' she accused in a tight voice, her expression gradually shifting from anger to fear. 'You read them, didn't you?'

Alisoun was puzzled. Had the documents concerned the identity of Clarice's father? It seemed a trifle, to have caused such pain.

'You believe that being his daughter should have brought you great privilege, more choice in your life, don't you? But at his rank, from such a family, he would never have openly supported you.'

'So my life is wasted so that he might rise to such heights and I'm to be content with that?' Clarice snapped. 'Is that your message, Lady Eleanor?'

'I am trying to explain by my example, Clarice, that as a woman you were never destined to have choice in your role in life. Except perhaps a woman such as my lady Princess Joan, with great beauty, with the blood of kings bringing the blush to her cheeks, with extensive lands in her name and a power over men that have led some to whisper.'

'I wanted to know who he is,' said Clarice. 'I wanted to see the man who'd fathered me. I did not expect a frail old man who treasures a love letter from a woman who died long ago.' Her deep-set eyes had cooled into a puzzled melancholy.

'When Alexander Neville becomes Archbishop of York you will see what an honourable man your father was in comparison,' said Eleanor. 'But then you know how devious Neville is, how ruthless.'

Dame Clarice was staring at Lady Eleanor. 'Did you kill Dom Lambert and his servant?'

With a shrug, Lady Eleanor dismissed the question. 'Princess Joan has sought His Grace's counsel because he knows many of the most important men in the realm and is a man whose judgement she trusts. I would be proud of such a father.'

Alisoun covered her mouth as a gasp rose up. They spoke of Archbishop Thoresby.

'And if he were not proud of you?' Clarice retorted.

'A father proud of his daughter?' Eleanor's eyes were cold, her smile cruel. 'You *are* a fool.'

While trying to remain silent and invisible, Alisoun wondered whether her sense of danger in the woman suggested that she was capable of committing murder.

'You have a child of your own, Lady Eleanor,' Clarice reminded her.

The statement brought tears to the lady's eyes and a hand to her waist, as if remembering her pregnancy. 'A son.'

'You are fortunate.'

'Yes, I was for a while happy with him. But he is not mine, he is his father's heir, and I have not seen him in a long while.'

No wonder she bowed her head and wept.

Clarice reached out for the lady's hand, and taking it, whispered an apology.

9

DESPAIR

THURSDAY AFTERNOON/EVENING

A strained silence closed round the four men when Princess Joan left the chamber, as if she had accidentally caught the air necessary for speech in her silken train and swept it from the chamber.

Richard Ravenser stood staring out the window, his silken robes reflecting the shifting light as the tree outside bent with the wind and rain, suggesting movement though he remained still. He clasped his hands so firmly behind his back that the blood could not wash across his knuckles; it was as if he forbade himself either prayer or labour. Owen imagined he was considering what it might mean to him, that Dame Clarice was his cousin; he seemed to find some significance in it.

Brother Michaelo still knelt at his prayers, now and then beating his breast. This news changed nothing for him, accorded him no grace.

Thoresby sat back against his cushions studying the canopy overhead, his hands behind his head; Owen could not recall ever having seen him in such a casual posture when he was aware that others were present. But then he had surprised Owen in many ways of late, most significantly with his choice of Magda Digby as his physician in his final illness. He thought perhaps Thoresby welcomed the news of another daughter, and one with whom he might share some of his final days.

For his part, Owen was agitated by what he'd heard and was

trying to keep his temper and clear his mind by pacing the chamber. He had known of Thoresby's provision for one daughter in his will, so he was not scandalised by the revelation that the archbishop had another child. What made him restive was trying to connect the theft of the documents and the murders of Lambert and his servant with Clarice's bungled search. He cursed Wykeham for his gross negligence in choosing such a weak emissary as Dom Lambert. The Bishop of Winchester had created a crisis that was robbing Thoresby of peace in his illness, confirming Owen's long held impression that Wykeham was a most self-absorbed man, a stranger to compassion. It seemed a profound lack in a priest. Princess Joan he also blamed, for her arrogant silence that had prolonged the search for Lambert's murderer, costing valuable time.

Thoresby interrupted Owen's angry thoughts.

'I wonder whether I sired only daughters? I think I might have a better chance of gaining the respect of a son, eh?'

Owen turned to find the archbishop smiling.

Ravenser had unclasped his hands, breaking his self-imposed bonds, and settled in one of the chairs by the bed. 'I agree. It would be easier to provide a good living for a son than to arrange a satisfying life for a woman. Women do not seem to consider it an honour to reside in nunneries. They feel they've been tucked away in an unused storeroom so that they might be forgotten. Though your daughter Idonea has expressed contentment in her life at Hampole.'

'True, Idonea has been a comfort, and for that I thank God, though I chide myself for having been so negligent in communicating with her. Which reminds me of Wykeham's emissary.' Thoresby lifted the leather case that Joan had brought. 'I would have Brother Michaelo read these aloud now.'

At the mention of his name, Michaelo bowed his head and crossed himself, and without a word moved to the chair Joan had vacated, taking the pack of documents from His Grace.

'I would like to stay,' said Owen.

'Of course,' said Thoresby. 'I want both you and Richard to hear what Wykeham went to so much trouble to tell me.'

'And failed,' Owen said beneath his breath as he settled onto the stool toward the foot of the bed.

Ravenser settled across from him. Thoresby lay back against his cushions, eyes closed, his hands lying at ease on his lap. Brother Michaelo began with the letter in which Wykeham explained what the other documents would reveal. It contained no surprises.

The temper of the remaining documents was clear. Alexander Neville inquired as to the nature of the family's agreement with the Thoresby family, Euphemia and her family expressed outrage over the implications and the intrusion into their private lives, the Bishop of Exeter assured the family that their secret was safe with him and that his respect for John Thoresby was undiminished. He advised them to keep their copies of this correspondence secure should they need to make use of them in future.

Owen mumbled a curse and added more clearly, 'For this two men have been murdered.'

'It does seem a great fuss has been made in an attempt at petty accusations,' said Ravenser. 'As Her Grace pointed out, Neville behaved as if he were dealing with guild members or schoolmasters, not an archbishop.'

'I would be alone for a while,' Thoresby said with a great weariness.

Owen was relieved. He'd heard enough and was anxious to question Dame Clarice. He and Ravenser left the room, but did not go far. Sir Lewis and Geoffrey were pacing in the corridor, the former with an expression at once grim and anxious, the latter plainly concerned for his friend.

'What has happened?' Owen asked.

'Lady Eleanor has been with Dame Clarice for a long while,' said Lewis. 'She has avoided me the past few days when it has been obvious that she has been much troubled in her mind. I come to you, Captain, because I suspect she has trespassed in some way with one of your guards. Gilbert. Several times I've come upon them in heated conversation and each time they've broken off at once and pretended they were not together. And now, this trouble with—I know who Dame Clarice is, Captain, but Lady Eleanor should not.'

'You need say no more. I would have you find my second, Alfred, and tell him to bring Gilbert to His Grace's chamber under close guard. I will bring Lady Eleanor there as well.' It was time to confront them. His conversation with Clarice must wait—indeed, it might prove unnecessary. 'Sir Richard, I would have you ask Princess Joan to allow Alisoun and the nuns to withdraw to her chamber for a short while, at least until I have escorted Lady Eleanor from there.'

'Have you a task for me?' asked Geoffrey.

'If you would accompany Sir Lewis, my friend, in case Alfred needs advice.'

With a nod, Geoffrey withdrew with Lewis Clifford.

'My uncle is weary,' Ravenser reminded Owen.

'He wants answers,' said Owen, 'and with God's grace we may this day deliver some.'

As Jehannes had risen from the table in Bess's kitchen he'd wondered aloud where to begin. Bess had suggested that he save time by talking to his summoner, Colin; he'd felt a little foolish for not having thought of that himself. It was a summoner's duty to keep abreast of the faithful, which involved sifting through the gossip that ran through the city. Colin was an unassuming, quiet, ordinary-looking man around whom people talked with ease, often failing to notice his presence. At this time of the morning he could usually be found kneeling in the minster near the chapter house to catch the gossip as the canons drifted out of the chapter meeting. Jehannes was not disappointed.

Grey-garbed and grey-haired, Colin often seemed a shadow or a reflection, not a flesh and blood being, but his conversation was full of the colours and textures of his observations of folk, great or humble, young or old; he had a gift for divining the subtleties of temper and a true affection for his fellow man. His pale eyes lit up at Jehannes's approach, and he rose at once to join his master in a quiet spot.

His head bowed to give his full attention to Jehannes's description, Colin nodded several times during the explanation and query.

'Yes, God be praised, I can help you with this, Dom Jehannes,' he said at last. 'The bearer of the brooch has been the topic of much gossip in the liberty and amongst the goldsmiths on Stonegate. A Neville he is, though he did not divulge that to the goldsmiths. He claimed the bauble no longer of use to him for his sweetheart had turned her gaze elsewhere.' He chuckled, his dimples showing.

'A Neville? You are certain of this?'

'Oh yes. He's also busied himself entertaining the canons while singing the praises of his cousin Alexander Neville. Why, this shall be the centre of God's earthly kingdom when Alexander becomes archbishop.' Colin's eyes were merry with his own wit.

'Did he name his sweetheart?'

'No, he is quite discreet, even going so far as to vary his manner of dress when on his own business.'

'Was he able to sell the brooch?'

'Oh, yes. It was a pretty piece.' Colin nodded decisively. Then he asked, 'Is it true that the princess's party is confined to the palace because a murderer is loose?' Before Jehannes could think how to respond, Colin added, 'It must be exciting to be there, in the midst of all that.'

'Dangerous would be a more appropriate description,' said Jehannes.

'So it is true?'

Rather than answering the question Jehannes asked instead for the name of the goldsmith to whom the man had sold the brooch, and once he had his answer rose in haste, thanking Colin and departing before he could ask more.

The goldsmith seemed to corroborate Colin's opinion of the clever Neville, for the man had apparently been quite convincing in his tale of wishing to gather enough money that he might go into self-imposed exile and heal his broken heart. The brooch was beautiful, and the goldsmith already had a buyer in mind.

Jehannes was grateful that he had plenty to report to Owen, for it was time to return to the barge. He regretted that he could not spare the time to tell Lucie and Bess what he had learned, but he must hurry in case something in his report might help Owen prevent another death.

In the days leading up to Princess Joan's arrival Thoresby had focused on regaining some strength, which had left him little time to anticipate how the visit might unfold. Certainly he had never dreamed that he might meet a daughter of his own. But now, lying in his great bed absorbing the news, he thought it a most appropriate revelation to receive as folk came to pay their last respects. It was, after all, his child's last chance to speak with him. Though apparently she had not come with that purpose, but rather to spy on him.

He tried to recall Euphemia of Lincoln, Clarice's mother. He'd often travelled to Lincoln, a lovely city. He set his mind the task of remembering his time there, perhaps twenty years ago. Feasts and processions passed before him, the steep pitch of the streets always making the latter a challenge. Twenty years ago that would have been nothing to him. He had kept his strength and energy long into old age. Twenty years.

John Gynwell was bishop there then, a man who had left little impression on Thoresby—on anyone, he suspected. Gradually a voice came to him, a strident voice, an attitude dressed in vibrant colours. Ah yes. A coolly confident, manipulative woman with a fierce sexual appetite who danced with a mischievous grin and teased him with her eyes. After one night of lively lovemaking she'd apparently had enough of him and had assiduously avoided him. She was the only woman who had so painfully bruised his pride. But other than that grin, those eyes, the energy and fire, he could remember little else. Perhaps her hair had been red.

Thoresby shifted in the bed. That a child had resulted from

that coupling saddened him. A daughter born of lust, not love—not even affection. No wonder the young woman had grown up bitter and cold. He and Marguerite should have had a child. Such a one, from such deep, abiding love could not help but be an exquisite, compassionate soul.

He grew melancholy. That was not a good thing when he was trapped in bed. He fingered the pack of documents beside him, the worn and creased leather representing the active life he had left behind. His life was now confined to blankets and cushions, physics and watered wine. He wished he could stir up a healthy rage about Alexander Neville, but he was too weary. Perhaps after a nap.

A strange sort of quiet had settled on the room. Dame Clarice lay with eyes closed, her breath uneven as if silently weeping; Lady Eleanor stood with a cup of wine in her hands but not drinking, seeming somehow undecided about whether to return to her seat or depart. Alisoun itched to seek out the captain and inform him of what she'd heard, but he had placed Clarice in her care, both to guard and to nurse.

She went to her patient, touching the back of her hand to the nun's brow.

'You are feverish.' She truly was, eliminating Alisoun's need to lie. 'Let me fetch Dame Magda's powder for a fever.'

Clarice's eyelids fluttered, but she did not open her eyes, merely reaching up with one trembling hand to press Alisoun's.

'I'm frightened,' she whispered. 'I don't want to die.'

'She said you were feverish, not dying,' said Eleanor. 'You have the benefit of several healers in the palace. Where are the midwife's powders?'

'In His Grace's chamber,' said Alisoun.

'Send the guard posted at the doorway for them.'

'He would not know what to fetch.'

Eleanor set down the cup and bent to Clarice to check Alisoun's report, nodding as she straightened. 'She is feverish, poor woman.' She stepped close to Alisoun, looked straight into her eyes. 'You will not gossip about what I've told Dame Clarice?'

In normal circumstances Alisoun would be insulted, but she understood why Eleanor did not wish her to repeat what she'd heard. Others would easily read into the recitation the possibility of her being involved in Dom Lambert's death. 'I have already assured you that I am not a gossip, my lady.' To report to the captain was not gossiping.

Eleanor nodded. 'I shall stay with Dame Clarice until you return.'

Alisoun stepped out of the room and into the arms of Captain Archer. She almost cried out, but smothered her impulse with a hand to her mouth.

'I would go in,' he whispered.

'Dame Clarice is dressed and presentable, Captain,' she kept her voice as low as possible as well, though it was difficult to judge the volume over the loud pounding of her heart. She'd initially merely been startled, but the grim expression on his scarred face now frightened her. 'What has happened?'

'See to the fever powder,' he said. She realised he must have been listening. 'I am moving Dame Clarice to Princess Joan's chamber. Bring the physick there.' He let her go. She hurried away.

As Alisoun reached the stairway she realised that the main meal of the day was being served in the hall. She'd not noticed that the morning had already passed. To her dismay Sir John Holand was standing in a small group at the edge of the hall and straightened with a grin as he noticed her. She'd had a disturbing dream about him the previous night and now, seeing him, she could feel the heat rising in her face. She hurried to Thoresby's chamber. She was surprised to find Magda there, sitting by the great bed, her hands folded on her lap, watching His Grace with a faint smile as he softly spoke. Alisoun thought she heard the words 'Clarice' and 'daughter'. So he knew. Magda rose when Brother Michaelo ushered Alisoun in, and assisted her in choosing the appropriate powder. She suggested that Alisoun also take some sprigs of rosemary to scent the water for a cool compress for Clarice's forehead.

When Alisoun stepped out into the corridor once more she experienced a frisson of fear that it was deserted. She chided herself for making much of nothing, for surely Sir John would not approach her again. But suddenly he was there, and in a few strides he was beside her.

'Shall we walk in the garden, Mistress Alisoun?' He slid his arm across the small of her back and pulled her close.

'I cannot, Sir,' she whispered, finding little air for speech. 'I must attend Dame Clarice. I've just fetched a powder for her fever.' She glanced around, desperate to catch someone's eye, but they were alone in the corridor.

He grabbed her free hand and kissed the back of it. He smelled of leather, horses and wine, a not unpleasant medley of scents, and he had his mother's beautiful blue-grey eyes with thick lashes, but Alisoun could not breathe, for she could not believe that he meant her no harm. As if he'd read her mind, he tightened his grip.

Alisoun gasped. 'Why do you want to hurt me?'

It was not what she'd intended to say, but it caught him off guard and he eased his grip round her waist just enough for her to spin away and pull out the dagger that Captain Archer had given her. She pointed it at Sir John's face as she backed toward the hall.

Throwing up his hands, Sir John asked with a laugh, 'What is this?'

'It is my protection, Sir.'

He laughed again. 'Why not just scream?'

'I did not wish to embarrass you or myself.'

'Embarrass *you*? You dim-witted, ungrateful girl. You should be honoured by my attention.'

Alisoun turned and fled up the stairs, sheathing the dagger as she reached the top. When the guard admitted her to Princess Joan's chamber she stood for a moment, uncertain which way to turn.

'Child, what has happened?' asked Ravenser, who stood near the high-backed chair on which the princess was seated.

Alisoun humiliated herself by bursting into tears.

CANDACE ROBB

With the assistance of Dame Katherine, Ravenser had moved Clarice to the princess's chamber. Now Owen faced Eleanor alone in the small room, which was now so quiet that he noticed how loudly his heart was beating and wondered how Eleanor did not comment on it. She was a study in the beauty of earth tones and woodland sunlight, her deep gold gown, dark green surcoat, and delicate deep gold veil rich against her dark hair and pale, luminescent skin. With a whisper of silk she stepped so close he could smell the rosewater in her hair.

'How everyone obeys you here,' she said with a teasing smile as she reached up and touched his scarred cheek. 'But is this not too bold, even for you? There will be talk about us, my love. What if your apothecary wife should hear of our being alone together in a bedchamber?'

'My lady, to my regret I come to you on official duty, not to make love to you.'

Her lips separated a little as she took a deep breath that sent a shiver through her, and she closed her eyes. 'I've thought of you so often, Owen.' She looked up at him and again touched his cheek. 'Why did we not leave Kenilworth together? Why didn't you save me?' Her dark eyes searched his face.

He was taken aback by the questions. 'Eleanor, you were never mine to save. We knew each other but one afternoon.'

'I meant nothing to you?'

'So much has happened since then.'

She turned away from him, and in a cold voice, said, 'I don't know why I thought you different from the other men I've loved, why I thought you would be true.'

'Loved? You cannot mean that, Eleanor.' He began to wonder whether she was a little mad.

'I have nothing to say to you.'

'In truth you have no choice in the matter, my lady.'

She turned to him, her cheeks flushed. 'What did that midwife's apprentice tell you?'

'Was there something to tell?'

238

'You play with me, Owen, like a cat with its prey.'

'I have no time to play with you, Lady Eleanor.' He took her by the forearm. 'You will come with me. We will both be more comfortable in His Grace's chamber.'

'His Grace's? Why?' She tried to shrug out of his grasp, but he held tight. 'You are hurting me.'

'I would not need to if you will accompany me without argument.'

'Why? What is this about?'

'You know full well what this is about, Eleanor.'

She stared at him for a moment, then bowed her head and ceased struggling. 'As you wish.'

As they passed the hall, Owen noticed Richard Ravenser quietly talking to Sir John, whose crossed arms and flushed face threatened an angry outburst. He hurried Eleanor to His Grace's chamber, not wishing to add the arrogant Holand to the already volatile mix.

Brother Michaelo's nostrils flared and his eyes narrowed at the sight of Lady Eleanor. 'His Grace is resting, Archer.'

'He will rest much better after seeing us, Michaelo,' Owen said loudly enough for His Grace to hear.

But it was Magda Digby who called out to him to enter.

He felt Eleanor begin to step away, and firmly taking her arm he guided her into the room.

'Michaelo, bring some wine,' he said. 'Your Grace, I present you with Lady Eleanor. She has been named by several as being likely to know something about the theft of Wykeham's documents and the death of his emissary.'

Eleanor gasped. 'Rumours, Your Grace,' she said. 'I call on your mercy.' She bowed her head to him.

'If deserved, you shall have it, Lady Eleanor,' said Thoresby. He indicated that she should sit on the far side of him, opposite Magda. 'I would have you stay if you will, Dame Magda,' he said. 'I prefer having another female present, and as ever welcome your counsel.'

'I would prefer a woman of the princess's household,' said Eleanor.

'No doubt you would,' said Thoresby, dismissing her.

Michaelo directed a servant to arrange chairs and pour wine, all the while watching Eleanor with curiosity. But he was called away as someone knocked on the door. It was Lewis Clifford, leading Owen's second lieutenant Gilbert, whose hands were tied behind his back. Richard Ravenser followed.

'This is a sickroom,' Michaelo protested when Owen joined him at the door.

'I would have you go see to Lady Eleanor's comfort and arrange three more seats, Brother Michaelo,' said Owen in a quiet voice. 'I believe that you will find some satisfaction in what you are about to witness.'

When Michaelo moved away, Gilbert said, 'God forgive me, Captain, I never meant to harm anyone in this household.' He did not meet Owen's gaze but kept his eyes on the tiled floor.

'But it sounds as if you did, Gilbert. What were you offered? Captain of Neville's guard?'

Gilbert lifted eyes filled with remorse and fear. 'Yes.'

'Fool.' Owen turned to Sir Lewis. 'Where are Geoffrey and Alfred?'

'They hope to deliver Lady Eleanor's accomplice to you,' said Lewis. 'Your man has directed them to him.'

That was an unexpected boon.

'Roger Neville,' said Gilbert. 'Lady Eleanor's cousin and lover.'

'A Neville.' Owen nodded. 'And you, Gilbert? What are you to my lady?'

Gilbert shook his head. 'Naught but her pawn, Captain.'

'Come,' said Owen to all three. 'We will see what satisfaction we may have this day. Say nothing unless I address you, Gilbert.'

'The nun is resting comfortably?' Owen asked Ravenser.

'She is.'

'I saw you with Holand.'

Ravenser's deep-set eyes seemed to sink farther into his skull and the set of his jaw spoke of a profound anger. 'He had nothing to do with this, though he be a knave. More of that at another time.'

Owen gladly dropped that line of inquiry.

As Gilbert took his seat, Thoresby looked to Owen. 'One of my guards? He has something to do with all this?'

Owen had watched Eleanor's face as he invited the three men to approach the great bed, and he'd felt both sorrow and relief to see her blanche and drop her eyes to her hands. She'd been restlessly twisting the rings on her slender fingers, but now she grew still. Gilbert kept his eyes fixed on the floor.

'Are we expecting more, Archer?' Thoresby asked.

His face was drawn and slightly pinched, his voice bordering on breathless, Owen realised. He prayed that this would not prove too much for the ailing man, and yet surely he could not properly rest until the murders were resolved.

'We may have several more to fit round your bed,' said Owen. 'Chaucer and my man Alfred are searching for Lady Eleanor's cousin, Roger Neville.'

'Roger?' Eleanor whispered. All colour fled her beautiful face and she swayed.

In a swirl of confusing colours Magda was beside her with a small cup of something she ordered the woman to inhale. With a sharp intake of breath, Eleanor began to cough. Magda held her shoulders until she breathed evenly. Then she handed her the cup of wine that Michaelo had set beside her.

'Drink. Thou wilt not escape by inviting a faint, Lady Eleanor.' Magda stood over the lady until she took several sips. Then, with a nod of satisfaction—Eleanor's colour was quite noticeably improved—Magda returned to her seat.

'Perhaps it would be advisable to begin at the beginning, Lady Eleanor,' said Thoresby, nodding to Magda in thanks.

Eleanor seemed to collect herself, folding her hands on her lap, straightening. 'My lord archbishop,' she bowed her head to him. 'As you have hooded me and hold my jesses, I have little choice.' Despite her description of herself as a hooded and tied falcon, she used her quite uncovered eyes to include all in the chamber. 'So be it. You shall hear my sad tale. And to begin, you should know that my husband is retained by Sir John Neville, Alexander's father. I owe the Neville family my life, much to my husband's displeasure.' A tremor in her voice seemed to contradict her air of defiance, though it might be anger rather than fear.

'His displeasure?' said Thoresby. 'And why is that?'

Owen admired Thoresby's courteous tone and demeanour. Yes, this was how to approach Eleanor.

'He believes that they have wronged him by supporting me, that they have proved ungrateful for his allegiance.'

'In what way has their support offended your husband?'

'Anything that eases my lot offends him,' Eleanor said sharply, her eyes a little wild. But she caught herself. 'Forgive me, Your Grace.' She frowned down at her hands, shaking her head as if reminding herself what she meant to say. 'To explain how I sold my soul is to ask you to reassure me that I had no choice. But that is a lie. I am finished with lies. I did have choices, and at each step I chose to go forward.' Now she raised her eyes to his. 'I stole Dom Lambert's documents for the Neville family.'

The air seemed sucked away by all present, and the room became unnaturally still, so still that Owen heard the subtle rustle of silk from Eleanor's now quite pronounced trembling.

'How did you do this?' asked Thoresby in little more than a whisper.

'I lay with him, God forgive me.' She blushed and momentarily looked away. 'Afterwards, as he slept, I studied the parchments so that my cousin who followed our company, a Neville kinsman as you already know,' she glanced at Gilbert, who blushed and looked away, 'so that Roger might supply me with the number and size of replacements.' She paused for breath, her hands breaking from the controlled grasp and clutching her elbows in an unconscious embrace. 'Again I lay with Dom Lambert, and again he slept afterwards, helped by the wine I'd prepared for him, and I traded the blank parchments for the documents that the family was so keen to prevent His Grace from reading.'

'If they had the documents, why did they want Dom Lambert dead?' Thoresby asked.

Michaelo's little sob caught Owen's attention, but the others were focused on Eleanor and paid no heed to the monk who stood at a distance, guarding the door. Michaelo bowed his head and crossed himself.

Eleanor shook her head and, regaining control of her hands, folded them once more on her lap. 'They did not want him dead. I had assured them that Dom Lambert had no idea of the content of his pack.'

'Such a naïve man,' Ravenser murmured.

Eleanor nodded toward him, her tension rendering the movement uneven, almost sharp. 'Yes, Sir Richard, he was. I had teased him that it was a simple matter to break a seal, but he would not be tempted. So I had completed my mission for the Nevilles.'

'Does this mean that you do not know who murdered him?' Thoresby asked, though he looked at Gilbert, who flicked his eyes toward Eleanor and nodded.

'God help me, I know all too well. I became so afraid.' Eleanor took a deep, shuddering breath. 'I lay awake at night thinking of Dom Lambert discovering the blank parchments.' She looked around at her audience with a yearning air, as if hoping to see their eyes light with understanding. 'I imagined him suffering humiliation before this man, the great John Thoresby, Archbishop of York. How could he bear such shame? I was certain he would think of me, of our time together, and would realise that it must have been I who had tricked him. Who else? He'd guarded that pack day and night. Except after lovemaking.'

'He said nothing of you when he discovered the documents had been stolen,' said Thoresby. 'He never spoke your name.'

'More worthy than the rest, God grant him peace,' she murmured.

She bowed her head. That was the moment when Owen knew for certain that she had murdered Dom Lambert, and his heart felt as if some demon had reached up from hell and clutched it in its blazing, inhumanly strong claw and yanked it, trying to wrench it from his body. That such a beautiful creature could so cold-bloodedly hunt a modest man who had approached an important mission with such simplicity of heart.

'Tell me that you did nothing to him.' When Eleanor glanced up at him Owen realised he'd said it aloud.

Now she spoke to Owen. 'I wanted to leave the company, run away, to a convent if that was what they wished,' the pitch of her voice rose and she spoke almost too quickly to articulate, 'but through Roger I was instructed to remain where I was, that as long as I did nothing I would not call attention to myself, and that was crucial because I must still watch what happened when Dom Lambert presented the blank parchments.' She looked around at the others as if hoping for understanding. 'My fear did not matter. I was never aught but an unwitting tool.' For a moment she seemed distracted, as if listening to something that the others could not hear. With her hands on her knees she leaned slightly forward. Taking a breath, she said, 'I see now that lack of sleep and—I was unwell. I needed a confessor.' She moaned, then shook her head. 'In faith, I don't know what would have saved me. I was convinced he must die before we reached Bishopthorpe. I had hunted him, now I would bring him down.' She nodded to herself and seemed to calm a little. 'I devised a way to loosen his saddle and I tucked a flask of drugged wine in it. He did not fall the first day. Nor did he drink from that flask. But the next day—it had not occurred to me that he would switch horses and saddles with his servant when the horse grew restive. But when he fell, I knew.' She hugged herself. 'I was furious! Not sorry, no, I felt only contempt for the man. He'd noticed something was amiss and left it to his servant.'

A loud voice in the corridor turned the attention toward Michaelo, who reluctantly opened the door once more.

'Eleanor.' A man in elegant though travel-stained clothing stood in the doorway between Geoffrey and Alfred. His features were sharply handsome, his eyes hot with pain.

'No,' Eleanor whispered.

There was a shuffling of chairs as room was made for the latest arrivals. Magda coaxed Thoresby to sip something she had been heating on the brazier. Owen ordered Alfred to keep his murderous look to himself or Gilbert might not speak up when they needed him. Michaelo splashed his face with some scented water. Sir Lewis moved toward the door, then changed his mind and returned to his seat.

All the while Eleanor stared at her cousin Roger, who grew quite plainly uncomfortable beneath her hungry gaze and shifted in his seat so that he might not see her but rather face Thoresby.

When all were settled, Thoresby said, 'So you designed an accident that took the wrong life, Lady Eleanor, and Dom Lambert's attempt to rid himself of an uncomfortable mount won your contempt. What then did you do?'

Still she stared at Roger as if dumbstruck.

Thoresby glanced at Roger. 'Why did you not rescue her from herself?'

Roger sputtered some inane excuse that Owen was too impatient to hear.

'Your Grace,' Owen interrupted. 'If it please you, might we hear the full story before picking it apart?'

Ravenser coughed into his hand. Geoffrey wiped his brow; Owen could not recall ever having seen him so ill at ease. Thoresby grunted and nodded to Eleanor. 'Continue, Lady Eleanor.'

But she was now glaring at Roger. 'Rescue me? Oh, but he could not do that or his powerful kin might discard him, the penniless cousin.' Her voice was thick with loathing.

'Lady Eleanor, thy temper does thee no favours,' Magda said with a little frown and shake of her head.

Miraculously, Eleanor dropped her gaze. 'I beg the pardon of His Grace and this company,' she said, though there was no remorse in her voice.

Thoresby patted Magda's hand.

'Once at Bishopthorpe,' Eleanor continued in a quieter tone, 'I convinced Roger that we must finish the task. It was easy to enlist one of your guards to assist me. All I needed was the bait of the Neville affinity.'

Gilbert crossed himself, keeping his eyes averted.

'So pious now, Gilbert,' said Eleanor, 'but you were so helpful then. It was from you that I learned that Brother Michaelo and Dom Lambert had withdrawn to the monk's small chamber and what that might mean. I'd no knowledge of Brother Michaelo's past sin.'

With a pained expression Thoresby glanced toward the door, where Michaelo stood with head bowed.

Now Eleanor also bowed her head.

When the silence dragged on, Owen took over.

'Lady Eleanor, did you kill Dom Lambert?'

She straightened a little, but her eyes, though turned toward Owen, seemed to be focused far away.

'You must understand. I can't bear you to think I had no cause. As your jongleur's mistress, having no chance to speak my pain.'

Her words momentarily silenced Owen, invoking the woman who had blinded him. But he could not allow himself to be played by her. 'You are confessing to his murder?' he asked.

His question seemed to chill her. 'Once I bore my husband a son, he wished to have no more to do with me. For my part I was much relieved, for I had no joy of him. He returned to his mistress and I felt free to give myself to—'

'Eleanor, no!' Roger said, rising from his chair.

Eleanor grimaced as she turned to him. 'What a fool I've been in my affections. Much joy I've had of you.' She turned to Thoresby, and with anger strengthening her voice and quieting her tremors she continued. 'When my husband learned that Roger was my lover he beat me and locked me away. Roger was frightened for me and informed his lord, and the family came to my rescue. Indeed, they brought my case to the court of the bishop of Lincoln, where my husband was ordered to mend his ways. I had been in Princess Joan's service for a brief time before my marriage, and they arranged for me to rejoin her household to give my husband and I time to think how we might best come together, what it was that caused our disaffection.' She paused, and almost too softly to be heard she said, 'As if it might be easily mended.' More loudly, she resumed, 'From time to time someone would ask me to find out this or that.

Small things. Until this journey. When we learned that the Bishop of Winchester was sending an emissary with our party, I was told that I would be working with Roger, who would be following us at a discreet distance, to steal the documents Dom Lambert carried.' She turned back to Roger, who had been ordered to resume his seat by Geoffrey. 'You never loved me. You sold my brooch to cover your expenses.'

'That is not true! I sold it—' he caught himself and dropped his eyes.

'I'll be well rid of you,' Eleanor moaned.

'So it was you and Gilbert who hanged Dom Lambert,' Owen said to Eleanor.

She gave him a curt nod. She'd separated her hands into angry fists.

'What of Brother Michaelo?'

'The fool followed,' said Eleanor.

'I take responsibility for that,' said Gilbert. 'I hit him and left him there.'

'But you take no responsibility for the death of Dom Lambert?' Thoresby asked in a cold voice. 'Or for betraying me?'

If Gilbert could have hidden beneath his chair, he would have. He cringed and hugged himself and hung his head so heavily Owen thought his neck might snap.

Yet another knock on the door distracted Owen for a moment—with tragic results. He'd not thought to check Eleanor for a dagger. He was so close to her, but it took a second too long for him to understand her cry of 'Enough!', Roger's shout, Gilbert's shriek, Ravenser's 'No!'

Blood pumped from her stomach onto her hands that still clutched the hilt of the dagger and pressed sideways. Agony and terror twisted her face, but no sound came from her open mouth. Owen did not know what to grab, her hands, all of her? It was Roger who knelt before her and quieted her hands, sobbing as he lifted her and took her to the pallet to which Michaelo and Magda guided him.

Jehannes stood just within the doorway. 'I am come too late,' he said, staring at the horror of the bloodstained woman.

'Pray over her, Jehannes. Pray over her,' Owen whispered. Sinking down onto a bench, he buried his head in his hands and stayed there for a long, long while, at first trying to stop his mind from its futile search for ways he might have save Eleanor, later merely praying for God's grace for all of them. He was drawn out of himself by Magda's warm hands on his shoulders.

'Thou hast done all in thy power, Bird-eye, and thou hast eased Old Crow's mind, there should be no more murders here. Speak with Jehannes now. He saw thy wife in York this day. That will comfort thee.'

She handed him a cup of wine.

'Have you added anything to it?'

She shook her head. 'Thou hast more to do this day.'

Now he was able to listen to Jehannes's report that the brooch had been sold in York, and best of all that Lucie and all his family were well.

Much later, Owen and Ravenser questioned Roger further. It had been difficult to wrest him from Eleanor's bedside, and they had to promise him that he could return. It pained Owen to see the noble Sir Lewis kneel in Roger's place, and lifting Eleanor's hand, gently press his lips to the inside of her palm. How many had loved her, he wondered, and she could not trust their love.

They withdrew with Roger to the small chamber that Brother Michaelo had been using. Oblivious to the blood caked on his hands, sleeves, the front of his gown, Roger sat cross-legged on the bed, his eyes staring sightlessly until they convinced him to drink some wine.

'We will not keep you long, I promise,' said Owen.

Roger finally focused on Owen and nodded. 'Thank you.'

'Are the Nevilles responsible for these murders?' Ravenser asked.

Roger hesitated for only a moment, as if his mind were catching up with the words. 'No, they had condemned Eleanor for going beyond their orders. They said she had ruined everything by killing Dom Lambert and his servant. They had shifted their sympathy to her husband, saying they now saw he'd had good cause to discipline her. You did not see her with her lip split, her face swollen and discoloured, and so thin. He'd been starving her.' His voice broke, and he bowed his head for a moment before he continued. 'I sold the brooch so that we might buy passage across the Channel. But she was so angry and we fought, and I did not have a chance to explain that she was wrong, that I meant to rescue her. I thought I had time. Time.' He whispered the last word, staring down at his hands. Owen wondered whether he had yet fully realised that it was Eleanor's blood that stained them.

'She must have believed that she had time to make amends, to perform penance to save her from eternal damnation,' said Ravenser. 'I will ask all in the palace to pray for her, that she has time and grace to make her peace with her Lord before she dies.'

Roger moaned. 'There are two healers here—what good are they if they cannot save her?'

Owen had seen how certainly Eleanor had ensured injury beyond repair. 'She does not wish to live, Roger.' Had he not trapped her into a confession with so many witnesses who could save themselves only by condemning her, would she have managed to escape with Roger, he wondered. Could she have found any joy with two deaths on her conscience?

'You are certain that the Nevilles had not called for Lambert's death?' Ravenser asked.

'If I could blame them for this tragedy I would, Sir Richard,' said Roger. 'I would. But they had no part in this.'

No part. Owen would not have chosen those words. But he was convinced that the Nevilles had condemned the murders. It was the poison in Eleanor's heart that had led to this.

'I should have stopped her. I should have taken her away as soon as she spoke of her fear. I can't remember now why I did nothing.' Roger stared at Owen as if expecting him to say something to comfort him.

'I have no words of comfort for you,' Owen said. 'I feel guilty as well. I should have thought she might have a dagger. I should have seen her reach for it and prevented her from wounding herself.'

'You will both drive yourselves mad with such self-flagellation,' said Ravenser. 'For pity's sake, accept that a beautiful woman for whom you both cared has been destroyed by her own demons.' He put a hand on Owen's shoulder. 'Come. Let this poor man go to his lady.' To Roger, he said, 'I am certain that Princess Joan will let you sit with Lady Eleanor.' They had moved Eleanor to Joan's chamber where they could keep her warm by the brazier and away from the draughts and the noise of the hall.

After Roger fled the chamber, Owen asked Ravenser about his earlier comment about John Holand.

'Twice he has grabbed Alisoun and frightened her. This time she pulled a dagger on him.' Ravenser sighed. 'Two daggers drawn in the palace this day by women, one so tragically, one so appropriately. But young Alisoun was frightened beyond anything that wretched man could have imagined. I had forgotten that she'd lost her family to the pestilence, that she'd been out on that farm defending herself for days. Apparently a man had threatened her. It was that memory that Sir John's aggression brought back to the young woman. Princess Joan comforted her. It did my heart good to see.'

'I am not so delighted by Princess Joan as you are,' said Owen, needing to vent some of his frustration. 'Had she warned us of Lambert's mission when his servant died or at least when we discovered the theft of the documents, I might have prevented one death.'

'Alexander Neville. God rot him. You blame the wrong person, Archer. Curse the devil himself, not those whom he has thrown into confusion. I would not have expected Her Grace to tell us of this until she deemed it the proper time. They are different from us, Archer, the nobles, particularly the family of the king. I learned that when I was part of Queen Phillippa's household.'

'Of course they are different—they wield the power over all.'

'Can you possibly imagine the responsibility they carry?' said Ravenser. 'The fate of the realm is in their hands. Their choices rule the fates of so many, not just themselves, their families, their friends.'

'Princess Joan's marriage to Prince Edward did nothing for the realm, Sir Richard.'

Ravenser grunted. 'I'll say no more of that. Young Alisoun would speak with you about Lady Eleanor's visit to my cousin Clarice. She is with the nuns in the small chamber next to Her Grace.'

They parted in the corridor, Ravenser headed for the hall, Owen for the solar.

Alisoun opened the door to Owen, stepping out and closing it behind her to recount to him Eleanor's tale.

'I am so sorry for her,' said Alisoun, 'and yet not. I understand her, but what she did righted nothing.'

Owen said little, numbed for the moment by all that had happened. But at least by the time he left Alisoun and headed for the chapel he felt he had most of the pieces to the puzzle of the murders. He would pray a while with Gilbert. Thoresby had ordered his execution at dawn—another tragedy to survive. Owen knew it was what any judge would decree—Gilbert had strangled Dom Lambert and then strung him up, attacked Brother Michaelo and left him in the woods, where he might have died. But it was hard to condemn a man who had been loyal so long. Very hard.

Towards evening, Magda returned to Thoresby's chamber, and he knew by a heaviness in her that Lady Eleanor was dead.

'How could she go so quickly,' he wondered, 'when an old wretch like me lingers so long?'

'She wished to die,' Magda said, 'and without the will to heal, the flesh succumbs. Her lover held her close. May he find some peace in that.'

'Would you have saved her if you could?' Thoresby asked.

'Thou shouldst know better than to ask that,' said Magda. 'There is no place for pride in healing. She did not wish to live. But thou shouldst know, the poor woman was with child. Barely, but Magda thinks that she knew.'

Thoresby crossed himself. 'Not her husband's.'

Magda shook her head. 'There was no joy in her future. No peace.'

Thoresby lay back against his cushions and said a prayer for the lost soul just released from its earthly form. Perhaps Lady Eleanor repented at the end, perhaps she would eventually rise from her penance and dwell in God's grace.

They sat quietly, saying little, sipping spiced wine from jewelled mazers, until Brother Michaelo announced Dame Clarice.

Magda patted Thoresby's hand and rose. 'Time for a walk beneath the sky for Magda. Embrace thy daughter, Old Crow, make thy peace with her.'

Alisoun had been glad when Dame Clarice asked her to walk with her to His Grace's chamber. Though she and the two nuns had been shifted back to the small chamber, the sounds of grief over Lady Eleanor's deathbed and the heavy stench of blood permeated the little room, weighing heavily on all three of them. The memories conjured earlier by Sir John had gnawed at Alisoun, and the sounds of mourning had pulled her even farther into that horrible time, as one by one her family succumbed to the pestilence. She had been too young to understand how completely unprotected she would be without her parents, how silent the world could be, how suddenly crowded with threats. When Clarice said she wished to speak with her father, Alisoun had jumped at the chance to escape her memories.

She did not know what to expect when she entered Thoresby's chamber. She had seen poor Lady Eleanor, had seen the man who had been her lover crumple in despair, had heard that the handsome Gilbert was condemned to death. Such tragedy would surely taint a room, echo and haunt any who walked there for a long while. But the room seemed as peaceful and inviting as it had before. It seemed wrong to Alisoun.

Magda left her seat next to the great bed, where Thoresby sat up, holding a jewelled mazer in his beringed hands. Alisoun had wondered whether his condition would deteriorate with the dramas that had played out around his bed earlier in the day, but from this distance he seemed undiminished. Dame Clarice would have a chance to speak with him.

To the nun she said, 'I shall sit here by the door. Go to him.'

As Clarice walked slowly over to the great bed, Alisoun tried not to watch.

'I would go to the chapel and pray with Gilbert,' said Michaelo. 'Would you stay here until I return?'

'I would be glad to,' she said, 'but have you already forgiven him? After all he's done?'

'I will not judge him,' the monk said, his long face drawn with grief but lacking any sign of anger.

Magda came to Alisoun and kissed her forehead. 'Thou hast come far, Alisoun, and Magda is proud to call thee her apprentice.'

As Alisoun settled in the chair by the door, her heart felt lighter than it had in a long while. She smiled on the tableau before her, Dame Clarice leaning over the great bed to kiss her father's hand, and being invited to sit.

10

WELCOMES AND FAREWELLS

THURSDAY EVENING THROUGH
MONDAY

With some trepidation Thoresby observed the tall nun with the deep-set eyes and his mother's broad brow as she approached his bed. He was uncertain how he should behave. He had received letters from his daughter Idonea, but he had never met her. His only experience with children was with godchildren, most recently Archer's young ones, and his wards, who had usually been young men.

Clarice's steps slowed as she neared, her expression uncertain. Though her pale Cistercian robe and plain wimple suggested a spiritual maturity her face was unlined and youthful, and Thoresby reminded himself that to her he was the powerful Archbishop of York, someone to whom to bow in obeisance, not approach as friend, as kin. How strange that she was flesh of his flesh, yet until the previous day he had been unaware of her existence. Not so for her—all her life she had probably wondered about him. So they were both ill at ease.

'Your Grace,' she said, hesitating a few steps from the bed. 'I humbly beg your forgiveness for my trespass.'

'Come closer,' he said, holding out his hand.

She stepped forward and bent to kiss his ring. He placed his hand on her head and whispered a blessing.

'Now sit and talk to me, child.'

She took a seat on the high-backed chair beside him, primly, hands in lap, back straight, eyes on Thoresby's hands, not his face.

'I see much of my blood in you, Clarice,' he said. 'My daughter.'

She dared to meet his eyes, blushed, and quickly dropped her gaze. 'I do not deserve your kindness.'

'You are my daughter, Clarice, flesh of my flesh. You deserve more than kindness, you deserve my love, my guidance. I regret that I had no opportunity to share your life.'

She frowned, his words obviously not what she had expected. 'I feel responsible for what happened here. Dom Lambert's emissary concerned my birth—'

'No more of that. I would celebrate your existence, not seek cause to regret it.'

'I have been an ungrateful wretch, Your Grace.'

'Perhaps you've had some cause.'

'Lady Eleanor tried to help me see how good my life is, how much freer I am than she has been. But I envied her—her lovers, her beauty, her silks and jewels.' She lifted tear-filled eyes to his. 'She cannot be evil. She reached out to me, to teach me how to be grateful for my life.'

'She spoke to you?' He saw in his mind's eye the proud face framed in raven-black hair, the defiant carriage, and then the self-inflicted wound, the blood. 'Then she gave you a precious gift, and I pray that God was listening when she did so. Now, Clarice, let us talk of happier things. I would not waste my last days dwelling on Lady Eleanor's self-destruction. How goes your mother?'

'She is well, Your Grace, and will be most curious to hear of our meeting.' Clarice blotted her eyes and cheeks with a prettily embroidered cloth.

Thoresby smiled at the little vanity. 'I am glad to hear it.'

'Do you remember my mother?'

'A little.' Thoresby described dancing with her, the mischievous grin and teasing words and gestures that had stirred him. 'But I am confused. Princess Joan said she was sent away to give birth so as not to ruin marriage negotiations, but I remember a more mature woman—' It seemed a better choice than 'not a virgin'.

'She was a widow at the time,' said Clarice.

'Ah. Yes, that fits my memory.'

They grew more comfortable with one another as they talked, and Thoresby tried to ignore the weakness that hoarsened his voice and prevented him from lifting his mazer. He was both sorry and relieved when Dame Clarice noticed that he was having difficulty breathing. She called out for Alisoun's help.

'A soothing tisane, Your Grace,' said Alisoun, helping him to drink. 'You must rest now.'

Working together, Clarice and Alisoun shifted his cushions so that he lay back with more ease, added covers and placed a warm stone at his feet.

'Rest, Father,' Clarice whispered, kissing him on the forehead.

For a moment Thoresby thought his heart would break, to feel her warm lips, her breath on his face. He did not want her to leave, he felt a surge of regret to have known her for such a brief time.

'If it please Your Grace, I would sit with you a while,' said Clarice, as if she had read his thoughts.

He felt a warm rush of peace and contentment. 'Yes, it would please me.'

He might never have met her, never have spoken to her, never have seen her hatred turn to love—or at least affection. God's grace was upon him.

The pain and unhealthy cold in his knees eventually convinced Owen to rise from his prayers for the souls of Lady Eleanor, Gilbert, Dom Lambert and his servant Will, Brother Michaelo, Thoresby—his list had no end. As he lifted his head his gaze rested on Gilbert lying prostrate before the altar, arms outspread in a mirror of the crucifixion, with several of his fellow guards from the night watch surrounding him, kneeling on the stone floor with heads bowed. Gilbert had begged Owen's forgiveness. Seeing the shame in the man's eyes, witnessing his torment, Owen had forgiven him and promised to pray for his soul. In truth, he felt responsible for having failed to notice Gilbert's discontentment. But Gilbert said he'd not been discontented but greedy and anxious about the future. He'd steadfastly refused to name those who had cooperated with his betrayal, insisting that he had lied to them and tricked them into disobeying Owen's orders. Nor were any guilty of murder.

'I take full blame, Captain,' Gilbert had insisted. 'You can trust the others without me to lead them astray.'

Owen was not entirely comfortable with that logic, having thought he'd chosen men for the guard who could be trusted to reject any orders contrary to what they'd heard from either Owen or Alfred, but he had given Gilbert more responsibility of late. He knew that with Alfred's help he could pick out the unreliable ones. Not that it would matter for long. The archbishop was dying, and with him the composition of the archbishop's guard.

'Had Sir Lewis anything to do with it?' Owen had asked. 'Did he assist Lady Eleanor in any way?'

Gilbert shook his head. 'No.'

Owen thought Geoffrey would be glad of that.

Leaving the chapel, Owen walked out into a gentle rain and the dim light of early evening. He tried to recall all that had happened since he'd given up on sleep and talked to Jehannes in the chapel very early that morning, but his thoughts spun out of reach. He needed food and rest, but he had no appetite and could not imagine quieting his mind enough to sleep. He thought of returning to the hall to ask after Lady Eleanor's condition, but he did not have the heart.

He headed, instead, toward the stables. As he passed the kennels the happy sounds of the romping dogs reminded him of Lady Sybilla, and he turned in that direction, thinking it possible he might find her there, that it was a likely place in which she might seek solace. Owen had yet to talk to her about Dame Clarice and Thoresby's letter, having had no heart for it after what had come to pass in His Grace's chamber. He did not think that Sybilla would react with such violence, but he had not imagined for a moment that

Eleanor would take her own life. Strange, he had understood why Dom Lambert might try to end his own life, he had understood the humiliation that the man had suffered in Thoresby's chambers, but he could not quite sound the depths of Lady Eleanor's humiliation or despair. That she had murdered, and had that on her conscience, he understood. But she had implied a much deeper despair.

On a bench in the little shed that housed the kennels sat Lady Sybilla, her gaily coloured clothes subdued in the light of a solitary torch. Two dogs sat at her feet, their attention riveted on her. She stared down at them, but did not seem to be watching them.

Owen stood in the doorway for a moment, waiting for her to notice him. But when moments went by and the dogs began to whine, he said, 'My lady, are you unwell?'

As if waking from a dream, she turned her head slowly toward the sound of his voice, not focusing on him at first. He stepped into the light. Now she blinked and gave a slight start, focusing on him.

'Captain Archer. Have you heard? They could not save Eleanor.' Her voice was flat, without life.

'God have mercy on her soul.' Owen bowed his head and crossed himself. 'I had not heard. I've been long in the chapel.'

Sybilla nodded, a jerky, graceless gesture.

'You were a good friend to her,' he said, moving closer and crouching to pet the two dogs.

'Not good enough. I had promised her I would say nothing of Roger Neville. Would that I had been more frank with you about my concerns, that I had broken my ill-considered promise.' She lifted her face, tear-streaked and swollen. He realised she must have wept a long while. 'You were there, Captain. Do you understand? What drove her to such despair? Was it the child?'

A wave of pinpricks across his blind eye robbed him of breath for a heartbeat. 'Child?'

'Dame Magda will have noticed. Her courses had not come, and she grew ill in the mornings. That is why I went hawking in her place. Forgive me. I'm talking too much.' She pressed a hand to her mouth.

'A child. God have mercy. It does not sound as if her husband would believe it his.'

Sybilla shook her head. 'No. She would not say whose it was, but I knew about her slipping away to see Roger. Would she have been put to death for her crimes? Surely Her Grace would not have allowed that.'

'We cannot know what might have happened.' He needed wine. This last piece of the tragedy sickened him. 'My lady, I would not have you suffer more, but I must ask about Dame Clarice and the letter.'

'Forgive me for lying to you. But when she fell ill I was frightened. God forgive me. And it was all for nothing. The letter was not what I had hoped. I knew that Dame Clarice had a secret. I knew that someone had a purpose in including her in our company.'

'So you took it upon yourself to spy on her?'

'Sweet Jesu no! As Lady Eleanor was here for the Nevilles, I am here for the Percy family. I am a Neville, but my aunt was married to the Earl of Northumberland. She has passed on, but the Percy ties remain.'

'What were you to prevent?'

'Nothing. I was merely to listen. They wanted to know whether Her Grace intended to suggest a southerner for York. They are not fond of Alexander Neville, but they believe it is important to have a northern family in control, as the Thoresby family has been.'

'A vigil of spies,' Owen muttered. Ravenser had said that is what Thoresby had called the princess's visit.

He left Sybilla in the company of the dogs, gentle, playful souls to whom she might whisper her sorrow. He drank good wine, talked to his men, ate a little, drank more wine, and slept the sleep of the exhausted. Dreamless.

In the morning, Owen woke to find Geoffrey sitting cross-legged at the foot of his pallet, his ink-stained fingers moving quietly along a string of paternoster beads, his eyes closed, his face relaxed, peaceful. Apparently sensing Owen's eye on him, he lay down his beads and reached for a mazer on a stool beside him, handing it to Owen.

'Alfred and Sir John's man Douglas have organised the men, constructed a gallows, and Dom Jehannes has spent the night with Gilbert, shriving him. They await us now in the clearing beyond the river garden.'

Hanging. It was a fitting form of execution, as Gilbert had done unto Dom Lambert. But Owen's stomach cramped at the thought of the man he had trained hanging from the gibbet. He crossed himself, then took a long drink of the ale.

'They tell me this is Tom Merchet's finest ale, and that he is your neighbour,' said Geoffrey. 'Jehannes brought back a fresh barrel yesterday.'

'What of Lady Eleanor's body?'

'Sir Richard has arranged for Roger Neville, Dame Katherine, and Master Walter to accompany her by barge to Lincoln. Her family will join her there. Her Grace is not pleased with Sir Lewis's insistence on joining the journey to Lincoln, but he reassured her that he will return with the barge on the morrow, when she intends to depart.'

'So soon?'

'She believes that she has disturbed His Grace's last days enough.'

'Amen,' said Owen. He drank down the rest of the ale and rose to face the sad conclusion to Wykeham's mission.

Although Thoresby had prayed for inspiration about whom to advise Princess Joan to trust, he seemed left to his own common sense. Perhaps God paid him a compliment—he did not need divine intervention.

The experience of her was once again a heady treat for his senses. How beautiful she was, how graceful, how sweet her temper, how gentle her touch. He drank her in with what senses he had left to him. The previous day had taken much of his strength.

'My lady, it is good to see you again after the storms of yesterday.'

Her smile was a benediction. 'Your Grace, you do me great honour to say so. And I am much relieved. I had feared that my delay in revealing Dame Clarice's identity might have offended you beyond forgiveness. But I believed it best to have the documents safely here before I spoke, and Clarice wanted you to hold the proof in your hands rather than being told that she was your daughter. Perhaps I should not have agreed to assist Wykeham by letting Dom Lambert join our company and stopping at Nun Appleton for Dame Clarice, but I did not imagine the tragedy that would unfold. Still, you must regret your hospitality.'

'At this late point in my mortal existence I hold no grudges, my lady. Nor do I care to dwell on the tragedies that have befallen your company in my palace.'

'God bless you.' She settled with a silken grace into the chair beside his bed. Again she wore the comforting blue, and he felt quite certain that she knew its calming affect. In her lovely eyes he saw remnants of weeping, a redness that artful powder had not quite erased, a puffiness that a soothing compress could not entirely ease.

'I will say only that I grieve with you for Lady Eleanor, and I pray that God grants her peace,' he said.

'My poor benighted lady,' Joan whispered. 'I cannot understand her violence—it is as if she emulated her beloved falcons.' She crossed herself. 'How I could be so blind to her suffering—it frightens me, Your Grace. I sensed a rift among my women and I withdrew from them instead of extending my hand to help. I responded to a threat when I should have offered solace and support.' She bowed her head. 'May God forgive me.'

What blinders she wore—Eleanor's lying with Lambert on the journey, slipping away to Roger Neville, and her flirtation with Clifford. But surely she must have noticed something. 'Lady Eleanor must have neglected her duties to have dallied with Lambert and her cousin on the journey. How did you reconcile that?'

'I told myself she was with Clifford. I knew of their attraction to one another.' Joan sighed. 'I was too fond of her. I shall not be so lax in future.'

Thoresby doubted that the princess would actually allow herself to become more involved in the lives of her ladies. In an effort to change the mood before cynicism overtook his good intentions, he noted, 'You move with more ease than when you departed my chamber yesterday.'

Joan looked up with a relieved expression. 'I am most grateful for the skill of Magda Digby, who has soothed my discomfort and convinced me to move about more and consume less. I would welcome her into my household, but she is unavailable.'

'She refused you?'

'With such wise words I would have sounded a fool to argue with her.'

Thoresby could well imagine the exchange. 'I cannot think of another I trust more than I do Dame Magda, yet I know almost nothing about her. Not for want of prying questions.' Despite the shadows of last night's grief he'd noticed a glow to Joan's complexion and a sense of fresh air when she moved. 'You have been walking?'

'Oh, more than that—I have been assisting your falconer—he is training a young hawk. Dame Magda inspired me to take advantage of your beautiful estate. I am curious—the young hawk—who is it for?'

'Owen Archer's children—my godchildren. On my death my falconer has instructions to move several of my birds to Freythorpe Hadden, the manor young Hugh will inherit.'

'Captain Archer's children? You have curious affections.'

'They are mine to have.'

She raised an eyebrow, but did not comment. 'The young hawk is fierce and graceful. He will please them.' She smiled on him. 'But you did not invite me here to talk of godchildren and hawking. Have you advice for me?' Her lovely eyes studied him, no longer smiling.

'I have prayed much on this, and I believe that John of Gaunt is a man who understands that his path in life is to support the king.'

Her husband's brother, the powerful Duke of Lancaster, second living son of King Edward. 'I cannot say that I have ever sensed in him a man who believes he's destined to be king of England.'

'There are many who would disagree.'

'His power and wealth frighten many, my lady. But you did not come to Bishopthorpe to hear their opinions.'

'No.'

'He is not always a pleasant man, or easy to deal with, but his sense of honour is profound and steady. I believe you would be wise to keep him near you.'

'I am relieved to hear you say so, Your Grace, for I've ever felt I could depend on John, as has my Edward.'

'I would warn you about your *son* John.' He raised a hand to quiet her apology. 'He needs discipline, he needs to learn respect for his fellow men. Some time in the company of a man like Owen Archer would do him much good.'

'I have asked Geoffrey Chaucer to stay behind, talk to the captain about his joining my household,' said Joan.

'Good.' Thoresby nodded. 'Yes. That would be good. As for whom to avoid, I warn you against Alice Perrers and her friends at court.'

'Even the Nevilles?'

'I've come to accept that they are a necessary power in the North. But of those in Perrers's circle, beware.'

She nodded. 'What of Alexander Neville? If he is named your successor, who in the Church might I trust?'

That was simple. 'Put your trust in William Whittlesey. The Archbishop of Canterbury is a good man. And Brantingham, Bishop of Exeter.' Thoresby coughed and paused for a sip of honeyed water, which she kindly handed him. 'As you have witnessed here, be wary of William Wykeham. As Bishop of Winchester he is powerful, but you will have support in resisting him.'

She nodded. 'Any others?'

'I do not wish to name too many, Your Grace, for you'll have Lancaster to guide you, and he will have the pulse of the nobility.'

Now she grew even more serious. 'And the other matter, Your Grace? The curse on my family?'

Thoresby took her hand. 'I cannot believe that God would curse Prince Edward for the sins of his grandparents. Nor do I believe that God would hold King Edward and Queen Isabella solely responsible for the crises of their reign. They were caught up in currents that each believed threatened their ability to fulfil their duty. As your own husband has, I am quite certain, itched at times to escape the long shadow of his most noble father the king, so must have your husband's grandfather squirmed in the shadow of his father, Edward Longshanks, a most formidable man. But that earlier Prince Edward had not the blessed counsel and gracious example of a mother such as was Queen Phillippa, your husband's late mother. As for Queen Isabella, though I respect your affection for France I suggest that in that realm's court she had been raised to believe herself superior to her fellow mortals, and was therefore unable to bear her husband's slights, nor did she consider it necessary to temper her own lust and ambition. I pray I have not offended you.'

He'd noticed that Joan had straightened a little, subtly widening the distance between them, and her hand had grown heavy in his.

'You think I have no cause to worry for my family, Your Grace?'

He read disappointment in her eyes and hastened to add.

'I did not say that. A pilgrimage to Canterbury, with the intention of making a vow to rule wisely and with God's guidance—that I would advise you to make, my lady. You might also contribute to the lady chapel at York Minster in memory of your husband's grandfather.' She warmed to his suggestions, pressing his hand. 'I shall do so, Your Grace. A pilgrimage and an offering. Yes, these seem fitting gestures of atonement. I am most grateful for your counsel, my good lord of York.'

After Joan's departure, Brother Michaelo brought Thoresby some more honeyed water, helping him to drink.

'I could not help but hear you mention your lady chapel, Your Grace,' he said with a knowing look.

Thoresby felt himself blush. 'Shameless, I admit. But it was worth it to see that look in your eyes once more, Michaelo. Well worth it.'

'What look, Your Grace?' Michaelo asked, feigning innocence.

Thoresby chuckled, Michaelo joining him, until Thoresby had a fit of coughing that reminded them both of their impending separation, and both grew solemn.

'I forgive you, Michaelo. How could I not, when faced with the results of my own surrender to temptation?'

'I do not deserve your forgiveness, Your Grace,' Michaelo whispered, bowing his head.

Irritated to have to use breath to force a kindness on his secretary, Thoresby said, 'I have no patience for humility. Accept my forgiveness and be done with it.'

'May God watch over you, my lord,' Michaelo murmured, and began to leave.

'Stay a moment. I am brusque because I am uncomfortable with my own part in your surrender, Michaelo. I have neglected your spiritual needs. Benedict said that your superior, and that is me, should use every curative skill as a wise physician does, bringing in wise counsellors for you, showing you the way to humble reconciliation. I witnessed your severe penance years ago and chose to believe that was enough despite the arrogance that gradually reasserted itself in your character. I recommend you to Dom Jehannes. He is a good man, and a worthy counsellor.'

'Your Grace,' Michaelo whispered, 'the fault is all mine.'

Thoresby shook his head. 'After I am gone, I pray you find peace in Normandy. Now go. I am tired.'

Michaelo covered his face and hurried from the chamber.

Princess Joan had said her brief farewells, accompanied by Sir Lewis, Sir John, and Lady Sybilla. Thoresby had managed to preside over the little gathering from a comfortable chair—it was pleasant to sit by the window and feel the sun on his back. He blessed their journey and bade them pray for his soul. As soon as they withdrew he admitted to Magda that he was ready to return to his bed.

As the sounds of the princess's departure receded in the hall, Thoresby gave a great sigh, settling back deeper into the cushions.

'I have survived the princess's visit.' He winced at the breathless quality of his speech.

'Quiet now, Thy Grace,' said Magda.

'She wants Archer to join her household, you know,' Thoresby whispered. 'What do you think of that? He would remain in Yorkshire—listening for her. Occasionally Sir John would ride north to receive his report. Do you think he will agree? He would be richly rewarded for his service. I'd need have no concern for the comfort of his family.'

'Magda has no opinion in this, though she thinks the princess might do best not to mention her young peacock when proposing it. As for thou, see to thyself. Rest. In a few days Bird-eye will return with his family. Thou shouldst save thy voice for the children, eh?'

'Michaelo tells me that Archer took it very hard, Gilbert's betrayal.'

'The princess's visit weighed heavily on Bird-eye in many ways, Thy Grace. He has much healing to do.'

'I would like to know that he's well provided for.'

'Rest.'

Alfred had suggested that Owen go home for a few days before returning with Lucie and the children.

'The men will be on their best behaviour, after witnessing a hanging of one of their own,' he reasoned. He looked haggard, his eyes bloodshot.

'You grieve as much as I do,' Owen said. 'When I return, you hasten to York to see your lady, eh?'

Alfred had agreed. Now he came to help Owen carry his packs out to his waiting horse. 'You have a companion for the journey.'

'I've invited no one to ride with me.'

'He says that you need the company. He's to cheer you.'

Slinging a pack over his shoulder, Owen stepped out into the yard. Leaning against a second horse was Geoffrey Chaucer.

'You were not on the barge this morning?'

'Apparently not.' Geoffrey grinned. 'I look forward to more of Tom Merchet's finest ale. And I want to confer with your wife Lucie about what I might use to clean the ink from my fingers—and clothes. My Pippa would be most grateful.'

To his surprise, Owen felt a little better about the journey. 'Then let us be off to York.'

For their journey by barge to Bishopthorpe, Lucie's family was blessed with a crisp autumn day, the foliage along the riverbank bright with colour, the garden through which they approached the palace a delight to Gwenllian and Hugh, with leaves to kick and toss. Lucie had dreaded this journey, but the weather and their companion had cheered everyone. She liked Geoffrey Chaucer the moment she set eyes on him, and she did not change her mind with longer acquaintance. His expressive face was almost always lit with amusement, even when of a sardonic flavour, his short legs and arms seemed always in motion, and his conversation always surprised her with perceptions that challenged her own. The children loved him, and he kept a close watch on Owen, yanking him out of his moods with japes or challenges that rarely failed.

She knew that the tragedy of Lady Eleanor and Gilbert's execution had shaken Owen to the core. In their lovemaking he had clung to her as if to a lifeline; she wished that he could weep and cleanse himself. Her own dreams had been haunted by memories of her mother's unhappiness, so like Lady Eleanor's. Both had met bloody, tragic endings, powerless to help themselves.

In the doorway to the palace stood Brother Michaelo, drawn and subdued. But he brightened on seeing them, warmly welcoming them, and he escorted them at once to the chamber next to the great hall where Thoresby held audience from a great bed with bright silk hangings and cushions. For a moment she caught her breath and could not breathe out, shocked at the sight of the diminished John Thoresby propped against a pile of cushions. But his smile was a benediction, and so was Magda Digby's open-armed greeting. Gwenllian was soon sitting on the bed beside her godfather, and Hugh at his feet, telling him about the wondrous barge journey.

Owen stood near the window, his back to it, with a fond smile on his face. Magda stood beside him, her arm round his waist. Alisoun sat on a chair beside Thoresby, Emma asleep in her arms. Jasper stood shyly next to Lucie on the opposite side of the bed, uncertain of his role. Geoffrey had stayed in the hall.

Thoresby had just announced to Gwenllian and Hugh that they were to have some hawks at Freythorpe Hadden, and that there was a young one that his falconer was training especially for Hugh. Lucie felt Jasper stir beside her, and when Gwenllian slipped off the bed to grab his hands and repeat the news to him he seemed as excited as she was.

Hugh turned questioning eyes toward Lucie. 'Can I play with a hawk?'

Lucie laughed. 'Jasper, why don't you ask Alisoun to escort the three of you to the mews to see the birds?'

It took little more urging. When the room was quiet once more, Lucie sat on the bed, taking Thoresby's bony hand.

'You are so good to our children, Your Grace.'

'It has been a great pleasure for me to watch them grow, Lucie. No doubt you have heard that I gained a daughter of late. You shall meet her at supper in the hall. She will leave soon to return to her convent. I shall miss her.' He paused for breath. 'Your stepson Jasper—I would like to give him something that would please him. You must look around in the next few days and choose an object— perhaps you might note what catches his eye? I regret that I've not accorded him the attention I have my godchildren.'

Lucie's emotions overwhelmed her at that request, and she lay her head on Thoresby's shoulder and wept, while he held her close to him.

'Sweet Lucie. You have repaid me a hundredfold for my patronage of you regarding your guild status. Your marriage, your family—thinking of you has comforted me in the darkest hours.' He lifted her chin and looked deep into her eyes. 'Blessings on you and all your family. I ask only that you think of me now and then, and pray for my soul's redemption.'

Behind her she heard Owen clear his throat, but did not turn to him, allowing him the privacy to weep if his pride allowed him to do so.

After supper, Owen was summoned to Thoresby's chamber. They sipped wine while talking of Owen's family and Alisoun's maturing, and then they grew quiet for a while.

'You've often sat in judgement over me,' Thoresby said, breaking the silence. He lifted a trembling hand to stop Owen's protests. 'I've no doubt that it was your righteous anger that protected you from those who would have kept you in Wales, that and your devotion to Lucie and your children.' He took a shuddering breath. 'I never regretted recruiting you, Archer. In faith, I never doubted your loyalty, no matter how much my orders chafed.'

'Your Grace.' Owen bowed his head, fighting for composure.

'How fitting for Wykeham to rake us through the coals one last time, eh, Archer?'

Owen heard the smile in Thoresby's voice and felt safe raising his head. 'One last time for you, perhaps,' he managed to say in a steady voice.

Thoresby chuckled weakly. 'I've written to him, and sent a copy of the letter to the Archbishop of Canterbury, strongly advising Wykeham to reward you for your efforts on his part, on these several occasions, with a manor that abuts some of the Freythorpe fields. I seem to recall he has land there, and if not he is the man to arrange it.'

'Your Grace!' Freythorpe Hadden was Lucie's inheritance from her father, which would pass on to their son Hugh. Owen owned no land.

'I think you would like having property of your own to leave to your children. Not that I imagine you retiring to your country estate. Your conscience is too strong—it will overrule your desire for peace. Princess Joan favours you, and I am certain the city of York will ask you to stand as bailiff. My successor will no doubt try to coerce you into being his captain—Gilbert was a fool to think Neville would prefer him to you. Even Wykeham might expect something in return for the land. You will have no peace. But you will thrive, Archer, you and your lovely family.' His breath had deteriorated into a pitiful wheeze.

'You leave me with a mixed blessing, Your Grace,' said Owen.

'You expected me to do otherwise?' Thoresby managed a weak smile.

'It has been an honour to serve you, Your Grace,' said Owen. He dared say no more.

'God go with you, Owen Archer.'

EPILOGUE

ST LEONARD'S DAY,
SUNDAY, 6 NOVEMBER 1373

Magda, Michaelo and Ravenser sat by Thoresby's great bed. The archbishop had been dozing for a while when suddenly he opened his eyes and requested a little wine to wet his mouth. Ravenser did the honour, gently lifting his uncle's head and holding the cup to his lips.

When Thoresby lay back against the cushions he reached for Magda's hand.

'Have you thought of what I might leave to you, my friend?'

'The memory of thy friendship will be most precious to Magda,' she said. But seeing his gathering frown she added, 'Sir Richard suggested an ass and cart from thy stables, and Magda agreed that she and Alisoun might make good use of that.'

Thoresby nodded and, turning his gaze on Ravenser, said, 'See that it is done.' He looked on all three of them with a trembling smile. 'God go with you, my dear friends.' And after a last shuddering breath, he was still.

Magda gently closed his papery eyelids. 'May thou rest in peace, Old Crow. May thy god embrace thee.'

Ravenser rose and kissed his uncle's forehead.

Brother Michaelo's long withheld sobs, though muffled, broke the gentle peace of the room.

AUTHOR'S NOTE

When I cast John Thoresby, Archbishop of York, in the first Owen Archer novel I did not expect to grow fond of him. Now here I sit mourning him. I've learned through him a drawback of writing about real historical figures—their lives can end all too soon, before I'm ready to part with them. Once he caught my heart I dreaded the years ticking over toward his historical death. He was one of those rare gifts to a novelist, a character who seemed to write his scenes. From the beginning, he flowed from my imagination. He was always reliable.

I have been aware for the past few books in the series that John Thoresby died on 6 November 1373 at his palace of Bishopthorpe after a long illness. In order to cheer myself, knowing that this book would encompass that sad date, I decided to fill his palace with interesting people. A visit from the beautiful Princess of Wales coupled with a last irritation from William Wykeham, Bishop of Winchester, seemed just the thing. For Owen, I wanted to introduce future possibilities—I did not want to suggest that the death of the Archbishop of York brought with it my main character's retirement. I'm not nearly finished with Owen and Lucie.

In the course of my research, reading about Thoresby's last days and the bequests mentioned in his will teased me with possible relationships. But for the sake of a manageable plot I might have crowded the palace with his relatives and others mentioned in that document. I settled for one enticing figure, Idonea de Brunnom, a nun at Hampole, to whom Thoresby bequeathed 100 shillings—I thought it plausible she might be his natural daughter.

As I contemplated the situation I'd set up—Princess Joan

and her company staying at the palace—I saw that I had all the ingredients for a type of book that Agatha Christie would recognise: the country house mystery, in which a group of people with wide-ranging motivations for visiting are in a sense marooned in a large house in the country and suddenly one dies, then another, in suspicious circumstances. The game was afoot. I enjoyed wrapping up the investigation with a variation on the classic gathering in the library in which the detective explains all—a nod to Hercule Poirot (I have a special relationship to Agatha Christie, as we share the same birthday).

The death of the Archbishop of York, the man who ranked second in the Catholic Church in England at a time when it was the religion of the realm, would have been significant at any time, but even more so when peace between Scotland and England was still fragile. The northern shires played a significant role as the buffer between Scotland and the government in Westminster, which of course means they also bore the brunt of the Scottish raids, and the Archbishop of York was often called upon to rally defence forces. This is why the northern families such as the Percies and the Nevilles had become so important—the king counted on them to secure that territory. The Percies had been prominent in the north for a long time, but the Nevilles, although they had held public offices for generations were only now rising to prominence in the central government. It would seem to follow that a Neville as Archbishop of York would increase the family's stature—whether Alexander Neville accomplished this will be seen in later books in this series.

The marriage history of Princess Joan, known in her lifetime as the Fair Maid of Kent, is complex. King Edward I had two wives— by his first wife he sired his heir, the future King Edward II; by his second wife he sired Edmund of Woodstock, Earl of Kent. Joan was Edmund's daughter. When he was executed in 1330 by his half-brother's queen and her lover, his daughter Joan was brought up for a while at court and then in the household of William Montague, Earl of Salisbury. In 1340, at the age of 12, already known for her beauty, she secretly betrothed herself to a member of Salisbury's household, Thomas Holand; but while her betrothed was off fighting in Prussia, her guardian married her to his son and heir, also William Montague. It's not entirely clear whether Joan doubted the validity of her betrothal to Thomas or whether she was merely too young and intimidated by her guardian to reveal her previous engagement. When Thomas returned in late 1341 or early 1342, William refused to give Joan up, and it was only after capturing a man of high rank in the French war and securing a considerable ransom that Holand could afford petitioning the Pope. Montague held Joan incommunicado for a while. When, at last, he was coerced to permit Joan to speak on her own behalf, she acknowledged her former betrothal to Thomas. Joan's marriage to William was declared annulled and she was allowed to marry Thomas in 1349. It was not long after Thomas's death in 1360 that Joan entered into yet another secret marriage, this time with Edward, the Black Prince. When King Edward learned of this he was angry, to put it mildly, as he had been planning to use the marriage of his eldest son and heir to form a powerful political alliance. But acknowledging that Joan and Edward were two consenting adults and therefore their vows were legitimate, the king resigned himself to the match—but he dissolved the clandestine marriage, ordered them to do a penance, and then had them retake their vows in an official state ceremony once papal dispensation was granted (for Joan and Edward were second cousins).

As foreshadowed in the novel, Joan is widowed in 1376. As mother to the heir apparent, she would have been grateful for advice such as Thoresby gave her in this book as to whom her son Richard might trust. He was eventually crowned King Richard II.

In Joan's company I included both real and fictional characters—Lewis Clifford, John Holand (one of her children by her first husband) and of course Geoffrey Chaucer are all historic figures, as well as Alexander Neville, who is on everyone's minds but never appears. The others are fictional characters.

I'll end with a lovely quote about my friend John Thoresby from *Fasti Eboracenses* (p. 449):

'John de Thoresby was one of those great and good men who were the glory of the fourteenth century. That was indeed, in every respect, an illustrious age. Whilst the chivalry of England was winning renown in the wars in France, every liberal art was being fostered and cherished at home, and John de Thoresby stood in the front rank of that band of worthies who signalized themselves by their taste and learning. It is with a feeling almost akin to veneration that I look back upon his many services to his country, his pious zeal and his open-handed munificence.'

FOR FURTHER READING

Davies, Richard G. 'Alexander Neville, Archbishop of York, 1374-1388' in *The Yorkshire Archaeological Journal*, 47(1975) pp. 87-101.

Dixon, W. H., *Fasti Eboracenses: lives of the archbishops of York*, ed. J. Raine (1863), pp. 449-494.

Dobson, R. B., 'The Authority of the Bishop in Late Medieval England: The Case of Archbishop Alexander Neville of York, 1374-88,' in Church and Society in the Medieval North of England (1996), pp. 185-193

Dobson, R. B., 'Beverley in Conflict: Archbishop Alexander Neville and the Minster Clergy, 1381-8' in *Medieval Art, Architecture and Archaeology in the East Riding of Yorkshire*, ed. C. Wilson (1989), pp. 149-164.

Highfield, J. R. L., 'The Promotion of William of Wickham to the See of Winchester,' *Journal of Ecclesiastical History* 4(1953), pp. 37-54.

Wentersdorf, Karl P., 'The clandestine marriages of the Fair Maid of Kent,' *Journal of Medieval History* 5(1979), pp. 203-231.

A recent accessible overview of the period is Miri Rubin's *The Hollow Crown: A History of Britain in the Late Middle Ages*, Penguin Books 2005.

The citation from the Rule of St Benedict in the prologue is from the recent translation by Patrick Barry, OSB in *Benedict's Dharma: Buddhists Reflect on the Rule of Saint Benedict*, edited by Patrick Henry, Riverheard Books, 2001.

MORE FROM CANDACE ROBB

THE OWEN ARCHER SERIES

THE APOTHECARY ROSE

In the year of our Lord 1363, two suspicious deaths in the infirmary of St. Mary's Abbey catch the attention of the powerful John Thoresby, Lord Chancellor of England and Archbishop of York. One victim is a pilgrim, while the second is Thoresby's ne'er-do-well ward, both apparently poisoned by a physic supplied by Master Apothecary Nicholas Wilton. In the wake of these deaths, the archbishop dispatches one-eyed spy Owen Archer to York to find the murderer. Under the guise of a disillusioned soldier keen to make a fresh start, Owen insinuates himself into Wilton's apothecary as an apprentice. But he finds Wilton bedridden, with the shop being run by his lovely, enigmatic young wife, Lucie. As Owen unravels a tangled history of scandal and tragedy, he discovers at its center a desperate, forbidden love twisted over time into obsession. And the woman he has come to love is his prime suspect.

Lovingly detailed, beautifully written, *The Apothecary Rose* is a captivating and suspenseful tale of life, love, and death in medieval England.

THE LADY CHAPEL

Perfect for fans of both Ellis Peters and CJ Sansom, *The Lady Chapel* is a vivid and immersive portrait of court intrigue and a testament to the power of the medieval guilds.

Summer in the year of our Lord 1365. On the night after the Corpus Christi procession, a man is brutally murdered on the steps of York Minster. The next morning his severed hand is found in a room at the York Tavern—a room hastily vacated by a fellow guild member who had quarreled with the victim.

Archbishop Thoresby calls on Owen Archer to investigate. As Owen tracks the fleeing merchant, he uncovers a conspiracy involving a powerful company of traders, but his only witness is a young boy who has gone into hiding, and his only suspect is a mysterious cloaked woman. When Owen discovers a link between the traders and a powerful coterie in the royal court, he brings his apothecary wife Lucie into the race to find the boy before he is silenced forever by the murderers.

THE NUN'S TALE

Based on an enigmatic entry in the records of Clementhorpe Nunnery, this authentic, gripping mystery conjures a 14th century ripe with forbidden passions and political intrigue.

When young nun Joanna Calverley dies of a fever in the town of Beverley in the summer of 1365, she is buried quickly for fear of the plague. But a year later, Archbishop Thoresby learns of a woman who has arrived in York claiming to be the resurrected nun, talking of relic-trading and miracles. And death seems to ride in her wake.

The archbishop sends Owen Archer to retrace the woman's journey, an investigation that leads him across the north from Leeds to Beverley to Scarborough. Along the way he encounters Geoffrey Chaucer, a spy for the king of England, who believes there is a connection between the nun's troubles, renegade mercenaries, and the powerful Percy family. Back in York, however, Owen's wife Lucie, pregnant with their first child, has won the confidence of the mysterious nun and realizes that there are secrets hidden in the woman's seemingly mad ramblings...

THE KING'S BISHOP

From the marshy Thames to the misty Yorkshire moors, murder stalks Welsh soldier-sleuth Owen Archer and one of his oldest friends.

On a snowy morning in 1367, Sir William of Wyndesore's page is found in the icy moat of Windsor Castle, and some whisper that the murderer was Ned Townley—a former comrade-in-arms of Owen Archer. Burdened with a reputation as a notoriously jealous lover, Ned cannot hope to clear his name; even Mary, his ladylove, is unsure of the truth. Hoping to put Ned out of harm's way while solving the murder, Owen places his friend in charge of a mission to Rievaulx Abbey at the edge of the moors. But when the travelers receive news of Mary's drowning, Ned vanishes into the wild.

Riding out in search of his old friend, Owen does not know whether he will be Ned's savior or executioner. With his one good eye, Owen sees more than most, but now he must find a way to penetrate the curtains of power that surround the Church and England's royal court and discover the truth of Ned's innocence or guilt...

THE RIDDLE OF ST. LEONARD'S

In the year of our Lord 1369 the much-loved Queen Philippa lies dying in Windsor Castle, the harvest has failed, and the pestilence has returned. In York, the atmosphere of fear and superstition is heightened by a series of thefts and violent deaths at St. Leonard's Hospita, as well as rumors that these crimes are connected to the hospital's dwindling funds. The Master of St. Leonard's, Sir Richard Ravenser, hurries north from the queen's deathbed to summon Owen Archer, soldier-spy, to investigate the scandal before it ruins him.

While his wife Lucie faces the plague-panicked townsfolk at the apothecary, Owen encounters a seemingly random series of clues: a riddle posed by one of the victims at the hospital, a lay sister with a scandalous past, the kidnapping of a child from the hospital orphanage, and a case of arson. The answer to the riddle of St. Leonard's lies in the past, and as Owen's family is caught up in the sweep of the pestilence, he must abandon them to race across the countryside to save the next victim.

A GIFT OF SANCTUARY

Under the pretense of escorting his father-in-law and the archbishop's secretary on a pilgrimage to the sacred city of St. David's in Wales, Owen Archer and Geoffrey Chaucer, in truth, are carrying out a mission for the Duke of Lancaster. England and France are at war, and the southern coast of Wales is vulnerable to invasion—Owen and Geoffrey are to recruit archers for the duke's army and inspect his Welsh fortifications on the coast, while quietly investigating whether the duke's steward at Cydweli Castle is involved in a French plot to incite rebellion in Wales.

But trouble precedes them in the cathedral city of St. David's. On Whitesands Beach beyond the city a young man is beaten and left for dead, then spirited away by a Welsh bard. Shortly afterward a corpse clothed in the livery of the Duke of Lancaster is left at the city gate, his shoes filled with white sand. Meanwhile, at Cydweli Castle, a chain of events begun by the theft of money from the castle's exchequer ends in a violent death and the disappearance of the steward's beautiful young wife. Owen and Geoffrey begin to see connections linking the troubles in city and castle, and learn they must unravel the complex story of betrayed love and political ambition to prevent more deaths. But in the course of his investigations in the land of his birth, Owen is haunted by doubts about his own loyalties...

A SPY FOR THE REDEEMER

Late spring in the year of our Lord 1370, and Owen Archer is anxious to leave Wales for home. His mission for the Duke of Lancaster complete, he attempts to arrange safe passage on a ship sailing for England, but the hanging of a stonemason interrupts his plans. On the surface it appears the young man was driven to suicide by a broken heart, but to Owen the signs all point to murder. As his investigation stretches on, however, Owen finds himself drawn into the influence of the leader of a Welsh rebellion whose manifesto speaks to his heart, and a choice is offered to him: join or die.

Meanwhile, at home in York, Owen's wife Lucie is troubled by rumors that her husband's long absence is permanent, as well as threats by a customer who claims she was poisoned by a physic from the Wilton apothecary. Meanwhile, Lucie is tempted by the attentions of a friend's steward, even as she uncovers a shattering betrayal in her own household.

THE GUILT OF INNOCENTS

Winter in the year of our Lord 1372. A river pilot falls into the icy waters of the River Ouse during a skirmish between dockworkers and the boys of the minster school, which include Owen Archer's adopted son Jasper. But what began as a confrontation to return a boy's stolen scrip becomes a murder investigation as the rescuers find the pilot dying of wounds inflicted before his plunge into the river. When another body is fished from the river upstream and Owen discovers that the boy Jasper sought to help has disappeared, Owen Archer convinces the archbishop that he must go in search of the boy. His lost scrip seems to hold the key to the double tragedy, but his disappearance leaves troubling questions: did he flee in fear? Or was he abducted?

On the cusp of this new mystery, Owen accepts Jasper's offer to accompany him to the boy's home in the countryside, where they learn that a valuable cross has gone missing. A devastating fire and another drowning force Owen to make impossible choices, endangering not only himself, but the two innocents he fights to protect. The bond between fathers and sons proves strong, even between those not linked by blood.

THE MARGARET KERR SERIES

A TRUST BETRAYED

In the spring of 1297 the English army controls lowland Scotland and Margaret Kerr's husband Roger Sinclair is missing. He'd headed to Dundee in autumn, writing to Margaret with a promise to be home for Christmas, but it's past Easter. Is he caught up in the swelling rebellion against the English? Is he even alive? When his cousin, Jack, is murdered on the streets of Edinburgh, Roger's last known location, Margaret coerces her brother Andrew, a priest, to escort her to the city.

She finds Edinburgh scarred by war—houses burnt, walls stained with blood, shops shuttered—and the townsfolk simmering with resentment, harboring secrets. Even her uncle, innkeeper Murdoch Kerr, meets her questions with silence. Are his secrets the keys to Roger's disappearance? What terrible sin torments her brother? Is it her husband she glimpses in the rain, scarred, haunted? Desperate, Margaret makes alliances that risk both her own life and that of her brother in her search for answers. She learns that war twists love and loyalties, and that, until tested, we cannot know our own hearts, much less those of our loved ones.

THE FIRE IN THE FLINT

Scots are gathering in Murdoch Kerr's Edinburgh tavern, plotting to drive out the English forces. Margaret takes her place there as innkeeper, collecting information to pass on to William Wallace—until murder gives the English an excuse to shutter the tavern. The dead man was a witness to the intruders who raided chests belonging to Margaret's husband and her father, the latest in a string of violent raids on Margaret's family, but no one knows the identity of the raiders or what they're searching for.

Margaret's uncle urges her to escape Edinburgh, but as she flees north with her husband Roger, Margaret grows suspicious about his sudden wish to speak with her mother, Christiana, who is a soothsayer. Margaret once innocently shared with Roger one of Christiana's visions, of "the true king of Scotland" riding into Edinburgh. Now she begins to wonder if their trip is part of a mission engineered by the English crown...

A CRUEL COURTSHIP

In late summer 1297, Margaret Kerr heads to the town of Stirling at the request of William Wallace's man James Comyn. Her mission is to discover the fate of a young spy who had infiltrated the English garrison at Stirling Castle, but on the journey Margaret is haunted by dreams—or are they visions?—of danger.

He who holds Stirling Castle holds Scotland—and a bloody battle for the castle is imminent. But as the Scots prepare to cast off the English yoke, Margaret's flashes of the future allow her to glimpse what is to come—and show her that she can trust no one, not even her closest friends.

A Cruel Courtship is a harrowing account of the days before the bloody battle of Stirling Bridge, and the story of a young woman's awakening.

CPSIA information can be obtained
at www.ICGtesting.com
Printed in the USA
LVHW090505230323
742298LV00004B/533